Praise for *Gilded M*

A Finalist for the Reading the West Fiction Award

"A stellar read from an acclaimed author."

—Bethanne Patrick, *Los Angeles Times*

"Kate Manning's fat, immersive novel transfixed me. . . . She builds her characters' challenges with such empathy, I didn't even realize I was getting a crash course in the history of labor relations. . . . There are views to admire, mysteries to be solved and love stories to escape into. . . . Awe-inspiring."

—Elisabeth Egan, *The New York Times*

"A rousing yarn."

—*The New York Times Book Review, Editors' Choice*

"A page-turning exploration of wealth inequality, organized labor, and young love in the early 1900s."

—Emma Athena, *Boulder Weekly*

"Unforgettable."

—Kristyn Kusek Lewis, *Real Simple*

"Stellar . . . Manning shines . . . This is one to savor."

—*Publishers Weekly* (starred review)

"Manning's bildungsroman not only provides a clear portrait of her young heroine; it captures the intensity of an unsettled time and place in American history."

—*Kirkus Reviews*

"Sweeping. A wild adventure."

—Robin Young, NPR

"An old-fashioned novel of big mountains and bigger than life robber barons."
—Sandra Dallas, *The Denver Post*

"Gorgeous sentences and a driving plot that keeps the pages turning."
—Alex Menard, *The Crystal Valley Echo and Marble Times*

"Utterly transporting. A novel that will sweep you off your feet with the promise of adventure, equality, freedom, and yes, love."
—Al Woodworth, *Amazon Editors' Choice*

"The writing is magnificent."
—Sandy Mahaffey, *The Fredericksburg Free Lance-Star*

"A steady-eyed look at the costs of justice, Kate Manning's latest novel is a solid, sweeping read."
—*The Christian Science Monitor*

"I adored this book for three reasons: the exquisite language, the organic twists and turns of the plot, and the riveting, brutal history of union organizing in the early twentieth century."
—Trish MacEnulty, *Historical Novel Society*

"An eloquent epic. Sylvie is a heroine and a half."
—Jesse Kornbluth, *Bookreporter*

"An expansive novel of passions: love, beauty, suffering; struggles for labor rights, women's equality, and the rights of formerly enslaved people . . . It contains romance, historical fiction, and inspired, high-minded thinking on important issues, [with] lovely writing about the natural world. . . . A painfully beautiful novel of big ideals, heartbreaks, and tragedies, sewn together by an admirable and unforgettable heroine."
—*Shelf Awareness*

"Here is adventure of the first order, as young Sylvie Pelletier finds herself thrust into a seething union dispute in a marble-quarrying town. There's violence in the wintry air, but also romance, as two charismatic men vie for Sylvie's attention. Dread and love entwine, as the forces and people that transformed the twentieth century converge on the town, all this rendered by Ms. Manning in prose as clean and sharp as the stone saws on the mountain. I raced through it. Sylvie is dynamite and *Gilded Mountain* is brilliant."

—#1 *New York Times* bestselling author Erik Larson

"Kate Manning is a master storyteller. *Gilded Mountain* is so immersive, so richly imagined, that reading it feels akin to time travel. Manning writes historical sagas like no one else; the dreamers, strivers, and opportunists who populate this tale possess a uniquely American desire to reinvent themselves, whatever it takes. An epic story of love, hope, and perseverance."

—#1 *New York Times* bestselling author Christina Baker Kline

"The best historical novels sing because, through them, we feel the reverberations of the past in the present day. Hard work, love, sorrow, revenge, joy— *Gilded Mountain* hums with all of this and more."

—Mary Beth Keane, *New York Times* bestselling author of *Ask Again, Yes*

"The gold at the center of Kate Manning's remarkably panoramic and meticulously researched new novel is one indomitable Sylvie Pelletier—an adventurer, a romantic, a crackerjack observer of worlds and hearts. *Gilded Mountain* is that rare thing: a historical page-turner that nimbly moves from gritty mining shafts to elegant drawing rooms of an earlier America with all its seething and striving, and where—then, as now—fates are decided by a stroke of luck or unluck, kindness and corruption, and reinvention."

—Carol Edgarian, author of *Vera*

Also by Kate Manning

My Notorious Life

Whitegirl

GILDED MOUNTAIN

A Novel

Kate Manning

SCRIBNER

New York   London   Toronto   Sydney   New Delhi

Scribner
An Imprint of Simon & Schuster, Inc.
1230 Avenue of the Americas
New York, NY 10020

First Scribner trade paperback edition October 2023

SCRIBNER and design are registered trademarks of The Gale Group, Inc., used under license by Simon & Schuster, Inc., the publisher of this work.

For information about special discounts for bulk purchases, please contact Simon & Schuster Special Sales at 1-866-506-1949 or business@simonandschuster.com.

The Simon & Schuster Speakers Bureau can bring authors to your live event. For more information or to book an event, contact the Simon & Schuster Speakers Bureau at 1-866-248-3049 or visit our website at www.simonspeakers.com.

Interior design by Wendy Blum

Manufactured in the United States of America

1   3   5   7   9   10   8   6   4   2

Library of Congress Control Number: 2022465732

ISBN 978-1-9821-6094-4
ISBN 978-1-9821-6095-1 (pbk)
ISBN 978-1-9821-6096-8 (ebook)

For Roberta Baker
and
For Amy Wilentz

In the monuments to the dead that stud my history,
it is I who am buried.

—Simone de Beauvoir

To the dead we owe only the truth.

—Voltaire

PART ONE

Moonstone

Oh Lord, set a guard at my mouth.
Keep watch over the door of my lips.

—Psalm 141:3

Chapter One

I NEVER TOLD A SOUL about the money. Not a word about the marriage or the events that led me to his arms. In those days I was a young *religieuse*, my mother pointing me toward a nunnery. But it was the transformations of love and ease I wanted, and when we went west, I went looking. There in the sharp teeth of the Gilded Mountains, where the snow and murderous cold conspire to ruin a woman, I lost the chance to become a delicate sort of lady, one of those poodles in hair parlors and society clubs. Instead, I got myself arrested as a radical and acquired a fine vocabulary, one more common to muleskinners and barflies, quarryhogs, witches. And I'm not sorry, for it was all of my education in those two years, about right and wrong. Here in the attic of memory, I sit with my trunk of ghosts, my pen, to put down those long-ago days in Moonstone, Colorado, to report at last certain crimes, my own included, of the heart and worse, and how they tried to smash us.

We never should've headed up there in that avalanche month, April 1907, but already had waited two years to follow my father. Our party consisted of myself, a tall, odd girl, almost seventeen; my mother, Cherie; my brother

Henry, age twelve; and the baby, François, who'd made it alive to a year and a half—old enough to travel at last. We called him Frankie, or Nipper, for he enjoyed the use of his new teeth. Already we'd crossed two thousand miles of country in a weary succession of train cars, on harrowing tracks tacked along sheer rock faces, up and then farther up into the excitement of the western peaks.

Behind us we'd left a squabbling maw of relatives crowded in dark rooms, the *petit Québécois* parish in Rutland, Vermont, the worn-out path to the church of Sainte Marie, its fog of incense and the Latin Mass interminable. As the railroad took us away from the granite towns of New England, I imagined my new life as a circus adventure or a tale of the Wild West, where I'd be transformed from a pious, studious girl into a bareback rider wearing spangles on a trick horse.

These were the laughable dreams from which I was soon to be waked.

We fetched up in the prettified coal town of Ruby, Colorado, and were now to travel the last eight miles into the fangs of the Gilded Range, to ten thousand feet of altitude. My father, Jacques Pelletier, had relocated to Moonstone in 1905, to escape a certain "unpleasantness," as the bosses termed a labor dispute. They'd found him organizing stone workers for a fair wage and ushered him out of Vermont at the point of a gun. Now he worked as a quarryman for the Padgett Fuel and Stone Company, digging out the world's finest grade of pure white marble, good for carving into statues and bank pillars, monuments. Gravestones.

"Come in April," his letter instructed, "when the worst of the storms has passed." "Won't Papa be happy to see us?" said my mother. She'd offered a version of these words every day of our travels and now pumped air in her voice to refresh them. (Won't he be happy to see us, *if he is still alive, not crushed by rockfall, frozen in a crevasse, jailed by the bosses.*) She was worn out to start with, and had turned stringy with travel. Still, she did not complain. *Complaints are the seeds of misery* was her belief. This philosophy was laced into me so thoroughly that what grievances I had were pressed behind my ribs as if by a wire corset.

At the reins of our sledge that morning was Hawky Jenkins. Fronds of yellow hair hung below his hat brim, a matching beard tucked into his coat. Weather had etched his face into a kindly expression that did not match his sour disgruntlement.

"Whattinhell's in here?" he asked, loading our crates.

"Books," said my mother. She arched an eyebrow in my direction, as I'd insisted on carting them all this way. Perrault and Grimm. *Arabian Nights* and *Robin Hood*.

Jenkins sniffed the box and sniffed suspicious at my father's fiddle in its case. Soon our papa would play it in the evenings by the fire and tell his stories of Ti-Jean and the *loup-garou*, a wolf-man who rode a flying canoe and devoured children in his dripping fangs. Papa called me Birdy, *p'tite Oiseau*, though I was no longer petite, but gangling and raw-boned.

We left Ruby with cold sun dazzling off the snow-covered land, the mercury at twenty degrees, and headed for a mule trail no wider than a string of gristle. The road led through quiet skeleton woods studded green with pines, then out again through clearings, a cirque of open range. The horses drudged up a slow grade and the cold froze our nostrils together on the inhale. We pulled our mufflers up and gazed at the fearsome towering peaks all around.

"*Magnifique, non?*" My mother pointed out the beauty as if to sell it to us.

"You people Frenchies?" Hawky Jenkins asked. "Belgiums? Canucks?"

"American," I said, to set the record straight from the start.

"*Québécois*," my mother corrected, to make sure we did not forget our roots. "We are French-Canadian."

"The Chinee of the East," Jenkins said. "Not a lotta Canuck Frenchies 'round up here. Mostly bohunk polack n'dago guineas. Wopslike everwhere. Coupla chinks'n nips on a rail crew. Course your swenskas 'n norskis and messicans. Notta lottanigras, though, exception acoupla slaveswork in the castle."

"Slaves?" I asked Henry in French. "I can't understand a thing he says."

"Can't understand a gotdam thing you people say," said Jenkins.

Nipper began to fuss. He was done with travel, squirming and quarly. I took him, then Henry took him, then Maman had him again. "Alouette!" he demanded. She sang to him in her soft churchy voice, "*Gentille alouette,*" about plucking a little bird, yanking out the feathers, the beak. The sledge went gliding over ruts and she wrestled Nipper under the blanket, where she nursed him.

The song turned Henry's thoughts to hunting. "I'm gonna trap grouse this summer," he said. "Set snares for partridge, whatever else they got here. Rabbits?"

"Ferrets," Jenkins said. "Weasels. Company'll let a man take an'elk offa the property if he got the price a bullets."

Henry thrilled to hear it. He had a fascination with our *voyageur* forefathers trapping for furs, axing the forests to stumps, thus forcing their descendants to emigrate for factory work. "Any moose-*là*?" Henry asked. "'Cause my sister gotta find herself a husband. Enh, Moose?"

"Not funny," I said.

He reached to swat at me behind our mother's back.

"Stop now. *Arrêtes-tu là,*" she said. "Sylvie, be good."

I bit my tongue and resented how she shushed me, not him.

We drove toward a ridge of sharp peaks. The path grew steep. Dread grew along the wires of our nerves. On one side was a straight drop down, on the other a wall of rock. Just before noon, the wind came up, wild and biting. A long gust buffeted the sled like a warning. The sky cast over with dishrag-colored clouds.

"Sheeeet." Jenkins cursed the air and hurried the horses.

Maman crossed herself and chewed her lip, her face skewed with fear. For Cherie Pelletier, danger threatened on a sunny morning, sin in a stray thought. But that day she was right to be afraid. "Go back. We turn back *icitte.*"

"We'll outrun her," Jenkins said. "Five miles more." He sipped at a flask from his pocket and drove directly at the storm.

The snow started steady and fast, piling on our hats and laps. The wind slanted sharp flakes into our eyes. Maman was rigid with terror. She handed me the sleeping Nipper and fingered a rosary in her mittened hands. She had at my age intended to take vows with the Soeurs de Grâce but met Jacques Pelletier fiddling at a barn dance and left the nuns with religion packed in her valise. She carried it now in our crates, in the *Lives of the Saints*, with their glorious suffering.

My own suffering was ordinary, for no purpose. I was merely hungry, merely cold, my feet blocks of ice. I held out a crystal flake on my dark wool mitten.

"A diamond for you, Madame."

"*Oh, là,* a diamond." Maman destroyed it with her breath. To teach me what lasts. What doesn't. "Poof, *invisible.*"

Even as they melted, the stars of snow in my hand provoked my secret longing, impacted like a boil behind the sternum. A red unspeakable greed. For what? To have, to keep it. The crystal beauty and the oxygen, ferny diadems of lace in the air. Such yearning hit me like a regular vertigo. I swallowed it down, so that my soul would not fall out of my mouth and wither away.

The horses struggled against the driving blizzard. Mats of snow clumped their manes and eyes. Hawky Jenkins got down and rubbed their snouts, clogged with ice. "Sweetie, there," he said. "Baby, now." When he got back up, he whipped their flanks. Blood striped their hides.

"Don't hit them," I whispered. "Don't."

"Shhush," Maman said. "He has to, or they won't go." For Maman, between carrot and stick, it was stick that worked, as there was no carrot in this life. *Silence is a woman's best garment,* she taught me. And because I loved my mother, I followed this philosophy despite how it chafed me.

"Oh, I'm light-headed," she said, suffering the mountain sickness. Our lungs were so tight we had to take sips of air. Frequent thin helpings.

The track narrowed still more, the rock wall of the trail so close Henry reached and touched it. The outside edge was a sheer drop to the ravine below. A glance over the lip made my stomach fall clear to the bottom, to the underworld miles down, where dark boulders jagged up through the snow and the Devil waited to catch me in his arms.

"Fugginshee fuggit whoa," said Jenkins. With a sudden sickening slide, the sled went sideways toward the edge. Maman clutched at Henry with a little scream. Jenkins hauled the reins in a hard turn, but the horses went too fast around the curve, and the sled swung straight out behind. A back runner hung half off the edge. We were suspended over nothing.

"*Je vous salue Marie.*" Maman did Hail Marys under her breath.

"Quit that," said Jenkins. "Shitgotdam bastidbitches. Don't nobody move."

We froze, balanced hideously over the lip. In the teetering moment Hawky whispered to the horses, "Sweetie, Baby, rightgirl, right." He pulled them in a carving turn till we straightened, and the sled switchbacked along a ravine worse than the last. Jenkins narrated over the howling bruits of the storm. "Was a whole party in a wagon fell down to death right here. String a jackmules pulled overside by the stumble of the lead animal."

The weight of fear and the cold pressed our lungs empty; the horizontal snow blew wasps of ice in our eyes, no breath between the flakes. You could not see ahead. Then in the solid white air came the fairy sound of bells.

"Mule string comin' down," Jenkins said. "Everbody out." We climbed down and sank in the drifts, pressed to the wall of the trail. Nipper whimpered in Maman's arms. Bells jangled. "Hallooo!" Jenkins hollered a warning, and pushed the horses against the mountain. "Don't make a move. You don't wanta startle 'em. Only an inch between a hoof and death overside."

The bells came closer, menacing. Emerging out of the curtain of snowfall was a ghost rider astride a ghost horse, whitened and furred. The trail was so tight we could've touched his leg through the flakes. His blanket was frozen and his hat pulled down against the wind. The horse's eyes bulged goggling with nerves, lashes beaded with ice.

"Jenkins, ya miserable fool," the rider spat as he passed. "Riskin' death with women and children." He and his horse carried on. After them followed mules roped together and strapped with barrels and crates, sacks piled on their backs. They snorted and plunged, flanks raw, patches of hair missing where the wide latigos cinched their ribs. One had a red sore festering. As the last of them passed, a blast of wind pinned us to the mountain, so loud Maman had to shout.

"Go back, *monsieur*. We turn back."

"Can't," Hawky said. "No turnaround. Too narrow. Better go on than back. That string tramped it down some ahead, anyways."

"I'm sorry for them," I said.

"Pah. Going down's nothin'," Hawky said. "Them barrels is empty. Up-hill, we load 'em to the ears. We brang pianos up. Heating stoves. A printer press. The Duke had all that mahogany wood toted here by mule."

Mahogany wood sounded to my ears like *Enchanted Forest*. In his letters my father wrote that in our new town of Moonstone there lived a Duke, with his wife, the Countess. Their house was a château, with turrets and marble columns, fountains and gardens. Picturing such luxury distracted me from the aching ice blocks of my feet. Hawky Jenkins handed us back on the sledge to hunker under solid blankets, our mufflers stiff with frozen breath. He retrieved his flask from the depths of his furs and drained it. We wrapped our arms around each other and went on silent into the jaws of the storm, up the face of Dogtooth Mountain.

In the middle part of the afternoon, the grade of the trail flattened. Out of the blizzard the shapes of buildings emerged. Lights glimmered in the windows of a warehouse. "Carving sheds, on the right," Jenkins said. "Millworks."

"Are we there?" Henry asked.

"Pelletier's up in Quarrytown. This is Moonstone," Jenkins said. "Your store yonder. Your church. Your barbershop. Jailhouse. You'll get the hang of her."

The smell of woodsmoke came through the snowfall. A whiff of meat roasting. Signs for Koble's Mercantile. Weeks' Bakery. We went gliding past small shacky dwellings sunk in snowbanks, sure we would stop now, and there would be the snug darling cabin. Hot supper. But the town ended and the trail went on in the white blowing curtains of the storm. Jenkins drove uphill again, past nothing and more nothing. Maman pulled the blanket over our heads. We closed our eyes and endured three miles more.

Jenkins said, "Here's Quarrytown."

It was not a town. It was a collection of huts affixed to the side of the mountain, a narrow alley strung on a precipice. Paths like tunnels were carved in the drifts, leading to buried burrows, only tin chimneys visible above the snowpile.

The wagon stopped. Hawky Jenkins pointed. "Cabin Six."

What we saw was a door in a wall of snow, a stovepipe sticking out. A sort of hallway was shoveled to the entry. Moles lived there. Badgers.

"Pelletier!" Hawky whistled.

"Jacques!" Maman shouted above the wind. "He is here?"

"He is," said Hawky.

But he wasn't.

With numb stumps for feet, we got down and sank past our knees, fighting to the steps. When Henry pushed in the door, the wind took it out of his hand.

"Papa?"

Jenkins dumped our last box in the drift and disappeared in the howling whiteout.

"Papa?" A green tuque hung off a peg by the door. His hat.

"Where is he?" Henry's voice rose in fear.

"Work," Maman said, not convincing.

We found coal in a corner and shoved it inside the stove. Wind through the cracks snuffed six matches, but we got the fire going and pushed close to it in our frozen coats, our violent shivering. The stove heated fast but we did not.

"Sylvie *icitte*, here's a pot," Maman said. "Get water for tea."

Outside again, I scooped a pot of snow, as light as nothing. It melted over the fire, but the water it made was not much and not yet boiling. The snug house was not snug. It was not a house. It was one room of batten and boards nailed with tacks. Strips of canvas and pages from the *Phrenological Journal* covered the walls. Newspaper chinked the cracks. The furniture was a table and three short stools. A cushioned chair. A dust of snow on everything.

"Tea won't boil," I said.

"*L'altitude*," my mother said. Exhaustion came off her like fumes.

Up a ladder was a sleeping platform nailed around the chimney pipe. Pelts of rabbit and weasel were tacked to cure in the rafters. Snowshoes hung on the walls with tools and implements. A flap of tar paper served as the door to a lean-to room just big enough for a shuck mattress, a washstand.

We thawed our fingers, the baby's toes, with our breath. Our hands and feet itched and burned, turned the bright red of raw meat. Maman found bread frozen in the cupboard, a can of oysters. A can of peas. She handed these to me with a tin punch.

I opened the tins and cut a finger on the sharp teeth of the lid. Blood tinged the oysters pink. We put the cans on the stove to thaw. Maman hacked the bread and heaped bloodied oysters on it. We ate these with spoonfuls of peas from the can and drank weak tea, stunned still in our coats, our hats. We got in the bed in a pile like a litter of animals and warmed each other by shivering till we slept. Papa was not in this house. His hat was not on his head.

Slivers of frozen sunlight came through cracks in the roof. A fur of snow lay across the covers. Boots stamped outside.

"Halloo, allo!" Our lost papa like a stranger flopped on the nested heap of us. "*Ma famille*, look at you!" He filled the room with his loudness, his happiness, saying all our names. "Cherie! Henry! So tall, Sylvie! So beautiful, my wife!" He wrapped his arms around Maman, around my gangled shoulders and Henry's. He gazed through the murk, light shining in his eyes, with his first ever sighting of his baby son. "*Oh, mon fils.*"

In the two years since we'd seen him, my father had altered, his blue-black hair long to the collar, his beard half down his chest. Nipper whimpered and hid his face in Maman's neck. Papa chinned him with his whiskers and burrowed under the covers, playing peek till Nipper laughed. Papa wrestled Henry. He pulled my hair and made the tail of my long braid into a mustache for the baby, holding it under his nose.

"Jacques!" My mother was rosy with shyness. Happiness.

He made a mustache for her too, and pulled the covers over our heads, roaring. "I'm a cave bear," he said. White grit powdered his eyebrows, the plates of his hands cracked and silted. "A quarryman's a dusty man," he said. It hurt to see how worn he was, haggard.

Maman brushed grit off him. He pressed his brow against her forehead and removed her pins. Her hair spilled down in a dark fall. "Jacques, *tétè où là?* Where were you?"

"In the quarry, Cherie." Papa pulled back, eyes on her. "I'm on graveyard-shift now. New rule. Same grievance. Same again—we organize."

"Please no more striking." My mother soothed her hand down over the edge in his voice, over the crown of his head, a new grizzle of gray at his temples. "You promised no more. You said it was no danger in April. But—the storm. We nearly died."

"*Non, non, non*, Cherie. You did not die, no. Mrs. Luck smiled on us."

"You mean *Lady* Luck," I said, and they laughed.

He arranged the strands of her hair, tucked it behind her ears. Her hand went up to him, and he caught it, kissed it. She rested her face against his chest. *Love* was not a word they said aloud, but there it was, what I wanted for myself, *un grand amour.*

Papa put new coals in the stove, his eyes shiny with emotion. He sang "Alouette" and cooked frozen bacon in the fry pan. He watched us eat, like it was a miracle that we chewed and swallowed. "Today, *mes poussins*," he said, "we go out and see the beauty up here in the rafters of heaven."

We emerged from our burrow into the sun, looking across the ravine at the vast landscape reaching in the distance like a sea. The peaks were waves cresting into the blue. The white glory of it blinded us.

"It's the Cathedral of God," said Papa in his showman's voice. He had traveled with the circus, which was why he could juggle, why he could hang off a scaffold with a chisel and swallow flames. He'd run with the Iroquois, which was why he could see in the dark and nest in the trees (he said). My father had lived in a tent all through a winter. Goldfinches nested in his beard. He spoke Canadian French, and his English was American. He could walk on his hands.

"This place Moonstone is named by the ancients," he said, "because a piece of the moon fell down from the sky and landed here." Half his stories were true and seventy-five percent of them were not, he liked to say, no telling which was which. He hoisted Nipper on his shoulders, took Henry by the stalk of his neck. "Let's go see the sights."

We followed the snowy boot-pocked track up the slope. I looked for a shop or a church or a school but saw only shacks clinging to the rocky shelf, as I clung, myself, to the hope that I was not now stranded up here on this pointy peak.

"Cabin Five is Setkowski," Papa said. "Cabin Four is Bruner. Stone house up the hill is for boss Tarbusch and his pocket watch. All these empties are for the summer crew." He pointed out a long tin-roof building nailed to a cliff face, propped on struts: the boardinghouse. Papa had lived there two years without us. "Mrs. Quirk runs the place. Her commissary can sell you coal or coffee, but get supplies in town. Everything in these Company joints cost a nose and ear."

I laughed.

He pulled my braid. "What's funny?"

"It's 'arm and a leg,'" I told him.

"Sylvie knows everything," said Maman. "She is top to her class." This was a rare show of pride; also a warning: not to be *Mademoiselle connaît-tout.* Know-it-all. What-all she wanted us to know was *la langue maternelle*, without the Yankee expressions that corrupted our French. She saw it on me like a rash, the wish for my own words.

We came around the bend and arrived on a flat shelf where workers and horses labored beside a gaping black hole punched in the side of the mountain.

"The Padgett quarry," said Papa, proud of it.

"That's it?" Henry craned his neck. "That cave?"

"*Ohh, là.*" Maman crossed herself.

The entrance was the toothless open mouth of a whale. Hung around it were platforms and derricks, ropes and scaffolding and ladders. Cranes rigged to the crag above poked up like antennae, dangling cables and a massive hook the size of a child. All around the yard, hunks of white rock lay piled like the sugar lumps of a giant.

"The most beautiful stone in the world." Papa beamed. "Pure statuary white. One big vein with gold in it. A mile long inside the mountain."

"Gold?" Henry's eyes lit. "Real gold?"

"Nah. It's the pyrite gives the marble the yellow streaks. Prettiest thing."

"Pyrite is the foolish gold," said my mother.

"Fool's gold," I said, unable to help myself, correcting her.

"Duke Padgett is no fool. He's seven times a millionaire," said Papa. "Watch how we make his money."

"Heads!" came a shout. A whistle blew shrill blasts. A clot of men surrounded a stone block the size of a grand piano, wrapped in chains. The crane above pivoted and lowered the dangling hook. One fellow leapt atop the stone, and as it began to rise, he held the lifting chains, performed a somersault.

"He's Setkowski," said my father. "He rides the white bird."

"I want to try it," Henry said.

Our mother closed her eyes. "Never," she said.

The crane maneuvered the stone over the lip of the cliff, where it swayed, suspended above the ant bodies of the workers in the yard, fifty feet below. The chain would snap, I thought. The block would plummet and smash the men. It lowered slowly, showoff Setkowski waving his hat, then settled on a waiting flatbed wagon. A six-horse team would haul it down the track to the mill in town.

"That stone, *là*." My father pointed. "A hundred thirty dollars a ton. Thirty tons for a Greek column. Figure how many columns in a bank. A library? Enough stone in this mountain for three hundred years. Add it up."

"Millions!" Henry said. "Can we go in the quarry and see?"

"No," said Maman. "The danger."

"The beauty," Papa said. "When the sun comes in, the dust in the air is gold, like the sparks of God. You'll be amazed. *La Comtesse* herself came for a tour."

"The Countess?" I said.

"The Duke's wife. From *Bruxelles*. She's Belgian," Papa said. "You ladies go on back. I'll take the boy for a look. Moonstone quarry is the Eighth Wonder of the World."

"Sylvie." Maman pulled me away from talk of countesses and wonders.

"But—" If I were a boy, I could ride the white bird. If I were a countess, I could go in the quarry to see the dust of gold. But I was a dutiful daughter and forbidden. What else could I not do? A long list. Even here in the Wild West, life would be a sentence of chores and boredom.

Papa saw my disappointment. "Wait for summer, Birdy. Summer is the time, you'll see. Always there's flowers on the hills, rainbows in the river."

"He means trouts," said know-it-all Henry.

"I mean rainbows," Papa said, and went off off to show Henry the sights.

Maman pointed to the dangling hook. "See the danger? He's always a fool for the risk, your father."

I would rather be like him is what I thought. And yet I was like her, obedient and quiet. I took Nipper from her arms.

"What would I do without you?" she said, grateful.

Get Henry to help instead, I thought, but understood it was my fate to help her with her burdens. Henry's was to go with Papa, to fly through the air on a white stone bird, to see dazzlements. My mother and I walked back toward the safe cage of Cabin Six, away from the Eighth Wonder of the World. My jaw slid forward on its hinge. Whatever marvels there were to see in the Gilded Mountains, I determined to see them.

Chapter Two

AFTER THREE DAYS THE CABIN was rank with smells of cabbage, of wet wool. Our sibling bickery leaked out through the cracks, and a cold rain leaked in with new jealousies. Henry blathered on about the marble quarry. The most stupendous, most astonishing sight in the universe. *Magnifique.*

"You would not like it," he said, lordly. "It's dangerous."

"And dirty," my mother said. "It's not for a girl."

I sat by the stove reading *Flowers of Evil*, trapped in a stew of resentment. I hated rocks. I hated mountains. Mud. Old snow like scab on the land. Nipper banged his spoon on a pot. Henry lowered a string off the platform where we slept, above, "practicing to fish." His hook was a crooked hairpin that snagged on the end of my braid. He pulled at it. I flung the book and uttered the *Québécois* curse, "*Tabarnac!*"

To insult the holy tabernacle was to risk perdition *éternelle*. Maman trembled at me. "You will say Contrition. You will be good."

I prayed to be good, and I was. Helpful, polite. Except not in my thoughts, where I was Mrs. Satan, bride of the devil. A spew of defiance was gathering in my craw. I swallowed. "Sorry, Maman. *Desolée.*"

I said the Act of Contrition, not contrite. After a minute she came to rest her hand on my hair. Perhaps she understood. Perhaps she once had strings pulling her toward some delight and they led her to the barn dance and my father, who landed her here on this miserable rockpile.

"God hears all things," she reminded me, and handed me the coal sling to fill at the commissary. "Go now," she said softly, and forgave me. That time she did.

Outside, I stumped along in disappointed boots. Steam rose off the snowbanks. In a matter of days, the temperature had warmed from twenty to fifty. On the Quarrytown path, rain had melted the top layer of snow to reveal black mats of ash frozen in front of the huts, dumped smuts of stoves emptied out of doorways. Pathways of mud threaded over ice pitted with boot prints, the ruts of wheels and runners. The sugar was dissolving, and now there was muck. Someone was staring at me.

A girl stood in the doorway of Cabin Five. She was nine, maybe younger, a sprite wearing overalls fashioned into a dress, her hair uncombed, a crust of yellow in her eyes.

"I don't see you around here yet," she said. "Where you came from?"

"Back east," I said.

The girl laughed. Her name was Eva Setkowski, she said, and kept laughing.

"What's so funny?"

"Nobody never should come here."

"Why?"

"It's a curse. It's a curse on it."

"What curse?"

"Indian Yoots put a bad spell here. This place used to be all Yoots, but the white man killed 'em and chased 'em away. So they cursed the mountains." She stabbed her finger at the four points of an invisible compass. "Curse, curse, curse, curse. You won't never leave here without bad evil finding you."

"I don't believe you."

"I don't care if you do," she said.

———

"What are Yoots?" I asked later, at home.

"The Ute people," Papa said. "U-T-E. Like Utah."

"Indians who lived here long ago," my mother said.

"Not long. Thirty years," my father corrected.

"That Polish girl said a curse is on the valley."

"That's only a fairy tale," Papa said.

Was it? At the time I thought so, that it was just a legend. But all these years since, I've wondered if the disasters that befell Moonstone were due to the Ute curse, Chief Colorow's prophecy, that any venture attempted by white people in the Diamond River Valley was doomed.

"Do not talk to that girl," Maman said. "Don't look at the men when they watch you. Keep walking."

But I did look at them, envied their swagger and ease, their loudness, jokes, and cursing, not allowed for me, who must not look and must not talk and not go in the quarry to see the Eighth Wonder. Fetching water or hauling coal, I looked, yes, to see—was one of these fellows a sweetheart for me, someone to free me, the Devil himself, from this boredom and obedience? I noticed their sledgehammer arms, their broken-nailed fingers raking their hair, and was in love twice a day.

"They are *primitifs*," my mother said. "Foreign."

"Ah, Cherie, they're good people," Papa said. "Except the boss, Tarbusch."

"Shh!" Maman put a hand over his mouth. She tied a cloth around his neck and cut his hair, trimmed his beard. In a week she'd shaped him up with clean overalls, and spruced Cabin Six with flour sack curtains in a rose pattern and a paper portrait of *Notre Seigneur* on the wall, golden rays of light spearing his head. She prayed for protection from primitives while I prayed for my deliverance from this rock. I could not get to town, not even for school, to finish and get my certificate.

"It is still a danger of slides," Maman said. "Mud and rock."

But it was the danger from men that worried her, the laborers in the loading yards, the artisans and stone carvers in the mill.

"Italians are the masters," Papa told her. "The finest artists for statues—"

"Naked ones," she sniffed. "*Complètement nu.*"

"Most of 'em stay down there in Dagotown," he said, "by the mill."

I did not like the way my parents talked about the foreign workers, for weren't we ourselves called *froggy* and *peasouper*, and weren't we migrants ourselves? How was anyone to be American?

"Company set them up separate," my father said, "so we won't plot for a union. But, *tant pis*, if the boss don't pay more—we strike. Tarbusch cheats hours off your clock. Makes us work Sundays."

"It's against God," said Maman.

"Turns stone into gold. Pretty good trick." My father's laugh was undercut by bitterness. He was not the Papa who played his fiddle in the evenings. He was too tired to read *Robin Hood* aloud or sing "Alouette" or whistle. He held the bridge of his nose pinched in his hand, massaged his dusty head. He went to work or went to sleep, and when he was awake, he argued in whispers with Maman. From listening in the eaves, we knew everything. Our debt for supplies at the Company Mercantile. The strike brewing.

Early one morning Papa came in after a graveyard shift of fourteen hours and sat taking big helpings of air, his hands outstretched to the stove. Maman brushed at him. Dust rose from his jacket and made her cough.

"It's sugar coating," he said, eyes closed. "I'm the sugar man."

"Don't breathe it," Maman said. "You're bones and skin. You rest."

"No time."

All their talk was of time. A day was twelve hours, or ten. Some days were at night. The lunch hour was minutes. Some hours were overtime, but those hours were dead.

"How can hours be dead?" Henry asked me.

"Dead work," I told him. "Not paid."

Their other talk was about money, never any in the jar. Wages by the hour. Rent by the month. Hospital fees for the year. Coal was four plunks per sack. Plunks were scrip, offered instead of cash, to spend at the Company store. By payday it was all down to *zed*. The talk of money made me want some for myself.

"The boys are set to walk out," Papa said.

"They will kill you this time," said Maman.

"Nobody kills me," he said, and fell asleep with his boots on.

One evening, two weeks after we'd arrived, Papa came home in the dark and left again after six hours of sleep. In his exhaustion he forgot his lunch bucket.

"I'll take it to him," I said.

"You don't," Maman said. "Henry does it."

But Henry had gone off to set snares for rabbits, Nipper riding piggyback. Maman threw up her hands. "Fifteen minutes. Give the dinner to the foreman. You don't talk. You don't go in."

"*Oui*, Maman." I headed out the door and the Devil whispered defiance in my ear.

In the load-out yard I went between blocks of stone, past the stares and whistles of the men, to a small shack by the quarry mouth. There in the open half of a Dutch door was perched Juno Tarbusch, timekeeper, stoop-shouldered and small-eyed.

"Here's dinner for my father," I said. "Mr. Pelletier."

"Frenchy's girl, are you?" He ran his finger down a page of his ledger, checked his watch. "Doesn't deserve dinner, that one. He's in the pit. I'll take that."

"I'll bring it to him. I don't mind."

"Not smart," he said, and cleared a long gargle of phlegm. "Been a long winter. These boys might just put you in a slag bucket, steal you off for a ride. We won't never see you again." His wet eyes gleamed. "You could slip and fall. Skirts like that."

You could stick that pencil in your eye, I didn't say, imagining eyeballs bursting like the vile jellies of Shakespeare. "My mother sent me."

"Go ahead, then," he said. "Only one way down, and that's Satan's Staircase!" He tapped his watch. "Better git. Time is money."

I went past him. Now I'd see it: the Eighth Wonder.

And it was true, what Henry said. *Magnifique. Incroyable.* I stood inside the cave at the top of the Devil's stairs and gasped. Men had hollowed the mountain into a white stone cathedral. Pillars and flying buttresses of marble held up the vaulted roof. Particles of glitter hung in sunbeams shafting through the entrance like God-light in a painting. Hundreds of feet below were clots of machinery, lumber, tangles of rope, chain, wire, the dark shapes of men and mules. Workers moved along ladders tacked to the walls, hung from scaffolding rickety as twigs. Hammer blows ricocheted off chisels amid a buzz of drills and stone saws. Smoke billowed up from boiler fires and stained the white ceiling of the cavern black with ash. The smell was of dampness and sulfur.

Satan's staircase was only thin backless boards spiked to stone. I gripped the railing in one hand, lunch pail and skirts in the other. A fellow shouted and pointed. Whistles and hisses, eyes on me like millipedes. Halfway down I arrived at a terrace of rock. Workers there hammered at the wall, trading blows. They stopped, leaning on their sledgehammers, gawking as if I were a mythical creature. I nodded hello and went on into the cold and damp whiteness of the cave. At different levels were carved rough letters, hearts, initials dug in the marble walls.

On the lowest landing, six men balanced on a long crowbar, levering up a cut block of stone. Two more pushed rubble over a three-foot ledge, rattling it into metal buckets below, shovels scraping.

One of them stepped in front of me, spectacled, young, oddly dressed in a collared shirt, a silk tie of gold and crimson stripes. Pale springs of hair were tamed to a side part. He was slight through the shoulders, hatless in a suit jacket, strangely out of place. Was he a geologist? A dandy? A prospector?

Are you lost? I wanted to ask him.

He adjusted the wire-rims on his nose and leaned on his shovel to blink at me. "Are you lost, miss?" he said, Southern vowels in his voice.

"No," I said, startled, as if he'd taken words from my mouth.

"Might I offer assistance?" His professorial air was bizarre in the dust and clamor.

"I'm looking for Mr. Jacques Pelletier," I said.

"Frenchy? Everybody knows Frenchy." He pointed below. "There in the green hat."

I had knitted that hat, *une tuque*, fitted around the head with a flop of extra space at the crown. *Pour attraper les pensées*, my father said, *so dreams don't escape*.

I myself should have escaped then, to avoid the impropriety of talking to a strange man, but the Devil had other plans. Though is it fair to blame the Devil? I was fascinated from the start by this odd fellow. He was owlish. Clean-shaved. His teeth white as his starched collar. His leather boots were new. He fussed with a bloody handkerchief wrapped around his hand, trying to tie it off with his teeth.

"Shall I help you?" I said, forgetting to slump into my bones, to appear petite.

"Why, yes, thank you." He held out his hand to show an open blister across the web of his thumb, flecked with grit. "Went off without my gloves this morning. I'd be obliged, miss, if you could secure this for me."

When I put down the lunch bucket, he handed me the handkerchief, monogrammed in blue initials, *JCP*. "This will have to do," he said, "unless by some stroke of fortune you happen to carry bandages in your dinner pail? A tincture of iodine?"

Dinnah payel, he said, as if it were a languid hot afternoon.

His outstretched hand, when I took it, sent a jolt through me. I had not gone to school with boys or known any boys except loud brothers and cousins, the uncles full of snores and guffaws, curses and drinking, fiddling and singing. This boy was refined and American, his hand pink and uncalloused, streaked bloody. He smiled directly at me, as if he knew my thoughts. "That looks painful," I managed to say.

23

"Those who would learn must suffer," he said, "as my father is fond of telling me. And I *am* suffering, truly. The old man would send us all to the school of hard knocks."

"Or hard rocks," I said.

He laughed as if my joke surprised him. I wrapped his hand, its long delicate fingers, and tied the cloth in a knot. I could not look at him, his hair the color of corn, both of us pink with awkwardness, not only me. Sweat steamed his glasses. He blinked behind them, considering me. "Thank you for coming to the aid of the suffering," he said. "Nobody told me they let angels down here."

"It's no trouble." Angels did not stammer as I did. Seraphim did not wear dusty boots. The other fellows ragged him. "Ohh, J.C., the ladies' man." Making kiss noises.

"In my dreams only." He grinned at me, and I had the strange impulse to take the spectacles from his face. To clean the fog off them and see the color of his eyes.

"Sylvie!" Papa beckoned below.

I nodded to JCP and carried on in a fluster to hand the lunch pail to my father. "You forgot this!"

"Cherie sends you?" he asked.

"She said give it to the foreman but—"

"*Bah, non*, if you give it to Tarbusch, he would eat it himself. He eats babies. He eats kittens. He'd cut the kidneys out of you and cook them for breakfast."

"He said that you do not deserve dinner," I told him.

"Did he?" My father's eyes narrowed. "You see, Birdy? Big shots don't like a man even to have his dinner." He glanced toward the hole of light above us as if it were the eye of God all-seeing. But who was looking down was that bandaged fellow, *JCP*, from the rock shelf. He saluted when he saw us notice.

"That fella"—my father pointed with his chin—"is Jasper Padgett. Son of Duke Padgett. His daddy has him playing quarry boy all summer."

This information interested me. JCP was royalty. Son of a duke. He looked as odd in that cavern as I did. He had called me *angel*.

Papa the showman held up his dinner pail and kissed it. The fellows around him laughed and came over to shake my hand.

"Here's my daughter, Sylvie." He pointed a warning finger at them. "Don't none of you dare. Or I feed you to the wolves." He swept his arm grandly overhead. "*Regarde*, Sylvie, our famous marble quarry. *Splendide, non?*"

"*Splendide*, yes," I said.

My father pointed with pride to a hulking machine that inched along a cut with a hammering screech. "There's my sweetheart. She goes through stone like the knife through jelly—but so slow we call her *l'Escargot*."

The Snail was a channeling machine on tracks, drill bits on either side like massive sewing machine needles. "She moves one foot an hour. She eats five hundred pounds of coal every day. She's a beautiful girl."

The Snail's grim industrial appearance did not match his worshipful description. He loved it for the chiseling work it saved him, his arms and back, but to me it was a burping pile of dirty metal. Black exhaust from its fiery boiler was the only hint that it might be the murder weapon that it was. That it came to be.

The fellow at the controls wore a blue kerchief around his neck, a cigarette in his mouth. "Sylvie," my father said, "here's Dan Kerrigan, our favorite troublemaker."

"Troublemakers, eh?" Kerrigan said, winking, "It's your dad who's chief rebel, and we thank him for that, don't we, now, Jocko?"

My father spooned up his dinner and shared it with the hungry-eyed Kerrigan. A whistle blew. The men on the floor looked up, wary as deer. High above, a man pointed theatrically at his watch.

"Tarbusch," my father said. "*Putain.*"

"One a these days," Kerrigan said, "gonna punch his doors in."

"Gonna *walk out* of his doors," my father said. "Then they pay." He noticed me listening. "Go on home now," he said, and returned to his sweetheart, the Snail.

Back across the quarry floor, my boots sucked in a gray paste of icy mud. I hoped to see JCP, but the only sign of him was a red spot among the white stone chips, the bloody handkerchief. I fished it out for a souvenir and started up the stairs. When I came blinking into the sun, Mr. Tarbusch tapped his watch.

"Thirty-five minutes," he said. "Lunch break is fifteen only." He opened his timekeeper's record and with elaborate theater, licked his red pencil, made a mark. "Hadda dock that crew twenty."

"Sir?"

"Like I said, time is money, so time is our enemy. Don't forget it."

What I don't forget is that Tarbusch was an enemy, the tool and agent and lapdog of the actual enemy. But that morning I was preoccupied by Jasper C. Padgett, his bloody paw, the southern flavor in his voice. *Angel*, he'd said. The word played a shiny harp in my life of dreariness and boredom. I'd seen the Eighth Wonder of the World and bandaged the son of a duke. How, I wondered, could I contrive another sighting of JCP? The quarry no longer interested me. One tour down in the mountain bowels was enough. I stowed the handkerchief in my shoebox of keepsakes, where the red bloodstains hardened and turned brown. I have it still, all these years later.

Chapter Three

THAT WEEK PAPA WORKED LATE, and slept, and left again. The rest of us sat out on the steps in the dusk, inhaling a new green smell in the air, of shoots and leaves unfurling, watery rivulets coursing downhill. The sinking sun made bands of blue shadow along the mountain flanks, till it was only a scarlet rind behind the stonehearted ranges to the west. The night filled in between the peaks. A swift arrowed through the dusk. Nipper hummed a tune. Henry took a piece of paper from his pocket and handed it to Maman.

"Mr. Tarbusch says he can use me in the quarry," he said. "Ten cents an hour."

In the lantern light, she read the paper, a certificate granting permission for a boy to quit school and go to work. It stated Henry's age as fifteen though he was only twelve. It gave his weight as a hundred pounds when he was not more than sixty, soaking wet. It was signed as fact by Colonel Bowles, the Company president. Bowles was also mayor of Moonstone and superintendent of schools, too.

"You'll sign?" Henry asked her.

For an answer, she tore the paper in bits. "It's lies," she said. "The age. The weight. You lied. In this life, all we have is our savior and the honest word."

"Other boys do it," Henry dared to argue. "The Duke's own son works there."

"He is twelve? *Non*." She stabbed the paper with a finger. "This colonel. He prefers you not to have education? To work in a mine? *Bon ben*, you go to school with Sylvie. To start tomorrow."

It was thanks to my brother and his sneaky attempt to earn a dime that I escaped from Quarrytown.

Monday morning at five o'clock, we started hiking to town. Eva Setkowski passed us going uphill to fetch water. "What about school?" I asked her.

"I got to work." She skipped off with her buckets. When she filled them at the sluice pipe, they'd weigh as much as she did.

We'd not seen Moonstone since coming through it in the storm three weeks before, and now we went along with excitement. The sunrise speared up behind the greening peaks. Echoing from the village came the barking of dogs, the bray of mules, alluring as a carnival. Around the shoulder of the mountain, we passed a sign marking Hairpin Point. Below, the turrets of a great house rose through the trees.

"The castle!" I cried. "Look, Henry! It's Elkhorne, the Padgett château—" If I could peer through the windows I'd surely see dragon piles of loot and that odd prince, JCP, at his breakfast of poached peacock eggs, roasted humming-bird tongues.

Henry ran ahead, uninterested. We walked downhill for an hour and crossed the bridge into Moonstone town, passing stock pens of cattle and pigs and the long tin-roof sheds of the mill. Blocks of marble were lined up there to be slabbed and carved, then trucked out by wagon.

Classes were held in the church (of apostates, Maman said). We followed a straggle of pupils who examined us with suspicion. The church, when we found it, was not pretty; it was Methodist, plain without saints. Henry went to the vestry room with the younger students. I climbed upstairs, following a paper sign that said *High School*.

A petite young lady wrote on a chalkboard, her shiny hair piled and pinned. Was she the teacher? Teachers were wimpled, stern as crows. This was a sunflower. "I am Miss Gage," she said, smiling. "Please have a seat."

From my desk I studied her bright American expression. A few girls sat up front in starched hair ribbons. In the back were older boys; among them, Carlton Pfister, big as a man, with small bored eyes and clenched hands, in training, perhaps, for his future as the lout he would become. My adversary.

"Please welcome our new pupil, Sylvie," Miss Gage said. "Mademoiselle Pelletier is from Quebec. She speaks French."

"Frenchy Frenchy," Carlton whispered, tipped his nose at me with his thumb.

"Please demonstrate for us, Sylvie," the teacher said. "*Parlez, mademoiselle.*"

To speak French would reveal me. The Yankee children in Rutland had mocked our accents, called us frogs.

"Sylvie? *Un peu de français, s'il vous plaît?*"

"*Salut,*" I said. "*Bonjour.*" All available blood was in my face. My plan to be American was spoiled now by this daisy teacher. Or so I thought then. But as it turned out, Miss Gage was the one who set me on my course, however unwittingly.

Sniggering stares and whispers crawled on my skin. It was the first time I'd been in a classroom with boys. Without nuns. I was shocked to see Carlton and another pocky student playing catch with a pinecone. Why did the teacher not beat them with a switch? In front of me, Millie Havilland drew elaborate hearts on her slate. In the middle row, a boy put his head on the desk and slept with his mouth open.

Disappointment pooled in my gullet. The school was for *imbéciles* and *enfants*. I would never get my diploma. Just before dismissal, Miss Gage said, "Tomorrow, boys and girls, let's all try to be as good and quiet as our new pupil."

I kept quiet not because I was good but because I lacked words to name the frustration throttled in my throat. How a girl could learn such words or dare to speak them would not be taught here. I'd have to find them myself. When the bell rang, I went out to see what the town might offer in the way of opportunity.

Moonstone was eight mud blocks crosshatched in a flat bowl, hemmed in by snowy mountains. Empty lots and sprouts of new buildings clustered on Padgett Street: a bank, a bakery, a saloon. At the butcher shop, Henry and I stared at sausages hung in the window, then lingered in front of Company Mercantile but did not go in. We had no money to spend, and if we missed our ride on the stone lorry back to Quarrytown, we'd have three miles to walk home.

Just before the bridge, we came upon a rack-ribbed donkey chewing a patch of weeds sticking up through old snow. A bunch of boys poked the poor creature with branches. Carlton Pfister and his friends, stabbing with sticks.

"Don't say anything." Henry pulled his hat low to hide his face. We passed them, silent, while the poor donkey fixed his baleful eye upon me, accusing. At the stone yard, we found the lorry had left without us and hiked uphill two hours.

Maman waited on the steps. Nipper charged us on his wobbling new legs. Henry caught him and swung him up. Voices came from inside the cabin. My father and someone. The door opened and a young man came outside. He had the scruffy look of a pirate; the white thread of a scar traced from ear to chin.

Papa followed out after him. "Sylvie, here's George Lonahan. From Denver."

"Not from Denver," said my mother, disgusted. "From the IWW." She meant the Industrial Workers of the World, the labor union that had caused my father's trouble in Rutland.

"With respect, ma'am, it's UMW, and I'm from New Jersey," Lonahan said. "The Garden State. We grow the world's best bog iron. I been sent west here to free the workingman by the strength of our own numbers. Pleased to meetcha, Sylvie."

My parents went inside to argue behind the door. George Lonahan stretched his arms overhead and sighed. I could hardly look at him, such a dashing, rangy fellow, brown hair too long in the back, past a frayed collar inside his thin city jacket. Under a sparse growth of whiskers, the scar was a bracket around one side of his face. Perhaps he was attacked by a swashbuckler. A cutlass. My shyness was acute.

"Mind if I sit?" he asked, and then did, beside me on the step, the long grasshopper bones of his legs folded and splayed. He loosened his necktie and leaned back on his elbows to chew a toothpick and look across the gorge. "Free the workingman," he muttered. "That'll be the day, Sylvie, won't it?"

He cracked his knuckles and assessed me sideways. A frisson of heat shivered through me for the second time that week.

"So, Miss Pelletier," he said, "here's a riddle: What are singular?"

"Singular . . . ?"

"Here's a hint: scissors." He waited for the answer, an amused expression on his face like a trap. Or a lure. "I'll ask again: What are singular?"

"Pants?" I said after a minute. "Pants are singular."

"Ha! Bravo! Your dad said you were first in your class. What else?"

"Suds!" I said, grinning.

"Ye olde *pluralia tantum*," Lonahan said. "Like measles."

"Also riches," I remembered. "You cannot have one measle or one rich."

"But you *can*." Lonahan sat forward with a sudden intensity. "See, right here you got a singular, measly, rich Duke, down there in his *château*, like you say in France."

"I'm American," I said. "I've never been to France."

"Let's go right now, then. You and me fly off to Paree, whattya say? Alley-oop." He flapped his arms like the wings of a comical goose. "The point ain't grammar," he said, serious now. "Point is, I need to have a couple words with the fellas up here."

"What words?"

"The singular truth. About the boot heel of injustice. Good hardworking people like yourselves deserve the fine and beautiful things, same as a duchess."

31

"We don't have a duchess. But we do have a countess."

"Same basic snoot." He took a cigarette from his pocket and smoked in the gathering dusk. "You tell your papa you won't wait another year for a roof that don't leak. You want milk for that baby. Roast chicken on Sundays. Tell him he needs a day of rest for the bones. Your mother does."

We listened to her whispers behind the door and watched Henry pitch pebbles to Nipper, who tried to catch them in his baby paws.

"You want a ball glove for that brother of yours."

"He'd kill for one," I said.

"And what about you?" Lonahan tilted his head to the side like a curious crow, to examine me. "What would you kill for, Sylvie Pelletier?"

"Murder is a mortal sin," I said, smiling.

"Tell that to the boss class." Tendrils of smoke came from his mouth, and I breathed it in with his words like a new kind of oxygen.

"What's sister want, then, eh? A sweet for the sweet. Whattya say?"

"Want costs money," I said. "Many plural monies."

"Plenty of that right here. Trouble is, how to get our hands on it?"

"Beg, borrow, or steal." I shrugged.

"Steal?"

"Not—I shouldn't have said that."

"Speaking is the start of doing, ain't it?" Lonahan said, and winked. "Not that you'd steal." Was that the moment when the idea planted itself in my mind? He drew on his cigarette so the tip flared red. The sun was a matching circle of fire, the sky mottled with flaming clouds, purpled shadows. "Beauty is free, anyway, in these mountains."

"Free beauty," I said. "Could we eat it for dinner?"

He laughed and smoked and assessed me as if deciding. "Help me out here, Sylvie Pelletier. Problem is, how to get a letter to Moonstone? If I put my correspondence in the mailbox here, there's a danger it won't get delivered."

"Danger?" He made risk sound attractive. The cigarette hung off his lip, and I suppressed an urge to reach over and take it, to smoke it myself.

"Certain mail to certain people goes missing sometimes from Quarry-town," Lonahan explained, mysterious. "I'd deliver it myself, but I wore out my welcome in Moonstone. Some magoof with a badge told me to get lost. Company calls me an *outside agitator*, which is their most polite term for a union rep. Going to town to drop a letter is a danger."

"I'd carry it for you," I said, intrigued. "On the way to school in the morning."

"Then you'd be a heroine," said George Lonahan.

"Or would I be an outside agitator?"

He laughed. "No, you'd be on the inside, of course." George handed me an envelope from his pocket. "Take this to the editor at the newspaper. The *Moonstone Record*."

I accepted it as if it were a solemn mission.

"One a these days we'll go to Paris for an adventure, whattya say? You 'n' me," George said. "When the workers of the world are free, eh?" He made it sound like a joke, but it was a struggle for the ages.

"Ha-ha-ha, sure," I said.

When my father came outside, Lonahan stood and clapped him on the shoulder. "Your girl here," he said, "bright as a new penny. I was just telling her: Strike while the weather's hot, as we say in the union halls. Summer's the time. Starve their profits."

"Starve ourselves, more like," said Papa. "Won't call it for summer. It's paying season."

"Jacques," Maman called from inside, "tell that man *les socialistes n'sont pas bienvenus icitte*."

Not welcome, she said. My mother had a terror of *socialistes*. She called them godless radicals, infidels. According to the church, a socialist was a kind of demon. I perused George Lonahan with new interest, to see if he had horns. The envelope burned like a hot coal in my pocket.

"Cherie's got the Red fear in her," Papa apologized.

"Whether you call us socialists, Reds, dogs, whether you're with us or not, Jocko, the slaves of the caves will free themselves." Lonahan exhaled smoke.

"We are not slaves," said Papa.

"You think?" Lonahan went whistling on his way, but halfway down the road, he turned and bowed to me like a chevalier of old, as if he knew I was sorry to see him go, and he was sorry too. I wanted to tell him my father was right: Slavery was abolished after the Thirteenth Amendment to the U.S. Constitution. Perhaps the *socialistes* of New Jersey had not learned this fact in American history class, as I had, earning an A-plus.

The truth is that in those days I knew almost nothing about the past. I was preoccupied with the present, this new world, where a duke's son worked in his necktie, a *château* towered above the trees, and a scar-faced radical smoked on our step. He trusted me to deliver a message, so I fancied myself a heroine.

Paris, he'd said. Would I ever see it? Already I'd seen the Eighth Wonder. There were seven more. All I needed was money, the price of a ticket. How was I to get it?

Before school the next morning, I found myself checking the notices in the window of the *Moonstone City Record*: All Printing Jobs Accepted, Inquire Within. Perhaps I would inquire for employment, though it was not likely that a newspaper would hire a girl. Perhaps I could sweep and tidy for a few nickels.

"Hello?" I called inside. Only an orange cat appeared, mewing. I left George Lonahan's risky envelope on the typewriter there. What was in it? What did an agitator have to say to a newspaper?

At school, Miss Gage had an announcement: "An essay contest!" she said, sparkling enthusiasm. "The prize is a dollar. The winning essay will be published in the newspaper."

What Makes the U.S.A. a Great Nation? was the prompt on the blackboard.

"You must use an example from our own local experience," the teacher said. The judges were Miss Gage herself and K. T. Redmond, editor of the *Moonstone City Record*. Likely due to the influence of the Bolshevik pirate George Lonahan, I chose "Freedom" for my topic and wrote with a fierce intention to win. I wanted that dollar.

For "local experience," I remembered the poor mules chained in a string and the pleading eyes of the donkey tortured by schoolboys, and got carried away writing a plea for fair treatment of these animals, "who have been domesticated to serve man and cannot survive free like wild creatures do . . ."

Freedom is our strength but comes with responsibility, went my thinking; it had to be tended and fed, or some such lofty idealism in a schoolgirl's musing.

"Is this a joke?" was Miss Gage's comment. "The assignment was to write about what makes our nation exceptional. Not to write about donkeys."

My second attempt was a patriot's cheer about the engraved words on the Liberty Bell: *Proclaim Liberty throughout all the land unto all the inhabitants thereof.* The U.S. was great, I wrote, because we had fought a despotic king. We had democracy—Moonstone town had its own election upcoming! And thanks to our revolution, we did not suffer taxation without representation. (Or so I believed then.)

My new essay was a success. "Much better!" Miss Gage wrote in flowery script. She did not suggest I expand on the idea that Liberty belonged to "*all* the inhabitants," not just some. We were not taught to question ideals engraved in cast iron. My writing on the greatness of the U.S.A. earned an A-plus. So had I qualified as a real American at last?

June 6, 1907. Prize Day. I would be awarded a diploma that morning, my seventeenth birthday. We students lined up spit-shined, and marched to the village square, a patch of dirt with benches arranged around a platform swagged with bunting. Miss Gage perched there, a bright bird in yellow amid the dark-suited town officials arrayed like a murder of crows.

The speaker was Colonel Frederick Bowles, a vested man with a brush-broom mustache. He started in with his important talking, while the students pronounced his name in sniggering whispers. Bowels, Mr. Irritable Bowels. He was called Colonel, though he had never been a soldier or commander of a military unit. He owned the only motorcar in town, famously hauled uphill in parts and reassembled.

"Students, parents, teachers, friends!" His voice rang in the valley. "To-morrow's leaders are sitting here among us."

Next to me, tomorrow's leader Carlton Pfister scratched the wooden bench with a jagged point of rock, carving an obscene word.

"Don't," I whispered. "You'll get in trouble."

Carlton gave me a malevolent smile and raked the stone along my wrist so it bled. I let out a cry of pain.

"Shh," scolded Millie Havilland, a giant white hairbow on her head.

". . . and so, for her strong argument about American liberty," said the Colonel, "the essay prize goes to Miss Sylvie Pelletier."

People clapped and craned to look as I went blinking to the platform. Miss Gage beamed. Colonel Bowles presented me a large envelope, smiling with kind wrinkles at the corners of his eyes, while I stood like a mutton absorbing the wonder of it. A dollar just for writing a page. Here was the president of the company congratulating me.

"Thank you for the honor," I told him. "I'm very grateful."

"That's the spirit we like to hear from our young people! Gratitude!" Bowles shook my hand, the smell of mothballs wafting off his summer suit. The applause petered out, but while it lasted, I savored it like a sweet and floated down the steps.

Awaiting me was a hatless woman in a plain burgundy dress. Her face had a veneer of freckles, a snub nose, sparse eyelashes.

"Congratulations, Miss Pelletier. I'm K. T. Redmond, of the *Moonstone City Record*."

This was Redmond? She could not be the real editor, I thought. Editors were men in eyeshades, not freckled ladies with scraps of ginger hair escaping their pins.

I shook her hand, dismayed to see that Carlton Pfister's scratch on my arm had left red streaks on the prize envelope.

"You're bleeding," she said, and gave me her handkerchief. She did not say she was an agent of disaster or of my transformation. She did not reveal herself to be a provocateur, a windbag or witch, or even a "knocker," as she was later accused.

Her lace handkerchief was quickly stained. "I'm sorry—I'll wash it."

"Keep it. And come to the newspaper on Monday to print your essay."

"Yes, ma'am." I tucked it in my sleeve and hoped to get the bloodstains off before they dried. I'd keep it with the other one. *JCP.*

At home, my mother ran her thumb over the golden seal of my diploma and took the silver dollar I'd won to put in a coffee tin for my savings.

"*Pis ben,*" she said, hiding her pleasure. "Don't let your ankles swell."

"It's *head,* Maman. Don't let your head swell."

"We say *ankles,*" she said, uncorrected. "*On dit là des chevilles qui enflent.* Finish your chores."

Monday morning I walked to town in a thin June drizzle. My coat was sopped, but my hopes were dry, my head swelled with the new resolve of a winner, to ask for a job at the newspaper. The fact that the editor was not a man seemed a point in my favor. If a woman could be an editor, why couldn't I—with my prize certificate—be an employee? *Ask.* I muttered my intention all the way down the slope.

At the *Record,* rivulets of rain ran down the glass. Through the blurred pane, I peered into the wide-open room, where I saw Miss Redmond standing behind a cart-size machine. She plucked a sheet of paper and fed it to the mechanical creature. With the pumping motion of her foot, she turned the gears. She saw me spying and beckoned. Inside was the smell of ink and the machine's loud clanking.

"Miss Pelletier," she called over the din. "Observe, please."

She wore an inky canvas apron. Her jaw showed a slight bulldog under-bite. When she was sure of my attention, she released a handle on the press and pumped her foot on the treadle. The machine opened and shut its jaws while she placed blank sheets of newsprint and removed the printed ones in a regular rhythm.

"I read your two essays," she said. "Which convinced me we might get along."

"My *two* essays ma'am?" Had there been a mistake?

"I asked your teacher for the whole rotten bunch. There were two by you."

"Miss Gage liked the one about the Liberty Bell."

"Well, I didn't," said the editor, "and I told her so. The one about the donkeys is superior. We'll print that one."

"I thought the one about the Liberty Bell—"

"The Liberty Bell is cracked," said Miss Redmond. "Did you know? Why not ask the question: Is freedom all it's cracked up to be?" She laughed while I stood stumped. "Never mind. You did well with the donkeys."

"Miss Gage did not think so."

"Miss Gage is a nincompoop," she said.

I clapped my hand over my mouth to keep from laughing and screwed up my nerve. "Miss Redmond, I'd be glad to do odd jobs for you here at the paper. If you need a hand, if I wouldn't be in the way—sweeping."

"Sweeping?" She peered over her spectacles for a long judgmental minute and humphed. "If you'll learn to operate this press, I could pay you something."

"I'll learn," I said.

Miss Redmond looked skeptical, as if I were, probably, also a nincompoop. "I'll give you a trial. If the verdict is in your favor, two dollars a week."

Two dollars. It was a fortune.

Miss Redmond showed me how to work the press, how to ink the platens, screw down the type. She was all business. "You'll do the local deliveries on Fridays," she said. "And there's eighty out-of-town subscriptions to mail. Any questions?"

"No, ma'am." My first error.

"Learn to ask, or you'll never make a newshound."

"Yes, ma'am." Did I want to be a newshound? The idea had not occurred to me as among the possibilities, which seemed limited to nun, wife, spinster. Now it seemed a pretty good bargain to get paid just for writing addresses on labels for the *Record*'s subscribers in Washington, Chicago, New York. I rolled the papers and stuck down the labels and pictured readers in their starched collars, reading about our town.

THE MOONSTONE CITY RECORD

LIKED BY MANY, CUSSED BY SOME, READ BY EVERYBODY

Tom Pringle and Lee Bedford engaged in a disgraceful row. Bedford shot and perhaps fatally wounded Pringle who clings to life at the clinic. Bedford is in the town jail.

_____

A recently acquired and valuable property, heretofore undeveloped, is the manganese mine in Grand County Tuah. The Padgett Fuel and Stone Company has erected a small tipple.

_____

Will any brother or sister editors of the Western Slope, knowing of a nice healthy cat, please express it to my friend "Cap" Daily of the *Aspen Times*. Cats having litters of kittens preferred.

_____

The unwatering of the Black Queen mine is proceeding slowly. Just what is to be done after the unwatering is not announced.

Who was the Black Queen? What was a tipple if not a drink of liquor? Why did Bedford shoot Pringle? Had my employer received the letter I'd delivered from the socialist Lonahan? I still wondered what it said, but didn't ask, for fear she'd think me affiliated with agitators.

I should not have worried.

One evening I was so engrossed in my typing practice that I missed the last lorry ride and had to hike. At home, Henry sat on the steps with Nipper. The look on his face stopped me short. "Something happened," he said. "An accident."

"Is it Papa?" A cold claw of fear clutched me.

"Pete Conboy," Henry said. "They were lifting a block and the jack snapped, and—kerplow!" He smacked his hands together with a hard crack. "It fell on his leg."

"He's dead?"

"Naw, just hurt bad. They had to pry it off him. Blood all over. Hawky took him to the doctor over in Rabbit Town. They're gonna cut it off. The whole leg."

We could hear our mother fretting indoors. "Every day I fear, Jacques, you are next!"

"Cherie," Papa said, "I'm fine."

We stayed outside and watched Nipper stack rocks in a tower. "How do they cut a leg off?" my brother wondered. "With a saw?"

I shuddered and brought the baby inside to report about my job at the newspaper. The promise of cash money put a smile on my mother's face, but the idea of her daughter working! in town! had only added fears to her collection: that I'd come under the influence of Methodists. Drunks or wild animals would attack me on the quarry road. *Attention*, she warned: A mountain lion had been seen prowling the boardinghouse ridge. Mrs. Quirk had tripped over loose scree and broken her wrist. A man had leered at Mrs. Bruner by the water pipe.

"Remember your prayers," she said, and the next morning, sent me off with hers.

———

It was enough to remember all the keys of the typewriter and how to work the handpress. By five o'clock on Friday, my head was full of lessons and news, light with hunger. Again I'd missed the last ride uphill and now faced the climb back to Quarrytown, only raisins in my pocket, beasts and leering roustabouts on the prowl.

"Knock off now," said Miss R. "We'll go to dinner over at the Larkspur."

"Oh, no thank you," I said. (It cost fifty cents a plate.) "I can't, I couldn't—"

"Stop hawing and get your jacket. My treat. I'll send you home in the tally-ho wagon."

Maman would be frantic and fingering her beads, but guilt and explanations fit into a pocket for later. I could not turn down a restaurant dinner. We went out into the June evening, the air silky and crisp. Two girls in gingham rolled a hoop along the street. A dog chased them, barking. Dottie Weeks came out of her bakery next to the *Record* office to sweep the sidewalk planks and waved at K.T. "Hello, Trina!" A pair of kerchiefed women passed us chattering in Italian, carrying sacks of flour, their arms muscular and sunburnt as mine. In my dusty school dress, I'd be an eyesore at the Larkspur Hotel, a two-story affair with a wraparound porch.

Miss Redmond greeted the desk clerk. "Hello, Hal! How's my old pal Halibut?"

"Why, it's the lovely Miss Inkstains. How's the gossip-and-lies business?"

"Fine, thanks, Halibut." She blew him a kiss.

He blew one back and introduced himself to me. "Hal Brinckerhoff, master of hospitality, at your service."

"Meet Sylvie Pelletier," Miss Redmond said. "My new assistant."

"Watch out, Pelletier," he said. "Don't trust her! She'll eat you alive!"

"Says you." Miss Redmond tried not to smile.

"She'll make you confess things you'll regret. She's a trickster."

"Still haven't tricked you to spill the beans about the bandits who hole up here."

"Bandits?" He placed a hand on his heart. Innocent.

"Padgetts aren't the only crooks in town, Hal, old pal." I waited for K.T. to say more, picturing desperadoes, but she didn't.

In the dining room my employer ordered a whiskey, and for me a Coca-Cola, the first one I'd ever tried. I was fizzing already, from nerves. She would eat me alive.

"Your father a quarryman?" she asked. "What's his opinion of the Padgett Co.? Is he a union man? A Wobbly? Does he go to the meetings? Did he talk to George Lonahan when he was up the hill?"

"We did see Mr. Lonahan," I said, uneasy. "He asked me to bring you a letter—"

"Well, I'll be skunked," she crowed. "That was you? George said he got chased out of town for trying to organize at the mill. He thinks he's got a fighting chance with the quarry boys. Does he?"

She besieged me with questions, and where they concerned my parents and their opinions, I didn't reply, for fear of putting my father in that danger Lonahan had mentioned. What was a Wobbly? Some kind of invalid or drunk. I didn't ask. "I don't know, ma'am," I said to all her queries.

"What made you write about the donkeys, then?" Her eyebrows arched in exasperation.

"I felt sorry for them."

"Right!" she said. "That's what I liked about your essay. Your sympathies are on the side of the underdog."

"The underdonkey," I said quietly.

"Underdonkey!" She slapped her thigh. "I knew I liked you."

It was news to me that she did, a relief.

"Here's what I don't understand," she said. "The majority of those essays appeared to have been written by oxen. Why are you able to write an English sentence?"

The nuns beat us, I did not say. "We have four crates of books."

"What books?"

Miss Redmond clucked approval at the authors I listed and recommended I read Jack London and Upton Sinclair. She ordered us meatloaf and gravy with mashed potatoes, and ordered herself another whiskey, and soon a third whiskey. She was well warmed up, with the questions and habits of a man, elbows on the table.

"When I was your age," she said, "I wanted to be a newswriter for the *Cleveland Courier*, like my father was. I worked my way up to copygirl, but they wouldn't have a lady newswriter. When I heard about a position at the *Post* in Denver, I applied under the name K. T. Redmond, and it wasn't till I was hired and walked through the door that anyone discovered the truth."

"What happened when they saw you were a lady?"

"A question! At last!" she said. "That's the ticket. Ask. Don't just nod over there like a wheat stalk in the wind. Notice the details. Pay attention."

"Yes, ma'am."

"No. Not *yes, ma'am*. You can't just be yessing and thanking and goody-gumdrops all the time, Pelletier. You'll end up like one of your donkeys, grazing prickers at the side of the road. In answer to your question: They took one look at me and turned me back into a copygirl." She tapped her fingers on the table, expectant. "So? Ask."

"Did you get to be a newswriter in Denver?"

"You bet I did," said Miss Redmond. "But it cost me." A flash of anger skidded across her eyelids. She swallowed the dregs in her glass.

The dinner arrived, gravy steaming. While chewing, she recounted how she'd bought a used printing press and enough type to set four pages. She'd carried the equipment to Moonstone by mule train and purchased a town lot for $125, then built the print shop with some local fellows.

"Eventually," she said, "we'll publish daily." She jigged her knee under her skirt and ran her hands along the sides of her hair, which sprang from its holdings in cinnamon-colored strings shot with gray. I martialed more courage while she talked and drank and seesawed the bowl of her spoon on the table.

"I'd be glad to assist however I can," I blurted. "You mentioned you might pay something."

She watched me blush and squirm a minute before she took pity. "Ha! You're already hired," she said, grinning. "Listen. What I need is a real go-getter, hear? A regular gal Friday—what we in the trade call a printer's devil.

If you could bring yourself to keep asking questions, that devil could be you."

It was some unholy alliance that she proposed for me. "What does the assistant . . . the devil . . . do?"

"See these?" She pointed to her eyes, then her ears and nose. "Use 'em. Take notes. Talk to the fellas, the women especially. What's happening? What's going on up there in Quarrytown? Who knows what shenanigans Juno Tarbusch is up to. You hear anything about management spies, if you get a whiff of a strike or see George Lonahan, you let me know pronto."

She needed me to be a snoop? I might speak to the women, but to speak to Juno Tarbusch was a risk. My father called him *une belette*. Weasel.

Miss Redmond waited, testing me. "What's the news?"

"My brother says they're getting up a baseball team in town," I said. "They'll have games against Carbondale and Glenwood and—"

"Good idea. Get the game schedule and we'll print it. What else?"

"A man was hurt yesterday," I told her.

"Hurt how?" She sat forward, alert. If she were a dog, her ears would prick. "A quarry block fell on his leg. They might have to— He might lose it."

"You don't say? No news of it here at the clinic."

"They brought him over the pass to Rabbit Town."

"To keep it quiet," she said. "Doc up there is a drunk old Confederate, so he knows how to use a bone saw. If those boys had a union, they wouldn't have these injuries, they would—" She stopped her fuming then and paid the bill. At the front desk, she spoke to her friend Halibut, and a man brought around the wagon to drive me home. She gave him a dollar.

"Listen, Pelletier," said Miss Redmond, "you bring me stories from up in those boondocks, I'll print 'em."

And that's just what happened.

INJURY AT THE QUARRY

Journeyman Pete Conboy was seriously hurt
June 5 when a lifting jack snapped and a block

weighing ten tons fell on his leg, pinning him.
It took crews six hours to free the trapped man.
Dr. Haines in Rabbit Town puts odds at 3 to 1
he will lose the leg, and meanwhile safety at the
quarry remains precarious.

When I had been a printer's devil for about a week, the *Record* printed my prize essay, about the burros of Moonstone. *Sylvie Pelletier, Contest Winner* was the byline. I was proud to see it but unprepared for the trouble it caused.

Hawky Jenkins spied me passing by his smoking post outside the saloon and blocked my path. "Young Frenchy! I seen your story about my good old mules."

I waited for him to compliment me, but he gripped my arm, swaying on his pins. "If the Company'd pay to feed those animals, I'd feed 'em. If the Company'd pay to shoot 'em, I'd shoot 'em. But they don't pay for feed nor bullets. Write that, why doncha?" His fingers clamped my bones, fumes of whiskey and tobacco off him. "Anyways, when Padgett gets his train tracks laid up here, it's bye-bye to alla us drovers 'n skinners. No more mules neither. Write that!"

"Mr. Jenkins—you're hurting me."

The barkeep came through the saloon door. "Let go of that girl, ya sonuvabitch." He pulled Hawky away. Two more drinkers came outside to help, started punching. It was a brawl now. The barkeep escorted me across the road. "Young lady, don't you walk this side of the street. Women don't belong here."

"Yessir," I said, well scolded. If only I'd kept to the other side of the road, kept my opinions to myself, if only the newspaper had not printed them, I wouldn't be in this trouble with the sour breath of the muleskinner in my hair, bruises on my wrist.

I went to tell K.T. To my dismay, she took notes.

"Don't print it!" I said. "The whole town will know."

"Exactly, child. That's the point. We run a newspaper. And why shouldn't you walk on that side of the street? It's your right."

She went out to ask questions, and I saw that to be a newshound was to sniff for trouble and run toward it. I admired that gumption and wanted it for myself—without the consequence of bruises.

The *Record* reported BRAWL AT LOCAL GIN HOLE, with an Editor's Note:

> The proprietor claims that such incidents
> would not happen if ladies would not exercise
> their rights to walk on the east side of the street.
> Any lady will tell you the east side is as good as
> the west if not for the men who violate those very
> rights.

"Next time, Pelletier," Miss Redmond said, "you'll write the copy yourself."

That prospect thrilled me. Increasingly, I saw stories everywhere; in all the houses and shops were secrets and histories, even of the Ute people, cursing us from beyond the grave. Even a Quarrytown girl had a story, and mine was about trying not to be cursed, striving toward a happy tale, hoping I was in one.

Chapter Four

IN THOSE JUNE DAYS, THE Diamond River overflowed its banks and rushed downhill, rooks sang in the trees, and leaves unfurled like new little salads on the ends of their branches. A corduroy of greens softened the hard folds of the mountains, and the meadows bloomed with swaths of blue columbine and dashes of yellow sneezeweed. *Beauty for the soul.* As long as I live, my own soul will find peace just picturing those endless waves of mountains, despite the tragic events that happened there among them.

At noon the sun blazed a white magnesium light hot over the deep canyons and pine ranges. In the evenings we Pelletiers sat out on our board steps in the elastic air, with our bowls of *soupe aux pois* and fried trout that Henry caught in his nets.

On June 24, we had a celebration for *La Fête de Saint Jean-Baptiste.* Papa and Henry built a big tepee of branches for the *feu-de-joie,* the bonfire. Maman gave us small *Québécois* flags made of blue and white flour sacks. After supper, she brought out her proud surprise, *tarte au sucre* made with sugar she'd carted from Vermont.

"*Ben, c'est ça là,*" said Papa, savoring it. "The taste of home, eh?"

"*Bonne Saint Jean,*" she said.

Lovely memories softened their faces. Henry lit the fire, sparks towering in the late-falling darkness as we marched around with our miniature flags. My father played his fiddle and we sang "Ô Canada," the cabin dwellers coming out to listen. Tears stood in my mother's eyes. When the whistle blew for the graveyard shift, her face set again to its stoic expression. The fire of joy was scattered to embers, and Papa went off to work through the night.

Each morning Maman thanked God that he had lived another day without breaking his neck or stirring up "unpleasantness" again, labor troubles whispered in the dark behind the cabins. He went to sleep just as Henry and I made our way to the village. We hiked or hitched on a stone lorry, our feet dangling off the back, leaning against the blocks of white marble. Henry went in search of baseball or some boys' mischief, and I went to apprentice myself at the *Moonstone City Record*.

In three weeks, my scratchings filled a notebook, my hands were blue with ink, and my typing showed rapid improvement. I brought my wages home and brought K. T. Redmond a story if I'd found one: The Hulbert boy had mumps. Mr. Sistig's dog had pups. A man was impaled in the quarry with an iron spike through his foot. K.T. deemed such events to be news, and now I was the one who wrote them up for the *Record*.

> Last week, Marcello DiRobertis, a stone-worker, was killed on the quarry road. On a steep portion of the rock his foot slipped, and he was hurled to the bottom of the canyon. He was buried Sunday. The deceased leaves a widow and four children in Italy to mourn his loss.

My employer had a fondness for disaster. I brought her reports about a quarryhog concussed by a rockslide and a millworker who lost an eye to a stone chip. These incidents incensed her. "I'm giving you the agony beat, Pelletier." She wanted accidents, epidemics, bones, and blood. I was to interview Doc Butler at the clinic, to see what I could find for my own new weekly column, called "Infirmary Notes."

C. P. Randall has a lacerated and contused head as a result of being caught between two cars of the funicular rail at the quarry.

_____

Doctor H. T. Carriell, one of the surgeons at the Padgett Company coal operation in Ludlow, warns of an epi-demic of typhoid plaguing the camps.

_____

Mr. & Mrs. Matthias Andreu mourn the death of their daughter Emilia, age 7, after she was drowned in Glassy Creek. Residents, please note that river rocks are invariably quite slippery.

Accidents were regular in the mountains, but the more of them I typed, the more I wondered: Why didn't anybody do something about them? Perhaps disaster was ordinary, unpreventable. Or perhaps people cared more about the items snooped up by K.T. in her popular gossip column, "Susie Society."

SUSIE was informed that Miss Alice Cartmell of Denver, visiting Moonstone in hopes of catching herself a Padgett Company man, was seen at the Elks Lodge, dancing in the company of Tom "Tiptop" Topham, architect in the drafting house.

_____

SUSIE heard tell that the two roustabouts who drove a rig off the quarry road had drunk too deep at Bacchus' fountains. They paid with broken axles and a day's work hauling the mess back onto the trail. Lady Luck was all that kept them from death over the side of the precipice.

_____

SUSIE REPORTS that E. Rutherford Havilland has returned from his "fishing expedition" and is said to have caught a 4-foot rainbow. He said nothing about the pot of gold at the end of it. Rumor has it he's invested in copper futures at Leadville.

"Here's a headline," said K.T. one morning, and flung a bit of peach-colored stationery at me. "Nincompoop's getting married."

"Good news," I said.

"Is it?" she said. "Rather too soon to say. Type it up."

I pecked the Underwood's keys until I produced suitable results. She ran the wedding item in the "Susie" column, next to one about a ladies' tea.

> SUSIE has learned that Miss Florence Gage, teacher at the high school, is engaged to marry Mr. Samuel Ward, of Cleveland, Ohio, in August. The citizens of Moonstone congratulate the happy couple.

Reading this, Maman announced: "Your teacher *va se marier* before it is too late," as if to suggest I ought to do likewise before I shriveled to a prune. My mother had married at my age, seventeen. My cousin Thérèse at eighteen. Here was Miss Gage now, marrying at twenty-two.

Miss K. T. Redmond had not married at all. Henry called her Old Maid. Hal Brinckerhoff called her Miss Inkstains. Mr. Koble at the Mercantile called her Trina Tattletale. What I learned: She had a cat she called Billy, "but his real name is Bilious." She hated Plutocrats, Nincompoops, and "Abercrombies." These were Company supervisors, out-of-towners with "outfits" ordered from New York. What K.T. thought of fashions or marriage seemed to be: not much. She hated lateness. She did not praise me no matter how hard I worked. Which made me work harder.

Five days a week I got to the *Record* at the crack of eight. I tended the press and delivered the paper. I wrote "Infirmary Notes" and stories about the Moonstone Slammers, including Henry Pelletier's three-run homer (which pleased him so much he cut out the article and stuck it to the rafters of Cabin Six). I wrote up the ice cream festival and interviewed the mailman about how he escaped a bear by singing "Yankee Doodle." I printed handbills and announcements and pecked the typewriter keys till the last wagon headed uphill. I liked it—not just the money but describing events in town. It became a habit for me to write things down, a compulsion. More and more it seemed to me that if it weren't written, it had not happened.

At sunrise, my brother and I carried buckets of water from the sluice pipe to fill the barrel. Evenings, we hauled coal sacks and swept dust, skinned squirrels or rabbits for stew. We chased Nipper. "Slivvie!" he cried. "Get me!" He careened around, chattering in French and English. When he escaped out the door, we corralled him so he didn't toddle into the stream or fall into the ravine across from our door. We had to work hard to save him from himself. Maman penned him in the wood box, toted him in a sling, tied him to a post. He was all over cuts and bruises, struggling out of our arms, putting stones in his mouth.

"He is raised on rocks," said our weary father. "A mountain man."

Maman seemed stricken to hear it. All day she worked with the boy strapped on her back. When her back gave out, I strapped him on mine. On the weekends my brothers and I left our father to sleep, our mother to her *travail* of prayers, and hiked feral all over the mountains. In town we ogled the houses on Bosses' Ridge, where the supervisors and architects lived. Colonel Irritable Bowles had a two-story affair with a stone chimney, a gabled roof, a garage for his motorcar, and a German shepherd behind a picket fence. Next door to him lived the Havillands, where hairbowed Millie from my school days kept a pony. I disliked her simply because I wished for a pony of my own, or a porch where my mother would sit in a rocker and I'd entertain suitors, as Millie did, over iced tea. At the Mercantile, we eyed the jars full of jewel-colored fireballs and lemon drops, slavering till Mr. Koble chased us off.

"Buy something or git!" He accused us as thieves, called us varmints.

Maman called us *sauvages*. She was maddened by our roving, no church for months now, no confession or catechisms but what she could improvise in our suffocating shack while Nipper fidgeted. Out I went from her nunnery, crackers in my pockets with her prayers. *Gloire au père, au Fils et au Saint-Esprit.* She could not keep me indoors. I was hatless and wild now with summer.

By the end of June we knew Dogtooth Mountain and Marvelous Lake and Moonstone town like we knew the freckles on each other's faces. From the heights we looked down at the turrets of Elkhorne Manor, but I never once glimpsed Duke Padgett or the Countess or JCP. At the lumberyard we made a seesaw out of boards and teetered Nipper till he fell off and got a goose egg on his skull. I got a nail in my foot, punctured through the boot. Maman poured whiskey on it, sure I'd get lockjaw, but instead I got poison ivy. I got sunburnt. Ropes of muscle in the legs from hiking the mountain, arms hard from hauling wood and water, hefting my brother. I got quieter than ever, muted by a secret chronic ache in my throat, as if I'd swallowed a grape, sometimes a plum, of longing without a name. To be *seen*, I think now, even as I hid.

At the *Record* I kept my mouth shut to disguise my ignorance from Miss Redmond, with her college education, American slang, and scalding opinions.

"What are you, a dressmaker's dummy?" she said. "Speak up!"

"Yes, ma'am," I said, typing faster.

"You're a whiz on the keyboard, Pelletier," she said, which made me happy: I was a whiz! But also I was a dummy, a numbskull, a scatterbrain.

At home I did not talk about Miss Redmond, how she cursed and smoked and went to the Larkspur for dinner with businessmen from out of town. I did not mention the time when, wearing a disguise of a ridiculous new mustache, George Lonahan the Bolshevik pirate had delivered K.T. a bottle of whiskey and a copy of *The Little Red Songbook*, "to fan the flames of discontent." He was proud to report that "Company beef" had not recognized him. But I was pleased when he recognized me.

"Why, hello, Miss Pelletier," Lonahan said. "When are we two off to Paree?"

"When the workers of the world are free," I told him.

He roared laughing. "Are you free now? Let's go for a sarsaparilla."

I wished to try a sarsaparilla, to sit at the soda fountain and drink from a straw and watch the rough way Lonahan smoked a cigarette, plugging it in his mouth to let the ash grow long, spilling while he talked about his life in the Pine Barrens of New Jersey. *How'd you get that scar?* I wanted to ask, but such personal questions were impolite. Instead, I said, "I'd better catch the last lorry," too shy to mention that I was forbidden to walk out with a man unless he met the approval of *ma mère*. Which he would not get. *Socialiste*. Her suspicion was practically an arrow pointing me in his direction.

"Thank you." I hoped my regret was showing. "Maybe another time."

"Another time, then," said George. "Say hello to Jocko and the boys at Quarrytown!" He went outside singing "There's Only One Girl for Me." I wondered who was his sweetheart. How was I ever to be a sweetheart myself? I was forbidden to go to the "hops and entertainments" I read about in Susie Society's column.

The Misses Havilland put on a fish fry at the lake on Saturday last, and it wasn't only the fish who got "fried."

A hoedown at the Woodrow Ranch drew 19 guests. They were greeted with refreshments of popcorn, cider, and taffy. There was dancing to tunes played by Woody Woodrow on his violin.

Summer in Moonstone was a party where I'd never be a guest.

Tuesdays, we printed. Wednesdays, I bundled papers. Thursdays, I hauled them in a hand wagon to the post office for subscribers out of town, and towed a separate load to the Bonnie Lynn Dairy for delivery with the milk in the morning. Now on my rounds, people greeted me by name. *Hello, Sylvie, hey, sweetheart.* Hal Brinckerhoff gave me a nickel when I left the paper on his doorstep, and so did K.T.'s friend Dottie Weeks at the bakery. Fridays, I delivered a stack of *Records* to Koble's Company Mercantile.

"Here comes the Gossip Gargler with the birdcage liner!" Mr. Koble said, smiling and hostile behind his cash register. Mr. Koble, it seemed, and others in town, did not much care for K. T. Redmond's paper. I heard remarks about *that suffragette, that labor symp.* She didn't seem to worry about it, so I didn't either. Subscriptions increased along with the town's population: A hundred new employees arrived in June. White tents bloomed on empty lots where families camped next to crews of "bachelors," workers at the mill. Laundry lines flapped outside and smoky fires burned in the yards. The sound of hammering went on all day.

___

"Donkeys can mate with horses," Henry announced at supper.

"*Monsieur!*" said Maman, affronted. "What else are you learning in this town?"

"Pitching." He demonstrated his windup. "Jasper Padgett brought a Negro man to show us a fastball yesterday."

"Jasper Padgett?" My ears perked.

"*Oh, là,*" said my mother. "*Un negre icitte?*"

"He's a chef on the Duke's private train," Henry said. "He used to pitch in the Negro leagues. Says I'm a southpaw!"

Papa let out a scoff. "Boss's boy does four hours in a *cravate*, then takes off to play ball." He simpered, mimicking the Duke's son, la-de-da.

"They built us a new baseball diamond," Henry said. "There was a ceremony with *la Comtesse* yesterday. She cut the ribbon."

"Oh, *la Comtesse*," said Papa. "Lady Bountiful, the angel of the mountains."

"A sainted lady," Maman said. "They say she rides the town to give apples for everyone in the fall."

"And in winter she flies south like the snow goose," said my father. "A baseball diamond? Pah. The diamond on her little finger would build a hospital or pay us for a day off. If you ask for overtime wages, you're *Bolsheviste*."

I heard more talk of Bolsheviks in the dark behind the cabins that summer, men whispering about overtime, my father and Dan Kerrigan huddled on the stoop. But there was nothing *safe* to report to K.T., only rumors of union organizing and strikes. Instead, the *Moonstone City Record* printed a story about the new baseball field alongside a simple question from the editor:

> Where is the money for the new hospital?
> Thousands have been taken from workingmen's
> paychecks to build it!

I worried my father would see this and realize I'd repeated his sentiments in the news office. But it was my secret pride that Miss Redmond had put them in the paper. She'd often found fault with me over a spill of ink or a mistake due to carelessness with the letterpress. I fed my spirit off every nod of approval I earned from the editor.

Just after the Fourth of July, I wheeled the newspaper wagon along Padgett Street. Approaching in a white summer dress was Miss Gage, my teacher. Because of my employer, I thought of her now as Nincompoop.

"Sylvie?" She carried a suitcase and set it down to embrace me. "I was hoping to run into you! Are you interested in a little summer work?"

"I have a job at the newspaper."

"I see, but this would be—a plum. So exciting! A job *á la château*."

"Elkhorne?"

"Mr. Bowles asked me, would I myself like to be social secretary to the Countess? She requires someone who speaks French, and he knows I parlay a little. But I can't accept—I'm getting married!" She wrinkled her nose adorably.

"Congratulations," I said, as if she had won a prize.

"So, Madame la Comtesse needs summer assistance. Her regular secretary—had to leave quite suddenly. So I thought of you, Sylvie."

"Me?"

"You speak *français* much more *mieux que moi*. The Countess is from Belgium. Your penmanship is neat. The pay is five dollars a week! With room and board."

"I would—live there?"

"Yes!" She beamed at me. "I told Colonel Bowles about you. That you parlay *français*, how you are such a good student, a quiet girl. You must run to the Company offices to see about the position. *Au revoir!*"

I never saw Miss Gage again, but I think of her whenever I hear the word *nincompoop* or ponder the consequences of a chance encounter.

At the office of the Padgett Company, Colonel Bowles presided at his desk, putting numbers into an adding machine.

"Miss Gage sent me," I said, "for a secretary position at Elkhorne Manor?"

"Minute." He punched keys and did not bother to look up. I picked a thread off my sleeve and observed him. He was built thickly in the way of an athlete gone to fat, his suit jacket strained across the shoulders, his hair and mustache salted gray. At last he pushed back from the desk and winged his elbows behind his head, smiling with a weary expression. He appeared ordinary, not cruel, as I came to understand that he was. Cruelty itself was ordinary.

"Mrs. Padgett needs a summer gal who speaks French," he said, and cupped his ear. "Let's hear you parlay."

"Mes parents sont de Québec et j'ai parlé français toute ma vie."

"Very good." He seemed impressed. "You know I spent a very happy year in Paris as a young man. Can't understand the Canadian version, ha-ha. 'Muskrat French,' they call it, right? Can you type?"

"Yes." *I'm a typing muskrat.* "Miss Redmond at the newspaper taught me."

"Hmmpf." His eyebrows quirked. "Redmond the Red. Well, no matter. And your father is Pelletier the machinist up the quarry?"

"Yessir. He's a master mechanic."

"Well, I don't suppose there's a pick of others in town who can parlay-voo on short notice," he said. "If you are interested—"

"I am interested. Thank you, sir."

"Mrs. Padgett is—a very charming lady. Lots of energy! Takes up a lot of my time with her little projects. Do your best to distract her, will you?" He chuckled. "If she likes you, no telling where she'll take you. You might find yourself in ole Virginny or even Paree. Or maybe she'll take you on as a *project* for her new sociological department."

"Thank you, sir, I'll do my best to earn her approval."

"Please be forewarned that this is a delicate position. Should you be hired, your arrangement with Redmond and that newspaper is terminated. There will be no gossip. You will respect the privacy of your employers. If you don't, there will be a penalty."

"Yessir."

"You'll start on Monday."

"You will live there?" Maman asked, suspicious.

"That's what he said."

"You will be *une femme de chambre*? The maid?"

"A secretary, the Colonel said."

We could not imagine. To do the hair, we thought, like a lady-in-waiting. To unpack the luggage, hang the ball gowns, fuss with the jewels, dust the pastries, or whatever it was *une comtesse de Belgique* might eat.

"They'll eat you for lunch," said Miss Redmond. "I just trained you!"

"I'm sorry," I said, hangdog. *If you had offered me a bed in a castle.* "It's just eight weeks. For five dollars the week. Plus room and board."

"I can't match that," she said, disgusted. "You're out the door and into the arms of the boss class, then."

"I can start again in September, if you'll have me, when the Countess goes back to—wherever she goes."

"Phhuh. She's not a real countess."

"She is, though," I said, wanting to be right.

K.T. snorted. "Don't be a dunderhead. She's a gold-digging French vavoom who snookered the old man on his travels to Belgium to nurse at the teat of royalty. He wouldn't know an actual countess if she were ringing his bell. Which she is, of course."

I blushed at her language and failed to ask questions. But K.T. saw an advantage and softened. "Apologies, young Sylvie, I got carried away. You come back here to good old K.T. when Countess Fifi has left you at the side of the trail like a chunk of riprap."

Kate Manning

"If you still need me."

"What I need is someone who'll bring me back a story from inside the castle. Will you do that? Sniff around. Report back."

"I'll try," I said, but remembered my promise to keep secrets or suffer a penalty.

"Invite me to the *château* for some fizz. I'll wear my pearls."

My bundle of scraps fit in a flour sack. My nightgown and spare dress, black lisle stockings and unders, wool cardigan. A clean blank notebook. I planned to write down everything, not for the *Moonstone City Record* but for myself.

"See ya, Moose," Henry said. "Write if you get married."

"*Bon ben*, don't get married," said Papa.

"Don't get your hopes high up," said my mother.

But my hopes were already at that altitude where the air is thin, where it's hard to breathe. I was headed to the castle for an appointment with the Countess, a glimpse of the Duke, an encounter with the strange princeling, JCP.

If they like you, no telling where they might take you . . . even Paree.

What did I know of Paris? Paris to me meant romance and ease—all the things we did not have and I wanted. Five dollars a week was a step in the right direction.

PART TWO

Sugar and Awe

The home of a workingman may be just as happy, just as ideal a home as that of a rich man. While a fine house, rich furniture, elegant decorations undoubtedly have a great value in rendering a home attractive . . . it is the cheerful, helpful, hearty, self-sacrificing spirit . . . that can render any home a paradise.

—*Camp & Plant*, Colorado Fuel and Iron Co.
Sociological Department

Chapter Five

Elkhorne Manor had the look of a dragon, windows like eyes lit up, spreading out in wings, squatting on haunches at the foot of Rosy Dawn Mountain. The house was built of silvery granite, with columns of marble, turrets, peaked roofs, mullioned glass in bay windows. Smoke rose from four stone chimneys. All around were lawns and gardens. A greenhouse and a gatehouse, stables and kennels. The long drive led between stone lions on marble pillars, roaring. The snoozing gatekeeper took no notice of me passing by in my coiled braids, with my parcel of clothes.

At the grand front door, a knocker in the shape of a bearded man stared through hollow eyes, a ring through the nose. *Go around*, it said out of its iron mouth, *find the service entrance*. In back, there was a carriage courtyard where gargoyles spouted water into a horse trough. I pulled the bell rope and waited with a tongue of dust.

"Yes?" The man who answered was brown-skinned, his gray hair cut close to the scalp.

I had never met a Negro. My surprise caused me to stare and stammer. "I—I'm sent for an appointment with Mrs. Padgett. I'm Sylvie Pelletier."

"And I," he said with a formal smile, "am Mr. John Grady. Come in, Miss Pelletier. I'll find Mrs. Grady." He ushered me into the kitchen and went out through a door swinging on hinges. His age was about fifty, and subtracting from the present year, 1907, the question came unbidden to my mind: *Was he born a slave?* Preposterous, that it could be true of such a gentleman in his fine suit, white collar, and cuffs. Enslaved people of my scant history lessons were tragic and ragged or singing in moonlight. This unsettling train of thought and everything about this new land of Elkhorne caused me profound unease.

I was intimidated by the kitchen. It featured a hearth so big I could stand in it and cook myself. Here were cupboards and glass-front cabinets of white china, a porcelain sink, and a contraption with a crank for what purpose? Mangling, making sausage. What was in all these drawers, I could only guess. Silver and meat. Chocolate and slabs of butter. Doubloons. A massive stove had six burners, two pots simmering. Two ovens. Jars and tins of provisions sat on the countertop. *Flour*, one said. *Sugar.*

Oh, sugar. Perhaps I would taste a spill of it. I would've been happy even to lick some off the floor if no one was looking, but here was Mr. Grady again, followed by a narrow woman more dark-skinned than he was, wearing a starched apron over a black dress, her hair pulled tightly back, her eyes bright as sparks off flint.

"Sylvie?" she said. "I'm Easter Grady. You've met John Grady?"

"Yes, ma'am." I stared while trying not to and decided it was right to curtsy.

"Are you feeling unwell?" she asked.

"No, ma'am," I said, in a flummox. The Gradys smiled at me and at each other with some secret delight. I smiled back, apologizing, my behavior wrong already.

"I'll take you to housekeeping," Easter said, "soon as I finish this." She opened a tin on the sideboard to reveal a golden loaf of bread. "Cut four slices. Help yourself if you're hungry, but I won't serve you. A knife is in that drawer there." John Grady went through the swinging door. Easter began to wash a pan in the sink. I wanted her to keep talking just so I could hear her voice, the southern inflections and where she put them.

I picked up the bread knife just as a young man burst in. "Easter! I need some sandwiches to take." It was him, JCP, son of a duke, in a rush.

Easter did not turn around. "Did I hear a rude man come in here?" she said. "Is someone talking at me, Miss Sylvie?"

He noticed me then. "Have we met?" His smiling eyes without their foggy spectacles provoked that frisson again. He took his glasses from his pocket and put them on, the better to see my red face.

"Introduce yourself properly to the young lady," Easter said.

"We have met once," I said, the knife in my hand.

"But not *properly*," he said, grinning. "I'm Jasper. People call me Jace."

"Or they call you late again," said Easter.

"Sylvie Pelletier," I said, with the American pronunciation. *Pell-tear.*

"Nice to meet you," he said, "despite how you're threatening me with that knife."

I put down the knife like it was on fire. My face was.

"You're that Florence Nightingale of the quarry." He held out his hand to show me the blister had healed. "See? Good as new."

"She's here for a job with your stepmother."

"La Countess?" He drew back and blinked in exaggerated fashion.

It seemed he did not like Madame. She was his stepmother? "Susie Society" would relish the information. Would it cause a penalty if I revealed it? I was fascinated by the exotic lot of them, gathering details before I was rejected as a hayseed. Easter prepared a lunch basket while Jasper Padgett struggled with his necktie. When he smiled at me—had he?—his whiskerless cheeks went red again, as did mine.

"Go," Easter told him. "Fix that tie. I'll bring the sandwiches out front. Next time you'll roll out of bed on time or I don't feed you."

"Yes, ma'am." He saluted. "Thanks kindly, my dearest Easter. Might it be too much to ask for a jug of iced tea?" Another grin, in my direction, as if he knew he was charming, performing for an audience. "A slice of cake? Two slices?" He blew her a kiss on the way out, while I wondered at the banter between them, and how I was supposed to comport myself, with the whirlwind of Easter whipping through the kitchen, crossing to an icebox where she got out liverwurst, pickles, mustard. She slapped these together on the sliced bread, a tuneless tune on her breath.

"Shall I help you?" I asked, getting out of her way.

"Wrap those," she said, and handed me the sandwiches with a roll of waxed paper. From under a tea towel, she exposed a tin of small yellow cakes, selected four, and handed me one. "Keep that for yourself."

"You're very kind." I put it in my jacket pocket. "Thank you."

"Well, at least someone was raised with manners." She appeared surprised by me somehow. She took up the basket and pointed to a row of hooks where I was to leave my things. "Come with me. I'll bring you to Mrs. Nugent."

Through the swinging door, we entered a great dining room paneled in dark wood. My eyes went everywhere. *Holy*— The ceilings soared up, painted with clouds, cherubs. Here was a marble mantel sculpted with fruits and florets. Above it was a portrait of a solemn white man in a white suit, white walrus mustache. Animal heads gloomed between electric wall sconces, lit even in daylight. A long table was set with silver candelabra. Marble statuary posed in alcoves and nooks, busts of naked infants and nymphs. A vermilion carpet under our feet twined with patterns of flowers and vines, soft as a lawn. I was timid to cross it in my dusty boots.

Easter bustled past the displays and led me into a salon full of upholstery, chairs and sofas and tufted footstools. Here and there perched a fern, an ornamental stag cast in bronze, an ivory ashtray in the shape of a monkey head. Sunlight blasted in wide windows bracketed by draperies of blue velvet. The walls of the next room were upholstered in leather. Following, I sneaked a hand to touch it, the wrinkled soft gray. Easter saw me do it.

"Genuine elephant hide," she said with a sniff. "Mr. Padgett shot them in Africa."

Susie Society reports, I thought. Was wall covering a subject for privacy?

We emerged into the grand front entryway, where Jace Padgett waited, reading a book.

"Master Padgett," Easter said.

He closed the book reluctantly and took the hamper. "Thanks. Gotta get going now, Ma."

"Don't you call me that."

He blew her a kiss and was out the door. "I'm late! Tarbusch is gonna dock me."

"Pphhh," Easter said when he was gone. "He won't get docked, no way."

"My father got docked," I said, "for taking more than fifteen minutes for lunch."

"That's how they do," said Easter. "Unless your daddy owns the place. He works at the mill?"

"The quarry," I said. "He's a master machinist."

"Huh." She led me back toward the kitchen, branched through a side door, down a narrow passage running behind the rooms, a mouse warren for servants, and knocked at a door labeled *Housekeeping*. "You'll see Mrs. Nugent," she said, and left me there.

"Come!" Inside, Mrs. Nugent sat behind a small desk. Her hair was a gray puff of spun cotton pulled tight behind her ears. By the drawstring scowl of her mouth, she showed she was displeased with me already. "I have enough untrained girls for the season, so don't waste my time if that's what you're after."

"Colonel Bowles sent me about the secretarial position. With Mrs. Padgett?"

"Tcch. Nobody tells me." Mrs. Nugent pushed her chair back from the desk. "Follow me, and pay attention so you can find your way back."

We went along the service halls through the endless house. "There are forty-two rooms at Elkhorne," she said. "Fifteen on this floor." She recited names as we passed: the Library, the Ballroom, the Salon Rouge, the Tearoom. Grumbling around a corner, Mrs. Nugent opened a door and we came into a vast hall, turned through an archway. "Here is the Greenery," she sniffed. "Or should I say the Jar-din-air, as she calls it."

"*Jardinière*," I said, correcting her pronunciation. She glared and I kicked myself. *Know-it-all.*

It was a room made of glass. Feathery ferns grew from Grecian urns. Palm trees from the deserts of Araby sprouted from a bed of indoor earth. A fountain simmered in a pond where orange fish swam between lilies. A little black dog came at us, yapping.

Mrs. Nugent flinched. "Mrs. Padgett, a girl to see you," she said.

The dog yapped ceaselessly.

"*Bisou!* Be quiet now." This was the actual Countess, calling the dog from a chaise, smiling at me in beams of welcome. Was she twenty-one or thirty-three? Her pale summer dress had sleeves made from diaphanous gauze. Her face was a white pearl set with blue eyes, surprising as a wild iris in snow.

The little dog sat at her feet, looking up in adoration. I was enthralled as the dog.

"*Bonjour*," she said. "Mademoiselle Sylvie Pelletier?"

"*Oui*, Madame."

Mrs. Nugent fled. The goddess patted the chair next to her, where it seemed I was to roost my scuffed and nervous bones. "*Reste ici, petite*," she said. "Permit me to introduce you to my little schipperke, Bisou." She took the animal's front paw and extended it toward me so I would shake it.

"*Enchantée*," I said, and shook the paw.

The Countess laughed. "*Dites-moi tout*, Sylvie."

Tell her everything? I sat tongue-tied in two languages but managed to say, "I have just received my high school diploma."

"Monsieur Bowles says you're the excellent student." She spoke English in a French voice with flutes and warm notes of cello. "You are *Canadienne*?"

"*Americaine*. From Vermont. But—I mean to say, *Québécoise*. My parents are."

"*Ah, oui*, Vermont," she said. "Many French at Montpelier?"

"Yes. And Rutland. Winooski."

This name was hilarious to her. "Winooski," she laughed with a hand covering her mouth. "It's funny, Winooski!"

"An Algonquin Indian name," I told her, then feared again I'd overstepped and would be seen as *Mademoiselle connaît-tout*.

In French, she asked about my father. "He works in the quarry? Your husband does also?"

"My husband? No. I am not—"

Pealing laughter. "Perhaps, maybe, you have *un petit-ami*? A sweetheart?"

I shook my head.

"*Enfin*, then, soon!" She unfolded herself from her chair, a delicate willow, as tall as myself. "Stand up," she commanded. "Turn this way and that."

In mortification, I turned as she inspected me, the shab and scuff of my shoes, my sunburnt arms and peeling nose, the weight of my bones.

"*Oui, très bien*. You will capture many hearts, I am sure, when the gentlemen arrive for the hunt."

Was I to be hunted? I suffered as she judged me, and stared at the floor, at her delicate beautiful shoes of yellow kid, a rosette of silk on the toes.

"Now," she said, "tell me about your papa. It's a terrible hard life, yes? You suffer very much?"

It seemed she wanted me to agree that it was a hard life, so I nodded, exposed as if naked in front of her.

"How are you to bathe? What is the condition of the *toilettes* at Quarrytown?"

"We bathe," I said, defensive. What kind of question was this from a countess?

"But how?" she insisted. "Don't be shamed."

I was mortified. At her insistence, I explained our arrangements, the water flumes the Company rigged from the river, how we filled the buckets at the pump, hauled them home, heating the water on the stove, pouring it into the washtub on a Saturday. She listened as if fascinated, and I could not think why she pursued such a subject. I would've liked to ask how she herself bathed. But my place here was not to ask, only to answer. I talked in halting sentences, transfixed by the merriment of Madame's eyes, the way the sun poured through the glass walls as if we were inside an aquarium.

"And you have a screen," she asked, "for the privacy? And what facilities? The lavatory? Where do you . . ."

"*Les béscosses.* The chamber pot." (Was it not normal?) I stammered under her bizarre smiling interrogation.

"*Enfin*, you're so cold in the snow, yes? Poor petite rabbits." Madame leaned toward me, excited. "You see, Sylvie, it is for the science. I'm interested to improve the village life. To build schools, install the plumbing for the health and hygiene, for *la modernisation*. You understand?"

"*Oui*, Madame." She was called the angel of the camps, and here was evidence.

"I'm told you write French? Demonstrate, please, *chérie.*" She found a pen and a sheet of paper, and I wrote: "Sylvie Pelletier, Moonstone, Colorado, le 7 *juillet* 1907."

She inspected my work with approval. "*Bon*," she said. "I hire you as summer secretary. *Tu as la main d'une artiste.*"

I had the hand of an artist but the heart of an imposter. I was not a real secretary and resolved to speak French as little as possible so she would not disdain my so-called muskrat version of the mother tongue.

"*Allons-y*," she said. "I will speak *en français* and also in my terrible English. You will write and translate to proper English, please. My spelling, bah, *c'est une catastrophe.*" She handed me a notebook. "You will take dictation."

"I've never done it."

"Whatever I say, you write. It will be fixed later. *Tranquille, petite.* Don't worry." She began, her eyes narrowed in concentration, petting the little dog.

My dear Colonel Bowles,

In the matter of the miners' housing, it has come to my attention that the cottages at Quarrytown lack sufficient plumbing. They are still deprived of electricity. The poor workers tremble in their hovels like rabbits. With the scientific hygiene we can fight the sickness and disease. Please take all measures to remedy insupportable conditions before the beginning of winter.

Sincerely,

Madame La Comtesse Ingeborg LaFollette deChassy Padgett

The Sociological Department, Padgett Fuel & Stone Co.

"The company's new philosophy," she said, "is to operate a sociological department in all the towns where we have the business concern. With science, we will improve the lives of seventeen thousand employees across the West. Did you know?"

I didn't.

"The Padgett Company have forty operations, not only here in Moonstone. Coal, copper, marble in the five different states. We are to make not *only* profit but the healthy society. You are familiar with *le Départment Sociologique*?"

"*Non*, Madame."

"It will soon be very famous. A philosophy model for the West. For America. You passed through the town of Ruby? The pretty cottages? The social club? All thanks to our work. For the welfare of the people. We will make such improvements here too. We will build kinder-schools, the hospital, a library. *Comprenez?*"

I nodded, in thrall to her elegance, her fragrance. She talked about the Company the way the church talked about our Lord. My mother talked of the Company this way too, but in fear of godly wrath. By contrast, Madame's idea of management was compassionate. I was ready to believe, to worship among her flock of sociologists.

"If we act in the kindness," she said, "these agitators, these terrible malcontents, will go away. No one will listen to them. We will be all together, *tous ensemble*, to make the town, the state of Colorado, for the future. For the profits. You see?"

She offered me little *pastilles* from a lavender tin. They tasted of violets.

The air around her was scented with rose water, her perfume like anesthetic. I forgot to observe with the sharp eyes of a printer's devil because my sight was dulled by sugar and awe.

That morning, Madame dictated three letters to Colonel Bowles on the subjects of moral character, gymnastics classes, and the prevention of disease. "Typhoid fever is epidemic in the camps." Instructing me, she was patient and showed me a stack of pamphlets—I was to include one in each envelope—titled "Hygiene for the Working Classes." This caused me a flicker of shame, that she thought me uncouth because I'd told her about the outhouses and tin washtubs of our toilette.

"Now," she announced, "we write the instructions to Mrs. *Ménagère* Nugent."

I chose a new page of my notebook and held my pen ready.

She leaned in to whisper, "I do not enjoy Mrs. Nugent. She is Mr. Padgett's old favorite. Twenty years she works for the family. But *elle me deteste*, maybe even more than she detests petit Bisou. Nugent is like the guard of the prison. Is she not?"

"I do not know, Madame."

"She needs to more, I think, make love!" The Countess giggled wickedly. "But Monsieur Nugent the husband is—" She sucked her cheeks in, to make fish lips. "Have you met Mr. Nugent? He is valet for my husband. A fish!" She kissed Bisou, a *comédienne*. "You try, Sylvie, to kiss a fish!" encouraging me.

I struggled in vain to remain serious but did not dare try the fish face.

"You are very *politique*, Sylvie," she said, seeming disappointed. "You will bring Mrs. Fishy Nugent all the *directifs domestiques*. Here is the list. Ready? 'Dear Mrs. Fish *Poisson* Nugent,'" she began, but leaned over and stopped my pen. "Please do not write *poisson*. Can you imagine if she read 'Mrs. Fish'?" The Countess's laughter bubbled over. "*Enfin*, continue: 'For the Hunters' Ball and royal visit the week of September the eighth, we require: rooms made up for thirty-six guests, twenty doubles and sixteen singles. The Bighorn Suite will be ready for His Majesty King Leopold II of Belgium . . .'"

"*Majesté?*" This could not be correct. Surely it was a missed translation. "Monsieur—King? Leopold . . . *le roi?*"

"Yes! The King is coming to hunt!" Madame whispered again: "And not just to hunt the animals. He seeks opportunities. The investments, etcetera. The Hunters' Ball is the finale of the season. *Majesté le roi des Belgiques.* Leopold will be our guest."

"The Queen too?"

"No, no. She rests at her castle in Laeken. Perhaps he brings his *copine*?"

I wrote on as she dictated: feather pillows only, sheets washed and ironed daily. "The King is very concerned of germs. So please note the staff to beware, to use the special gloves, the soap. But never ammonia!"

She held her nose with delicate horror and moved on to a recitation of menus: roasted capon. *Truite à l'anglaise.* Crown roast of pork. Then came paragraphs of procedure: tables set up for whist and backgammon after dinner; luncheon for the Grand Quarry Tour on Wednesday; another luncheon Thursday for the hunting party. "The musicians must arrive by noon on Saturday," she dictated. "And Nugent must make a schedule for the carriages to bring the guests from the train depot."

"The depot at Ruby?" I asked, to avoid a mistake.

"No! To here!" she said. "Our own new railroad will go direct to Moonstone Station, ready in time for His Majesty's arrival."

A king! In my fairy tale–addled mind, a king was not human but chosen by God or some anointing power to be above us lesser people. A royal visit would allow us to breathe the same air, would lift us as if we too had been anointed. What a lot of horse manure, I see now, but at the time I labored under notions of worthlessness that worked as a spell to disarm thinking.

I took down Madame's words, distracted. All in one day I was secretary to a countess in a castle. I had talked to Negroes, to the son of a duke, and shaken the paw of a schipperke. With any luck, I'd soon observe a king in Colorado. All this fortune from writing an essay! A schoolgirl effort about the greatness of the U.S.A., our magnificent land of natural resources and freedom. At that moment, sucking on violet *pastilles*, I forgot the burros at the side of the road and saw that American greatness was vast as the land spreading out beneath our perch in the *château*, beyond to the high peaks, up even to Quarrytown hanging by threads off the rocks. Mrs. Luck was smiling at me now.

"*C'est tout*," the Countess said at last. "Tomorrow when you have copied the correspondence to English, bring me the results." She showed me to a little rolltop desk and gave me printed examples of schedules and letters "to copy from." She left with a fluttery wave, Bisou trotting at her heels. "*À tantôt!* I'm going for my ride on the lake trail. How I love the mountains here, *l'air pure.*"

As she loved the air, I loved the little desk, the neat compartments for stamps, for ink and envelopes. The typewriter was there for my use, she'd said, pleased that I knew the keys already. I copied out her letters, careful not to smudge. Finished after two hours, I left the correspondence for her approval and went through the back halls to give the household lists to Mrs. Fishy Nugent.

"Miss Pelletier," Nugent said, "I'm instructed to hire you at the rate of five dollars a week. Madame will not require your services more than half the day and some days not at all. It is therefore agreed that when you are not occupied, we will enlist you in the kitchen and with general housekeeping. There are twenty-five fireplaces to manage."

From a closet in the corner, she removed a black dress like her own, with a starched white apron. She inspected me for size. "You're quite a tall girl," she said, as if it were news to me. "Let the hem down. The uniform is the property of the household. You're required to launder it and pay for damages. Understood?"

Her eyebrows lifted, lowered. I was dismissed. On the way back to the kitchen, I sucked in my cheeks and made fish lips in the air. I already counted Nugent an enemy and vice versa. Strange, how we fail to recognize our real foes: the greedy high *chapeaux*. Mrs. Nugent was one of the toilers same as myself, turned mean due to the effects of servitude.

———

72

"Your bed's in the Cardboard Palace," Easter said, and brought me outside to the barracks. It was hidden behind the pines, so the Manor's inhabitants would not have to see it or think of us sleeping, having dreams or colds, indigestion or homesickness, love affairs or grief. It was *a medieval arrangement built on the bleached bones of the workers*, as K. T. Redmond once wrote in her newspaper. I loved it.

Easter led me up the stairs. "Pick any bunk," she said. It was a room of new pine planks under bare rafters, my own bunk in a vast array of bunks. The barracks, Easter explained, were sparsely occupied, except when the Padgetts' guests brought their own servants or a crew was hired for some stint of labor. Musicians from Chicago stayed here when they came to entertain. It was a long plain dormitory divided in sections: upstairs for women, downstairs for men, separate entrances, locked doors between. Also downstairs were the Nugents' private apartment and "the white kitchen," as Easter called it, for white servants.

She pointed through the woods. "Over there is where we stay." She flexed her eyebrows in some quick revelation. Of disdain. It was a small movement that caused a rupture of discomfort in me that I ignored, because I was distracted by the lavatory. This was a luxury of porcelain sinks, flushing toilets in private booths, showers with hot water from a nozzle. Soon I was to see the Padgett larders, the barns of livestock, the stables and hothouse, the swimming pool; then later I saw the dirt-floor shack that the Gradys were assigned for housing; and tasted oranges, like the fruit of the tree of knowledge. It was that summer when the first seed of resentment began to form, like a pearl in my chest.

Two pasty serving girls with odd blunt haircuts slept in the row of bunks by the door. Albina and Domenika. Mrs. Nugent had hired them for the summer.

"I am nice to meeting you," said Albina that evening.

"Sisters." Domenika pointed to Albina. "Us."

"Croatia," Albina said.

"America," I told them with, I confess it, a superior attitude. I was not the foreigner for a change. Perhaps I'd be their friendly guide. But they stayed apart, shy of me. I chose the bunk farthest away and knelt to say my jumbled prayers. *Laisse-moi, aide-moi. Save me now and forever,* merci, *thankful for my luck, and do not let me bungle it, please,* Grâce à Dieu, *now and at the hour of our death. Amen.* I blew out my lamp and listened to the scuttlings outside, the wind in the aspen leaves, the rocky *soupire* of the mountains. It was the first night of my life away from home, but I was not homesick.

Chapter Six

AT SUNRISE, FOLLOWING NUGENT'S ORDERS, I went to the kitchen, where I helped Easter juice oranges. "I've never tasted orange juice," I said, hoping.

Easter laughed. "Help yourself." And I did, like drinking sunlight. Domenika carried the pitcher to the dining room, and when the door swung open, I heard the Countess laughing. At ten o'clock, I went to the *Jardinière*, ready with my notebook, and there she was, reading a magazine, Bisou beside her.

"What is this you are wearing?" she said. "I don't like to see a secretary attired like the maids, Nugent knows it."

"*Desolée*, Madame."

"Don't be sorry. Only to understand, clothes, the fashion, is very important. Please tell Mrs. Nugent: Give you Adele's dresses. Sad, she left so many behind."

"Adele?"

"My secretary before. *Enfin*, she grew out of them. A disappointment."

"Madame?"

"She was tall like you. I'm sure they will fit. Write this please, now, to Mrs. Nugent, and tomorrow come dressed properly."

"*Oui*, Madame."
"And not *Madame*, Sylvie. You must call me Inge. We will be friends."

We were not friends, but I was given Adele's dresses so the Countess would not be seen as the companion of a servant. Uniforms, I saw now, were made to set us apart. If everyone wore regular clothes, no one could tell who served whom in the castes of the castle. Still, even if Inge had worn the white apron and frilled cap of a chambermaid, she would be a class unto herself. To me she was a creature from a star, bird-boned, a waist the span of two hands. I was her acolyte from the first day. I studied the small mole below her nose. The line above her lip that curled when she smiled. Were her eyes violet, or were they the wavering blue of a match flame? I sat with my spine straight, my legs crossed like hers, my head tipped to the side. "Friends," she said. But my friends did not wear a pearl necklace on Wednesday morning, like a choker of white berries, did not sit on a couch dictating letters about real estate management. "Please tell Nugent: 'The Richmond house should be made ready for residency in late September. The trip to Paris is scheduled for January. Nugents and Gradys to travel steerage. Steamer tickets arranged on the White Star line. We'll have Christmas in Richmond. Please not to forget the oysters, to ship alive from Wellfleet.'" The gamekeeper's lodge required *une douzaine* of wool blankets. Four spittoons. "And six rocking chairs for the porch. My husband likes to smoke outside regarding the moon."

Sometimes she spoke her letters not to me but to the little dog, in a baby voice. He licked her face and she kissed him on the nose. I took notes and typed them later. My typing was quite fast now, without mistakes.

It took a week to learn the routine, the layout of the house. I collected snippets of information gleaned from dusting portraits, from Inge's chatter and stories in the kitchen, writing down the details in my notebook to remember them.

"I get lost in all these rooms," I said to Easter while we made egg salad for twenty.

"You're not the only one," Easter said. "All kindsa ways to get lost in this house. You know he built this place for the second Mrs. Padgett? As a gift. But she spends one summer here, then goes off with one a them ragtime fellas."

Ragtime fellas? Mrs. Padgett II had absconded with a jazz singer! Too bad I was not at liberty to divulge this morsel to Susie Society, but it whetted my appetite for scuttlebutt. "And the first wife?" Carefully, I shelled another egg.

"Jasper's mother. Died in childbed," Easter said. "I did as best I could with that boy. And wasn't he a little old colicky baby. Crying for his mother to break your heart."

I'd dusted her portrait in the library with its plaque: Opal Braden Padgett, 1868–1887, a dark-haired young woman holding an armful of magnolia blossoms. Dead at nineteen. I collected such details like puzzle pieces. The painting of the boy in cornsilk curls holding his toy horse was Jasper, motherless, age three. The white-suited gentleman over the mantel was the Duke. The stern soldier in gray, sword at his side, was Brigadier General Sterling Padgett, the rebel Confederate ancestor. I stared at them, prospecting for information: the sad eyes of the child. The merry smile of Opal. The prominent ear of the Brigadier, like an oyster shell on the side of his head.

When I'd been two weeks at Elkhorne, the Countess dictated instructions for a fishing expedition (pâté, *chocolat*, lemonade, two men to portage the lot). "My husband," Inge mused, "do you know? The last wife never will go fishing with him. She detest *les montagnes*. She detest the forest, all of nature. But me, I adore to be in the open, the wild! The wife before? *Non.* She had the love affair, and that was the end."

With a ragtime fella? I didn't ask.

She smiled and whispered, "Of course, Duke had the love affair for himself. *Et voilà*, here is me now, Madame Padgett number three. Everybody's happy."

On the page, I was drawing small daisies, little hearts with Cupid arrows.

She sat forward and put her hand on my pen. "Do not write that, Sylvie, about the wife before!"

"I'm sorry," I said, fearing a *faux pas*. "*Désolée*."

"No, no, *ange*. Don't be sorry. Inge must learn not to think aloud."

But she didn't learn, and mused to me all that summer as if I were her confidante. Perhaps I was. Who else was there, in the mountains, for her to talk to besides the little dog? Her husband, the Duke, was away, traveling on business. After two weeks I had yet to glimpse him. Inge went out on horseback in the afternoon with Cedric, an English riding instructor. He wore bizarre trousers ballooned at the hips called jodhpurs. Inge adored him. He sat with her in the afternoons reading while she painted watercolors. In the evenings, she dined with him at the big table or with guests from town, Mrs. Colonel "Bunny" Bowles, and two others whom she called *Mme Ennuyant et Mme Étouffante* (Mrs. Staid and Mrs. Suffocating). You could hear her yawn through the swinging door. Another lady was deemed *Mme Bonté Chrétienne* (Mrs. Christian Goodness). Inge refused to invite her again after the woman spent the afternoon discussing Bible verses.

"Pah," she said. "All that religion is only *fantasie et folie et mensonges*."

Fantasy and madness and lies.

The Countess was an apostate! Surely she would burn in the fires of hell for such talk. But it thrilled me. That she would insult the Holy Word of God aloud. *Could she be right?* I wondered, but in the next moment I trembled at my own wicked thoughts and crossed myself for protection. Slowly, her daring began to alter me. No chance of a nunnery in my future now.

"Religion is not modern," she said. "Sociology is modern. Science is. Facts, not fairy tales." She wished, she said, to talk to Jasper about the Sociological Department. "But his head is in the clouds."

It was true the stepson was absentminded, in a rush, his shirttails loose, tie askew, a book in his pocket. His blushing smiles intrigued me. From afar I entertained notions that I was the cause of his flustered state.

"For a man who reads all them books," Easter said, "he sure can't please those professors. If he don't pass that one class, he's out again."

"What class?" I asked.

"He says he don't care for Latin, so he failed. Can you imagine?"

I did not care for it either but had passed Latin with honors and could do all four conjugations and five declensions. *Servus vīnum ad vīllam portat.* (The slave carries the wine home.) I imagined saying this to Jasper Padgett, his surprise to hear me. Perhaps I would tutor him and he would pass with highest marks. We'd be friends.

The truth was I lacked courage to talk to him. I watched him rushing or reading, giving me a wave or a wink. He was not lordly or terribly handsome, nor was he that Western type of rugged man you saw swagger in town, chewing tobacco. He was solitary, built on a thin-shouldered frame. He left on horseback to work his shift at the quarry and returned late. He ate his dinner at the Larkspur Hotel, or who knew where? Not with his stepmother.

"Likely he's out drinking buzz juice in that saloon," Easter said, a crease of disapproval on her face. Or worry.

One morning the Countess sent me to the manor library to fetch a magazine, "and borrow what you like." I dawdled, fingering the titles along walls made of books. I fished out *The House of Mirth*, *Little Women*, and then stood still, reading *Great Expectations*.

"Hallo there!"

I jumped out of my skin. Jasper Padgett peered around the back of a wingchair.

"If it's not that sainted angel from the quarry," he said in his drawl.

"Saint?" I said. "Hardly."

"I don't forget your good deed, bandaging the wounded. And then there's your service to my stepmother."

"She's very kind."

"Kind like a spider," he said.

What he meant I couldn't guess, but an image of Inge with eight legs, spinning a web, lurked now in an attic corner of my mind. Jasper came to stand beside me, looking at the wall of books. He drew his forefinger along their spines. "Poor things. All for show. Nobody ever cracks 'em. Except me. Now you."

"I'd like to read all of them."

"Which do you have there?" He peered at my choices, leaning over my shoulder. "*House of Mirth.* Ha! Not this house."

What did he mean? Inge was full of mirth, always laughing.

"I haven't read it," Jasper said. "Tell me if it's any good." He displayed the book in his hand with distaste. *The Aeneid.* In Latin! To think I'd imagined myself tutoring him when he was reading Virgil in the original. "I prefer Jack London," he said. "The best is *White Fang.* But I'm forced to break my teeth on this rock 'cause if I don't I'll be the shame of the family. I detest Latin."

"I also dislike it," I said. "The verbs give me a headache."

"We hate the same things!" Jasper said. "Kindred spirits."

Not hardly. But I wondered: What else did he hate that I also hated? Some more loathings that we could share.

"I'll read the Wharton after you finish," he said. "We'll compare notes." He settled by the window with his Latin epic, and I went to the magazine rack and found three issues of *Country Living* for his stepmother.

"Sit." Inge patted a spot beside her. With Bisou across our laps, she turned pages of the magazines till she found a photograph of an alpine castle perched among mountains, a petite Swiss village at its feet.

"*Regardes*, Sylvie. This is the dream we will bring here for Moonstone. So many amusements, the lake, the fishing and riding, the hunt *surtout*." Her finger traced the picture, the dots of sheep. "The workers happy."

At the time I was enthralled by the dream, convinced by her plans for social betterment. But now I remember that she pointed to the sheep when she said *workers*.

"Next season," Inge said, "all Richmond society, New York society, *les petites noblesses* of Newport, will arrive to see: Elkhorne Manor is the premier estate of the West. Moonstone village will be *exacte* like the alpine villages, and Elkhorne is our American castle to equal the *grands châteaux* of Europe."

"It's exciting to imagine."

"But it is difficult to execute, this sociology. I am exhausted." She sighed mightily and leaned her head against me.

I stayed frozen with the head of the Countess listing on my shoulder.

"My worries and trials." She sighed again. "The Sociological Department, and the household staff to manage, and the menus! The furnishings and decor to oversee—"

Complaints are the seeds of misery, I almost said.

"My husband," said Inge. "He voyage everywhere—with I don't know who. What do you think he is doing when he is away?"

Riding camels in the desert, slaying dragons, shooting elephants.

"I expect he's . . . working," I said. "My father went far away for work. He came here without us for two years. *Ma mère* had her baby alone after he left."

The Countess sat up. "You're right! My husband is a businessman. He sacrifice for the good of the Company, for the workmen. You are wise to remind me how they suffer. Your poor mother. We must aid the people."

"They call you the angel of the camps," I said from my shyness.

"Angel? Phh. You know, *en fait*, I'm the devil? The American ladies think so." She sighed with the burden of it all.

How strange it seemed to me that she was unhappy. "At least you have the *grand fête* in September to look forward to," I said. "It will be marvelous."

"Do you think so?" she asked. "You have no idea how—the King's visit, the work to organize. The guests. To plan so many details. This is the first time for me, the responsibility. I don't sleep. I have the nightmares *effrayants*."

"Poor Inge."

"The guests! Everyone is so important. Mr. Rockefeller! Mr. Osgood . . ."

She lowered her voice. "What the King requires . . . It is very delicate. Can you imagine?"

I could not. Even now I prefer not to.

"These are very rich men. They are the railroad money. Oil money. Coal money. My husband wants to show the gorgeous mountains, the fresh air, his vision to the future. The guests will see the opportunity and make the investment. The sociology—everything we dream depends on the money. I tell Duke, *mon cher*, what use is the money without goodness of the heart? But if the gentlemen don't to invest—it will spell *catastrophe*."

"Same spelling," I said. "In English too."

"You are very clever, Sylvie." She laughed. "And we *must* be clever to show these men the vision, the beauty, of the Western living. This new world."

———

Dear Maman and Papa, Henry and baby Nipper,

I am sorry I have not sent word sooner but I write so many letters
all day in my job for Mrs. Padgett I have hardly had time.

The truth was I did not know how to translate the people of Elkhorne, its porcelain lavatories and elephant-skin wallpaper, the taste of orange juice, into language that would not hurt them. They would see I'd been corrupted by plumbing and library books, blasphemous thoughts and a craving for luxury, for the admiration of a duke's son and his glamorous stepmother. It was best to leave out the details. I wrote those for myself, in my private notebook, and sent a plainer version to my family.

I think of you and wish that you could see this place with your
own eyes. It is grand and beautiful. I live in a dormitory with other
girls who are summer servants. Mrs. Nugent is the housekeeper.
She is very strict! I prefer to work with the cook Easter Grady who
is teaching me pastry. I will tell you more, but for now, know that

I'm keeping well and have done my work to the satisfaction of my employers. Please write and tell me how are things at home.

Yours in Christ's love,

Sylvie

Maman wrote back in French with English smattered in, the way she spoke.

Ma chère fille,

Your father works many shifts even Sunday. We prepare for winter. I grow peas and have put a fence against the animals. I have pickled 53 eggs, malgré we have now only the four hens. Mrs. Rotisserie was carried off by the weasel. Nipper is growing too fast and talking un vrai bavard. A bear two nights before was strolling the quarry road. I wish your father to shoot him but it's forbidden to hunt in the Padgett property. Henry wants to set the bear trap. You are in my prayers. Bless you and keep you dans l'amour du Christ.

Maman

Below her words was a funny drawing by Papa, of a girl mouse in an apron, brandishing a feather duster. It made me laugh. I missed them, far away on the point of Marble Mountain. I worried. About Henry setting traps. Nipper tumbling off a crag. Maman falling down from exhaustion. Especially about my father in the pit. The *Moonstone City Record* was full of disaster:

ESCAPE FROM DEATH: Clifford Radcliffe was hoisting one of the new 75-ton cranes, standing on an iron beam about 50 feet from the ground. The hoisting rope broke and swung with a great deal of force. It knocked Radcliffe off the beam, and wound around his neck. He fell and struck the ground with about a foot of rope to spare. Had the rope been shorter the fall would've hanged him. He was unconscious a few hours but is set to go back to work on Tuesday.

DOUBLE DANGER: Tommy Gilbert, a mill-worker cutting marble mosaic for tile floors, had part of a left-hand finger cut off by a stone saw not two weeks ago. Returning to work Tuesday, he had the misfortune to lose the entire fore-finger of his right hand to the very same saw. The young man is a gifted pitcher for the Moon-stone Slammers. Sadly, he is unlikely to play for the team again.

While the marble workers risked necks and limbs breaking rock, I sat with the Countess, taking dictation and watching her feed bits of ham to Bisou, teaching him tricks. He could roll over on command.

"Hold him!" she said one morning. "We will brush his teeth."

The dog struggled and shed dark hairs on my starched shirtwaist while I held his snout and Inge poked a little toothbrush in his mouth to scrub the long vicious canines. "*Shh, p'tit coocoo,*" she said.

No one would believe it.

I addressed invitations while we gossiped about the guests, the Richmond society figures invited for the Hunters' Ball, especially the most important, Mrs. Randolph Sherry, president of the United Daughters of the Confederacy.

"Thanks to Coralee Sherry, these daughters give the Company a contract for one hundred thousand dollars," Inge said. "It's true! They want to build a monument on the National Mall in Washington out of Moonstone marble."

I imagined bills of money falling down like snow and forming a marble temple.

"It is a statue to honor the Confederate soldiers and loyal slaves of the war," Inge said. "But really I think it is for Coralee—to win Mr. Padgett for her *lover!*" Her eyes were large and spilling secrets as she whispered: "Because—do not repeat—she tried to marry Mr. Padgett before I stole his heart."

"Not stoled," I said, giggling. "Stole."

"Ah, *merde*. Stole." Inge cursed to shock me, and she did, even as I loved her scandalous gossip, while she talked *intime* like a sister. She had begun to call me Sugar, or Silly, short for Sylvie. Her names made me laugh behind my hand.

"What is funny?"

"Silly, in English, *ça veut dire ridicule.*"

"I call you Ridiculous because you are too much Mademoiselle Professeur. It's dull to be so serious. You are too pretty Silly girl for just books and paper."

Pretty, she said. *Jolie.* The word lodged like a dart in the shallow regions of my soul. The sin of vainglory was a direct path to damnation. *Pretty* had never applied to me, and now it was a sugared pastille to savor.

"For myself," Inge said, "I prefer to commence the party right *now.* September is too long for waiting." She fretted and sent letters to society ladies in the East. "Do you think they will come? It is so far to travel. But the *grand bal* will be like nothing they've ever seen. We adore to dance and drink champagne under the mountain stars."

"I'd love to try it," I said.

"Oh, yes!" Her eyes shone with a plan. "I invite you as a guest! Sylvie, I think you would like to meet *le Roi.* The King. Am I right?"

She knew she was by the naked wish on my face.

"*Oh, là,*" Inge said. "Mademoiselle Pelletier would like to meet the King of Belgium! So you will." She clapped her hands like butterfly wings beating. "There are never enough young and beautiful women here in the mountains. Only the roughnecks men. You will be fantastic. You will sweep."

Sweep? Her idea was to have me be a servant. To brush crumbs and observe.

"You know, Sylvie," she said, "it was in the court of King Leopold that I met my husband. I sweeped him off his toes."

"His feet."

"Yes, at just such a party at Laeken. He was fallen for me. Right away we elope to get married." Her face was lit by the memory. "We'll dress you up, silly mountain goat," she said fondly. "To see what happens."

——

85

The next morning Inge took my mountain-goat hand and pulled me from the writing desk up the grand staircase. We traveled down a wide corridor, past paintings of foxhounds. It was a hallway of doors, all of them closed. "There is the Jasper suite," she said, pointing through an arch toward what appeared to be a separate wing. "Here's my own chamber. And . . . *voilà!* My closet."

She opened the door to a room the size of Cabin Six, hung around with racks of dresses and costumes for hunting and dancing, lounging and dining. Above were shelves for hats and below for shoes and boots and slippers. An inner door led to her bedchamber. Two armchairs flanked a window overlooking the gardens. A vanity table held a vase of greenhouse gardenias. From a mirrored alcove, three Inges reflected back and beamed at me, expectant. Three Sylvies stood beside her in the mirror, struck dumb as potatoes.

"Which dress for Mademoiselle?" Inge asked. "We find one to match your eyes." She began to slide hangers along, as if turning pages. A rose pink, a midnight blue. A linen, a satin, a taffeta. She skipped the wintry woolens, the velvets, saying the names of the Parisian designers as if they were her friends. Poiret, Paquin, Callot Soeurs. She pulled out a long green dress of sheening silk, the color of new grass.

"A beautiful silhouette." She held the gown under my chin, checking it against my face. "The green for the green eyes. Try it!"

"Oh, no, I couldn't, thank you," I performed the modesty of a nun but prayed to the Devil that she would insist.

"Off with everything, silly Sylvie, to try this one."

My embarrassment was no match for my love of that dress. I went behind a screen and let fall the navy-blue secretary skirt, then stood in my slip, scarlet with discomfort. The gown went over my head, light as nothing. Where were the sleeves?

"Do not be *timide* like a goose. Come out and show."

I stepped forth blotchy and bare-armed, and there she was, pulling up a sheath of lilac satin over her stark-naked body, shocking and white as a Roman statue. I cringed back behind the screen to protect her privacy while she convulsed with laughter.

"Don't be shocked, Silly. It is only woman flesh." She buttoned herself and assessed me. The green gossamer fabric draped over my moose bones and hung with the hem just off the floor.

"It suits you," she said. "Take off that slip. It bunches."

I wrapped my arms around my exposed shoulders.

"*Arrêtes*, Sylvie. Stop, the face, you look painful—in pain." She turned me around, judging, humming. "In the palace at Laeken, we girls played all day long with the clothes." She rummaged on a shelf and found a spring-green shawl of chiffon, emerald sequins in swirls along the border. She put it around my shoulders and tilted her head to judge the effect. "Maybe yes?" She turned me to the mirrors.

There I was, standing like a taxidermied trophy.

"Permit me?" She unpinned my braids and combed her fingers through the plait so my hair fell down in ripples. "*Magnifique, oh là*," she said, inhaling. "You're fortunate."

That morning as she dressed me up, I felt fortune shining like a star over my head, as good as if I were a manger in Bethlehem. At her vanity she painted my face, twisted and pinned my hair. I was the mannequin plaything of a mountain fairy. But even as I was dazzled at the effect, I felt a whiff of cruelty in the way she adorned me with gems I'd never have, that image in the mirror like a false promise. Did Inge have the power to transform me? I did not realize yet how I'd have to transform myself.

"You have the American beauty," she announced. From her velvet-lined boxes she lifted a rope of sparkling stones. "These are only paste, but who can tell?" She fastened them around my constricted throat. "Behold Mademoiselle Sylvie *la belle*. The gentlemen will be at you like bees to a flower."

I hid my face so she wouldn't see the effects of her flattery.

"But why do you hide?" she asked. "The gentlemen will like you to show them, *non*?" She thrust her chest out and lifted her uncorseted bosom in two hands so the breasts rounded and spilled from the V of her dress. "Like this, *va, va, va*."

I could not bring myself to hoist my chest as she did, brazen and fleshy. To obey her was to wade into a lake where my feet would not find bottom.

"Oh, don't be *stupide*." With a sudden reach of both hands, she cupped and lifted my bosom, giggling with delight. I squawked and recoiled, laughing despite myself. "You'll learn, *chérie*, to enjoy, because they will anyway appreciate. Your beauty."

"*Vous me faites rougir*, Madame. Inge."

"So beautiful, your blushings, your smile." She hugged herself, excited. "Now the party will be more amusing. You'll enter the room, *très élégante*." She fluttered her eyelashes and thrust her chest forward. "That's how it's done. All the men will ask, 'Who is she? This beautiful *femme mysterieuse*?'"

"I doubt it," I said, but thrilled to think so, sure they would laugh.

"They will chase you and fall in love if you only smile at them. Smile, yes. Like that." For two hours Madame continued her lessons, throwing gowns over our heads and off again, tutoring me about flirtation, about bodices and ruching, drape and pull. Half the dresses were too tight across my back, but she put them on me anyway, leaving the buttons open across my woodcutter shoulders. When I would not remove my slip, she pulled it over my protest and over my head, inspecting me.

I crossed my arms to hide my chest. Inge was bizarre, lewd. Or perhaps she wasn't. What would I know of royal behavior? Perhaps it was normal to converse half naked. Despite my shock at her talk of love affairs and hunting, I was stirred by a new thrill in the blood. Enchanted by the mirror where our lips were pursed, painted red. *Jolie*, she said, that worm of a word. Pretty. My mother would be scandalized. K.T. would snort. *Just some French vavoom*. But I was on my own now, and Inge was irresistible. Delightful. What was the harm in a pretty dress or having fun? One singular fun.

She pulled more gowns from their hangers for us to try. "It is a lark," she said, and then pondered. "Why do you call the fun times—'it's a lark.' What is the lark?"

"A lark? *C'est une alouette*."

"Aha, right, a lark, to dress up. We are the birds, and these are the lovely plumes."

I did not mention the song "Alouette," about plucking feathers, the beak, the head. Was I to be plucked? At last Inge chose the green dress for me. "A gift for you."

"Madame?" It was wrong to accept charity. This dress was the pity of a butterfly for a grub. If I wrapped myself in chiffon, would I turn into a *papillon* and flutter off enchanted? "*Non merci*," I said, but I still wanted the dress.

"You will accept," she said, like an order. "The King. He will like you. Maybe even he could prefer you. He has not had ever . . . an American friend." She hesitated, as if deciding what to say, then spoke in earnest. "A long time ago, Sylvie, it was *le Roi* Leopold who noticed me and chose me for his court. If not for him, I would never meet Mr. Padgett, I would not be here in this house. Do you understand? Maybe you don't!" She laughed. "A dress, a king, any wealthy gentleman—he can change the circumstance. For me, it's true. And for you, I hope."

"The circumstance for me is already changed," I said, "thanks to you."

"You're welcome, my dear. I enjoy to lift people from the low station to the better one," she said. "I had hoped, maybe, for Adele, but—you under-stand?"

I nodded as if I did, but at the time I did not, despite all insinuations.

Later, when I remembered that summer, I saw Inge without the goggles of naïveté that I wore then, and understood that she wanted to make me over as she'd done for herself. That summer, La Comtesse Ingeborg LaFol-lette deChassy Padgett was only twenty-six years old, the closest to a sister I'd known, and I was under her spell. When she left me alone to pick up the discarded finery off the floor, I twirled in the green dress and admired myself reflected in a pattern infinite as the future seemed to be. I lifted my bosom in my two hands as she had done, burning with new flames of daring. *They will chase you.* Her words lurched in my stomach like the sickness of hope, not to be a dressmaker dummy or a printer's devil, but a butterfly. Silence would not be my best garment then, not if there were green silk, satin slippers, a choker of rhinestones.

Chapter Seven

THE DUKE ARRIVED IN A great flurry one Friday evening, with guests from New York. "Important guests," said Inge. That weekend I stayed in the backstairs and did not get a glimpse of her husband, only heard his bluster and sneezes in the house, his wheezy cigarette laughter. I was glad when Nugent assigned me to the kitchen with Easter and went off to church on Sunday morning with the Croatian sisters. Inge was out riding with her instructor, Cedric. So I jumped when a bell rang from the lower quarters.

"That's old Padgett," Easter said, in a bad mood. "Go see what he wants."

I went in my apron to the new territory of downstairs, imagining the lower floor as a damp dungeon of rats and skeletons. But here was a saloon, a game room with a billiard table big as a hay wagon, red leather couches conspiring around a fireplace, elk heads on the walls. Brass spittoons. Chips and cards piled on a credenza. I took a wrong turn and found myself in a wine cellar. The bell rang again, and I followed it to the end of the corridor to arrive at a suite of offices, empty on a Sunday. Beyond these was the inner sanctum of Jerome "Duke" Padgett, the door ajar.

He was on the telephone and held his finger in the air for me to wait. I stayed just outside and observed. He had a big head of white hair. The wiry caterpillars of his eyebrows rose above spectacles hooked behind prominent ears like whirligig propellers. A cigarette was clamped in his teeth below a luxurious mustache. Smoke curdled above him as he spoke loudly into the handset. "How the hell do you plan to get that shipment to Cleveland by October if the track's not finished? Work it out, Colonel. Tell those guineas to settle down, half of 'em blotto half the time. Put 'em in tents. They won't freeze, they're hot-blooded. Goddammit, Bowles, if you can't figure it out, I'll figure it out for you. Get the troublemakers out of town. Ten o'clock. Here. Yes, yes. Elkhorne."

What did he mean, *troublemakers out of town*? Did he mean Lonahan? Papa?

Mr. Padgett hung up the earpiece violently. "Goddammit."

"You rang upstairs, sir?"

He startled. "You're not that Bohemian gal—what's-her-name?"

"No, sir. Sylvie Pelletier. Mrs. Padgett's secretary."

"Well, well, nice to meet you, Miss Pelletier." He stretched his arms forward, fingers laced, to crack his knuckles. "All the reports on you are favorable. My wife is happy. Keep up the good work, and I'll be grateful." He spoke pleasantly to me with those soft Virginia vowels in his mouth. "Please tell Easter: send breakfast. Then lunch at noon for three men. Thank you."

"He would like breakfast," I said, back in the kitchen.

Easter still appeared angry, beating eggs, chopping herbs with loud thwacks of her knife. When I passed behind her to set the tray, she did something that astonished me. As long as I live, I won't forget it. She cleared her throat and coughed into her palm. Then she wiped a gossamer stream of spittle like albumen into the dish of eggs and beat them fiercely with a fork. She did not know I'd seen her. Maybe I hadn't? I did not trust my own eyes. She shook the skillet, adding the eggs, then cheddar cheese, and turned the golden omelet onto a plate, adorned it with parsley and a slice of orange cut like a flower.

"Here's this," she said, strangely cheerful now. "Duke's special."

I carried the tray downstairs, afraid I might trip on the shock. I didn't yet understand about revenge, or know Easter's reasons. But that morning I began to pay attention, watching to discover them.

Mr. Padgett was preoccupied, papers in front of his nose. As I poured coffee, he stood up, reading a document, and went to the corner of the room, where he slid back a red curtain, revealing a heavy steel door. It was painted black with a gold crest of fighting lions on a shield. In the center of the door was an elaborate lock. He spun a dial, distracted, but then stopped and noticed me. "That's all now," he said with a smile of dismissal. "Thank you kindly."

And was he kind? He appeared so, whistling low under his breath. Reports on me were favorable, he'd said, so I was inclined to like him. But I would not dare say anything about the adulterated eggs. Not to him or to Easter either.

Instead, I asked her about the metal door. "Where does it lead?"

"To the money, honey," Easter said. "That vault is steel and cement. Nobody can't get in there except maybe by a stick of dynamite."

But, as I was to learn, there was an easier way to get in. From the first time I saw it, I dreamed about that safe. Surely it contained piles of gold and jewels, like Ali Baba's cave of the forty thieves.

After an hour Easter sent me downstairs to clear the breakfast tray. The Duke was in conversation with Colonel Bowles and another man: Juno Tarbusch, boss at the quarry, who had dressed up for the occasion in a string tie and vest.

"Your son does a fine job," Tarbusch was saying, his voice oiled as his hair. "The quarry boys all like Jasper."

"He's not there to be a pal," said the Duke.

"Well, he likes to talk." Tarbusch grinned. "He's a young professor."

"Do your best to cure him of it," the Duke said.

"We'll knock some sense into his head," said Tarbusch.

"When it's time for knocking heads," Bowles laughed, "I know who to get."

"You get me," Tarbusch said. "And I get the Pinkertons."

"Best agency for hired muscle in the U.S.A.," Bowles said.

Duke Padgett examined the backs of his stumpy fingers. "None of these union scum will last a minute in this town, am I clear?" He pointed at me.

I jumped as if he'd seen me twitch at the mention of Pinkertons and *union scum*. Was my father in danger? I'd have liked to report the conversation to Papa or tell K.T., but could not afford to lose five dollars a week. My loyalties gnarled and snared me.

"Could we get these gentlemen more coffee?" the Duke said.

"Why, bonshooor, Sylvie," said the jovial Bowles. "Comment alley voo?"

"*Bien, merci*, thank you, sir."

The Duke laughed. "These gals. My wife insists on the company of her French mademoiselles."

"My wife would talk the ears off an elephant," said the Colonel.

"Mine's her own gaggle of geese, I tellya," Tarbusch said.

The men cracked themselves up while I poured coffee and wondered what it would be like to send scalding streams directly into their laps. How they would leap up, *a gaggle of geese*, squawking. The seed pearl of resentment grew larger.

The next afternoon, I was typing Inge's correspondence in the Greenery.

"Young lady! Must you make that infernal racket?" There in the doorway was the Duke, smoking.

"I'm sorry, sir, I was—"

He massaged his scalp and snuffed his cigarette in the potted fern. "You must excuse my temper, miss, I am overwrought." He departed with a watery smile.

"Where should I type, then?" I asked Inge later.

"Pay no attention," she said. "He's not staying long—and always at the office, the mill. He is very *préoccupé* with the finance. Also the train rail is not finish, so he's not happy. Make as many rackets as you like."

"As much racket," I said. "Only one."

In the vast house was a carpeted silence, punctured by the bell when servants were summoned, muted footsteps along the back passages, Inge plinking at the piano. In the Cardboard Palace at night was only soft wind and animal rustlings outside, the laughter from the men's quarters where the grounds-keepers drank whiskey. Their tobacco smells and strumming guitar boiled up in the darkness into a stew of loneliness. I looked forward to the hours in the kitchen with Easter Grady, the pot-clanging, dish-rattling afternoons and evenings when I helped her.

In truth, she helped me more. That summer she taught me pastry. She taught me sauces. She taught me dishes like grits and scrapple, sweet potato pie, ham with gravy, oyster stuffing. Those recipes made me feel American even as Easter showed me how to make fish *en croûte*, how to make a *roux*, French things I'd never heard of, each requiring a week's worth of butter. It was from Easter that I learned food could be decorated. "Tastes better if it's pretty," she said.

"Where'd you learn all this?" I asked, marveling.

"From an old Guadeloupe woman worked at Belle Glade till she keelt over dead at the stove one day. The old grandfather, General Padgett, said she died on account of whipping all that cream, but it was the whipping she got from his own hand on the lash." She hacked a melon in half with her cleaver.

What I know now about retribution is that we use what tools are at hand. I would soon discover my own. Easter had her cooking, her kitchen tools for chopping and boiling. Knowing what I came to learn about Duke Padgett, I wouldn't have blamed her if she had put arsenic in his stew, but she did not poison him or smash the china. She cooked revenge in the eggs.

Despite what evil and sorrow had happened to her, she was kind. She was sovereign in herself. She was a tiny honeybee, alighting on her tasks of slicing, kneading, washing, muscles flexing her ropy arms. She looked out for us. When Albina had a cold, or I had a headache or female pains, she had a nostrum or an herb or a tea to offer. If I dropped a dish and broke it, she would only say, "Never mind, just sweep." If Nugent scolded one of us, Easter would put a sugar lump in our pockets or give us a wink. As we worked, I asked questions and heard stories, how she gathered eggs as a child with her sister in the sweet Virginia morning, splashing in the river. "Same river where my boys played with Master Jace."

"You have two sons?" I asked.

"Caleb and Marcus. Them boys was mischief. Jasper one time got himself stuck in the middle of the creek. He was only little then, and Caleb went in after Jace to drag him out. Next thing you know, little Marcus is in the water too, the pair of 'em hollering. And Caleb saved 'em both! Got one under each arm and took 'em over to dry land good as Moses." She shook her head, smiling and lost in the memory.

I invented reasons to stand at the counter and chop things just to listen to her talk.

"Where your people from?" she asked one afternoon. "Canada or where?"

"My parents are from Canada. But I was born here, in Vermont."

"What does your mother cook?"

I told her, *soupe aux pois* and *boudin* sausage, *pâté chinois* and *ragoût de boulettes*, sugar pie and *pattes de cochon*.

She laughed. "What'n hell is that?"

"Pig foot."

"Padgetts don't eat that." She laughed again. "You have a brother? Any sisters?"

"Two brothers," I said. "You have a sister and . . . ?"

"Two brothers." Then, after a moment, "Tilly, my sister, was sold away."

The air of the morning coagulated around the words, as if she'd told a tall tale that was true. As if the *loup-garou* had flown through the air in his dugout canoe and stolen a child, stolen happiness itself. "Sold away," she repeated, and went on peeling potatoes. The skin with its pocks of eyes fell into the sink.

It was a tragedy from the past. A private subject. My upbringing and instinct vibrated with warning: *Do not pry.* At the same time, I was afflicted by curiosity. K. T. Redmond's orders were to ask questions, but I could hardly bring myself to practice with Easter, held off by something unspeakable. And by dread—perhaps it was better not to know. Better for me? For Easter? Carrot peelings fell away from my knife in curls. In the silence, while we worked, I thought maybe a story would spill out of her, same as a recipe or instruction on how to juice an orange.

After a minute, she drew a long breath. "Tilly was most of ten years old when Padgett sold her. That was Mr. Duke's father. General Padgett." She gouged a sprouted eye from a potato.

"How old were you?" I said carefully. "If you don't mind me asking . . ."

"Maybe four, five," she said. "And I don't mind telling you. You oughta know. That's what I always told Master Jace, don't go on pretending like it didn't happen. We all saw with our own eyes."

"Saw?"

"They took Tilly from us and sold her with six more people off Belle Glade, to pay a *gambling* debt. Old Padgett sent 'em away walking out the gates, on down the road to Louisiana."

"They walked? From Virginia to *Louisiana*?"

"We didn't hear different." Easter sliced potatoes into white bloodless rounds.

"Tilly didn't write to you?"

Easter peered at me as if at an imbecile. She arranged the potato slices in overlapping circles like the petals of a rose and poured a roux of milk and flour into the pan. "When he was a boy, Master Jace was all the time pestering me about that story. He swore he was going to find Tilly one day. That child always want to act a big man like his father. I won't say he don't have a big heart. But how's a child gonna go down there to Louisiana? Find a needle in a haystack."

"It's a lot of Acadians in Louisiana," I said, flailing. "Like my family. French people." And for some reason I told her the story of the English Yankees driving the French Acadians out of Quebec and casting them out to sea.

"They were free?" she asked sharply.

"Well, yes, but—" But it was not the same, I saw. Not an equivalency of wrongs. "They were forced away from their homes and migrated south," I said. "To Vermont and Maine and Louisiana."

"So, you say maybe your people have some kin in Louisiana? Who we could inquire to find Miss Tilly Padgett sold out of Richmond in around about 1857?"

"Eighteen-fifty-seven is a long time ago."

"Not to me it ain't," she said.

Chapter Eight

A COUPLE OF WEEKS BEFORE the Hunters' Ball, Mrs. Nugent gave me the newspapers to take in to breakfast. "And give this to the cook," she said, handing over a letter.

In the kitchen Easter and John Grady were laughing about something, but when I came in, they rearranged their faces. "Good morning," John Grady said, as if they'd been caught. I gave Easter the letter.

"Oh, thank the Lord," she said. "It's from Marcus. Our younger boy. He's a chef at the Prince Hotel down in Denver. Both our sons are chefs."

"College men too," Mr. Grady said. "Both got degrees from Hampton Institute."

Easter opened the envelope and let out a cry, a hand on her heart. "Will you look at that! John Grady, you see these two." The beaming Gradys examined a photograph. "See, Sylvie," Easter said, "the older one here is Caleb, and that one's Marcus."

The two young men were posed formally, Caleb standing behind Marcus, a hand on his younger brother's shoulder.

Mr. Grady laughed. "You just know Caleb made Marcus sit down in the chair so Cal looks taller."

Easter smiled. "Caleb never could tolerate how his little brother grew right past him." Their sons wore tailored suits, stiff-collared shirts, and ties. Marcus had a strong resemblance to his father, grasping his lapels like a politician. The older son, Caleb, looked at the camera with a certain veiled amusement in his eyes, a watch chain across his middle and a thick book in his hand. His ears stuck out like cup handles.

"Very handsome," I said, smiling.

Easter examined the letter with reverent attention. "Miss Sylvie, don't suppose you could read this out for us? I went and lost my glasses like a fool. And John Grady needs to get some spectacles. Can't see the nose on his own face." She handed the letter to me, and I began to read it aloud.

DEAR MOTHER & FATHER GET CALEB TO READ THIS LETTER.

"Wait," I said. "Shouldn't you let your son read it, then? Instead of me?"

"Cal won't be up to Elkhorne for another few weeks," Mr. Grady said.

"He's the chef on Padgett's private rail car," Easter said. "They sent him to Denver to cook for the King when he travels here."

"Mother can't stand to wait till then," said Mr. Grady. "Might as well read it." So I continued with Marcus's letter.

When brother Cal was here in Denver, we had this photograph made for Mother's birthday. We hope you like it. (I'm the handsome one.) The news is your sons have a plan to buy Colorado land west of Ft. Morgan, $100 for a lot. We can't shake the idea since we heard a speech from Mr. Oliver Toussaint Jackson. He proposes to build up a new town in Weld County, all for colored people, with a school, doctor, barber, post office. Everybody owns a piece of land, a house. This is the new way, following the teaching of Booker T. Washington from Tuskegee College. Caleb argues with me over Booker T.'s philosophy but we are agreed on the remedy. We have savings enough for homesteading and mean to start in September.

As I read, the two Gradys wore constricted expressions. Their eyes darted back and forth from one to the other, then to me. Easter's laugh was nervous. "Marcus always has some fool notion," she said. "Going off about how he's gonna get himself a town, the moon and stars. Can you figure? A town! That's a fool talking."

> Given the danger now with the news from Richmond, if you're still anxious to get away, Cal could fetch you in September and we'll get us a piece of ground and some seed wheat. The place is called Dearfield. Caleb's idea is to start a college there. We both endorse the plan with utmost determination to succeed. Mother, you could run that luncheonette you always dream about. Dad, we plan for you to raise strawberries and peaches to eat with cream.
>
> Your devoted son,
> Marcus

"He's crazy, for sure, that Marcus." Grady shrugged and went out to the stables.

"Now, Sylvie," Easter said, "you appreciate the privacy of a letter."

"Yes, ma'am. My mother taught me not to mind other people's business."

"Then she raised you right."

Jace Padgett came into the kitchen and threw his book on the table. Easter folded the letter into her apron pocket. "Good morning, Master Padgett."

"Please don't call me that," he snapped.

"I call you what I call you."

"You do it because you like to," he said. "To remind me."

Easter gave him a soft look, tousled his hair. "What's eating you?"

"If I could study, maybe I'd pass that exam," he said. "But Father has me working dawn to dusk—"

"Hmmp," Easter said. "What would I know about that?"

"All last month it was shoveling quarry rock," he said.

Easter muttered, "All last night it was you out drinkin'."

"This week I'm assigned at the mill," Jace continued. "Worst is, tomorrow I have to take darling stepmother around the town. She wants a tour for her Sociological Department. The whole thing's a joke." He helped himself to bread and butter. "Why should I go touring for some lady project? How'm I going to study? I have to stand on my own feet."

"You standing right on *my* own feet now. Excuse me." Easter shunted him out of her path, put the letter in a drawer.

"Is that from Marcus?" he asked.

"It is," said Easter, caught again somehow.

"Want me to read it to you?"

"No, thank you," she said. "One of the girls read it out for me this morning."

"Well, how is he? How's Marcus?"

"He's keeping well in Denver."

"Let's write and tell him come on up to Moonstone with Caleb. I want to take them shooting, bag some elk. Shall we write back?"

"No time now." She took the breakfast tray out to the dining room.

I stood at the sink peeling a bushel of peaches. Jasper eyed the drawer where the letter was stowed, then went over and took it from under the folded clean dish towels, reading it. "Huh." He put the letter back where he found it. "'Anxious to get away.' Whattya suppose that means?"

"Beg pardon?" I said.

"Weren't you the one who read that for her?"

I nodded and dropped a peach stone in the rubbish, peeled another.

"See, Easter always gets me to read her letters," Jasper said. "Criminal that she can't read 'em herself."

"She lost her glasses."

Jace stood by the sink and watched my knife flense a long curl of skin off a peach. "They caught her with a book when she was about six or seven, and punished her. They'd be whipped—for reading."

I shuddered, my hands slick with peach blood.

"Apologies, Miss Pelletier. I shouldn't've started on it. It's not a topic for the breakfast table."

Jasper sat behind me, buttering toast. The air was stiff as canvas. His father and stepmother were drinking coffee in the dining room, clinking spoons on saucers, talking beyond the door. Jace stayed put. I felt his presence as if a boulder had rolled in the door and filled the room. He pushed his glasses up his nose and read his book. The hair at the back of his head was damp and curled like ducktail feathers.

"I hope you don't mind me sitting here," he said in his elegant drawl. "I'm asked not to read at their table." He nodded toward the dining room. "It's impolite. But reading's how I escape all that yap. All their projects. Of which I'm the main one." He ate his egg and turned pages. Occasionally, he made a note in a margin or underlined a sentence.

"You write in your books?" I asked, curious.

"I do, yes. Don't you?"

"I'd be scalped if I did."

"That would be a terrible shame." He took off his glasses and peered at me. "All that beautiful hair of yours."

The knife slipped in my hand.

"Last week I heard your daddy sing," he said, still regarding me.

"You did?"

"He sure can sing, Jocko. He plays the fiddle too, I heard."

"He does." I smiled, thinking of Papa fiddling. "He's a good musician."

"Frenchy's a good *man*," said Jasper. "Everybody likes Jack Pelletier."

Not boss Tarbusch, I didn't say.

Jasper finished his coffee. When he pushed back his chair, he pointed to the drawer storing Marcus's letter. "So let me ask you again," he said. "'Anxious to get away.' What do you think that's about? Why would the Gradys want to leave us?"

The question intimidated me. Jasper himself did, a college man reading Virgil in Latin, the princeling of Elkhorne, asking my opinion. It seemed a risk to offer one.

"To be with their sons?"

Kate Manning

"But 'anxious to get away'?" Jasper said, sounding betrayed. "It would be a hardship if they left. See now, Easter raised me right alongside Cal and Marcus. Gradys have been with us—forever. They're loyal to our family because—Easter's even been to Paris with Dad, to show off her cooking. My father *paid* to send Caleb and Marcus to Hampton Institute. And now they think of leaving? If it weren't for my father, Marcus wouldn't've ever have met this Dearfield fellow—Toussaint Jackson, or Booker Washington either."

"I am not familiar with who that is," I said.

Jasper picked up the *Moonstone City Record* and pointed to a headline: BOOKER T. WASHINGTON AT DENVER. "Even our local rag recognizes him as the most famous Negro in the country! Right alongside this Professor Du Bois. W.E.B. Du Bois." *Due Boyce* was how he said it, tapping his book.

"Du Bois?" I said (*Dew Bwa*). "Is he French?"

"He's American. Negro. A Harvard man. Wrote this book. Caleb Grady gave it to me." He showed me the title, *The Souls of Black Folk.* "When I'm done with it, I'll loan it to you."

"I'd like that. Thank you."

The moment turned strange. Jasper's neck flushed as if the subject were not a discussion of books but something else, the heat in my own face.

"Say, Sylvie," he said, "will you be going around town touring with Madame tomorrow morning? For this project of hers?"

"She asked me to take notes."

"Well, lucky me," he said. "I'll be glad to have a fellow sufferer along."

Suffering how? A drive on the red leather seats of the Countess's high-wheeled carriage sounded nice. After he left, I picked up the *Record* to see what K. T. Redmond had reported.

BOOKER T. WASHINGTON AT DENVER

White men, prominent in Denver circles, showed respect by their attendance at a recent lecture by Booker T. Washington, the brilliant colored educator. It may be safely said that Mr.

Washington shows in his makeup much of the Divine. Emancipated at 10, working in a coal mine, as a child he showed serious thirst for knowledge. He heard of the college at Hampton and walked 800 miles, working along the way, and, reaching the school, was made a janitor. He went on to become a leader, an example and benefactor to his own people and the same to the white race. Those who refuse to recognize Mr. Washington are sadly deficient in the virtues they refuse to honor.

Mr. Washington was certainly inspiring, but I didn't understand then why Jasper Padgett would be so interested in him, or in the Gradys' plans for their own town. What interested me was Jasper himself.

Chapter Nine

Ours was a surrey carriage of mismatch that morning. Our stalwart leader was the Countess in her summer whites, her ruffled parasol. Beside her on the velvet upholstery was myself in a preposterous nuisance of a hat she gave me "to protect your milky complexion." Bisou perched wagging between us. In the backseat was Jace Padgett, glowering behind his spectacles, brooding over that book about souls. On the bench in front was John Grady driving in his formal suit, with the steady cheerful expression he always wore.

"Good *morning*! A fine day, a fine day! How you feeling, Missus Padgett? Miss Sylvie? What a day, Lord."

At the time I thought John Grady was the sunniest man. But after my education at the hands of Gradys and Padgetts, I understood his cheer as a deception or mask, a shield or a way not to go mad: his soul and his very body protected behind songs and whistling, to disarm threats and worse. Smiling was a disguise of appeasement I'd used myself, and was advised to do more of it. We wheeled down the drive and into town. Grady hummed and Inge narrated. "Today, *mes amis*, we interview the people in the camp, to ask how the Sociology can make improvements, to see with our own eyes how they live like *les misérables*."

"Can't wait," said sarcastic Jasper.

A basket of candy boxes sat at Grady's feet. Madame and I had spent the previous afternoon tying them with gold ribbon. Inge's idea was to hand them out to the families, "to make friends of the *habitants*."

"To make dupes of them, you mean," said Jace. "Bribes."

"Bribe?" she said. "*Non*, it is scientific. Kindness is proved to make the people attach to the Company, to be loyal. It is to keep out the terrible *syndicats de travail*."

Unions, she meant. The insult rankled me, but I still did not defend my father or George Lonahan, silenced again by money. At five dollars a week, I'd have a lovely nest egg at summer's end, and was not ready to risk losing it by opening my mouth.

As we rode along, Inge pointed out how Moonstone was prospering: the crews hammering up another mill shed by the river, the schoolhouse with its white stone foundations rising next to the bank. "The Company donated that marble," Inge said proudly.

"Not like you can't just pick it up free off the ground around here," Jasper said. "Lying around for the taking."

"That would be stealing," Inge said, "off Company property."

"How about school books?" Jace asked. "Did we donate books?"

"Good idea, *monsieur*. Books, of course," she said. "Write books, Sylvie."

"Write books." That's how the words are printed in my notebook, like a command.

Outside the Mercantile, Mr. Koble stood smoking in the sunlight; Inge waved. "Good morning!" she called to K. T. Redmond's friend Dottie Weeks, who stood outside the bakery, shaking a white cloud of flour out of her apron. I pulled my hat brim low for fear K.T. next door would poke her long nose out the window to sniff, questions blazing like guns. But the shade was down, the sign read *Closed*. Likely Susie Society was rootling around town, foraging for stories. Perhaps she would like to write about Inge's philosophy of Industrial Betterment. (Later, when I told her about it, she derided it as *welfare capitalism* with a disgusted shake of her head.)

The Countess went smiling at everybody we passed, seeming to enjoy their gaping at the red leather seats and fringed canopy of our surrey.

"See there, the new streetlight!" Inge pointed to a bulb dangling from a wire across the intersection. "Soon we will have the sewer and electric all through town."

"Swell," Jasper said. He turned a page.

"You are not impressed?" Inge said. "Surely it is impressive to make a town only in two years! Sylvie, *ange*, don't you agree?"

"*Ange* is French for angel, no? Sylvie the angel," Jace said. "Not like your friend Adele." He whispered in my ear: "Beware the houseguests, angel. Beware their continental ways."

"*Arrêtes, monsieur*, stop," said Inge, "you are terrible."

Maybe he was terrible or arrogant, but also, he was fascinating. His eyes pricked my back through the upholstery. I stole a look at him, and he grinned as if I were in on a joke. I was happy to be in on it, but—his warning did not feel funny. *Beware*.

Inge announced: "Here we are at the Little Italy."

"You mean *Dago*town," Jace said. "As my father calls it."

"My father too. I wish he wouldn't." I spoke without thinking and then regretted it. It was a risk to talk about my family while these Padgetts were discussing *les misérables*, the squalid homes of the workers. They might propose a trip to Quarrytown, where they'd see our rickety shack, casting their judgment and charity candy. If they saw, even that platter of a hat could not hide who I was.

The cabins by the mill were nailed out of logs and canvas. Plank-board paths led over the mud to dark doorways. Chickens scratched in the dirt behind mesh wire fences where lines of laundry hung in the breezy sunlight. Women in kerchiefs tended their kettles over outdoor fires, yelled threats at the children rolling in the dirt. Two mongrel dogs panted on a porch, strings of drool off their jowls. Bisou snarled at them from the safety of the bench.

"Stop here, please, Grady," Inge said.

Mr. Grady handed us down. Charcoal fumes mixed with the stench of the outhouse. Flies buzzed around a barrel of garbage. Inge wrinkled her nose and went up the walk, knocked on the door. "*Buongiorno*," she called. "Hallo?"

A sunburnt woman with pale eyes answered, her cheekbones shiny with sweat, her head wrapped in a scarf. "*Cosa vuoi?*" she asked, alarmed to see the elegant Inge on her porch. Her hands were stained purple. When she dried them on her apron, the color came off in red streaks. "*La Contessa!*" She ducked her head, overcome. "Oh, I don't believe. *Benvenuto!*" Children crowded behind her. Her apron rounded over her swollen stomach. "*Sono Signora* Santorini."

"Please don't worry, Mrs. Santorini," Inge reassured her. "We are here only for the social visit, *non ti preoccupare*. Here is Mr. Padgett."

Mrs. Santorini stared at Jasper in astonishment. "The son?" she asked, striving for English. "Mr. Junior? *Il figlio.*"

"Jasper Padgett," he said. "Nice to meet you." He bowed so elaborately that Mrs. Santorini giggled like a girl and covered her mouth of missing teeth.

Inge invited herself inside. "Observe, Jace. Write everything, Sylvie." But Jace excused himself to read his book on the porch. "*Il me fruste*," Inge muttered.

Frustrated, I wrote, and followed into the Santorinis' house, full of children.

"Filomena, Giovanni, Margherita," the signora introduced them with a hand on her heart. "Maria, Anna, Pietro." The two littlest ones played with no pants on, like Nipper, putting rocks in a bucket with a clatter.

Inge smiled and touched their curls with a tenderness that made me miss my brother. "Do your bambinos have a bath?" She mimed a scrub. "*Il bagno?*"

"*Sì, sì.*" The signora wrung her apron. Embarrassment hung in the air like the smell of grease and clung to me. I thought of hiding by the stove in the big barrel. It was full of dark red juice, pips and skins over it in a sieve, the pressings of grapes.

"Make note," Inge said, pointing.

Grapes, I wrote. *Wine.*

The Countess inspected corners, sniffed the air, darted a look at a chamber pot, the settlement of flies on the screen, a row of wine jugs on a shelf. "Make note."

I did so whenever she lifted her eyebrows to signal me. What did not warrant her notice were the flour-sack curtains in a rose pattern, the mason jar of daisies on the sill, the *bargello* embroidery on the table runner, the picture of the Virgin tacked on the wall. When I passed it, I crossed myself by habit. Hail Mary *pleine de grâce*, but I was not full of grace, only squirming and uneasy, as if a bucket of eels swam in my bloodstream. The children stared. At me writing, at Inge swiveling her benevolent blue gaze. How did these Santorinis see us? As invaders, I thought, judges who could hurt them.

Mrs. Santorini pinched her lips between two fingers. She appeared desperate to speak but afraid of the words in her mouth. "Please, *signora*. Already we pay rent. I have *ricevuta*. We pay."

"Don't worry," Inge repeated, her face alight with the calm of her station, the power of her kindness. "We're the Sociology Department. *Siamo amici.* Sylvie, the gifts!"

I took the cover off our basket to remove one of the small candy boxes. Inge presented it. The children crowded around as Mrs. Santorini opened the packet and gasped at the sweets in their colored foils.

"*Caramella!*" Mrs. Santorini fanned herself and placed her hand on her throat in a choke of gratitude. "Oh, *La Contessa*, thank you. *Mille grazie.*"

"Now, Signora," Inge said brightly, "be sure to bathe the bambinos three times a week, with plenty of soap. Here are the instructions. Sylvie? Please, *la brochure.*"

I thrust forward the pamphlet: "Hygienic Practices for the Family."

Mrs. Santorini waved it away. "Sorry, sorry. No English."

"Leave it anyway, Sylvie." Inge whispered, "Make a note: *traduisez tout.*"

Translate, I wrote, but knew that to interpret between the cabins and the manor was nearly impossible. How could you wash with soap if you had no soap?

Back in the carriage, the kind Countess waved the air and wrinkled her darling nose. "You should have seen it, Jasper!" she said. "*Déguelasse*, like the pigs' house. Maybe better tear it down. At least they must move the latrines more far away!"

"But the winter, Madame," I said quietly. "The snow is so deep. If the privy's far, you could freeze." Her words had flushed me with shame and a wish to defend them, the Santorinis, all of the cabin dwellers.

"You're correct," she said, reconsidering. "That is *exactement* why we need the sewer system. Everybody so crowded. Eight of them in that cabin! Nine? Those naked children. They don't even have a toy. And the liquor! Did you see? The bottles? These Santorinis are, what do you call? Bootlickers."

I tried not to laugh. Later I'd recognize the actual bootlickers: toadies who did the bloody work of the bosses. "It's boot*leggers*," I told Inge.

"Heaven forfend! Bootleggers!" Jasper cried from the backseat. "Demon rum! Bathe them all in champagne, I say."

"Jace, please," Inge said. "They're making wine out of anything—even weeds!"

"Let's turn around," Jace said. "Let's see if the *vino* is as good as the Bordeaux in the old man's cellar. I'm thirsty."

I stifled a smile, and he saw he had me as an audience. *Kindred spirits.*

"The main problem in every camp is the liquor," Inge said.

I wish I'd said: *The main problem is the danger. The pay and the prices. The crowding and the cold.* But I believed it wasn't my place. My place was in the cabins or the Cardboard Palace, unless I could find a better one.

Jasper rested his book and, as if he'd read my mind, said, "The main problem is the men are not paid beans."

They aren't! I cheered him silently.

"Of course they are paid!" Inge turned on him. "Who tells you this idea? They drink all the wages. Spend it on whiskey."

"And why shouldn't they?" he said. "What's so bad about that?"

"Because we dry the town. Those type of people—they drink all day. They get an injury. They don't work. Sociology is the answer! I said to your father, we need a clubhouse for the men. To only serve cider. We'll have the amusements. Billiards and card games, baseball. That's what they need."

"Let's ask Sylvie what they need," Jasper said.

"I just take notes," I said, dodging, still hoping the notes themselves would be a tool, to prove what was needed, a way to get it. "It's not for me to say."

But Jace Padgett could say whatever he wanted, and he did. All that afternoon in our bickering wagon, he held forth. I liked listening to him, his learned righteousness. "Men can't live off scrip and scrap and fourteen-hour shifts," he said. "But my father doesn't want to hear it."

"It is not true. I am right, Sylvie?" Inge pressed me. "They are paid, of course."

"Tin," Jasper said. "Scrip for the Company store. Am I right, Miss Pelletier?"

Pinned between them, I shrugged, my answer revealed by my hands tipped open, empty as my father's pockets. I smiled at Jace, then smiled at Inge, listening with the attention of a spy.

"Inge, if you would read the local news—" Jasper started.

"That paper, pah!" Inge said. "She hates the business. She hates the success."

"What she hates is that we don't pay the boys overtime. She hates that Bowles charges workers rent—to live in tents. In the dead of winter."

"Where else can they live?" Inge cried. "We build as fast as we get lumber." She fumed on the seat beside me, her effort to convert Jasper to the sociological cause melting in the noonday sun. "Anyway, *this* winter we'll have a skating exhibition. And the ski races. Just like our villages in Europe."

"We'll all have to learn to yodel." Jasper gave a comical yodeling call. Inge burst out laughing. Grady slapped his knee. The air felt lighter now, even as they argued.

"I want for you to appreciate the *sociology*," the Countess said. "If we make the comfortable village, the habitants don't strike. They work."

"Like slaves," Jasper said.

"Slaves, phh," she said. "That's the past."

Perhaps that past is where the bosses got their training, I did not say.

Jasper brandished his book. "Dr. Du Bois would say it's not quite past."

"You're a parrot to the Yankee *professeurs*," said Inge. "Your father despairs it. I need you to persuade him: The sociology is the future. He'll listen to you."

"Never has before," Jasper said.

All that morning, Inge and I toured the village while Jace stayed in the carriage, talking with John Grady in the shade. At times he read aloud from that book by Du Bois, while Grady tolerated him, nodding politely, *Ummhmm. Uh-huh. You don't say.* It was plain there was nothing Jace could say about *The Souls of Black Folk* that Grady didn't know. It was Jace (and I myself, later) who found revelation in those pages, and the inspiration that would set him on the road to folly.

In and out of the cabins, the Countess questioned the residents. *What do you need?* She listened, her face an agony of compassion, her hand on a shoulder, a forearm, the Samaritan's touch. The little ones sat on her elegant lap and played with her necklace and picked their noses. They kissed her cheek with smudgy lips. She combed their hair with her fingers.

"Do you go to school?" she asked. "You must go every day! Do you have any toys? What should I tell St. Nicholas is your heart's desire?"

Make note: For all little girls a baby doll, the boys to get toy trains.

She was Christmas in summer. Bisou ran about yapping while the anxious mothers watched, telling the children in Czech or Polish and Italian, *Behave. Be good.* Smacking them away from the fine lady. Inge tickled their skinny ribs. Perhaps their mothers wondered, like I did, why she didn't have any bambinos of her own.

The women poured out wishes from their frazzled hearts, told her what they lacked: shoes and milk, meat and medicine. I wrote it down. One cabin had no door, another a leaking roof. *Make note.* Whole families slept on mattresses that filled smoky rooms shared with flies and chickens, a goat wandering through. Cesspits. Dust. *Make note.* We saw tents with tin pipe chimneys, a baby sleeping in an apple crate, as Nipper had done. Inge interviewed a girl, my age, an infant strapped on her back, a toddler at her skirts, gaps where her teeth used to be.

"What do you need?"

"A good sleep!" The girl laughed so the black holes showed.

Six or eight kids followed our carriage as if we were a circus parade. "Hey, *Contessa*! *Dolci, dolci.*" "Please thank you." We doled out caramels.

"A lotta good that does," Jasper said. "Give 'em cash, not candy."

Again he caught me smiling under my hat.

"Oh, phooey to you, Jace," said Ingeborg. "The men talk already of a strike on the mill. The *Colonelle* will smash their heads like at Ruby. Do you want that?"

My stomach lurched. Strikes seemed a world apart from this wagon, these fancy people talking about head-smashing. Such violence was what my mother feared, the reason she would not talk of unions and did not welcome Lonahan the organizer.

"We try to keep the people happy," Inge said. "Why you are so gloomy?"

"Must be the mountain air," Jace said. "I prefer the damp fog of New England."

It was a fog: his sarcasm and argument, the sidelong glances he threw at me. I was riveted by their talk and disappointed when he found an excuse to quit us, "Ladies, I'm forced to go back to my studies."

"*Enfin*, then leave," said Inge, pouting.

Jace winked at me and jumped off the carriage. At the corner, instead of turning toward Elkhorne, he went the other way, toward the saloon. Grady watched him go, shook his head.

"He isn't happy, that boy," Inge said.

Why he was not happy in a *château* with all that orange juice was a mystery to me. I stayed quiet so she might explain.

"His father says he was always a nervous child," she mused. "Of course, he never had a mother."

"I saw her portrait," I said. "She was beautiful."

"Duke loves the beautiful women," Inge said, not without vanity. "But Jace, he is alone." In French she whispered, "He was raised by these people, just poor Negroes." She cut her eyes at John Grady driving, at his straight back, the reins loose in his hands, as if the Gradys were at fault for raising a motherless boy. "And then the second wife—!" Inge continued. "She sends the boy away to the Massachusetts academy, he is only eight years old. And now? Phh. At the university he learns many wrong ideas. He talks against his father, against even the grandfather, who was a general in the war, you know? He was wounded at Manassas." She had switched to English.

"I saw his portrait too. The Brigadier General, right?"

"Very famous, yes. He lost his leg, lost everything. All their lands, and property."

John Grady began to whistle without any tune.

"That is why my husband will build the monument to the Confederate. For honor to his father. My husband cannot forget, his own papa home from the war, his leg cut off, can anyone imagine?" Inge shuddered.

I thought of Pete Conboy, the surgeon's saw. Mr. Grady whistled loudly.

"But Jasper—he does not care. He's too shamed. He prefer to forget. For my husband, the son is a grief. He is . . . *difficile*, for me too. Three years I try for him to be my friend, but he is angry to me. He's a frustrate."

"A frustration," I said.

"Yes. A frustration." She leaned against me.

With trepidation, I patted her silken head. "I'm sorry, Inge."

She wiped her eyes and straightened up. "Never mind. It's nothing."

But it wasn't nothing. Jace was difficult and morbid and sarcastic. Also charming and bookish and witty. He had winked at me as if we shared some understanding.

Chapter Ten

RAIN SLUICED OVER THE GLASS roof and down the walls of the Greenery. We were fish in a bowl, the fronds of palm leaves and ferns a seaweed around us.

"Please write up all the notes from our field trip," Inge said, languid on her chaise. "We make a report about the conditions in the camp for recommendations. First: to close the saloons. Number two: to plan the sewers systems. Number three: what else?"

I paged through my notebook. "To translate?"

"Yes, translate." She waved the air to clear it and yawned. "But not now, please. A report is too tedious. We worked too much yesterday, *non*? Today something fun." She patted the chair next to her. "I'm so boring."

"Not boring," I said. "Bored. *Ennuyée*."

"Bored, I mean. Monsieur Padgett is at Denver. He wished me to come along, but—" She dropped her voice. "The ladies there do not care for me. They say the rumors about me. They're sheep. *Vaches et moutons*. They don't like the European way or how I swept him, my husband. They prefer to talk about church. About nothing. Just recipe. They don't care for the music, the dancing. Do you know, Sylvie?"

The only dancing I knew was the aunts and uncles stomping in their hard clogs to the sound of my father's fiddle in the barn, the cousins hopping, possibly primitive. "Not proper dancing," I said.

"You don't know how?" She jumped up with alarm. "But Sylvie! You must prepare for *le Grand Bal*. Three weeks is plenty of time. I will teach you."

"I don't think it's a good idea."

"Stand up." Facing me, she held up her left hand and curved the opposite arm at my waist. Delicate Countess fingers laced my thick knuckles. She drew me toward her in a clamp, ushering me forward and backward, humming, "*Un, deux, trois!* Step step step, around and step!" She broke away and danced by herself, laughing her bubbles of laughter. Bisou began to bark, so she picked him up and danced with him a minute, then returned to steer me, laughing and whisking around. I followed, looking at the loaves of my feet as she waltzed with the oaf of me.

"Look up! Don't be stiff!" She sang waltzing notes. "Ta-ta-ta-ta-TA! You are skating, you are flying on ice, *glissade*. You are so light as a feather, Sylvie!"

Then, as if dusted by fairies, my feet got the hang of it. We careened about, both of us humming, skating out into the vaulted hallway. "Waltz, Sylvie!"

I abandoned myself to the rush and glide on the polished floors. Uh-oh. There was Nugent, clacking along the parquet in her disapproving heels, eyebrows alarmed, as if we were debauched in an opium den and not infected by imaginary music.

"Dancing lessons!" Inge cried.

"Yes," said the housekeeper, ice in her voice.

"Join us, Mrs. Nugent!" Inge sang out.

The housekeeper reared her head. The sight of her pinchface convulsed us in fits of laughter. Behind her back, we sucked in our cheeks to make fish lips, only to see Nugent turn and glare. She had caught me. *Tant pis*, I did not care. Inge waltzed us backward into the Greenery in hysterics. We collapsed on the divan, holding our sides.

"Sylvie, *ange*, you dance like the circus elephant."

"I'm a clodhopper."

"Clod-hoppaire," she said, howling. "What is this, clod-hoppaire? Never mind. You only make yourself a feather in the arms of the man, and he twirls you like you're nothing."

"Well, perhaps I am nothing," I said, testing.

"Hmm. I don't think so. Here in the American mountains, you are—whoever you say, *non*? As I am the Countess, and Monsieur Jerry Padgett from Richmond, Virginia, is called Duke. What do you desire to be? You say it, *et voilà*, it's true."

What did I desire to be? The possibilities seemed limited. "You cannot just wish something and have it be the truth," I told Inge. "You can't just decide what to be—"

"Oh no?" Inge took a tendril of my hair between her fingers and played with it. "Six summers ago, I had a wish. And then I met Jerome Padgett, dancing the waltz. So you realize, Sylvie, that it's important for you, the Hunters' Ball. All the society will arrive with their money. A hundred guests. The gentlemen will ask you."

"I don't think so," I said, to fight against hope infecting me. I knew only one so-called gentleman, but Jace did not seem the dancing sort. Would he whirl me about if I made myself a feather in his arms?

"*C'est sure*, they will," Inge said. "Take the advantage, *les opportunités*."

Over several afternoons at my desk, I typed up the notes from our expedition, studying the Sociological Department report about the town of Ruby, written by Adele two summers before. At Inge's suggestion, I retained passages from the eminent Dr. Richard Corwin, father of the movement for Industrial Betterment. Certain fragments of his ideas I edited out, in small acts of subversion, like an inside agitator.

BUSINESS ADVANTAGE

The company's parental solicitude and the employees' filial subservience and loyalty will increase tranquility, and keep out union rabble and Socialist influences. Profits will increase. We

do not seek credit as philanthropists, but aim to
carry out business ideals, as a corporation with
a soul. The Golden Rule of brotherly love is the
foundation of Social Betterment in all Padgett
Company camps.

I typed in Inge's commentary from our field trip. Adele's report was my
template, and the prettified Padgett coal camp in the town of Ruby was the
model for Moonstone.

VICES: Vices, especially drunkenness, common
in most mining towns, could be reduced to the
minimum by an ordinance banning liquor and
careful surveillance exercised by the company.

SHOES: The Company must provide an exchange of children's boots, etc., at the Mercantile
to keep students appropriately shod.

I wrote on in this fashion, quoting Inge's ideas. I was half in love with
them, with her philosophy of kindness and candy boxes, the way I'd once been
in love with the goodness of Jesus washing the feet of his disciples, cleansing
lepers. Lady Bountiful Mrs. Padgett would build a theater. A hospital. She
would bring light and sparkling health, caviar and roses and toilets. She'd have
a library and a playground, a Moonstone Orchestra playing Mozart.

CHRISTMAS: The Company will provide an
annual Christmas party for the employees, with
roast turkey and a pudding. Every child under
the age of eight will receive a gift: baby dolls for
the girls, little train cars for the boys.

Moonstone was a dream city shining on the mountain, the way Inge described it, the way I wrote the philosophy of Industrial Betterment, even as
a voice whispered, *Don't be a dunderhead.* Caramels and Christmas turkeys
would not last long; clodhoppers like me would never learn to waltz. I ig-

nored that whisper, trusting that soon there would be skiers *schussing* down the snowy alpine meadows. Ambrosia and nectar. Rainbows.

Instead, there would be unrest and bloodshed and death.

"It's excellent, the report," Inge said on Monday morning, looking it over. "You have written me *exactement*. I made only a few notes. You must type-writer it. Colonel Bowles will come to dinner Friday, and I will give him the recommendations."

I shut myself in the Greenery and typed the ten pages of "The Padgett Company Sociology Department Report on Conditions in the Moonstone Camp, with Recommendations for the Betterment of the Populace." By Wednesday, I was finished. Thursday morning, Inge pronounced herself satis-fied. "Tomorrow I show the Colonel."

Friday, likely as revenge for my fish-lips face, Nugent assigned me to the kitchen "in uniform." She handed me the black dress and a mobcap, hideous and ruffled. "Colonel and Mrs. Bowles are coming to dinner with some Den-ver people. Look sharp."

Instead, in that hat, I looked like a toadstool.

All day Easter had me peeling and hulling, shucking and chopping, for two dozen guests. I soaped trays and spoons, the slicks of gravy and glazes, the white dollops of *pommes de terres à la Normande*. My arm was sore from churning butter. Easter molded it into pats shaped like flowers. I brought these morsels to the icehouse and sat stealing time in the cool shade with the river running below.

"Where'd you get to?" Easter said when I returned. "Just when I need a girl to watch the oven, you dawdle out." She was cranky and hot in the steam off the stove pots, wiping sweat on her apron. "Twenty-five guests to dinner, and you go missing?"

"Sorry, Easter." She never stayed mad long, but that day she was irked. When John Grady came in the kitchen for a glass of water, she handed it to him without a word.

"Mrs. Grady," he said, "breaks my heart when you scowl like that."

"Then I'm a sorry woman," she said. After he'd gone, she drained a pot of scalded onions for me to slip free of their skins—a good trick she taught me. "Truth is, I don't deserve that man. If you get one half as good, you'll find yourself under a lucky star."

"How'd you get him?"

"Way back," she said. "When we was small, we played in the yard. But Grady's people run off Belle Glade the minute the war came. His daddy signed up for a Yankee soldier, but the Rebs shot him and gave Ma Grady and the children no choice but to came on back." The memory riled her. "Ma Grady never got over it, but for me, the luck of it was John Grady set his eyes on me, and they're on me to this day." She softened, thinking of it. "There's a wheel turning in my heart for that man still."

That the human heart had wheels was news to me. Ever since she said it, I have felt the wheels of my own, turning, turning.

When the guests were seated, the Croatian sisters carried supper into the dining room. Mr. Nugent stood at attention in his butler clothes, ready to fill three different kinds of glasses with claret or champagne or ice water from the Diamond River. When the swinging door flapped open, we heard the clank of silver on china, fragments of the guests' loud talking.

"Typhoid!"

"Oh, not at the table, please."

"We had that mule by the ears."

"Oh, stop, Jerome, *mon amour*." That was Inge, laughing.

For dessert we decorated individual *tartes au citron* with sprigs of mint. I snipped the leaves while Easter planted them like delicate flags, placed frosted rosettes no bigger than forget-me-nots on her handmade chocolates. She was an artist of sugar and pastry, intent on her creations. Just as dessert was ready, the kitchen door swung open, and there was Jace Padgett in his dinner jacket, blowing steam. He loosened his tie with sideways pulls.

"You leave that," Easter said, wrangling trays. "Go on back and sit."

"I can't tolerate it! All these people rattling on about copper futures and stock portfolios. If I mention just one word about the incident last week in Richmond," Jasper fumed, "they change the subject to the markets—"

"You try one of my lemon tarts." Easter cut him off as if distracting a child.

Jace plucked one from a tray and leaned over the counter where I snipped leaves. "Hello again, Sylvie. Sylvester." His grin like a challenge. "Sylvester. Your new nickname."

"Yours is Jester, then," I said.

"Jester! I like that." He laughed. "But listen, you heard what happened—"

"Not now." Easter rapped the counter with her spoon.

Jace sighed and regarded me with a lopsided smile. "You can do without that cap," he said, and plucked it off my head. "The better to display your crowning glory."

"Hey!" I grabbed it back.

"Stop that now, hear?" Easter said. "Go on in to your company."

"I'd rather poke myself in the eye with a meat skewer," Jasper said, but returned to the party, casting plaintive looks over his shoulder as if I might throw him a rescue line. I wished I had one.

"Some people never satisfied," Easter said, disgusted. I wanted to ask, *What incident in Richmond?* But it was plain she didn't want to talk about it.

After dessert, Jace returned to the kitchen and parked himself at the table. He watched me scrape plates into the slop bucket for the pigs. "Glad that's over," he said. "What a bore."

Easter sat down next to him, took her shoes off, and blotted her forehead with her apron. "What all has you so aggravated?"

"First, the incident no one will discuss," Jace said. "Second, those people get on my last nerve. Dull as dishwater."

"What you know about dishwater?" Easter rubbed her small delicate feet.

"Are you all right?" Jasper asked her. "You tired, Ma?"

"Don't call me that. What's griping you?"

"They keep on asking me about my *plans*," he said. "What about my *prospects*?"

"I got some prospects for you." Easter rose from her seat and went to the pantry, returning with a sack of walnuts. "Tomorrow I'm making my prize walnut pie." She set the sack on the table and handed Jasper a nutcracker. "So, get on with this."

"I will, if Sylvester pitches in."

"You call her by her right name," Easter said.

"I don't mind," I said, "I like it."

Later, the name Sylvester would serve me as an alias.

"Whatever your name is," Easter said, "come on over here to lend a hand to this grown man whining."

"Get comfortable, Sylvie-ster," Jace said, and held a chair. "A lotta nuts here. And not just in this bowl either." Wine roses bloomed in his pale complexion.

I sat, wary of his attention but also preening in it. He'd ignored the serving girls, who left to smoke cigarettes behind the Cardboard Palace with their roustabout suitors.

"Leave the bowl on the counter," Easter said. "And Master Jace, you leave the bottle!" She headed out the kitchen door.

"Leave the bottle empty, is what she means." Jasper went to the sideboard and poured two glasses, handed me one.

"No, thank you." I cracked a walnut.

"A good girl, are you?" He sighed as if I were a disappointment, and cracked walnuts, while goodness like a hard shell around me cracked under his warm glances. I returned his smiles and picked out nutmeats, like wrinkled brown butterflies, and resolved to be less disappointing.

"Hell's bells," he said. "How'd you do that? Get that one out whole."

"By not breaking it."

Jasper laughed.

"What was the incident in Richmond?" I asked.

His face fell. "Two weeks ago back home—a mob hanged a man off a tree just outside town. A blacksmith named Orion Peterson—was a friend of Caleb Grady. White lady said something about him—" Jace was agitated, his face red. "See, when I was a kid, my old man took me and the Grady boys—to see a man lynched. 'For a lesson,' Dad said. A whole crowd watched."

I listened hard, a hand over my mouth.

"Some neighbor men hanged Peterson right near Belle Glade, and the Grady family—it's dangerous now. It could happen to them just for no reason, it's—" He broke open a shell and then another, the sounds cracking the air. "I'm sorry to dwell on such a gruesome topic. But thank you for listening." He drank more as if to wash the subject down his throat. "We'll attempt to speak of pleasant things. Of pie and walnuts." He chewed one, musing. "Did y'ever notice how walnuts taste like metal? Like sucking on a penny? Tastes of copper. See if I'm right." He fished pennies from his pocket and cleaned them with a handkerchief. He handed me one and put one in his mouth, where he rolled it around like a lozenge. "Try the copper. Tastes like walnut. Go ahead." Like a dare, the way he said it. He was a strange bird.

"But money is not . . . sanitary." I held his gaze.

"Ha! Tell that to the gents in the smoking parlor." He waited till I placed the penny in my mouth as if it might poison me. Maybe it did. Perhaps it gave me a taste for bigger sums.

"It has a walnut flavor, you're right." I removed it fast and dried it on my apron.

Across the table, he savored his own penny like a sweet. It clacked against his teeth. "Copper now, to me, tastes like the future."

"The future has a taste?" I asked. He was possibly deranged, not just drunk.

"Copper futures is all they talk about in there. My daddy and his pals." He removed the penny from behind his teeth. "Copper, copper, blah, blah. Some fool's trying to corner the market. Somebody else trying to run up the price. Another fella's short-selling. All that garble."

"I don't have a head for finance," I told him, *I just like money.*

"Me neither. See? We hate the same things." He removed his glasses and smiled at me in such a way that I wished to hate everything he hated and love what he loved. His boredom and anger like my own. His face as flushed as mine. We cracked nutshells and the air crackled with heated looks, awkward smiles flaring.

I held up two unbroken halves for inspection.

"Geez," Jasper said, "another perfect nut. Like my stepmother, eh?"

"She's not a nut! I like her."

"The Sociological Department? Please. A joke."

"But it's a real philosophy."

"Just tonight she handed the Colonel her so-called report and forced it on us as a topic for conversation. He does not enjoy having a lady tell him how to run a company."

"Her ideas will help."

"But they won't. Because her sociology is a fantasy. My father plays along. To give her a toy. Keeps her busy. He'll never do those improvements they promise. He tried it at Ruby, and the men went on strike anyway. Billy clubs do the work, candy doesn't."

"You're very negative," I said. "Also, I wrote that report."

"You did?" He smacked his head with the heel of his hand. "Excuse me. Pay no attention to my rantings whatsoever. I'm a rude unhinged son of a gun."

He was. He was provocative and disheveled and strange, eating pennies. I liked him for all these reasons. He seemed to like me too, grinning. "I apologize."

"Apology accepted," I said, and liked him more.

"You wrote it, then? Quite an accomplishment," he said. "The Colonel praised it, and I can tell you he is not easily impressed. Congratulations."

The compliments worked on me as compliments do. He opened another bottle and poured, his eyes narrowed in a challenge. "Sure you don't care for a swig?"

The Devil whispered, *What harm in a swig?* "All right," I said.

"Atta girl." Jace watched me drink with approval, as a teacher watches a fast learner. When we'd finished with the walnuts and dusted our hands, I found myself in a pleasant state of intoxication, weaving a little as I hung my apron by the back door.

"Let's go out!" he said. "To the river."

"It's dark, though."

"That happens at night," he said. "Let's go!" He gestured for me to come along, scooping the air with his whole arm. He knew I'd follow, that I wanted to.

How could I resist his grins and attention, his charms and offers of— what? I pressed down warnings and hopes, so my lungs were tight, and learned then why desire is called a crush. To be crushed. I would die of it.

"C'mon, now, Sylvie girl, step on it."

It was a risk. *Alone with a man.* I dismissed caution and listened to my demon friend, who said, *Allez-y.*

Outside, the moon was a round eye above the sloping August lawn, watching us. The mountains themselves watched, silent and silver all around. Jasper strode toward the trees with the bottle and pulled aside low branches to make a path. We could hear the river talking to itself on its way to the sea, singing and rambling over the rocks. We bent and ducked under pine boughs till there it was, streaming in the moonlight, the Diamond River. Jasper took his shoes off, rolled his trousers above thin shanks. I undid my shoes and stockings, trembling, but not from the cold.

"Be careful, darlin', the rocks are slippery."

The word *darlin'* flashed like a firefly in the dark. Jasper took my hand, and we waded in, our bare feet in the riverbed. *Mother of God.* The water was melted ice off a glacier, cold to the marrow.

"You're shivering." He handed me the bottle. The liquor burned down, scalded beneath the ribs, woke secrets where the immortal soul resides in its bony cage. Revealed what I wanted. Surely he saw it. I drank more, giddy and laughing.

"Thatta girl," Jasper urged me on. "Drink up and drink down deep at every opportunity. That's my philosophy."

Everyone had a philosophy, it seemed. I needed one.

We traded the bottle back and forth, our feet numb. "Drink!" Jasper encouraged me like a teacher.

"Your turn."

"No, no, *your* turn," he said. It was hilarious, our elaborate drinking. I was never so happy, barefoot in the river, the two of us conspirators, cackling at ourselves.

"Ready?" he said. "On the count of three."

"Three and then what?"

"Sink down. Swim."

"Sink or swim," I said. Perhaps that would be my philosophy. I repeated it for courage. "Sink or swim." Devil may care, but in the moment, I didn't.

"One. Two. Three!" He fell backward into the water and I fell too, anointed beside him in an ice bath, spluttering upright till his hand flew out, pressing me down in the frigid water, an arm across my shoulders.

"Stay!" he commanded. "See the stars." The dome of the sky was brimming with sparks. We lay freezing in the riverbed till, with a thump, Jasper kicked up a spray of water and the drops showered down on us, lit by moonlight. Screeching, we leapt up and shook ourselves like dogs, both of us drunken and laughing. He howled at the sky and I splashed him in the stream, throwing water and caution to the wind.

"Damn," he said. "I thought you were such a good girl. A goody-good quiet girl. The angel. Saintly Sylvie."

"Don't count on it." I kicked water, danced away.

He went after me, splashing. It was a full-on water war, a play fight that was an actual fight, me in strange combat. To win him. He ducked me under.

"I'll fix you!" I cried, throwing big handfuls of river like joy in the moonlight. He splashed and dodged, and then we quit and jumped to the bank. We stood there dripping and winded, happy as spring ponies in a field.

"Pelletier," he said. "You're a wild demon."

I felt the weight of his judgment, appraising me as a demon when I'd aspired to be a butterfly. I wrung the soaked skirt pasted on my legs, and crossed my arms over my chest, shivering.

"Oh, no, you're cold," Jace said. "Go like this." He jumped and jackknifed his arms. We leapt around on the gravel, slapping ourselves for warmth, and traded the bottle till it was drained. He took his dry jacket off the branch where he'd hung it and wrapped it around my shoulders. "You're still cold. Poor Sylvie."

"I am not poor." *I have twenty dollars.*

"Sorry. I didn't mean—" It was not pity but kindness he was offering, with the warm jacket he drew across my shoulders. The silence filled with the sound of the pulling river. Cicadas in the trees. My limbs trembled on alert, and there was Jasper looming, his breath raw. "Sylvie?" He brushed my cheek with his whiskey lips.

I stumbled, light-headed, so he caught and held me up in the wrapper of his coat, braced together, listening to the water as it pulled over the rocks. When I swallowed, I meant to speak, but he stopped me, kissed me with eyes open, his face silvery.

I did not know about boys. Men. Only the rules to be a daughter of God, that to kiss him was to choose danger. Possible damnation. And I chose. He was doubled in my vision. Two Jaspers. Two rivers. Two moons. What to do about the weakness and liquor in my blood. Was it the fear, or the thrill, or something worse that caused this—overpowering. The crush of it. *So this is it.* Love swallowed by mistake or circumstance. Romance and the moon conspired to make a summer fool of me.

"*J'espère qu'on va pas se perdre,*" I whispered, close to tears.

"What?" he asked.

"I don't want to get lost."

"No, no, no, sweet, you won't. If you get lost, I'll find you."

And I was so happy to be found, to stand by the river with Jace entwined as if we slept standing up, peaceful and soaking wet. I could feel his heartbeat along the side of his throat where my cheek rested.

"I never did kiss anyone before," he said, as if it were a miracle.

A great wild eagle of feeling spread its feathers in my chest. "Not me either," I said, and held his face in my two hands, kissing him wanton and brazen and fallen, all the words for wrong, and did not care about the Devil, only the wild raptor ahold of me. In the swoon I braced for the wrath of the Lord, the bird to fall, shot from the sky.

"Sylvie." He said my name with amazement. Both of us so surprised at our hands smoothing along cheeks, along shoulders, the gooseflesh of our young and green trembling.

"It's so cold," I said, in a fluster. "It's late."

"No. All right. Yes." He found his glasses in the pocket of his jacket. "Here," he said, and put them crooked on my nose.

"No, like this." I hung them off his ears, under his chin.

"No, like this." He arranged them on the back of his head and groped backward, as if he had hindsight. He squinted and clowned. We were howling with laughter again. I'd never laughed so much.

"Ready? Set? Race you back." He gave me a head start.

I leapt and ran in his beautiful coat through the silvery leaves, while he whooped and chased after me. "Sylvester!" I was a fast runner with strong legs and came out of the trees to the lawn ahead of him, safe, but then he broke into the open, streaking past like a racehorse in the moonlight. He stopped at the top of the hill and watched me catch up, breathless and giddy. He put his arm around my neck, his finger across my lips, looking toward the house. "Shhh."

Hidden in the shadows, we watched. A woman came out onto the porch. Inge. She stood for a moment in the moonlight between the marble columns. A man came to join her. Jasper's father. He put his arms around her shoulders and she circled hers around his waist. They looked up at the glittering sky.

A carriage pulled in front, the horses waiting. The Colonel and Mrs. Bowles came outside, saying their good-nights. The women embraced, the men shook hands. Their voices carried over the lawn in the stillness.

"Your report is most excellent, Inge, my dear," the Colonel said. "You can be sure I'll act on it immediately."

Hearing that, *excellent*, a leech of pride attached to me.

"Oh, you are too kind," said Inge. "*Merci bien*, Colonel."

"No, thank *you*," he said. "*Merci*."

We waited in the shadows. The guests' carriage passed us by, wheels on the gravel. The Duke and the Countess gazed up at the stars. "Where's that boy Jace got to?" his father said. The lit end of his cigar glowed in the dark, the foul smell in the breeze. "I worry about him."

Jasper whispered, his breath electric in my ear. "Go around the back way. Don't let them see you." I slipped his jacket off my shoulders and he took it. "Now you're cold again. Poor Sylvie—you're trembling." He squinted and sagged against me, kissed my cheek. "Good night, angel." He went backward up the hill in a crooked line, a finger to his lips. "Shhhh," he said. "Quiet."

I watched till he turned and strolled up to the porch, where he came into the light next to his father.

Chapter Eleven

THE NEXT MORNING, INGE SENT me to mail her correspondence at the proud new Moonstone branch of the U.S. Post Office. Walking down the drive in the dappled sunlight, I feared to meet anyone in town. An encounter with ordinary mortals would break the spell of myself transformed, kissed, enchanted in a rainbow bubble. A secret was hidden in a new layer under my skin. I was hungover and rearranged, as if I'd been hit on the skull with a mallet and enjoyed the swooning stars. I especially did not want to run into K. T. Redmond, but there she was, sniffing the breeze.

"Sylvie Pelletier!" she cried. "Are you back in town? I could use a hand."

"Not until the end of September, but then—"

"Too bad, because that Havilland girl working for me now is a Giddy Gertie."

Certainly K.T. had talked about me behind my back, but now I nursed a mean-hearted pleasure to think of Millie Havilland suffering in her hairbows under the sharp tongue of Redmond.

"What's the news from the castle? Have they got you fanning them with palm leaves? Feeding 'em grapes?"

"I only take notes."

"Save them! Every scrap! Find the ledgers! Keep a diary!"

"I am only a *secretary*. A social secretary."

"So I see." She perused my clothes with a jaundiced eye. "What's the news? What's on the social calendar at the manse? Human sacrifice? A bacchanal?"

"King Leopold," I blurted in surrender.

"King *Leopold*?" Her eyes went wide. "Of Belgium? That one?"

I made excuses, but she wormed information out of me: the royal itinerary, the guest list. The more thrilled she was, the more I said, leaking like a bad pair of boots.

"The Elkhorne hunting party *week*? An entire week? Pity the poor wild creatures. It'll be a slaughter. Leopold is called the Executioner for a reason."

"It's not *only* hunting," I said. "There's a quarry tour, picnics, dinners. Lectures. The Hunters' Ball is held on the last Saturday."

"Oh, la-de-da. The Bloodbath Ball. And I'm invited?"

A sinking doom took hold of me. Susie Society would show up and ruin everything. The music and the dancing. The gossamer green dress. The spell. She hopped up and down on the boards of the sidewalk like a mad Rumpelstiltskin.

"King Leopold! Of all bloody tyrants," she marveled. "Did I tell you that the office is now hooked up to the telephone? A party line all around town. I intend to use it for the purpose of fact-finding." She hurried away on a mission.

My new *amour* Jace Padgett sat unsettling me in the kitchen, reading the *Moonstone City Record* with his toast. Since our grappling at the river, he had lingered at breakfast. After dinner. A zone of tension around him kept me taut and clumsy and distracted. "Hiya, Sylvie," he said, and I jumped. The river expedition was there between us. The baptism and whispers. The kiss. While he sat reading, the air vibrated without noise. His eyes were heavy on my back. Once, when no one saw, he caressed my hair. A voltage of current hooked between us, soft glances, sodden looks. At the sight of me, he smiled. Easter fixed us with stares as if to ask: *What are you up to?* We pretended not to notice that she noticed.

Hiya, Sylvester.

It was his name for me, so I liked it, liked our talk of books—*Did you read the Wharton? What'd you think?*—and liked him, the pale curls at the back of his neck, the flat broad fingernails drumming on the table. His luxurious yawn. I watched, waited for the minute he would say, *Steal out with me behind the icehouse*, and we would steal. For five nights we went out in the dark, kissing and drinking with a drunkenness that felt like love and sin, craving and danger. Which was it? All these but sin.

A girl of no means has to be doubly careful with a rich man, not to become a broken toy, as such people have so many. They don't repair what they break, or mend their shoes. They want a new pair and discard the old. But I did not know that then.

At breakfast one morning, I was bleary-eyed and distracted. Easter navigated around the kitchen in a routine to get breakfast served, but I got in the way, spilled things, and dropped a handful of spoons with a clatter.

Jace startled in his chair. "Jesus, Sylvester."

"Sorry."

We smiled. He turned a page, then drew the newspaper close and became immediately furious at something he found there. "Appalling," he said.

"What now?" Easter asked him.

"If you didn't want to talk about what happened in Richmond, Easter, you won't want to know about this." He threw the newspaper in the trash. "Tell them I'm going up to the lodge for a few days before I blow a gasket." He grabbed his hat. Next to me at the sink, he whispered, "I'll see you when I'm back."

But Jace did not come back for two weeks. Later he explained: He'd gone to the woods to clear his mind, to stop himself from saying something rash to his father. When next I saw him, he'd failed at both.

Easter fished the newspaper out of the bin and thrust it at me. "What was it set him off? What's he talking about, 'appalling'? See if you can figure."

I scanned the various items, reading snippets aloud to Easter. The Moonstone Slammers beat the Glenwood Grizzlies 5 to 4. The price of marble holding steady. Grouse plentiful for hunting. Susie Society Reports . . .

Uh-oh.

"What is it?" said Easter. "Read it out, Miss Sylvie. I worry about that boy."

I saw the reason he was angry. And knew that it was caused by my leaking sieve of a mouth. I swallowed and read aloud to Easter:

> SUSIE has learned: Our own Duke Padgett will soon play host to Royalty. His guest in September will be the Barbarian King, Leopold II of Belgium, which is called a country but is actually a dogpatch not half the size of our own grand state of Colorado.

"Dogpatch." Easter laughed.

John Grady came in then, blotting sweat off his head. "What's the news now?"

"She's just reading us about the King," Easter said. "Our son Caleb's cooking for him on the train," she added, in case I had forgotten.

Mr. Grady exchanged some coded look with his wife. "Go on," he said, so I read out the rest of K.T.'s hilarious—then chilling—description of the King of Belgium.

> Surely Leo is coming here to sniff out opportunities to enrich his larded coffers, and he is well equipped for it: The Monarch is said to have a nose as long as the trunk of one of the elephants he hunts in the deeps of Africa. Susie Snoop wonders what profit His Majesty sniffs in our rich rocks. Will our local Duke scent opportunity of his own in the King's deep pockets?
> Citizens beware! Our visiting Monarch is a man of infamous cruelties. According to the

> *New York American*, the King has enslaved
> countless Africans in the Congo and murdered
> countless thousands in his quest for rubber and
> copper. In his bloodlust for a colony of his own,
> he has used all the variety of torture familiar to
> American slavers of our shameful past.

Here I stopped. A disturbance had come over the clenched faces of Mr. and Mrs. Grady. But they urged me on, so I kept reading in a horrified stammer:

> Leopold's men have chopped off the hands of
> Congolese children . . .

"I can't read this," I said, faltering.

"Read," Mr. Grady told me.

> . . . whipped women and shot citizens just for
> sport, as in a hunting party. A sample of his
> legendary barbarity can be found in the testimony
> of one unlucky Congolese captive, Mr. Lilongo,
> who recounted to the U.S. Congress the many
> tortures by Leopold's men.

John Grady pinched his lips to a grim line of anger. "Go on. Read the rest."

"It's too—gruesome. I can't."

"Read to the end, please, Miss Pelletier," said Grady in a fierce new voice. "What else did Mr. Lilongo say?"

But I couldn't say the next bit aloud, and spared them the details of how the men were tied to trees and hung alive, beaten by Leopold's sentries. "Only Mr. Lilongo lived to testify before Congress," I said.

The kitchen filled with brittle silence. I could not look Mr. or Mrs. Grady in the eyes. They didn't speak, but their shocked faces said what was plain. The house would be host to a monster.

"Hmmp," Easter managed. "You put that back in the trash."

"Where it belongs." Mr. Grady went outside, shaking his head in stunned fury.

I buried the newspaper under the coffee grounds. Easter trimmed the fat off a rib roast and frenched the bones. I minced parsley to specks. We worked in the silence of our thoughts till the weight of them became too unnatural. There was nothing I could think to say that might offer solace against the words I'd read.

In an effort to change the subject, I ventured to ask: "Mrs. Grady, when do you and the Padgetts return to Richmond?" The question was designed to discover Jasper's plan, not hers. "Will you go back with them in September?"

Easter startled. Perhaps she was thinking of *the incident at Richmond*, for her face took on the frozen smiling expression she employed with Mrs. Nugent, her voice bright as ice in the winter sun. "Why, yes. This year we're going on the train, ain't that somethin'? Master J.C. says they don't have but a mile of track to lay down before it's a railroad straight from here to Ruby and back to Virginia. Padgetts have a train car like a beautiful little old house, with a dining room, sleeping beds, and my son Caleb cooking in a galley kitchen. It's their own private car. They call it the *Sunrise*."

And it was the *Sunrise* that carried the Barbarian King to us that autumn in the Gilded Mountains.

Chapter Twelve

His Majesty Léopold Louis Philippe Marie Victor, of the House of Saxe-Coburg and Gotha of Belgium, arrived in our hamlet of Moonstone with his beard and his medals and his elephantine proboscis. He came up from Denver on a golden afternoon, ensconced in the velvet of the *Sunrise*, hitched to the main locomotive of the newly finished Diamond River Railroad, delivered to Elkhorne's private rail spur below the brand-new town depot. A carriage greeted the royal guests, Grady at the reins in full livery. In the long violet shadows off the peaks, His Majesty came through the gates, past the lions, and up the drive to Elkhorne.

The household—porters and chambermaids, cook and butler, head housekeeper and gardener, kitchen assistants, and me—assembled in the hall to welcome him. I did not see Jasper. When I craned my neck, it was not only to ogle the King but also to search for Jasper's pale head, a gleam off his glasses, any sign of him.

The gravel crackled under the wheels of the carriage. Mr. Nugent opened the great heavy doors. Sunlight came shafting in through these portals and then the shadow of the King and then the King himself. His boots were black leather stems for the long stalking height of him. His chest was adorned by the foliage of a beard worthy of a mountain man in its length. Unlike our wild Western samples, the King's beard was squared, a shovel snipped straight across. It lapped over a uniform full of gold and silver stars and medallions and *palmes d'or*, ribbons in purple and scarlet. A sword strapped on his hip banged against his shins as he walked into the Great Hall. That he was a monster was not apparent in his thin smile or his imperial air. The bones of my wrists ached at the knowledge of his hideous hacking crimes, but we staff bowed low, as Nugent had instructed us, and kept our heads down until he passed by. Then we were free to stare at him sidelong as he went up to his quarters in the Elkhorne Suite, to rest before the hunt.

The manor was alive with arrivals, guests and luggage noisy in the entryway, greetings and the barking of hounds in the air. Carriages left the stables for the depot and returned filled with Statlers, Adcocks, Astors, and Vanderhoevens. Wagons arrived with sides of beef, barrels of apples, fish on ice, jugs of cream, berries packed in straw. Extra servants. The Cardboard Palace bunks filled with girls in starched white aprons over dark uniforms. It was my assignment to show them the backstairs. I ushered groups around the kitchen, wine cellar, icehouse, and laundry. Mrs. Nugent hovered with her lists, her schedules. Inge did not summon me. Her plan was for me to be part of the general staff until the last minute of the last night, when I was to follow specific directions. To wait for the appointed time. To dress. To descend. To make my entrance.

Nugent was not pleased to read Inge's note explaining: *Sylvie will be our guest.* "You've certainly insinuated yourself," she said.

At dawn, Mr. Grady drove the royal party into the hills, to the gamekeeper's lodge, for the hunt. The Padgetts went riding alongside, Inge *sportif* in a little bowler hat and leather gloves, a bamboo riding crop. I spied from the backstairs window and wondered if they would meet Jace there, on Prettyman's Ridge. The noise of his absence kept me awake in the night, forlorn in the daylight. That he would kiss me in the dark and then disappear was a slight I added to a pile of suspicion: that he thought nothing of me. Alternately, I feared he was killed, or lying fractured in a ravine, delirious with pain, calling for help. More likely he'd gone to Ruby to the cathouse, drunk in a saloon somewhere. That was Easter's theory: "Drinking himself stupid, no doubt."

News reached us at the manor that the royal hunting party had killed six elk and a bobcat. Leopold had brought down a bighorn sheep off a ledge. It took four men to retrieve and haul its three hundred pounds across the scree— thirty pounds for the horns alone—to the lodge, where the King posed for photographs, his foot on the head of the animal, its tongue lolling.

The *Record* reported the excitement, informed by roustabouts and porters, interviewed by K. T. Redmond. She was inspired to include editorial remarks.

> Perhaps Leopold perfected his hunter's aim
> in the jungles of the Congo, where his Belgian
> mercenaries have shot many citizens, including
> women and children, from river steamers, pick-
> ing them off where they stood on the shores.
> What his aim is, here in our own peaceful hamlet,
> Susie Society will do her utmost to discover.

Mrs. Nugent directed me to destroy the paper, so the guests wouldn't see it. But upstairs at the Cardboard Palace, the servant girls got hold of it and passed the story around. "The King is come here to shooting little children," said Albina, wide-eyed.

"It's only lies!" one of the guest maids scolded. "He has never even visited Africa. His Majesty is after only the big games. He's *un chasseur*, the hunter."

This was Annelise. She was the attendant to the King's companion, the Baroness Caroline LaCroix. With her imperial posture and *froideur*, Annelise now reigned over the maids in the Cardboard Palace. She'd rigged a cordon around her corner of the dormitory and curtained off her lower bunk, her baggage stowed on the top one so no other girl could sleep above her. Every one of the *filles de chambres* dragged their pillows around late at night to hear her talk.

Annelise held us rapt with stories about how her mistress, Caroline, had met King Leopold in Paris. "At only age sixteen, she was brought to the hotel at Les Places des Pyramides, where the King found she was his heart's desire. He bought her jewels and many clothes from Callot Soeurs and carried her to

Austria. He built palaces for her at Cap Ferrât and Laeken. My mistress's allowance is *un million de francs* every year. He calls her *Très Belle*," Annelise said, "and she calls him *Très Vieux*."

"Tray what?" one of the visiting girls, Biddy, asked.

"It means Very Old," I told her.

"She's sixteen and she's his *wife*?" asked the giggling one.

"Not his wife!" Annelise laughed. "The Queen is old like the King. My Lady Caroline travels everywhere with His Majesty—however, she dislikes to hunt. For her, only the fine luxury. But His Majesty adores wild country, the virgin country, all the kinds of hunting." Annelise flapped her lashes as if to announce a double meaning.

A queasiness rose in my throat. I did not sleep well during these nights, for pondering such strange people and their foreign ways. Troubling me was the plan, Inge's instructions. And Jasper. His name like a whisper or a gasp. He was nowhere in the mix of the guests, not a word of him from the hunting party.

The hunt lasted three days. Inge returned after only one, because the men had business to parlay without the women. At the lodge, the gentlemen smoked on the porch and argued politics and dipped naked in the river. In the kitchen, Easter talked rapturously of her son Caleb. He'd gone to the hunting camp and constructed a roasting pit, lined with rock. "All day he turns the spits," she said. "Roasts the whole animal." From the windows of the Cardboard Palace, we could see the smoke rising out of the far trees, smell the meat in the wind. "You'll meet our Cal any day," she told me, so thrilled that you'd think her son Caleb was the King, not the barbarian monarch from across the sea.

The ladies stayed at the manor, strolling the gardens or reading their novels. One painted watercolors. Another took photographs with a box camera. Mrs. Adcock and Miss Crandall wrote letters for me to take to the post office. The women spent a morning in Ruby, admiring the chalet-style cabins, the Industrial Betterment design of the town. Inge brought them all on a wagon tour of Moonstone, pointing out its progress and potential. They played cards in the evening and listened to musical recitals, a string quartet, an opera singer screeching at the piano. In the kitchen we mimicked her.

"She's got a bellyache," Easter said. "Get her some bicarbonate."

Another night the guests were entertained by Lew Dockstader's famous troupe of minstrels. These were three ridiculous white men with bootblack on their faces and outlandish mouths painted in white zinc oxide, shuffling through the kitchen with banjos and a gutbucket on the way to perform in the ballroom. Dockstader wore enormous shoes like boats on his feet, a giant polka-dot bow tie with his saggy patched trousers.

I laughed at their clownish appearance but was chastened when I saw how Easter stared at them with bald contempt. One of the troupe mocked her, bugging his eyes. She confronted him with poison in her glare, and lit the stove burner so the gas fire flared, as if giving him a piece of her mind. My own mind expanded, seeing Easter's opinions expressed without words, flame on a cast-iron pan, as if she would sear the man. Soon the minstrels' banjo music seeped under the kitchen door accompanied by howls of cruel laughter from the guests, as fat white Mr. Dockstader sang "Everybody Works but Father," cakewalking in his top hat. Easter slammed a skillet and sent an eruption of cream sauce toward the ceiling, where it stuck.

John Grady put a hand on her shoulder. "Only a week to go, Mrs. Grady," he said.

One week left of summer. It hit me with a pang. The house would close and they would all go back to Richmond. Or would they?

"I'm ready right now," Easter said, livid. "Take me out of here."

"Me too," Grady said, and retreated outside.

The sauce remained on the ceiling. For all I know, it is still there.

In the early dark of Wednesday morning, I came in the back door to the pantry and heard low talking in the kitchen. It was the Gradys with a man whose voice I didn't recognize. I stood inside the pantry and listened.

"Mother's ready to go today, Caleb," John Grady said. "Right now."

"Can't leave till Sunday, Dad," the stranger said. "Gotta get paid."

This was their son, the famous Caleb Grady. I stayed quiet so as not to disturb the family reunion. Also I was a veteran eavesdropper, having practiced on my parents.

"I don't know now," Easter said. "Leave the rest of the family at Belle Glade? Why don't we go on back home, say goodbye to brother and Uncle Fred and them. Leave next year, maybe."

"Ma, we can't go back to Belle Glade," Caleb said. "You think a mob won't string up any man—me or Marcus or Dad—swung from a branch same as hanging up a hat? Couple weeks ago they cut Peterson down off the live oaks by our creek. They do like that on no excuse to any black man all over the South. Woman too. Like a virus. We can leave that place now for good. We'll get set up at Dearfield. A new start. The cousins can come out west next year. Plenty of good cropland for everybody."

"All right, Cal," Easter said. "I sure can picture it the way you talk. That luncheonette. I'm gonna call it the Sunshine Café."

"What about you, Dad?" Caleb asked. "You gonna grow peaches?"

"Son, you know I'm just hoping to live like a man," John Grady said. "Go to sleep at night and not be afraid to be killed in our own beds. Live to ourselves, work for ourselves, in peace. And yessir, I'm thinking peaches *and* strawberries both."

Caleb started to say something else, but a board creaked under my foot to announce me lurking.

"Good morning," I said, coming from the pantry as if innocent.

Easter and John Grady sprang up from their breakfast. Caleb rose and examined me with a curious smile. He was a wiry man of twenty-three or -four, in a crisp white chef's coat, double-breasted.

"Here's our son Cal," Easter said, beaming. "Cal, this is Sylvie."

"Pleased to meet you," Cal said. He had long eyelashes that curled around some amusement in his expression, and he carried a book in his back pocket, same as Jace.

"I can make some more coffee if you like," I said.

"Can't sit," Cal said. "Got to get these trophies in the icehouse for the taxidermist." He took two big sacks from the sink, where something dark bled through the burlap, flies buzzing.

"I don't like to think of it." Easter shuddered. "All them heads."

"So don't think of it, Ma." Cal went outside with his parents. Their talk was none of my business, but I could not help spying.

Easter fretted her apron. "Somebody's gonna see us get on that train."

"And what if they do, Ma?" Cal said. "Just tell Duke you quit."

"Your mother got nothin' to say to that man," said John Grady.

"You tell him, then, Dad."

"What I got to say, he don't want to hear." John Grady slammed a fist into his palm. "Only prayer help me get through."

"Sunday morning come to the rail spur," Cal said. "I'll set you up in the cookhouse. Nobody'll see you. Marcus will meet us at Denver." He folded Easter to his chest and held her tight, small and delicate in his arms. "Leave all this, Ma. Don't scare off."

"You know I don't scare," she said.

Father and son went away toward the icehouse, carrying the bloody sacks of animal heads. The King would take his bighorn sheep back to Belgium as a trophy.

All afternoon Easter was distracted. She burned a tray of croquettes, cut her thumb on the jagged lid of a tin can. She did not sing or joke around.

Neither did I. *Seize the opportunities*, the Countess had said, but it seemed to me certain opportunities were like horses bolting wild, and I did not know how to grab the reins or how to steer if I got them.

For entertainment that day, the royals had a tour of the mill sheds, the stone saws and polishing machines, and were treated to a demonstration of statuary carving. That evening they heard a lecture presented by a geologist from the Colorado School of Mines about the Riches of the Mountains, the silver and gypsum, copper and bauxite, tungsten and gold and uranium ore. After a supper of watercress soup, trout *filet à l'anglaise*, roasted parsnips, and Easter's pecan tarts, they played cards and then retired, resting up for Thursday's quarry tour. At dawn the party was driven up to Quarrytown in five wagons, to marvel at the grandeur and the Eighth Wonder of the World. A crane lowered groups of the tourists in a newly rigged gondola to watch the men pounding spike, jumping the quarry bar. I could picture it. My father driving the Snail. Tarbusch checking his watch, leering at the ladies.

The quarryhogs put on quite a show: a twenty-ton block fresh-hauled out of the mountain, lowered to the yard in a circus feat of engineering genius. Oskar Setkowski, it was reported later in the *Record*, "rode the white swan," performing acrobatic tricks on the dangling stone. Nobody was crushed by rockfall. Nobody lost an eye to a stone chip. Nobody got burned by a steam blast. Nobody's leg was mangled in a lifting chain. Nobody fell off a scaffold or slipped on ice. Not that day.

Caleb Grady and his crew served luncheon on the flats by Hairpin Point, with its vast panorama. Twenty porters carried the spread from wagon to table—ham sandwiches and deviled eggs, lemon bars and iced tea—'a picnic' beneath a tent erected for royal protection from the hard sun of midday and the curious eyes of Quarrytowners.

Would Henry see the spectacle? Would Maman take Nipper's little paw, wave to the King? *Voici l'roi!* My father would come home to perform his imitation of His Majesty, a pickax like a sword, his chest puffed and his mouth in a sneer, *la-de-da*.

On their return, the guests napped. That evening they dined on hearts of palm while my own heart was consumed by worry. The ball. The King. The plan and the *opportunities*: to transform myself into a butterfly. I lurched between fairytale incarnations. I was a spy. A dupe. A wild demon. Cinderella. The goat girl of Quarrytown. All these and what else?

My jaw ached from clenching resolve: to smile, to be *élégante*, to flutter the eyelashes. To speak up, to stay quiet. To thrust the chest forward, to cover myself. Not to be a know-it-all. Not to envy. To be sweet and pure, a good quiet girl. To be an inside agitator and suffer for a cause instead of unrequited love or the blister on my heel. To take notes. Not to lose a chance, at least, to waltz.

All week we staff followed the schedule of assignments that Mrs. Nugent posted on the door of her office. In the kitchen Easter showed me how to skin the spikes off a pineapple and core their yellow hearts. I sliced them in rings, decorated each one with the bull's-eye of a cherry, guilty for the ones I stole and ate. They tasted of liquor and were called *maraschino*. A jar of these cost eighteen dollars, the price of three months' rent for Cabin Six. We used the entire order of two dozen jars. I liked to read the receipts tacked to the kitchen corkboard, pronouncing the names of delicacies, terrapin and gorgonzola, aghast at the cost: a hundred dollars for six bushels of iced fresh oysters from Norwalk, Connecticut. Crates of burgundy and zinfandel, champagne and brandy, Châteauneuf-du-Pape, Veuve Clicquot, their names like poetry, the price tags equations in my head. In fact, I *did* have a head for finance: A dinner for thirty at Elkhorne cost quadruple a quarryman's yearly salary. The cost of the Hunters' Ball would cover the Company payroll for a year.

How would I describe such sums to my family, the Pelletiers of Quarrytown? It was as impossible as translating to the Countess why Signora Santorini could not bathe her children daily. Or explaining to Jace Padgett why one could not deface the margins of books. These people did not know the value of things. Or of me, Sylvie, who could conjugate Latin verbs. I'd won a *prize*. I was published in a *newspaper*. The Colonel was impressed by my report. So there.

As I chopped and peeled and whipped the cream, small eruptions of resentment formed like the blisters that burst in my shoes as we girls worked double time, breathless, running. The ladies reclined yawning while we servants picked up their dresses off the floors and tidied sixteen rooms upstairs, where we laid fresh fires in the morning and evening, the lavatories swabbed, new posies on the nightstands, hothouse lilies and roses arranged in the entrance halls. The end tables and credenzas were abloom like the tropics.

Jasper did not burst into the kitchen or linger half-asleep at breakfast. "Where's Jace got to?" I blurted it to Easter.

"He stayed up at the Lodge," Easter said. "With Cal, you know. Master Jace and Caleb is good friends."

Easter was preoccupied with one of them and I was preoccupied with the other.

"J.C. never said nothing about Caleb?" she asked, pouring batter for cake.

"Not really." Caleb gave Jace a book, of *Souls*. Was that the sort of information she was after? "Like what?"

"Nothing particular," Easter said, nonchalant. "Never mind what these Padgetts say. You don't know what devilment people get up to with all that liquor—" Distracted, she spilled a spoonful of batter on the floor. "Look what you made me do," she said, annoyed.

"Sorry, Easter, I'll clean it."

"Don't you pay me any mind, hear? All this royal business got me in a state."

My own state was preoccupied by Saturday night. Nine o'clock. The plan. All week Inge flitted in and out of rooms, Bisou yapping behind. When the dog saw me, he wagged his tail. But the Countess carried on as if I were a statue. She was on the terrace, in the gardens, at the table with her guests, talking in French, burbling in English. She did not summon me or send me on errands. Just once she fluttered her eyelashes when she spied me around a corner. Once I said *Bonjour*, Madame, as she passed me setting tables on the terrace. She waved her fingers as if playing piano in the air and only went on laughing with a pair of women in white dresses, their hair coiled and adorned with tortoiseshell combs, cloisonné clips. One of them—Miss Susanne Crandall, of

Newport, I don't forget her—bumped against me as I cleared a table. She gave me a look of such menacing hauteur that it melted me down like a pool of wax.

"Are you an ox?" she said, and brushed herself off as if she'd been contaminated. As her form receded laughing down the lawn, I had a mind to tackle her and pull her hair out by the roots. The violence of my own impulse frightened me. Envy and Anger boiled in my entrails. Watching Miss Crandall, the vavoom gold-digger she surely was, flounce and swish, I could not summon Meekness or Humility to overcome my vengeful thoughts. Inge had not deigned to say good morning. Likely it was my own failure to understand that her instructions, to "help with Housekeeping," meant that she would not acknowledge me until the *fête*, until the Hunters' Ball Saturday night, when I was instructed to arrive at her closet at five p.m. to dress for the party, and to remain there until my *entrance* at nine o'clock. Ready.

For what? Dancing, I hoped. Transformation in the glissade and the whirl.

Silly girl, I would say now to my young self with the wisdom and superiority of the old, *did you think you could simply vault over the moon? That you might sprout wings?* Yes, I did.

Chapter Thirteen

Mrs. Nugent was counting forks when I went to remind her I would not be on the kitchen schedule that evening. "Madame has asked me to stay with her."

"Why she wants you tonight of all nights."

"To take notes for her Company newsletter."

"Tcch. You've made me lose count." Nugent rattled the silver. "Since you interrupted me, you'll stay here to tally every last spoon. There are pieces missing. Someone is a thief! And I suspect that big Croat girl." Albina could be heard weeping. Nugent went out incensed, muttering, "Newsletter!"

I would fork her in the gills, spoon out her eyeballs. I counted cutlery, full of vengeful thoughts, queasy with nerves. I had no intention of stealing anything myself. Not then, anyway. I'd yet to learn that the silverware, as well as the sides of beef and bottles of burgundy, the linens and crystal, were themselves stolen, bought as they were with dollars filched from the paychecks of miners and cooks. The clock ticked on toward five. Mrs. Nugent returned to me in the scullery.

"It's all there," I said. "Sixty pieces of each, including demitasse spoons."

"Then you've done it wrong." She practically spat, enraged, as if she kept

151

venom in the pouch below her jaw. "Count again. Albina knows full well. Knives are missing."

They weren't. Three times I counted sixty sets of cutlery, the spoons like rosary beads, but I remained resentful. Albina was not a thief.

At five-thirty, I ran to find the Countess in her dressing room, arrayed in a frothing lavender gown that matched her eyes. Her beauty made me stammer. "Madame, *désolée*, I am late."

"Ah, Sylvie." She did not appear angry with me, only maddened by the slippery clasp of the bracelet glittering at her wrist, held out for me to fasten. She could not even dress herself. *Like a child*, I thought. But hers was merely a performance of helplessness, required of a butterfly. *Snap it yourself*, I didn't say.

"There's your gown," Inge said, pointing. "You will arrange the hair like I showed you." She kissed me on the forehead, so I loved her again, wanted to please her. "You will be stunning. He will adore you."

"*Merci*, Inge." *Who will adore me?* I didn't ask.

"Nine o'clock," she said in a rush. "You must arrive down the big staircase, slowly. That is how everyone will remark you, like *une vrai Cendrillon*." She threw me a kiss, as if tossing a coin in a fountain, and was off to the party.

So she had said it. Cinderella. I was her toy, an experiment or a joke for the guests' amusement, like a bighorn sheep in delicate shoes. Alone I was to go down the grand stairs. The skirt would tangle. The fluttering scarf a possible noose. *Moose, noose, a ruse, you lose*, a rhyme of disaster. The plan was a setup . . . for what? *Beware the houseguests*, Jasper had said, some hint about Adele. Annelise's story of the Barbarian King and his sixteen-year-old *copine* was another alarm. Cramps pricked my linings as if they were bleeding. I'd guessed the reason Adele outgrew her dresses.

In Madame's closet, my thoughts lurched *bouleversées*. Sounds of revelry drifted from below, great roars of laughter. Rustle of silk in the hall. Someone at the closet door? I'd flee down the backstairs. Escape into the night and up the road to the cardboard barracks where I belonged. Summer was ending. I shut my eyes over the sight of the elegant clothes hanging in their thin candied stripes, and printed it inside my lids to last me my life. I see it still, can smell the tea roses. These were the last moments of the last days. God forgive me for the shallow vanity of what I wanted: Beautiful things. To twirl in society. To win the admiration of ladies and colonels, editors and an American prince.

The virtues of my past life, Meekness and Humility, would get me nowhere in this brash new wilderness. Such training had frozen me in a closet, afraid of judgment by party guests. *Who does she think she is? What are you, an ox?*

But why should I not be bold? If I tripped on the stairs, made some *faux pas*—what would I lose but my pride? At the least, I could report all to K. T. Redmond for the *Record*, the ice sculptures and glittering array. The excess and debauchery. My girlish young fabric suffered rips of longing for the music, petit fours with white sugar icing. Jace Padgett was still missing. He'd sweet-talked me by the river, pawing and drunk, but must've realized that I was too tall, too Catholic, too willing. Unrefined. *Sylvester.* Oh, I was nervous. The clock hands ticked: eight-sixteen, eight-forty-one. Go. Stay. *Don't just sit there like a poached egg on a wet plate,* K.T. would say. *Go to the party! Take notes!*

Fast, I removed the black uniform, peeled the hot stockings down my legs like shedding a skin. The green silk sheath went over my head in a whisper of grass. I pinned my hair, painted my lips, and combed my eyelashes, fastened on the sparkling necklace, the ear drops like hanging baubles of hope and dread.

And there she was, Sylvie altered. The glass image made me cold. She was a pretender in a costume. It was not too late to keep her here, secret. I could plead illness in the morning. What would I miss? Humiliation. Also, the party. *Les opportunités.* A change of fortune. What other chance would there be to sip champagne? "*Putain*," I cursed aloud, and smiled at the imposter. She flapped her lashes like butterfly wings. "Go now, *imbécile*," she told me in the mirror. "Go meet the King."

Surely this was the actual Satan's staircase, where I stood on the top step listening to the bubbles of the party rising in a frightful froth of laughter that stole my nerve. To make a grand entrance, as instructed, would be to hurl myself off a cliff. *Go down.* I teetered precariously on the precipice of the top step. I could not do it.

I turned and went shoeless down the backstairs, holding the petals of my skirt above the risers. I put on the dainty slippers and emerged through the service door hidden behind a ficus tree in the grand hall. The better to observe, not be observed. At the time I was ashamed of my cowardice, but now it is a secret point of pride that I resisted the Cinderella plan, Inge's method of elevating me.

The house was full of luminous people in organdy and satin, stiff white collars and cuffs. A pair of guests considered me, little question marks in their eyes. Was I someone? In a clutch of revelers was Colonel Bowles. He tapped my scandalous display of shoulder—to turn me around and throw me out, I thought.

"Good evening, Miss Pelletier," he said, bemused. "*Bonsoir.*"

"*Bonsoir.*" I slipped and slank through the moiling party. Across the great hall was His Majesty the King, an eddy of importance around him. He was stationed in his medals by the grand staircase down which I had not descended. From the outskirts of the room, I watched him speaking to Inge, her throat and wrists and hair glittering with diamonds. By her side was rotund Duke Padgett in a white tie and a pintucked shirt, laughing, the King chuckling, all of them har-har-har, hoisting flutes of bubbles, the very Veuve Clicquot I had unloaded in the icehouse that morning to chill.

A catering fellow came along, carrying a tray of golden elixirs, to ask, "Would you care for champagne?" and I would care, "Yes, please," arming myself. A swallow went down my throat like a zipper unzipping, the taste of fizz. Inge glanced frequently toward the staircase. She stood on tiptoe and whispered to the tall monarch. He nodded. She took the Duke's watch from his pocket and checked it, swept her gaze around the party. There. She spied me in the corner, widened her eyes in puzzlement, then beckoned me with a lift of her chin. I threaded through the throng.

"Madame," I said.

She pulled me near, her warm arm on my cold skin. "Your Majesty," she said in French, "I present you my young friend Sylvie. The one I have mentioned. This is the girl. *La favorite de l'été.*"

The favorite of the summer. I curtsied low, head dipped as she'd instructed, and did not shake his hand. Inge had warned me not to, because the King feared poisoning by enemies or contamination by microbes. "*Enchantée de vous connaître, Majesté,*" I said.

The King's eyes glittered small in his old ruined face as he measured me. From under my suspicious lids, I sized him back. If you encountered him on a mountain road without his trappings, you would think him a wild man of the hills, his beard a blanket. I could not stop marveling at his nose, the long slope of it. I had never seen one of such impressive dimension. "*Mademoiselle,*" he said, looking down the length of it at me, so green in my green dress of nothing. "You are *Canadienne.*"

"*Mes parents sont de Québec,*" I said.

Inge looked on, her eyes amused as she told the King, "*Une fille vraiment élégante, non?* She is only sixteen."

Seventeen. I did not correct her.

"*Seize ans?*" he said. "She is tall."

"She has such the charming American air of innocence, *non?*"

"Is it an air?" The King smiled with an arch of his eyebrow, half his mouth.

"No, Majesty, she is just as she appears."

Leopold looked me over, his eyes cold peas in their sockets. He said something in Inge's ear. She laughed and curtsied. A shimmering silver-clad woman appeared at his elbow. "*Ma Belle,*" he said.

She lifted her chin to gaze at him, adoring. "*Mon Vieux,*" she said.

"Dear Caroline!" cried Inge. The women traded kisses, and the Baroness Caroline slid her merry dark eyes over me. "*Jolie,*" she pronounced to the assemblage. "So many pretty girls in America, yes?" She steered the King away, her silver dress trailing behind like moonlight on a lake.

Jolie, jolie, jolie, the Devil tunneled that word along the channels of my vanity.

Inge watched the royal cluster proceed into the ballroom. "I knew he would like you," she said. "He invites you to visit later, for conversation. If you care for the adventure." Her smile was lopsided by drink or some wicked suggestion.

"Madame?"

"I think you care for it. Yes? The adventure? *L'éxperience?*" She touched my bare arm. "You will not regret."

"Inge—?" I coughed.

"Do not pretend you're shocked. Too bad you did not *descendre l'escalier*. The King is not the only gentleman at the party to see you. There is one Astor. A Rothschild. Lord Ashforth. They're crazy for the West. For Americans. It was a chance for you—"

"*Désolée*, Madame—"

"Phhf, it's not too late!" Inge put her arm around my shoulder to whisper. "For me, it makes no difference what you choose, because, myself, I did sweep. That's my lesson for you, to try. Your chance I give you. But I have maybe mistaken young Sylvie. You're not the hungry girl, as I was. *Pas assez faim.*"

Not hungry enough. That old lecher with the terrible beard would like me to visit him. If I were bold. If I had such appetite. That King was wrinkled as a walnut, the barbarian of the Congo. His *copine* Caroline was a silvery electric eel. I knew nothing about foreign customs or the habits of royalty. Inge did not mean—"conversation," did she? What would we discuss? *Mr. Lilongo of the Congo.* What Inge implied repulsed me. I was seventeen. *Une naïve.* I preferred hunger to the meal ticket she offered.

Mr. Nugent rang the chimes. Music started in the ballroom, and the guests floated toward the violins as if pulled along a river. The Duke whispered something to Inge. She laughed and toggled her fingers at me. "*Bonne chance, Mademoiselle.*" In the wake of the King, on the arm of her husband, she went on to the dancing.

Towed in the stream, I was flanked by men in dark jackets. The air was flavored with champagne fizz and the scent of *L'Origan*, while my head was full of helium and disbelief, tipped to gawp at the crystal chandelier sending shards of light onto the party. When I left off craning, there next to me was Jace Padgett without his glasses, dressed in a tailcoat, a white tie, the marks of a comb in his hair. When he noticed me, he pulled his head back on his neck in surprise and, I dared hope, delight?

"What the? I didn't expect—" He beamed.

"Jasper," I said. Not smiling.

"Oh my! So glamorous, Sylvie."

Champagne and his comical squinting foiled my intention to frost him. "I thought you were killed," I said.

"There are some who'd like to murder me. But look at you! You're re-arranged."

"*Ben oui, je suis la favorite de l'été.*"

"Speak English, Sylvester, please, I am in no condition."

"Inge says I'm her favorite friend now."

"Not me! I've disgraced myself." His face was pale and miserable above a brimming flute of bubbles. "I am a discredit to the Padgett line."

"Why?"

"First, I'm entirely inebriated. Number two: I stayed in the woods in order to avoid—this party, the hideous guest of honor. But I could not stay away. From you."

"And that makes you a disgrace?" I said.

"No, it makes me lovelorn."

My face broke a smile, I could not restrain it.

"My disgrace is—" Jace sighed. "At dinner I made the mistake to remark that perhaps His Majesty would like a large platter of roasted hands served up to him fresh."

"You didn't."

"Which was overheard by my father—"

"At the table?" I said.

"Our kingly guest, Leopold—in case you don't read the newspaper—is the Devil." Heads turned in the party crowd that eddied around the small rock of us.

"Shh," I said.

But Jasper carried on in exaggerated whispers. People stared while he ranted.

"Old Leo has killed ten million people in the Congo. Enslaved them for the rubber harvest. His overseers chop off their hands! Their feet! They kill infants with ax blows. Hang the women and cut off their—"

"Shh. Not so loud." I put my hand over his mouth, but he removed it. Held it in his own. "Stop."

"Don't shush me," Jasper said. "My father says shush. Everyone says shush. But it's true. Ten million. I have seen photographs."

"Jasper, you're shouting."

"I knew he was a king and a devil," he whispered, "but I did not know he was in cahoots with Lady Bountiful and her sociological experiments."

"They aren't experiments," I said, not yet ready for the scales to fall from my eyes. "The school is under way. The Company has donated a marble stone foundation—"

"A foundation of *slavery*," Jasper said. "They're building a monument to it out of our fine marble."

"Why don't you do something about it, then?"

"What would you suggest I do, Silver Sylvie Pelletier? I can't—how?"

"When I can't change something, I try to not think about it." In truth, the more I tried *not* to think about what I was powerless to change, the more I chewed the problem. For one night, I wanted to revel in the party, waltzing to my transformation in hopes that dancing and champagne held a power like alchemy. "Don't think about it," I said.

"What *should* I think about, then?"

Me? I smiled at him, bold as brass. "Think about whatever makes you happy."

"You make me happy." He listed toward me. "Happy you're here in this . . . beautiful, lovely, dazzling frock. I did not dare hope."

Oh, hope. It was still green that night as my dress, silken and fragile.

The musicians played quick time, and the guests went whirling, one-two-three. "Let's get out of here." Jasper grabbed a bottle of champagne from the passing waiter and steered me away from the music, the dancing, away from the fountain of punch where a cherub carved in ice slowly melted.

A little rueful, I looked over my shoulder like Lot's wife at Sodom. Was I changed by regret to a pillar of salt? Not regret, exactly, but I do wonder sometimes what might've been had I followed the plan. I shudder to think. But I went with Jace. He was not like them, not like his people, obsessed with copper and gold frivolity. He was angry. That anger drew me, because I was angry too. We did hate the same things, I think, the unfairness. I was not cut out to be a plaything of kings, a project of countesses. If I left the party now, I would have to be simply myself. Belong to myself alone.

Chapter Fourteen

OUTSIDE, THE BRIGHT BAUBLE OF moon cast shadows on the colorless grass.

"Look! It's a pearl." I pointed up.

"It's a silver dollar," said Jace.

"Not everything is money."

"Tell that to my father." He held the bottle at my waist and we began to waltz, clowning, amused by our bad dancing, twirling and giddy, then stopped to look up at the vast mysterious heavens. Stars like silver midges of happiness and possibility swam across the dark. "Oh-la," I whispered. "*C'est magnifique.*"

Jace danced me farther on, toward the woods, the river. "Sylvie, come along, now, like a good girl!"

A good girl. What was goodness? Obedience? Chastity? Listening to editors and countesses and cooks, I was grappling toward some other sort of goodness to claim for myself. The hem of my thin silly gown trailed down the slope of the lawn in Jasper's crooked wake.

"To hell with them all!" he cried.

"To hell, yes!" I savored the taste of *hell* in my mouth with the champagne fizz.

Jace took my hand as if we were conspirators, as if, by leaving the party, we'd struck a blow against the barbarism of a king, when really we wanted to find the kissing rock by the river. Under the pine trees, we crept over soft carpets of needles toward the water, a gleam of foil in the moonlight. Crickets and cicadas grated in the trees so the very air vibrated, tense and trembling with sound. We sat again on the riverbank, on that same flat stone worn smooth.

"Where have you been?" I asked, plaintive.

"In the wilderness."

"While I was left in the dark."

"I'm in trouble, Sylvie." Jasper put his head in his hands. "Big trouble."

"Trouble is a pebble, my mother says. *Un caillou*." I picked up a little stone and held it in front of my eye. "See? Here it fills your whole sight. You throw it—" I tossed it away. "*Et voilà*—it's nothing."

"That is fatuous," he said. "We're not talking about *pebbles*. We are talking about *boulders*. About big blocks. Of stone. We are talking about a fifty-foot monument to glorify slavery." He drank a long pull from the bottle. "Despicable. Shameful."

His distress caused tender feelings in me. "Are you all right?"

"I'm advised to leave it alone. But I can't."

"Tell me, then. I'd listen." If he confided in me, his confession would be a secret I could keep, a hold on him akin to the power of priests.

"Since you are kind enough to care, here's the trouble: I told my father, 'Do *not* build that travesty. Do *not* bring that King here.' And—do you know what he said? 'You are a disgrace. Get out.' *That's* my trouble. But the *subject* instead is: Jasper has insulted a king. Jasper has brought shame upon the house of Padgett. I am banished."

"Banished?" I cried. Did it mean he would leave, depart the kingdom? I'd never see him again. The melodrama of my imagined plight increased my ardor and the hope that we would commence kissing.

"The Old Man took me aside at the party, sentenced me to spend the winter here in Moontown. I'm to work in the quarry in the snow till I learn the value of hard work or get rocks in my head. Same as his. I'm forbidden to go back to school, as Father does not see any benefit to the study of philosophy. He believes it's corrupting my mind."

"But I'm glad you'll stay."

"I'll drink to that." He toasted and passed the bottle, and we drank.

"Why are you so mad at your father?" His anger made me strangely happy.

"The idea that he would court the devil, King Beard of Belgium, for money. That he would marry—her." He drank a long pull on the bottle.

"Inge is kind to me," I said, still defending her. "She taught me to waltz."

"I bet she did. Three years ago she waltzed my father straight out of Belgium. They say old Leopold found her in a brothel and she went shopping for a sugar daddy among his guests."

"It's only gossip." *The French vavoom.* Maybe K.T.'s story was true. "Inge's very refined. She can speak three languages."

"She speaks a certain universal language, for sure," he said. "We heard about it in Richmond. Richmond heard it from Paris. Surely my father heard it, but he didn't care. The country-club crowd snubs her. Inglebork DeWhatchamacallit has no social-register pals this side of the Atlantic, so she invites a King as bait." He blew a low mournful note over the lip of the bottle.

"Inge is known for her kindness," I said. "Her charity—"

"It's not charity that gets the stone out of the mountain. It's the lash and the stick. And men. Like your father. Like Frenchy."

I smiled to think of *mon père.*

"Look at you, Sylvie Pelletier. Mention your papa, you smile your radiant smile. Whereas I think of my old man and I get a murderoush—murderous anger."

"Jace, you shouldn't say such—"

"Because the *gossip.*" He held his head like a melon and shook it in his hands. "Everyone's heard it."

"I haven't."

"I'd never heard it myself until—because Caleb is—" He let out a groan.

"Caleb Grady, you mean?" I had no idea what he was going on about.

"Never mind." He put a finger across my mouth. "Ignore the gossips and snoops."

"Busybodies," I said, to ally myself with him. "People have nothing better to do than make up stories."

"I have something better to do." He threw his arm around my shoulders and pulled me against him. "Sweet, patient girl Sylvie. You are kind to endure my ravings about the old man. Thank you."

That he was in need of kindness was a revelation. I was in need of it too, some reassurance that I was more to Jace than a shoulder to cry on. I stayed in the crook of his arm, impatient for us to kiss again.

"Now *you* talk," he said. "Tell about your father instead."

"My papa is a wizard," I said, to show him my father not just *Frenchy*, covered with dust, driving a Snail. "He's a magician. He can juggle knives. Also swallow fire. He taught me how." Now I would impress the prince of Elkhorne. "Do you have a match?"

Jasper rummaged his pockets for matches, struck one, and held it out.

"You eat pennies," I said, tipsy still. "I eat flames." I took the lit match with the drama of a sword swallower and put it in my mouth, closed my lips till the fire snuffed.

"Whattya know?" Jasper was aghast. "The girl has an appetite for fire."

"Your stepmother says I have not appetite enough."

"What was she suggesting you consume? I'd guess, but I'm a gentleman."

"Thank you. Don't guess."

"And what has she done to your hair?" Jasper brushed his hand along the nape of my neck and pulled out pins so the arrangement uncoiled. "Crowning glory," he said, and ran his hand along the loose length of hair and talked all southern and soft, kissing. "Sylv. Sylver. Sylverie. You taste of fire."

"You taste of liquor."

"Dangerous," he said. "We might ignite."

I pulled my legs under the long dress and bound my arms around them, frightened by my own dangerous combustion of heat and yearning. Biblical warnings did nothing to quell the force of it, though I struggled as we were taught to struggle, against our very nature.

"Hey, now, come back. I told you, I'm a gentleman," Jace said. "Don't worry." His mouth on my mouth again. Moonglow shone metallic on his face, the tendrils damp at his temples. We kissed so fiercely it could not be love. Love was tidy and chaste, a romance of poems and roses, not this possession of teeth and lips. This was something else, a molten greed that defies words.

"Sylvie." Jace suffered and shook. "Save me."

My heart went out like a sparrow and was caged. The flat stone where we grappled was unyielding, but I was not. The skin scraped off the knobs of my backbone. I buckled, drunken, and lost against the swoon. It was the liquor again and the weakness in me. *Forgive me, Father, for I have.* The liquid river pulled over slick stones, and I stopped him just on the precipice of ruin, in fear of it. The dress wrinkled around my waist, despite my pulling it down, pushing the weight of him off me.

"Stop," I said. "We should go."

"Stay." Jace held on. "Stay, please, forever on this rock."

In the murk I searched his face for a sign to trust, and hid in the hollow of his neck so he wouldn't see my secret wish: not to lose him. Not to lose. This night, this wild transporting.

"Do you hate me?" he said.

"No! Why would you say that?" I stood up and brushed off grains of river sand stuck to my skin.

"Well, that's someone who doesn't, anyway." He threw the bottle into the river and got to his feet. With elaborate chivalry, he draped his jacket over my shoulders and took my hand. We went weaving through the trees while Jasper sang a little snatch of song, "Oh, my darling Clementine." He embraced me, "Good night, Sylvester," resting his head on the bone of my clavicle. "Sylver. Sylvation. I'm lost without you."

Was he? His lostness answered something in me. As if each of us were trying to forge a new way to be in this new West, but neither with a path to follow. I was his salvation, Jace said, needed for my sweetness, a quality I wasn't sure I possessed. I righted the glasses on his nose and brushed the curls off his forehead. He could've seen down to the roots of me, had he looked.

"You do care for me, then?" he said.

"I do, yes, Jasper."

"Also I care. For you, my lovely." He kissed me so I could not breathe. "Sweetheart, good night," and backed away toward the stables, singing. "Oh, my darling Clementine".

Clementine drowned, I did not say.

In a dishevelment, I went up the path to the Cardboard Palace, altered and surely riddled by damnation, as a sack of millet is by worms. I had made myself a disappointment to my mother and to *Sainte Marie*, but still it was pure happiness that flooded around the boulder of my transgressions. Jace Padgett was lost without me. I was smiling and atwirl in the dark. To be called lovely. To be kissed and intoxicated in the moonlit mountains. Through the trees came the music of the Hunters' Ball, the clink of crystal filtering across the scree, claps of laughter. The sounds carried up into the village and on up the slopes and down into the hollow cavernous quarry where the men worked even now, by carbide light and bare electric bulb, to pry stone out of the mountain on the graveyard shift. The fumes of the party washed into the night, into the secret grottoes and crevices where the cold was gathering, the leaves were turning, the animals bracing for winter.

Chapter Fifteen

As the sun rose, the royals and the Padgetts and their guests drifted to bed. The rest of us cleaned the wreckage of the party. A wire of pain pulsed in my temples. Cigarette ash mingled with dregs of champagne at the bottoms of glasses. The ice cherub was dissolved into the punch bowl. Crumbs flecked the white linen, stained red with crushed berries and burgundy wine. Shards of kisses were spikes in my blood. The air smelled of oil soap and evaporated spirits; a whiff of shame leaked out the windows into the pine wind. A new chill was in it, a turn of the weather.

The breakfast was on all morning. Bloody Marys. Blood sausage. We cleared the plates and washed them as the partygoers packed up, their luggage hefted down the stairs, the carriages waiting in front. We lined up to bid farewell to the royal party. The King left with his entourage, his trophy bighorn, and his fervor to invest in the riches of the Colorado peaks, or steal them. Leopold II took the *Sunrise* out of Moonstone. Years later, local people only remembered with pride that a *king* had visited their town, never the atrocities he committed in the remote Congo.

Inge appeared at last, with the Duke. Twice she toggled her fingers at me and smiled, gave a little wink, held her head in her hands to show how it throbbed. I worked in the kitchen. Jasper did not appear.

In the Cardboard Palace, the Croatian sisters spent the day weeping, denying they were thieves. They packed their bags and walked to the new depot to catch the afternoon train. Mrs. Nugent ranted. The house was a ruin. The Croats were light-fingered. Easter and John Grady were missing.

"They've disappeared," Nugent cried. "Easter said she'd be out one hour to say goodbye to her son. Nobody's seen the Gradys since the royal party left this morning. Where on earth could they possibly have gone?"

It was a good question, I see now. Where on earth was safe for them, what with hooded mobs rampaging *like a virus*. Dearfield, the town was called. I said nothing about Marcus's letter or what I'd overheard. *C'n'est pas mon affaire*, as my mother would say. I would not betray them.

Nugent pressed me into service to replace the departed housemaids and had me putting covers over the furniture, closing shutters upstairs in the guest rooms. I stripped beds and hauled armloads of sheets to the laundry, hung wet linen on the line. In Easter's place as cook was Mrs. Quirk from the Quarrytown boardinghouse. She was a freckled cheerful woman who specialized in making big pots of stew, chili and beans. "Your mother, Cherie, is filling in to cook up at Quarrytown," she told me. "If the boys like her grub too much?" She waved her knife. "I may have to chop off her nose."

The Padgetts went into Moonstone town to dine at the Larkspur Hotel rather than eat Mrs. Quirk's glop. Without John Grady to drive them, Hawky Jenkins was hired to bring them home in his wagon. Jasper was not with them.

It wasn't until the next afternoon that Inge summoned me. She sat enervated at her vanity, brushing her hair. "The party, Sylvie, *t'es-tu bien t'amusée?* Did you dance with the gentlemen? It was fun for you?"

"It was wonderful."

"I remember—zero!" she said. "*Rien.* My head is pounding still. And now we have to pack." She waved at her collection of trunks. She was returning to Richmond for the fall, then going on to Europe for the winter. She handed me dresses, hats and wraps, lingerie and shirtwaists. I folded them layered in tissue paper. "This one," she said, sorting the racks, "and this." Occasionally, she stopped and gaily tossed things in a pile on the floor. "*À la poubelle!*"

"The trash?" All summer I had rescued treasures from the wastebins of Elkhorne: pencil stubs, magazines, ribbons, safety pins, a glass jar of pink face cream, half full. All of us scavenged like pack rats. Inge threw out her copies of *The Smart Set*, unaware that the magazine's pages—the articles about the new drop-waisted gowns, the photographs of society dames at croquet, the gents enjoying a sail off Cannes—would travel with me to Quarrytown to serve as privy paper. She could not imagine that her torn stockings would be mended for a new life hiking Digger Mountain on my two legs, another layer of warmth.

Onto the discard pile went a lace-trimmed blouse, a houndstooth riding jacket, a crimson petticoat, a sky-blue cardigan. A lambswool coat with a fur collar.

"Do you want? It is from last season, so . . ." She gestured at the pile, where Bisou was making a nest for himself.

"Are you sure, Madame? It is—"

"It's nothing, phh." She shooed the coat toward me, "*Pour toi, ange,*" flapped her hand backward in the air, rummaging the closet. She pulled the green dress from where I'd hung it after the party. "A little bit of mud at the hem?" She lifted her eyebrows as if to suggest she knew why.

My face flushed to betray me.

"It's a shame you could not take advantage to the royal visit," she said. "I was forced to tell Leo you caught a germ. He was disappointed, but—all for the best."

"I am sorry—if I am a disappointment."

"Poor Sylvie." She sighed. "I hoped you to find a gentleman. It is how we—the ladies—elevate out of a poor circumstance." The scarf in her hand fluttered to the floor.

I picked it up, folded, and refolded its weightlessness.

"But all is not lost for you," Inge teased. "I observe: Jasper."

The name made me smile. All winter he'd be here, working for the Company, and—what? I don't know exactly what I expected, just that we would go forward. We would carve our initials in a tree and go skating on Marvelous Lake. I'd teach him the trick of swallowing fire.

"It's a shame," Inge said. "He went so soon back to the university."

The news was a block of stone dropped off a crane.

"Gone?" I said, flattened. "But—Jace said he would stay the winter."

"His father wished it, but I make Duke change his mind. To give the second chance." She wound strands of her hair around a finger, musing. "It's better for him to return and finish the school, than to stay here to *combattre* with the father."

I turned away to pick at a sticker on one of her trunks. *Thessaloniki*, it said. I wished myself there or anywhere else.

"Oh, I thought you knew," said Inge gently. "Jace did not tell you *au revoir* this morning?" She expelled a small angry pouf of air. "*Insupportable!* He does what he likes. At the dinner he insult the King. Deliberate! To cause embarrassment. He does not care about his father or me. Or anyone. Maybe Duke cannot forgive him. Maybe I cannot. But we will try, and you'll try, won't you, *chèrie*? He is a troubled boy. He suffers a *dérangement*."

She changed the subject then, to distract me. "One more letter." She handed me pen and paper and made a disgusted face. "To the United Daughters Confederacy Club in Richmond, to say thank you again for the honor."

"Which honor, Madame?" My voice was detached.

"The Company have won a contract for the memorial to the loyal soldiers and slaves, et cetera, *tu sais?*"

I did not care about the *putain* statue; I was twisted by the news of Jace absconding. Inge went on about Mrs. Randolph Sherry and the monument for the National Mall in Washington, the same one that had put Jasper in his ridiculous torment. *A statue.* I picked up the pen to take down Inge's fawning note to Mrs. Sherry.

"'My Dearest Coralee,'" Inge began, then stopped. "*Ah, merde.* I can't stand that woman," and resumed dictation.

> We missed you this week here at Elkhorne. How you would enjoy
> the scenery and the fine company! We had as honored guests His
> Majesty King Leopold of Belgium and other prominent visitors
> from Europe and New York. Perhaps next summer you will grace
> us with your charming presence. In the meantime, this is a personal
> note of gratitude for your choice of Moonstone marble to build the
> statuary in Washington. Mr. Padgett could not be more pleased!
> And (I will tell you in confidence) he hopes that when you see
> the beauty of the stone, you and the United Daughters of the
> Confederacy will select it also for the monuments in Florida and
> Alabama. It is simply the purest white marble in the world. Next
> summer, please come see for yourself. We will be home to Belle
> Glade next week!
>
> Fondly,
>
> Inge

"Duke says I must win Coralee Sherry as my friend." She made a nauseated face. "These Daughters are planning memorials across the country to the old rebel soldiers. You see, Sylvie? We must win the contracts. Please write the best you can."

"*Oui*, Madame," I said, hollow. My notebook closed on the last words of summer.

We filled five trunks with Inge's fashions and accoutrements. Into the one labeled *Thessaloniki*, we folded the pile of cast-offs. It had a broken hasp, so Inge did not want it. "It's yours," she said, "with all these things, and also . . ." She produced a small drawstring bag, dangled it in my direction. "*Voilà.* For you. To survive the terrible winter. My poor rabbit, Sylvie. I wish I could take you with me."

So take me with you, I didn't say. *Invite all of Quarrytown to live in your empty* château. I was to be a rabbit again, left behind, despite that I *was* hungry, certainly starving to escape winter on a mountaintop. After all her sociology, she had no idea how it was to exist there. "If you need a caretaker for Elkhorne," I said, not too proud to suggest it, "I could work—we—perhaps my mother—to live in the bunkhouse—"

"*Ce n'est pas nécessaire, chérie,*" she said. "We close the house."

It was a radical kind of crime that the house of forty-two rooms would stand empty while people froze in tents. My consolation dangled from her fingers, a flannel sack the color of mouse fur tied with gold string. Fifty silver dollars inside. Later that evening, Mrs. Nugent paid me forty more in crisp green bills.

"Is there a mistake?" I asked her. "It's ten weeks at five dollars a week."

She blinked at me. "Ten dollars for the clothing."

"I thought it was given—"

"Nothing is given," she said. "You will learn."

I did learn. Nothing was given, certainly not money. It had to be earned by drudgery and toil, or another way: taken.

Paid out and tucked into my rucksack was nearly as much cash as a quarryman was owed for three months of hard and frigid toil. And yet this bitterness. My lips pressed down on it, and I saw I was in danger of becoming mean as Nugent unless I did something to prove myself. Amount to something more than a rabbit.

In the Cardboard Palace that night, I was the only one left. With a paring knife I'd filched from the kitchen, I set to work in a corner behind the bunk and carved my initials in the baseboard. It was no monument of stone, but it was a mark, a proof of existence. *S.P. was here.* Next morning, I took my trunk of cast-offs for a ride on the new trolley up to Quarrytown, and lugged it home with my threadbare illusions.

Survive, the Countess had said, like a warning.

PART THREE

Quarrytown

When Something stronger than you holds your hands in the fire, don't let it burn you. When Something pushes you into a river of ice, don't be cold. When Something draws a cutting lash across your naked shoulders, don't let it concern you—don't be conscious that it is there. This is great wisdom and fine, clear logic. It is a pity that no one has ever been able to live by it.

—Mary MacLane,
I Await the Devil's Coming, 1902

Chapter Sixteen

HENRY SAID, "HELLO, MOOSE! ARE you married?" Maman said, "What kind of French you are speaking? Like the foreigner!" Nipper cried, "Slivviie!" and ran to butt his head at my knees. "I am the fighting sheep!" His clamor woke my father, who emerged yawning from the lean-to. He appraised my secretarial *blouson*.

"What have they done to your braids?" He ruffled my head so the hair fell out of its pins. "Where's *ma petite Bichette*?"

"She looks like one of those Abercrombies," Henry said. "Snoot snout snob."

"You better not be," said my mother, admiring me.

"Where's your beard, Papa?" I asked.

"Shaved off by the sword of an Arabian bandit." He rubbed his chin.

"The men have to shave now," Henry announced. "It's the *policy*! Company docks you if you don't—"

"*Tais-toi tu*," Maman stopped him. "You don't speak about *la Compagnie*."

They were sunburnt, all of them, with clear eyes cleaned by summer on the mountaintop. Henry was taller, his trousers too short, the shins exposed above his boots. His voice cracked and squeaked. Nipper's knees were scabbed, his arms scratched, from his adventures among the rocks. They were dear and familiar yet strange to me, despite how I was a stranger to them now, and to myself, judging the tar-papered cabin with critical eyes. *Make note.* The commode in the corner, the flies on the pan grease, the sacks of coal leaking black dust.

And how was the castle? they wanted to know. What did I eat? And did the royals drink out of golden goblets? I told them about the closet of dresses, the porcelain sinks, the electric light. "The Countess has a philosophy of sociological improvements. The hospital, a library—"

"Pfft! I'll believe it when I see it." My father performed his imitation of the Duke, looking down his nose, mincing, to teach us mockery as a defense against resentment.

It is a strange human need, to feel we are above the rest. We look for reasons to tell ourselves our ways are correct, better, and that others are lesser, wrong, deluded. I've never figured out why. Perhaps it is because the golden rule, of *do unto others*, is so difficult to obey when greedy, odious characters won't follow the commands of kindness. In truth, we enjoyed the sneering.

We ate our supper of trout Henry caught that very morning, fried in lard, while I remembered butter with lemon, and amused them describing Elkhorne's decor of elephant-hide wallpaper and velvet, the flush toilets indoors. They howled laughing when I told about the dog with a toothbrush and did my imitation of Nugent and her fish lips. My Countess-accented French was hilarious to them. Our faces hurt from smiling.

Nipper banged the Thessaloniki trunk with his fat fists. "Open!" He climbed on it to do a monkey dance, making faces. By laughing, we only encouraged his darling antics. He flexed his arms in a pose like a strongman. "Open!" he said in his baby voice. "Open a damn box!"

"See what he learns?" Maman cried. "*Les sacres.*" But she forgot to be wary of bad influences when I handed out presents. The discarded paint box of a houseguest, a tin of *pastilles*, magazines. For Nipper, a broken pocket watch. For

Henry, Jasper's old baseball glove, plucked from under the coffee grounds in the kitchen garbage where Nugent had pitched it—the stitching had unraveled.

"Mine?" Henry was reverent. "Hell's bells, Moose, thanks." He socked his fist in the leather and would fix it with a rawhide lace, good as new.

I presented the lambswool coat to my mother. She lifted the fur collar against her cheek, wonderment like a kind of sadness on her face. "But it's not for me," she said. "For you, Sylvie."

"*Non, pour toi*, Maman."

"It is too beautiful." She did not know whether to wear it or pet it, slipping her arms in the silk-lined sleeves. Papa said, "*Jolie là*, Madame." She brought a hand to her throat to hide the swallows of emotion there.

Nipper snatched the Countess's green chiffon scarf and danced away with it around his head, singing, "Hallelujah, I'm a bum."

Henry joined in, then Papa. "Hallelujah, bum again."

"Shush, *tais-toi*," Maman scolded. "Do not sing that wobbling song."

"Wobbly song," Papa said, "the proud strike anthem of the IWW." He pinched her cheek and admired her coat, so she softened and paraded in it girlishly, smoothing her hand along the soft fur. No more was said about unions, but the tune hung in the air like news of unrest.

Last, I handed over the envelope from Nugent. "Here, Papa, my salary."

"Not bad," he said, impressed, even as a flicker of wounded pride crossed his face at the insult of a girl earning U.S. greenback money doing soft indoor work. His pay, a man's pay—for hard labor and risking his very life—was scrip, to owe right back to the Company in rent and supplies at the Mercantile, no savings. He returned me twenty dollars with a magnanimous flourish. "Keep for your trousseau."

"Ah, *non merci*, Papa." My conscience scraped with subterfuge, since I'd withheld Inge's secret purse full of silver. Yours, she'd said. For a ticket somewhere, away. I returned the twenty to him. "*Non*, Papa, I don't need it."

When Maman was out of earshot, I told my father how Duke Padgett had said *union scum* and how the Colonel would be smashing heads. About

Tarbusch bringing in Company beef. Hearing it, my father thrust his chin forward and worked it side to side, as if his mouth were full of hot coals. "*Maudits bâtards*," he said. "I'm sick of them."

I was alarmed by his cursing, the red spider lines in his eyes, fearing what he might do. "Papa?" But he smiled in his old way and reassured me.

Rascal Nipper escaped, running down the Quarrytown lane, delighted at his own mischief. The green gossamer scarf streamed behind as he ran.

"François! Nipper!" Maman called. "*Oh, qu'il est méchant.*"

"I'll get him." Henry took off and caught the boy, hoisted him up, laughing. They went off singing "Hallelujah, I'm a Bum," to pitch rocks and try out the baseball glove and wave at the new trolley on the downhill run. Healy the motorman would toot the whistle for the boys if they timed it right.

"*Bon ben*, Sylvie's home, all's well," my father said, as if it were. He put on his hat and went whistling to the quarry for his shift. Maman went to the creel in the corner and lifted out a dripping string of Henry's fish. "We'll salt them down for the barrel," she said.

We sat on the steps outside and slit open the fat trouts, called cutthroats. We scooped out their guts and filled their bellies with salt and layered them down in their white grave: fish, salt, fish. All winter there'd be a fry reek in the cabin, seeping out into the murderous wind. As we worked, my mother flared her nostrils at the fish odor and some suspicious fragrance off me, off my new hairstyle or some whiff of transgression in my strange accent. "Did you say your rosary every day?"

"Of course." I lowered my lying eyes to the gravel.

My mother went inside just as Oskar Setkowski sauntered up the Quarrytown road. "You are back, Sylweea," he said, and kissed the air.

Home a few hours only, and already I was trapped in a fish-blood apron, Oskar Setkowski leering. The kiss of a rich boy had turned me into a snob. Despite his departure without so much as a fare-thee-well, I was pining. The cabin now was insupportable; Quarrytown was. I was spoiled as that fish would be if not salted fast. Tomorrow I'd ride the tram down to Moonstone town and beg K. T. Redmond for my old job.

———

Her familiar smirk was a fond welcome when I came in the door. "Pelletier! Wasn't sure you'd show, now you're pals with the nobility."

"They're not actual nobles. Duke is only a nickname."

"Won't say I told you so. Did you bring me anything? Rumor? Scandal?"

"I was a secretary," I said, "not a spy."

"But you spied anyway." She grinned. "Who wouldn't?" She drummed her fingers on the table. "Well?"

In defiance of my pledge to keep the Padgetts' secrets, I produced the secretary notebook from my rucksack, my first small act of spite.

"You wrote it down!" K.T. crowed. "Oh, God bless you, child."

I flipped the pages to determine what to surrender, what I could trade for a job, and there was the letter to Mrs. Randolph Sherry.

"Padgett Company has a contract pending," I said, "worth a hundred thousand dollars, for a monument in Washington, D.C."

She whistled. "Holy smokes. A monument to what?"

"To the soldiers of the Confederacy," I said.

She reared back in disbelief. "A monument to treasonous traitors, you mean."

"And to the loyal slaves."

"The *loyal* slaves? Well, tie me to a pig, honey, if they find even one such person. A hundred thousand dollars' worth of stone, you say? It's my kind of story, all right."

That story. The monument. It was not done with me yet.

Her offer was for two dollars a week, and I was grateful. Eager for the money and the work itself, a printer's devil again.

K.T. stared into the middle distance, shaking her head. "The *loyal* slaves. For Chrissake. What a crock of horse manure." She sat down to type, speaking aloud: "'Dear Mrs. Randolph Sherry, I would be grateful for an opportunity to correspond with you about your plans . . .'" For a few days she went around singing in a sarcastic twang, "'Oh, I wish I was in the land of cotton, old times there are not forgotten! Look away, look away, look away, Dixieland . . .'"

Dixieland might look away, but Miss Redmond? "Never," she said.

I resolved to be more like her, as it was clear I'd failed as a butterfly.

The air grew chilly with autumn. The aspens turned, brilliant slashes of yellow on the mountainsides. Their leaves shimmered in the wind with a sound like water rushing. In the gusts they rattled, shattering into bright smithereens, showers of gold coins streaming through the blue and marvelous air. I rode the new tram downhill in the cool mornings with my brother and the few Quarrytown schoolchildren. We sat on the back of the stone car, resting our backs against the marble that our fathers had hewed out of the mountain. It was my job to watch the little ones, to be sure they did not fall off. Henry liked to stand with Tom Potts, the wigglesticker, watching the connection to the overhead wires. Healy, the motorman, let him blow the whistle at Hairpin Point.

On the morning of September 30, we took the early train: just pure luck we did not take the following one. K.T. asked me to write up the tragedy for the *Record*.

FATAL SMASH ON TROLLEY

Four persons met death as the result of an accident on the new line:

Patrick Healy, motorman; Robert Lytle, brakeman; Atansio Negrete, a Mexican; and Mary Tonko, a Polish girl, age 8, were killed when Healy lost control of a heavily loaded train near the mill yards. Doubtless the brakes failed and the train attained a frightful speed. Just before the bridge, the runaway cars left the track and smashed to splinters. Tom Potts leapt to safety.

Rush Lytle, sixteen-year-old son of the brakeman who was killed, was working on the riverbank when the cars hit the cliff, and he ran in time to hold his father in his arms. The boy said his father spoke and gave him word to carry to Mrs. Lytle before the end came.

Pat McCann, a young man employed on the track, saw one of Healy's hands sticking out from beneath a block of marble and took hold of it. He said the hand grasped his firmly but then relaxed, and McCann knew it was over for poor Healy. The coroner was notified so that an inquisition might be held. The Company will bear the expense of assisting the families with burial costs.

In Quarrytown, Mrs. Tonko had slammed the door in my face, refusing to speak to me; I could not blame her. I did talk to McCann, the horrified track worker, and to poor Rush Lytle, whose father was killed. Atansio Negrete had no family in town to interview. I wrote out the copy from my notes and could not help weeping as I typed. No one could remain unaffected by such events. After that, I passed the site of the accident and crossed myself in re-membrance of the dead.

One afternoon in early October I missed the last car up and set out to hike home. Snow was already a cap of white on the far peak of Mount Sopris. Any day storms would bury this road under my pinching boots. At Hairpin Point I rested, to look down over the town. The turrets of Elkhorne speared up above the skeleton trees. No smoke came from the chimneys. The Diamond River gleamed in a silvery thread, carving past the slope of lawn and the flat stone where Jasper Padgett had kissed me under the summer moon. The sight of these places hurt me. I was ruined now, by pineapple and electricity, cham-pagne in flutes, the drunken swoon by the river. *Wherefore gird up the loins of your mind. Be sober and hope for the grace that is to be brought unto you.* Such Bible advice was useless. I could hardly sleep for the turmoil of my rumination and heat. No letter, no sign, no trace in the quilted pattern of mountains in the endless distance. Jasper Padgett had not said goodbye. In my notebook I wrote him letters I didn't send. I would not be that pitiful jilted woman. It seemed pointless to write to a college man far away at a mythical university, far above my station, remote as *le pays de Cockaigne*, where rivers ran with wine and buttered larks fell from the sky at supper into a pie.

The conifers creaked in the cold wind. A dervish of marble dust whirled in an eddy of brown leaves. My guts twisted with longing, not for buttered larks or riches but for a name I would not say aloud.

"Did you bring the milk?" Maman said when I came in the door.

"Sorry, *désolée*, Maman. I forgot."

"You forget your own self," she said. "What is wrong with you?"

"Nothing. I am tired from work."

"Work." She snorted to show she doubted that what I did all day at a newspaper counted as labor, while she boiled the clothes and hung them in the wind, piled stones around the outside walls of the cabin, an extra layer against winter, as high as she could reach. She hauled coal and water strong as an ox. She shaved Papa's chin and trimmed his hair, cooked beans and mended britches. She chased Nipper when he tried to follow Henry to school. All day long the little boy wrestled her for his freedom. And I did the same. Her eyes were swagged in dark half-moons, her hair unraveled and curled in the steam of her boiling pots. The air was thick with cabbagey odors and the threat of snow.

"Rest, Maman."

"We rest when we die, eh?" She brandished her darning needle at me. "Idle hands are the Devil's tools."

My hands were not idle, but the Devil would soon find other tools to fix me. I did my chores in Quarrytown and rode the tram to the newspaper, where I did the printing and mailing, keeping my eyes peeled, as K.T. advised. I walked the delivery route bundled against the winds of October, greeting our customers: "Hello, Mrs. Weeks." "Here's your paper, Mr. Koble." "Good morning, Colonel." I was cheerful, handing the news around, unaware that a certain story on page one was a flame. The match lit by me.

THE MOONSTONE CITY RECORD

"LOVED BY SOME, CURSED BY OTHERS, READ BY EVERYONE."

PADGETT COMPANY WINS
LUCRATIVE CONTRACT
$100,000 WORTH OF STONE
FOR CONFEDERATE
MONUMENT IN NATION'S
CAPITOL
TO HONOR DIXIE
SOLDIERS, AND SLAVES
"WHO REMAINED LOYAL"
OUT OF "LOVE FOR THEIR
MASTERS"

———————

Mrs. Randolph Sherry, president of the United Daughters of the Confederacy, awarded the commission. In a statement to the *Record* she wrote: "Many is the slave who longs for those happy, carefree years to return. This monument will recall for them their service to a great cause." The *Baltimore News-American* has suggested a more fitting tribute: "Why not a statue depicting a Negro family, with the inscription, 'In Grateful Memory & Sincere Apology to the Ones We Never Paid a Cent of Wages to During a Lifetime of Service Building Our Nation.'"

I thought of Easter and what she'd have to say about the "loyal slave" idea, if she'd even discuss it. Probably she'd slam pots and save her thoughts for when she was away from us white people. The article continued.

> BONUS REWARD:
>
> The *Moonstone City Record* offers a $100 PRIZE to anyone who can produce a former slave willing to testify to those alleged "happy & carefree days" that the Confederate Daughters seek to immortalize by whitewashing truth.

Colonel Bowles charged into the newsroom, mustache twitching. "Redmond!"

"Colonel?" She came from behind the press, arms folded across her chest.

"You want a reward?" he said. "I'll give you a reward, you bet I will."

"Excellence is its own reward," she said with her provoker's smile. "The *Record* is proof. Our circulation's doubled. There's my reward."

The Colonel spat: "If. You. Don't. Have. Anything. Nice! To Say! Say nothing!"

"Nothing," she said, full of sass. I loved it. Perhaps I could cultivate my own sass.

Bowles pointed a trembling finger. "Listen, Redmond, our company is engaged in an honorable enterprise, and we are doing our goddamnedest to make a go of it in extraordinarily difficult conditions. This company has accomplished astonishing feats. A heroic effort! You, madam, have no idea of the skills and courage required to get tons of stone down from these mountains. Fourteen feet of snow on the road. Slides. Freezing temperatures. Why are you such a knocker? Why can't you stand with us and contribute to the people of Moonstone, to Colorado, and to this nation, by supporting our efforts?"

"Our job here is not as a sales booster," she said. "This is a journal of record."

"You'd do well to bite your tongue, woman. Don't say I didn't warn you." He took himself out the door.

My employer poured a capful of whiskey into her coffee. "If it's only children and fools who tell the truth," she said, "then count me a fool." She toasted me with her mug and settled down to report what she called "all the new news."

Not a week later, what was indeed new news, was the *Moonstone Booster*, a rival newspaper. On the morning of October 15, K.T. came from Dottie Weeks's bakery, waving it like an enemy flag in her furious fist.

"This!" she cried, and thrust it at me, "is a declaration of war."

ANNOUNCING THE BOOSTER
MOONSTONE'S NEW JOURNAL OF RECORD
TO CHEER THE EFFORTS OF OUR MAGNIFICENT CITIZENS

AND APPLAUD OUR HARDWORKING EMPLOYEES &
EXPERT CRAFTSMEN

"The Phelps boy was delivering it all over town this morning," she said. "Go out and see what you can see."

On Padgett Street, a storefront window boasted a gilt-painted sign: *The Moonstone Booster*. A crowd stood around a table outside, where Colonel Bowles himself was serving free hot cider and corn muffins. A bow-tied young man in tweeds handed out copies of the new paper.

Bowles called me over. "Young lady, meet Frank Goodell, editor and chief correspondent. He has just joined the *Booster* after graduation from Princeton University, where he was editor of the *Princetonian*."

"Hello," said Frank, with the cheerful face of a choirboy. "And you are?"

"Sylvie Pelletier." I shook his hand. His bow tie was striped and his hair was slick with tonic. He had on city shoes, very shiny. *Not for long*, I thought.

"Sylvie has been working for that Red rag, the competition," said Bowles. "But perhaps she's come to her senses? Are you here for a job?"

"No, sir, I was just curious."

"I could use a gal assistant," Goodell said. "The Company has been most generous with the funding. Cider?"

"Thank you, I'm late for an appointment." I put two muffins in my pocket.

"Let me know when you change your mind," said the Colonel. "I predict you'll see the light."

What I saw was that the *Booster* was full of glad tidings: The mill is operating at full capacity! The Company has secured a contract for the American Bible Society building in New York! The Masonic Lodge hosted a successful raffle! The children of the Moonstone Elementary School held a spelling bee! Mr. Phelps went hunting for bear and came back with a beard! Ha! Ha! Ha! And then this:

PUBLISHER'S NOTE, FROM COLONEL
FREDERICK D. BOWLES:

> The *Booster* expects, before it has become
> very ancient, to uncover a few knockers, for
> what town is without them? Like death and
> taxes, the knocker cannot be avoided. But they
> can be placed in such a hopeless minority that
> they cannot profitably open their yawp. The
> boosters are in the vast majority here. More
> power to them!

"It's a Company paper," K.T. said. "You won't find any real news in it,
only the Panglossian ramblings of Padgett stooges." She crumbled the newsprint and fed it to the fire. "Outrageous claptrap."

This local outrage, however, was soon buried by a nationwide catastrophe
that hit us in the little town same as if an avalanche had cracked off a cornice
to bury the inhabitants.

The Financial Panic of 1907 began on October 22 with a failed swindle to
corner the copper market. In under three hours, $8 million was withdrawn
from the Knickerbocker Trust, Fifth Avenue, New York. The news came over
the telegraph, where K.T. stood reading grim headlines. She got on the phone,
scribbled on scraps, typed madly:

> The sidewalks of Wall Street were crowded
> with weeping ladies and grim-faced gentlemen
> snaking in lines around tall buildings, calling
> for their money. J. P. Morgan and his top-hatted
> secret cell of plutocrats are holed up day and
> night, trying to rescue the bankers and head off
> a market failure and an avalanche of woe.

Copper. Jace had ranted about it. The dinner-party talk, the taste of the
future. My spiteful heart harbored a penny-size wish that the Padgetts would

lose their fortune. *Serve them right.* The telegraph was full of dire occurrences, but I relished the thought of such ruin. When a girl is spurned, the loss of $8 million may appear as divine justice. I had no idea yet what tactics a millionaire might employ to get his money back, how he would take the bread from our mouths, cash from our bones and blood.

RUN ON BANKS AS STOCKS CRASH.
RICH MAN PUTS BULLET IN HIS HEART.
STOCK EXCHANGE CLOSED DOWN.
J. PIERPONT MORGAN PLANS TO HALT PANIC.
ROCKEFELLER PLEDGES HALF HIS WEALTH.

It was exciting to set the pages as K.T. tore them out of the typewriter. When Henry came to the office after school to collect me, I told him, "Go ahead. I'll leave in an hour." But it grew dark, and we were not finished running copies off the press.

"You won't go back up slope tonight," K.T. said. "Stay here. I'll telephone the quarry line to get a message home. Wouldn't want to alarm anyone."

But: PANIC! was her headline, in twenty-four-point type.

We worked well past midnight. I slept two hours on a pallet, then ran around town to deliver the news ahead of the *Booster.* That cheerful paper printed only a small paragraph: "Stocks Take a Tumble." HALLOWEEN PARTY SET FOR MASONIC LODGE was the *Booster*'s headline.

For most of the one thousand souls in our little hamlet, that first week of financial collapse proceeded as serene as the newly frozen surface of Marvelous Lake. The October snow fell and fell again so the sun sparked off every crystal stick and branch. It was impossible to believe trouble was real or could affect us in the midst of such dazzlement. The Ladies' Auxiliary sold raffle tickets to raise funds for a new gymnasium. The schoolchildren carved jack-o'-lanterns and drew pictures of ghosts and witches. The quarryhogs—"our heroes!"— wrote the *Booster*—met the deadline for the Michigan statehouse contract. My father worked double shifts in the white cave, and the new tramcars brought giant stone sugar lumps down to the mill easy as dreaming. I rode home on the last run with Henry after he was done with school, our breath frosty in the darkening afternoon. My brother and his buddies had made a bobsled run, having convinced the women of Schoolhouse Road to dump dishwater along the east side, so it would freeze and slick the course with ice.

"A bobsled is a practice coffin," Maman said, and prayed to avoid disaster while she chinked the cabin with the newsprint I brought home, filling the cracks with words: *Collateral. Liquidation. Collapse.* The house and our fates were sealed by these things.

She was more worried about cold than collateral, distressed by my father's secret meetings with his fellow quarryman Dan Kerrigan, their loud disdain for *crétin* Juno Tarbusch. More than once Tarbusch docked my father for some invented infraction: "One minute late? Docked. Two extra minutes for lunch 'hour'? Docked."

"You promised," Maman said. "You sign the contract never to join the union."

"That was a yellow-dog bargain," my father scoffed. "Disregards the law to turn us into minions of the boss. It permits him to arrest us for organizing even a card game."

"But you have signed it, *non*? Then you and Kerrigan try to make the union! Why? They will kick you off the town again."

Out of town. I didn't correct her. Sometimes I dreamed that if we were evicted, we could go somewhere without winter. Cold had seeped into my mother's bones and turned her gray with worry. If we stayed in Quarrytown, I would grow haggard as she was, as Papa. He was the color of dust and frost, working in the cavern, stone tonnage dangling over Satan's icy staircase. When I brought him his dinner, Maman did not have the energy to warn me of the dangers. She only wanted him to have a hot baked potato in his pocket to keep his hands warm. When the potato grew cold, he ate it.

My own preoccupation was the festering silence of Jasper Padgett, who still did not write to me. My apparent fate would be Oskar Setkowski. He eyed me on the road. "Halloo, Sylweea, you smile for me maybe once?" I avoided him, plotting some way to stay in town for the Saturday dances at Moonstone Lodge. There was a regular ragtime piano player and a punch bowl. *Non*, my mother said, so back and forth I went on the trolley. I preferred the wild down-swoop and dreaded the uphill grind to Cabin Six, where the air was thick with fumes of coal fire and discontent.

In a blizzard on the first of November, I wrangled an offer of hope: A cot in the supply closet at the *Record* could be mine. "It's a whiteout," I told K.T. "Would you mind if I camped here tonight?"

"Hell, stay till spring," K.T. said. "Once you're snowed under there in the boondocks, you won't get out till May. Just move the boxes into the hallway."

I spent one night on the cot, then went home to plead my case. "I'm invited to stay the winter."

"*Absolument non*," Maman said. With her blackbird eye, she checked me for signs of apostasy, afraid of K. T. Redmond's libertine indoctrinations. "Mademoiselle Redmond does not go to church." Moreover, she lived alone, was known to advocate for women's suffrage, and harbored dangerous opinions.

These were among the very reasons I liked K. T. Redmond, despite her moods and rantings. She did not need a servant to fasten her buttons, to write her letters or boil her tea. She did not need anyone to buy her a dress or dinner, or to *elevate herself out of the ordinary life*. She had bought the press, the land, her house, with her own money. I wanted money and that freedom she had, to do what she liked, to speak her mind.

At the same time, I did not want to pay the price she paid, alone and courting trouble, sniffing for it. Her nose had gotten red with the cold, her cheeks chapped to a raw rhubarb. When she typed, she muttered aloud. About the stock panic, she appeared almost gleeful, firing off letters to financiers back east. She began to subscribe to publications such as *U.S. Investor* and *Market Communications*, where, she pointed out, Duke Padgett's friends—the Knickerbocker Investment Syndicate—placed ads. Ads for salesmen. Ads for investors. Ads for "opportunities."

"Ads for suckers and dupes," K.T. said, and published a "Warning to Fools":

> Stock dumping, which has been the great source of revenue to our own gigantic local swindle, has been stopped, thanks to the efforts of newspapers sounding a note of warning. However, there's a new crop of fools coming on every year.

A week into the market disaster, K.T. got off the telephone, her face gray. "The Company's wiped out," she said. The banks had called in their loans. The brokerage house had used the Padgett Company stock as collateral. Her explanation was gobbledygook to me, but one thing was clear: The Duke and his investors had lost millions. "Won't say I told ya so," said K.T.

"Now maybe Padgetts'll have a taste of it," I said, spite in my mouth.

"A taste of what?"

"How it feels to lose."

"Ha. Careful what you wish for. When these people catch a cold, the rest of us get pneumonia."

The Panic barreled toward us in our placid village, but the slab saws hummed in the mill, and the grit machines polished. The rotary mandrels turned column drums for the so-called Loyal Slave monument in Washington, D.C. The payroll was "delayed," but artisans carved the frieze for the entry of the Bible Society Headquarters in New York. Sal Proccaccino hefted a newfangled air chisel to point details in a statue of a baby for a grave. Big Mike "Michelangelo" DiChristina bloomed stone into delicate rosettes for a marble mantelpiece, a *picarillo* hammer in his long tapered fingers, adding baguettes, palmettos, cabled fluting. The *Booster* boosted, citing record sales of stone.

But the *Record* reported a different story, wherein the Company did not pay a single worker in real coin, only doled out "plunks" for buying beans and salt pork, in a minimum amount to keep the men just alive enough to work:

COMPANY HARD-PRESSED FOR MONEY

> There has not been a payout now for four weeks. According to Kunnel Bowles, the "short-fall" will be made right by the end of the year, and credit is meanwhile extended at Koble's Company Mercantile for winter supplies.
>
> A cautionary note to Readers: The Padgett Company is begging stockholders to buy corporation notes. Without such funds, it cannot yet be stated what will be done to recover from the October Stock Panic and allow workers to be paid.

At Quarrytown all the talk was of the payroll. Mr. Tarbusch said money would come next week, then the week after. As my father read the paper, he flicked his thumbnail off his teeth, clicking a threat. "Come spring, these thieves, they get the payback. The boys go on strike."

"You don't," my mother said. She chewed the inside of her lips and crossed herself, kissed her thumb, prayed her rosary. "The strike, the resistance, is useless."

"Not useless," my father told her. "I invited *Monsieur* Lonahan to come back in the spring. By then we will have many songbirds ready to fly out the quarry."

A small evil bubble of hope formed in my throat that Papa was right. George Lonahan would arrive. The union would take charge. The men would strike and win. The Padgett Company would lose. Jace would lose. Thoughts of payback and vengeance were a solace. Of course, if JCP had knocked on the door, I'd have changed my tune.

Chapter Seventeen

On Saint Catherine's Day, the twenty-fifth of November, I was kept from town by six feet of snow covering the tram track. Crews of roustabouts shoveled it out alongside Hawky Jenkins's mule teams hauling plows and a big grievance: Nobody got paid.

"Dead work," Tarbusch said. "You boys don't clear the track, stone can't be shipped. Can't ship? No money to cut more. Simple."

"Even more simple?" said my father. "No pay, no cutting." He reported to us, sitting by the fire with his big feet steaming in damp wool socks, a tang of sweat in the air with the pea-soup odor off the pot simmering same as tempers in the pit. "No more dead work. In spring we walk."

Maman distracted the conversation away from *les combats* by reciting a list of winter supplies for me to put on the tick at the Mercantile: flour, kerosene, cooking oil, sugar, mutton, thread, a tin of carbide for the headlamp, hide leather for skinning skis and palming mittens. We needed yarn and tea, matches and coffee; beans, onions, cabbage, and potatoes. Salt pork and cured beef for the barrel. Provisions could be bought on credit till payroll cleared.

"Payday's the first of January," said Papa. "So says the lying weasel boss."

"Get everything now," Maman said, "before that track is closed for good."

"Phh. Pelletiers are *raquetteurs*," Papa said. "On the webs we go anyway."

Henry had found a pair of skis abandoned behind Cabin Three and wrangled Christe Boleson the Swede into giving me his old ones. I tried to fall in love with Christe, his cheeks bright red in the cold. But he was too serious, did not like jokes or conversation. Kindly boring Christe fixed the skis for me and greased the bottoms with boiled tar. Henry cut pine poles for balance. I pulled old trousers over my stockings and divided my skirt into *culottes*. "*À tantôt*, Maman."

"Don't fall," she said. *Do not die*, she meant.

We flew in a long swoop, a free glide in the flats, another swoop to the bridge. I was cautious and slow, but Henry zipped straight down, half the time airborne. He left a trail scalloped in the snow behind him and later set the speed record in a race from the quarry to town. I skiied along singing "Hallelujah, I'm a Bum," thinking bum Jace Padgett could jump into Boston Harbor in his own private tea party for all I cared. Perhaps he'd drown himself in a bourbon swill or be crushed by a stampeding herd of Confederate Daughters in hoopskirts. The blue sky and these thoughts of violence cheered me.

At the Mercantile, Mr. Koble tucked his chin into the bullfrog pouch of his neck where he kept his toady lies and flattery. "Only two bushels of potatoes per man," he said. "Two of onions." He wrote the charges in his ledger with red ink.

"Why red?" I asked. "Five weeks' pay is owed my father."

"Everything's on the tick," Koble said. "Till the payroll's in, you'll have a debt here. I'll ship your box on the trolley."

For the rest of the year, the Company paid not one actual nickel. In Quarrytown the crews lived off promises, and the Pelletiers lived off rations of beans, salt fish, and pickled eggs. By mid-December the track had been shoveled out twice. Winter was only just getting started.

The Christmas blizzard of 1907 began on the twentieth of December with a fury out of the North, the wind solid with snow. Through the howl of it, we heard the siren whistle for the first shift. My father put on his long red drawers and his overalls, his woolens and his two pairs of thick knit socks. He laced his boots.

Maman gnawed her cheek, her face in a twist. "Don't go," she said. The wind rattled the boards and guttered the flame in the lantern. "*Trop frette*."

"Cold? Bah. It's nothing." He put on his hat. "Normal."

It was normal for us to be frozen, to ache to the marrow. At the top of Marble Mountain, the mercury read minus one. In the quarry, minus ten. The pit generator burned coal in the boiler day and night to flush water through the pipes, to keep the machines from freezing. Every hour the men were allowed a steaming cup of tea to flush the veins, to keep the blood from congealing. The floor was ice, Papa reported, the ladders and steps slick with it. Soon the quarry would close till spring, and only a skeleton crew would remain. Machinist Jacques Pelletier was among the crew of skeletons assigned to spend the winter at Quarrytown. And us with him.

That morning, when he opened the door, the wind wrestled him for it. He got it shut and left my mother to her prayers. The storm raged all day till it seemed the shack itself would lift off like a cumbersome goose and whirl above the mountain. There was no going out, not on raquettes or skis or the flying canoe of the *loup-garou*.

That night and the next, the blizzard screamed and rattled and groaned. The snow grew around us, over the boarded window, four feet on top of three, then up to the roof so only the pipe of our stove came through the drift piles. Our shack was a layer of batten board around a smoky pocket. Henry went out to shovel. An hour later it was my turn. We dug out Setkowskis' place, Eva helping, and then dug out Bruners'. But the snow dumped down and buried our efforts.

"What about Christmas?" Henry said.

"Here do you see one single church?" Maman asked. The state of our souls plagued her, a year almost since our last confessions. Our Nipper did not remember the Christmas Mass or *Réveillon*. He did not know the uncles with their big noses and flourishing eyebrows dancing, swinging the aunts in their white stockings and black shoes. He did not know the feast or the *tourtière*, the *oreilles de Christ* piled on the table, the cousins hiding under it, eating sugar pie, the air flavored with maple and pork. These were things of an old dream.

We did not dream now, as none of us could sleep for worry. Papa did not come home. Was he lost and frozen in a drift? *He's sleeping at the boardinghouse*, we told ourselves. For three days we could not go out to find him.

The morning of the twenty-third, we woke in the quiet. We pulled open the door to a wall of snow and chopped through it, tunneling out of our burrow. The sun was a pale pock in the gray skin of clouds. And there was our papa, tromping home in the drifts. He dropped his webs and fell in the door, icicles on his beard. We thawed him by the stove, wrapped his frosted feet. He winced and drank tea and slept for twelve hours.

Christmas Eve we stamped out into the frosty dark on *raquettes*, Nipper riding Papa's shoulders. The stars and a crook of moon hung like ornaments in the sky, the snow lit with pearly light. The air punctured our lungs with cold. Climbing after us, the neighbors were a firefly parade of lanterns. The Bruners. The Setkowskis. Eva carried the small boy on her hip. Oskar carried the little sister.

"Sylweea, hello!" he called ahead to us.

"Happy Christmas, Oskar!" After the boredom and cabin fever, I was even glad to see Oskar.

Inside the boardinghouse, Mrs. Quirk and her stingy ladle stood guard to dole out grub. "It's got to last us till the road's open." A Christmas smile could not crack her face till Nipper pulled on her skirt. "Merry Christmas, Madame." He smote her with his sweet brown eyes.

"Oh, my sakes, youngster." Mrs. Quirk rooted in her apron and doled out peppermints to the few children. The fifty-four winter souls of Quarrytown sat down to eat in the din of tin plates and curses, buffeting laughter. My father told the story of how he once killed a skunk in the woods of Beaupré with a billy club.

"One of these days," Dan Kerrigan said, "we kill the weasel Tarbusch just the same." The men made guns with their fingers, triggers of their thumbs, bullet noises.

"*Enfin, messieurs*, please," said Maman. "It is Christmas."

"Damn Tarbusch slave driver," Kerrigan said.

"But the Duke, Monsieur Padgett, is a decent man," said my mother. "And Mrs. Padgett, *la Comtesse*, is a saint!"

"Oh, Lady Bountiful." Papa hoisted his fiddle and sang, "'I had a girl and she was good, one of her legs was made of wood, her hair was false and she was too . . .'"

Tchachenko on accordion and Bruner with his trumpet started up "Valse de Réveillon." The tables were shoved to the walls. The musicians played a *grondeuse* and "Whiskey Before Breakfast." Henry kept time on the spoons, his worshipful eyes on Papa, racketing along. The men clowned, dancing, raucous and competitive. They circled us women, while Maman guarded me with eyes sharp as barbed wire. The little ones ran around the fireplace and fell down laughing in hysterics.

No sign of the baby dolls or toy trains promised from the Sociology Department (though later we heard that the mill children got those at the party in town).

Maman sang *touralouralou*, her choir voice floating over the thump and whistle. My father rested his fiddle and danced her across the room while the men clapped, half of them jealous and the other half homesick. She fell back onto our bench, winded and girlish. The place filled with pipe smoke and the hot cooped breath of the dancers.

Then the door flew open, and Juno Tarbusch came in with a blast of cold that stopped the music. "Merry Christmas, boys," he said, drunk, flourishing a gallon jug. "Here's free grog, courtesy of Duke Padgett." He stood around pouring. Maman frowned across the room at me when I took some in a cup. Later she said that was the moment when she knew I was lost to her and to God. In the end, I was not the one she lost, which loss had nothing to do with liquor, and everything to do with the man who came unwelcome to the *Réveillon*.

Over the neck of his furious fiddle, my father eyed the boss. Tarbusch stared at him, then put down his jug and walked across the room to grab my mother around the waist. He twirled her, laughing. She endured it with a frozen face, then sat down to take Nipper from my arms.

Then Tarbusch sat alone, drinking and clapping to the music, violence in the way his hands smacked. I spared a moment of pity for his awkward friendlessness, the price of his toady truckling to the bosses. But that sympathy passed in an instant, never to return.

Henry and Papa exchanged a smirk. "*Vraiment maudit connard*," Henry said.

"*Chien humain*," said my father. "*Boss des bécosses.*"

"What say there, Frenchy?" Tarbusch approached, slurring.

They'd said he was a miserable idiot and a human dog, the boss of a toilet.

"I said Merry Christmas, boss." Papa swung his bow across the strings to start up the "Marché de Madame Robichaud." Tarbusch stared at him and chewed tobacco with a fierce intention. Henry's spoons clacketed along. Oskar Setkowski stood by the wall, a red kerchief knotted around his throat. When my mother turned her back, Oskar held out his hand to me as if it contained a delicacy. "Dance," he said. "Princess Sylweea." He pulled me around by the waist so fast, it seemed I'd spin out into the air like a drop of water off a wagon wheel. Dancing, he was graceful, easy in the knees, happy in the fast tempo. We were winded, hopping and red. I was passed from man to man, spinning and steered through the crowd so I was released from my bookish reserve, whirling uninhibited, laughing. *Joyeux.* All of us smiling so hard our faces ached.

"Air!" cried Oskar. "We need air! We see the stars!" He careened me toward the door and pulled me outside to the cold. The Christmas heavens went wheeling over us. Oskar grinned at me, hatless. "Queen Sylvie."

"Touralouralou," I said, but he pulled my sleeve and I tripped into a drift.

"Ooop!" He fell down heavily on me. "Merry Christmas to you," he said, and stole a kiss on the mouth. "You're my girl now."

"Not." I punched at him and wiped my face. "Get off me!" I got to my feet, snow down my neck, in my hair.

He followed me back inside and grabbed me to dance again. I broke away and went to stand next to my mother. Her eyes were fervid with prayers to save me from the fires of hell. The kiss of Setkowski burned on my lips, flamed my face.

The music paused. My father began to play alone. Dan Kerrigan stepped up and sang in his trembling tenor, a slow ballad from *The Little Red Songbook.*

"'Oh the banks are made of marble,'" Kerrigan sang, "'a guard at every door . . . and the vaults are full of silver that the miner sweated for . . .'"

"You can wail on, day 'n' night," Tarbusch yelled, "but you won't never get Padgett caught with his pants down for a Bolshy union." He raised his glass. "So Merry Christmas. Here's to you boys."

"'We'll own those banks of marble . . .'" Kerrigan sang, ignoring him.

"Yessir, we will," said Tony Mercanditti.

"You won't own nothing but your dago name," Tarbusch said, and dished out similar insults till the air was blue with cursing.

"Get your brothers," Maman told me. "It will be trouble. We leave."

"Calm it, boys," my father said. The music died out.

The men bristled like dogs. Tony stuck up a middle finger. Tarbusch swung. Tony punched him. Three men came to the boss's defense, to curry favor, and within seconds the drunken quarryhogs went at each other, delirious with violence, brawling. Mrs. Quirk swatted a broom at the pile. A bottle shattered. The floor was a glitter of glass where the men rolled and clawed, breaded with it. Then it was over. The fighters stood heaving and bleeding. Tarbusch swayed on his feet and bent to pick something off the floor. A watch. His prize possession, crushed.

"You boys will pay," he said. "Count on it."

"We count on being paid," said my father. "January first. We're owed."

Tarbusch said, "I don't owe you a damn thing, Pelletier."

Maman pulled me and Henry toward the door. "This godforsaken place."

We left Papa and carried Nipper home. The wind creaked in the trees, scudding clouds past the moon. "*Primitifs*," said Maman. "He will kill him now." She did not say who would kill, or be killed.

We lay awake worried until Papa came home, singing *touralouralou*. I heard him rattle the coal bin, whispering in the lean-to, "Chérie, Chérie."

"*Assez*," Maman hissed at him. "Enough."

"Never enough," my father said. "More heat, more whiskey, more money. More Chérie. More amour, mon amour. Happy Christmas."

"Jacques. Tarbusch is—"

"It will be fine."

"Fine, fine, you say always. Setkowski is a wolf. He has your daughter."

But he did not. I scrubbed at my mouth to get that kiss off. It was not the one I wanted.

Chapter Eighteen

JANUARY CAME AND SAT ON us. Snow fell, relentless, piling against the walls and over the roof to entomb us alive. Eight feet of it on the track, then fifteen. A horse could not get through. The tram couldn't. Nobody got paid and nobody had hauled coal to Quarrytown in the two weeks since New Year's. We dug a passage to the jacks. Water froze in the pitcher. Eggs froze in their pickling brine. Ink froze. Spit. Tears. "Out!" Nipper cried, and climbed the walls, climbed on our laps. "Once upon a time!" he demanded. I told him stories— "Robin Hood: Prince of Thieves," "The Little Match Girl"—till I was ready to light the cabin on fire with the tedium. Henry practiced the fiddle in screeches and tapped spoons, drummed us all to madness. We could not ski to town or clamber very far, even on *raquettes*, due to the danger of slides.

I was itching to resume life as a printer's devil, angling again for the cot at the *Record*. "I could ski down, stay with Miss—"

"Your patience will improve with prayer" was all Maman had to say about it.

I did the rosary in silence, each bead an unholy wish, for a letter, a job, a word, a dove with a kiss in its beak. There was no mail. Also no coffee. No tobacco. Only a few liters left of lamp oil and a coal ration. On the daily menu was beans, but we said, "Pass the strawberries" with mocking Belgian accents and did not mention our cracked lips, the skin of our fingers broken and bleeding, our boots soaked through. *Complaints are the seeds of misery.* We Pelletiers were stalwart and silent as sides of meat in a meat locker. I wrote down the boredom and the bile in my journal.

January 10, 1908: *If the Devil would come to take me away I'd leap into his arms.* I did not bother to erase this.

George Lonahan had not replied to Papa's November letter. "Maybe Tarbusch stole it out of the mail sack," Papa mused. "Maybe he has bigger fish to fry than us bony minnows. Maybe George has given up." Or my father had.

But not me. In the throes of winter doldrums, I pondered George Lonahan. Doldrums and throes: *pluralia tantum.* Lonahan's specialty. He was an agitator, and wasn't that what we needed? He wanted my father to call a strike in summer, but summer was too long to wait. I recalled the way George smiled around a cigarette, his offer of sarsaparilla. Would he return if I asked him? Why shouldn't I write to request that he come back and organize the workers? They were worn to nubs.

Inside the mountain, the fires belched smoke out of the cave, ash on the snow from the blacksmith forge. Plenty of coal was available for the machines while we in the cabins were on a ration. Tarbusch would not stop work. Colonel Bowles, warm in town, in his beaver coat, was determined that the quarry would produce stone year-round, in all weather. Orders for tons of marble were due to ship from the mill in February. The temperature in the pit dropped to twenty below zero. Break time in the warming hut was fifteen minutes, but no amount of time was enough to thaw the blood.

"Cold enough to freeze the match flame to the pipe," my father said.

The men worked wearing canvas over wool, rubber over leather, hats on top of hats. The rest of us stayed in our dens, wrapped under blankets. We heated rocks in the stove, took them to our beds. The path to the jacks was treacherous, the privy holes frigid. We emptied the commode out the door, where the night soil froze in foul ice, to be covered by layers of white.

My father went out into the solid wind and into the quarryhole, where he chipped ice off the Snail and checked the compressor, fired it with coal, ran its slow pace along the cut. He filled his pockets with anthracite lumps that fell from the barrow to bring home, and told us how Tarbusch caught him: "You're a thief."

"And you're a weasel," said my father in French. *Une belette.*

"Dock you, frog bastard, for insubordination and theft."

"Can't dock half of nothing. You owe us nine weeks."

The men were set to quit, Papa said. Once they were paid, the crews would slide down the mountain and leave for the warm suns of New Mexico or Arizona, never to return. We burned the stolen coal. "It's not a crime. It's a right," he said.

His words were a gift I've kept all my life as a justification and a defense for what I did, and later took. More than a few lumps of coal.

All the cabin dwellers stole from the brimming coal cars in the Quarry-town supply shed, while dreaming of a desert sun. We were never warm. We slept in our coats all in one bed. The snow fell endlessly, like a white darkness.

I wrote letters of grievance in my notebook: to Jace Padgett, to Inge, to the gods, to Satan, and to Beatrice Fairfax, advice columnist.

Miss Fairfax, I suffer a broken heart.

Dear Satan, come and get me at least it is warm in the fires of hell.

All of these I ripped from the bindings and burned. Pleading and self-pity were kindling for the fire. But there was one letter I did not burn.

Dear Mr. George Lonahan,

The situation at the Padgett quarry in Moonstone is bad: The men are on a twelve-hour shift but no pay since October. So far they've been sent three times to clear track on shovel brigade, so-called dead work. They can't get supplies here from town due to the snows, and we are shorted provisions. There are no safety ropes, and the ladders in the pit are so icy that yesterday a man fell and was concussed. It is twenty below and the foreman only allows fifteen minutes to get warm. They do not have good work boots. It would help if you would please return to do what is required for a union.

Sincerely,

I intended to mail this letter only as a last resort and told myself my motives were strictly business. In truth, the tedium of winter had nurtured my interest in sarsaparilla.

On January 26, the weasel Tarbusch closed the quarry for the season. My father would not work there till spring. He went to bed and slept two days straight. When he woke up, he said, "I'm a new man," and seemed to us his old self, whistling and roughhousing the boys. He mended *raquettes* with rawhide leather and wired the broken door hinge. He told Nipper the story of the *loup-garou* so the little boy crawled around with teeth bared, growling. He taught us songs from *The Little Red Songbook* despite my mother's warnings. "'There's power in the union boys,'" he sang, and gave Henry fiddle lessons that grated our nerves. "The neighbors will murder us," Maman said. Papa sat her on his lap and sang "À la claire fontaine" so she wilted against him and talked of her old dream of Quebec, where we'd live on a little farm in Beaupré.

"To grow potatoes," she said.

"And petunias," he said. "And parsnips and peas."

I stayed up on my shelf and wrote terrible poetry. The snow fell. Quarrytown was cut off same as an island in the Pacific, only it was not flowering vines hanging from the eaves but icicles like daggers ready to spear us in our beds.

On the first of February, the screech of the shift whistle woke us in alarm, for the quarry was closed. "Somebody's hurt," Maman said.

Papa strapped on webs and went to see about it. Twenty minutes later he was back. "On with your boots. They're ordering us out to shovel track."

The order was due to a break in the weather, a thaw to a tropical thirty-three degrees. Colonel Bowles was hell-bent on getting stone to the mill. Three miles of track to shovel. All hands would dig. Out we went, wrapped in layers of wool, stamping on webs over the drifts to the loading yard, where a boil of men trampled snow. Mr. Tarbusch handed out shovels. "Froggy's here," he said when he saw us. "With his tadpoles."

Papa pointed at us. "These two get paid. Dollar a day. Men's rate's two-fifty."

"It's dead work, Pelletier."

"Don't see any corpses here," my father said. "Payroll's overdue."

"You boys have a complaint? Get the hell out," said Tarbusch. "Vamoose."

"We dig, you pay." A hardness like stone dust hung in the clouds of my father's breath.

"You're paid to quarry rock," Tarbusch said. "Trackwork's dead work."

"We ain't dead," Kerrigan said. "Put it on the clock."

"How you gonna get paid if the rock don't sell? How it's gonna sell if it don't get to market? How's it get to market if you don't clear track?"

The men took up their shovels. My father began to whistle his ominous happy tune, "Hallelujah, I'm a bum. Hallelujah, bum again." Code for a walk-out coming.

"Don't you boys even think it or you're done, Pelletier."

In the worst foul French, my father cursed him and turned on his heel, whistling his Wobbly tune. We followed, and I filled the holes his boots made with whispered blasphemous words.

"Sylvie, shush," Henry hissed. "Girls can't say swears."

"I can, *putain*," I said. Profanity, no doubt, makes a hard task easier, but this assignment was near impossible. At first we were giddy to be outdoors in the blueness and sparkling sun. A couple of roustabouts threw snowballs, wrestling in the drifts. But then Tarbusch blew his whistle and we dug without ttalking. We cut steps to toss snow over walls of it higher than our heads. Jenkins's mule teams followed, dragging plows. We rested leaning on our shovels, arms and backs lit with pain. Burrs of snow stuck to my skirts. At noon we drank tea at the warming station by Hairpin Point. Mrs. Quirk had a fire going there, roasting potatoes.

"Free spuds!" Tarbusch said, as if offering a luxury. We ate them, ravenous, muscles burning, holding red hands over the flames.

After six hours, we heard the mill crews digging toward us from town, and then, around a bend, we met the whole population of Moonstone working shovels. The mill hands. The barber and the doctor. The new schoolteacher. And there, rowing toward me with her shovel, was K. T. Redmond, winded and chapped. "Pelletier! Why in hell don't you move to town for the duration?"

Hope sprouted. But before I could jump at the offer, Colonel Bowles climbed up a snowbank for a speech. "What a fine town!" he cried. "Here in Moonstone we all pitch in to get the job done. Nineteen-oh-eight promises to be the best year on record for the Company. Every darn one of you boys is a hero. Why, even some of you gals made your little effort too."

My little effort boiled in my sore bones. I resolved to mail that letter to Lonahan, first chance available.

"Thanks to all you stalwart volunteers—"

"We ain't volunteers," Kerrigan said. "We don't want none a your thanks."

"We want a paycheck," my father shouted. "Ten weeks and counting."

The Colonel pointed to distract them. "Look, fellas! Thar she blows. The first block on the way. The first block of 1908."

A loaded flatcar inched down the clear track. The color of the cargo matched the snowbanks. The driver tooted the whistle. Oskar Setkowski stood up on the stone, holding its chains like a trick rider, flourishing his hat.

"Hip-hip!" said Bowles.

"Hooray," said the exhausted men, not cheering.

"Bastard sonuvabitch," muttered my father. He stepped toward Colonel Bowles. Steam came off his blue-black beard in wisps of danger. "Crews were on the clock twelve hours, Mr. Bowles. Mark each man, two dollars for the day."

The Colonel stared as if amused. Miss Redmond watched. Men crowded closer.

"We dug you out this time. We won't do it again." My father wheeled around and beckoned us to follow.

K.T. caught my sleeve. "Stay in town, Sylvie, why not?" Then, with a lift of her eyebrows, she said, "By the way, I have a letter for you." She smiled wickedly.

The train whistle sounded, my father beckoning. "Sylvie! Now!"

"Thank you, K.T.," I said. "I'll—come for it tomorrow, now the track's clear—" I ran for the trolley and climbed the hill with the load of exhausted Quarrytowners. The news of a letter plagued me.

"Papa?" I said. "I'm asked to stay in town to work for the newspaper."

"She pays you?"

I nodded. "Did you write to the union man to invite him? Lonahan?"

"Months ago," he whispered under the clacketing noise of the tram. "But maybe the invitation went missing?" He jutted his head toward Mr. Tarbusch, riding behind us in the cab. "Don't worry, Birdy. We'll win this time. I'll take care of it." He pulled me against his solid bulk, under the warmth of his chin. "*Eh, Oiseau*, you're a good girl."

The next morning I heard my dear papa crack the ice on the bowl, his creaks and groans of stiffness. My own back was rusted with pain. Nipper coughed. Maman whispered in the lean-to. Across the raised platform where we slept, Henry snored softly, his head covered by the blanket. My breath rose in cold smoke toward a frosted spiderweb in the corner like the weaving of fairies. Shards of sunlight lit the spokes, and I remembered: *A letter for you.*

Below, Maman was arguing, "It's a danger."

"It's a newspaper," said my father. "Paid work."

Maman could not argue with money. My father put on his layers and went up to the boardinghouse to parlay with the men. I did not say thank you or tell him *au revoir*. God forgive me, I didn't. I sat up fast out of the warm nest of my bed into a torture of cold and climbed over Henry, the heat leaving me, teeth rattling. Down the ladder, the fire was embers. At the coal bin, I scraped the last lumps. Nipper came shivering toward the stove. "Slivvie," he said, reaching up. I held him and wiped his nose and got layers on him.

"So you leave?" Maman said, martyred in her thin brave smile. She'd have to do the washing and cooking, all the hauling and mending, without me now.

"Two dollars a week," I said, but faltered at the sight of her twisted face, gnawed by anger, and saw we were not so different, that she chewed and swallowed her complaints. Up the ladder, I packed my rucksack, and followed Henry into the blinding day. We skiied down the clear track and stopped to look across the knobby backbone of the Gilded Range. Tendrils of smoke rose from the buried burrows in the village, dissolved in the blue sky. Elkhorne's chimneys were cold.

"It's about time," K.T. said. "Thought you turned to icicles up there."

"So you missed me?" I grinned at her.

"Don't give yourself airs."

I hung my coat on its peg. *You mentioned a letter?* I'd say. But before I could get the query out, she put me to work rolling newspapers, the front page outward.

MILL COSTS EXCEED $1.5 MILLION
COMPANY HARD-PRESSED FOR CASH

The Padgett Company is on record for the year
1907 as having paid $1.5 million to build the new
mill, while employee checks are held.

"So why is there no money for payroll?" I asked K.T.

"Child," she said, "that company never missed a dividend of profit, 'cause they never paid a living wage."

"My father said the men will strike this summer," I said.

"What're they waiting for?" said K.T. "Hearts and flowers from a Padgett?"

Precisely what I'd waited for all winter. Did I really imagine that some letter would contain that fantasy? *Imbécile Sylvie.* To prove to myself I wasn't some romance-addled birdbrain, but still an agitator, I tore my invitation to George Lonahan out of my diary and found his address in the *Record*'s subscription ledger, c/o United Mine Workers in Denver. I rolled the letter inside a newspaper and stuck the label down. Let Mr. Lonahan come to Moonstone and fix things. Maybe then the dividends would accrue to others, not just Padgetts. To my father. Me. Off to Paris.

"I'll head to the post office now," I said. "Anything else?" Hoping.

"Almost forgot," K.T. said. "Came last week." She dug through a stack of papers and held out a long envelope addressed to *Sylvie Pelletier, c/o the Moonstone City Record.* I took it outside and opened it, shaking in the clear cold.

December 20, 1907

Dear Miss Pelletier,

I have written two jolly letters to you, care of the general P.O. in Moonstone. Did you get them? I have not heard one word from your pen. Perhaps you are too angry with me, or prefer some local man with a tolerance for snow and ice, unlike those of us who prefer bourbon and rye. The Cambridge crowd don't much care for Southern boys like yours truly, so I write from this boozery where the good man at the bar pours a generous glass of the amber to assist me in my dipsomania. I should be hitting the books, but instead nurse my sorrows, thinking how swell it would be to discuss this detective yarn *Hound of the Baskervilles* with you. It concerns a family curse, and it reminds me to ask, do you know about the Indian hex on the Diamond River Valley? I'd like to know what you think of such things, or anything at all, so tonight I write

209

you again, hoping this will reach you at the newspaper. I had to swallow several medicinal doses to screw up my nerve. Here goes nothing.

I'm aware I was less than a gentleman last I saw you. I offer my apology if you'll accept it. That gala evening marked the beginning of my troubles. When I woke the next day I took my headache over to the depot where I found Caleb Grady with his parents. Easter confessed the family was headed to Weld County to start up some Negro utopia. They would not be returning. I tried to talk her out of it but their minds were fixed.

In my distress at this news, I was seized with recklessness and decided to help the Gradys set up in the new town of Dearfield. I'll go with you, I told Easter.

She did not take to that idea. It's a town just for us, she said. Her look was so firm it prompted an impulse in me to step in front of the train to stop her. Instead, I wrote a check to her and Grady in the sum of five hundred dollars, which was nearly all my allowance for the remainder of 1907. It seemed a paltry gesture. Caleb wrote me later to say that the money bought the Gradys a pile of lumber and a grubstake in their new town.

I don't tell you this to make myself out a benefactor. And I'm not a lunatic, as my father fears. He believes I am overly influenced by the writings of this Professor Du Bois. Perhaps so. But if I'm honest, I will say that I meant to spite my father. Thanks to interventions of my stepmother, he's allowed me to finish school here in the "wrong-headed North" as he calls it. The fees were already paid, so he put me on a train that same afternoon and I had no time to find you and explain. He's now in Paris with my stepmother. Thus I drink my lonely bourbon and think of Sylvie and summer along the Diamond River. Dare I hope to see you there again in June when the meadows bloom and the wind sighs in the aspen trees?

I think you are cross with me. Why else did you not answer my
letters? If you'd only write. What about it, Sylvie? Drop me a note,
and if you are mad, say so. A Merry Christmas.

Yours as ever,

Jace

The letter was three pages. But following those was a fourth. A wet glass
had left a ring of blue ink, so the sentences had run and dried in streaks. A
bleeding blue X crossed the page so it appeared sent in error. The blur of sentences
made me dizzy, but I deciphered even the bluest of profane words. Out of
decorum and for privacy, I will not write what they said, what he did in his
bourbon dreams of me, would wish of me, were I there with him in his dark
room.

Chapter Nineteen

ANYONE PASSING ME OUTSIDE THE *Record* office would see clear through my coat to the bones, lit from within by unholy flames. High above, the Lord God and my mother surely saw and condemned me for the carnal thoughts that seized me on the sidewalk, my knees turned to sponge. I could hardly trek through the town for the wanton images the letter provoked. He was banished and had written from a saloon—he claimed he had—other letters that hadn't arrived, but when I inquired at the post office, there was nothing for me. Not a postcard. So what about those *two jolly letters*? In the moment, it was enough to grapple with this one. I'd spent the winter believing him a bum, but now, if he wished to discuss novels or—my legs were weak. He would return in June and I'd leap into his arms. Would I? Ten minutes ago the Padgetts were the enemy, but now I would defect again just to kiss by the river.

I put all the newspapers in the mail sack and sent them off, forgetting that one of them contained the letter to George Lonahan rolled in its pages. The afternoon passed distracted. At the Mercantile, I got a sack of coal and supplies to send to the Pelletiers of Quarrytown, penance for my desertion. Cough syrup for Nipper. Cans of peas and peaches. A pound of bacon. When

I paid with my summer silver, Koble looked askance. "Where'd you get this?" he said, like an accusation.

From my fairy godmother. I smiled politely and put the box of provisions on my sled with a note to Maman: "I am advanced two weeks' pay." Henry took the box when I met him by the mill. "Bacon!" he said, as happy about it as he was cross over the homework in his rucksack. "Eva Setkowski and me are tied for the most absences of anyone in the school," he said. "Thirty-eight days each."

I watched him hitch a ride uphill on his skis, holding a rope tied on the back of the tram. He fell once, but Potts stopped and waited for him. That day my brother invented the world's first ski tow. He is known for it still, in parts of Colorado, the Pelletier Tow. It did not get much use that February: The track was soon closed again by blizzards.

Miss Redmond stomped up and down stairs, fetching blankets to furnish the supply closet that was my narrow room. She poured herself a glass of whiskey and settled by the stove, in an uproar about the town elections. "Candidates handpicked by the Company! Every one of them, from mayor to sheriff, is a Company stooge."

I prayed for her to leave me to the letter burning in my pocket. I yawned theatrically in case she would take the cue. But instead she read from the columns of her hated rival, the *Booster*, cursing Colonel Bowles and his editor, "Goodyboy" Goodell. "Listen to this! The *Booster* boosting the Company slate."

> The people of Moonstone, given a chance to
> express themselves at the polls, will not hesitate
> to put their stamp of approval on the ticket that
> bears the endorsement of the Padgett Company.

"What the hell else can they do?" she cried. "Might as well get folks to vote at the point of a gun." At last she went to bed in disgust.

In my closet I removed Jasper's letter from my skirts to read and reread the sodden blue last page. His question, was I angry? Yes I was. No I wasn't. *Drop me a note. Yours as ever.* I set out to write to him, risking sentiments and confessions of my own. I crumpled six pages. One was a prayer; one said *love*. One of my attempts was proper and formal, a bid to save my pride. I burned these and wrote lighthearted about the weather, then ruined the effort by saying *dream in the night,* by saying *lonely,* by writing down *this longing.*

My heart, I wrote, and burned it.

There was no safety in writing anything. Even weather was not safe, but was it safety I wanted? *If you are hungry enough.* Here was my chance at some sort of a declaration. Writing in the dim light, I took it.

February 4, 1908

Dear Jace,

I was happy to get your letter of December 20. I did not receive the other two you mentioned. I'd have written back if I had. Firstly, I accept your apology and confess that your disappearance hurt me. I was ready to forget about you, but now, reading your letter, I am upside down again. The other behavior that you mention (on the last page) needs no apology because for myself I am not sorry. If that is too bold, I will risk it, as you risked writing what you wrote. Perhaps you did not mean to post that part. But I don't take offense.

I will try to find a copy of the Baskervilles novel you mentioned. Is it about a dog? Another thing: While I don't claim to understand the ideas of your professors, I believe that your generosity to the Gradys was very kind.

Lastly, you asked if I were mad, to say so. Very well, I'm not angry. Not anymore. I hope you'll write to me again, so I'll know you are sincere.

Your friend,
Sylvie Pelletier

In the morning K.T. came downstairs, her eyes small and puffed with sleep. That I had made the coffee seemed to touch heartstrings I did not know she had. She put a quiet hand on my shoulder. "Thank you for the morning fuel."

"Thank you for the lodging."

"Sorry the slop closet doesn't match your Padgett Palace accommodations. Let me know what else you need."

"I don't like to ask."

"Ask, for cripes' sake."

"Can you spare a stamp?"

She pounced. "A stamp! I see your correspondent resides in Cambridge, Massachusetts. A sweetheart? Susie Society wants to know."

"Susie Snoop! Is there no question you won't ask?"

"No," she said, thinking about it. "Questions are a religion for me."

"Many would consider it a sin to say that about religion."

"Who cares about that sort of sin? Not everyone is cut out to be a saint like you."

"If you only knew."

"If only you'd tell. Here's your stamp."

I mailed the letter to Jace, then went around preoccupied with the return mail. Too late, I looked up the word *dipsomania* in the dictionary: *the irrestible, insatiable craving for intoxicants*, which definition convinced me that Jace's correspondence was the result of alcoholic fever. My own sentences haunted me. *A saint like you*, K.T. had said, while I pondered her notions of sin and sainthood. Apostasy or lust? Which was worse?

As events unfolded that winter, I got new ideas about what was sin and what wasn't.

TROLLEY LINE BLOCKED

February 15. For three weeks, the quarry has been shut off from the outside world, so far as getting supplies up to the place. A number of

men made their way down from the boardinghouse yesterday on foot or snowshoe but have
refused to go back, and are awaiting a train to
take them away. It is reported only 25 remain in
Quarrytown.

"Somebody up there's gonna die," K.T. said.

Did she forget that four of the twenty-five were my family? I used the
town party line to call the boardinghouse weekly and was assured all were safe.

"Your papa says to tell you don't worry," Mrs. Quirk told me, wheezing.

Living those weeks in the storage room, I was grateful not to be stuck
in Cabin Six, despite the guilt that gripped me. I'd left my Pelletiers to
freeze while I had the luxury of a private cubby, the expanse of town, where
the streets were plowed by mule teams. K. T. Redmond loaned me a Kodak
camera, and Hal Brinckerhoff gave us a closet at the Larkspur Hotel for a
darkroom. I was entrusted to handle printing jobs and collect subscription fees, becoming a regular wizard of assistance, learning the tricks of the
trade.

Learning anything about Katrina T. Redmond herself was another matter.
I'd only once been invited up the stairs to her quarters to envy her cozy room,
her armchair and shelves of books. How had she acquired such a place of her
own? At night among the reams of paper and boxes of ink, I fell asleep to the
sound of her footfalls above. Her shotgun sneezes, six or seven in a row. I heard
her sing sometimes. I heard a bottle drop and roll, a glass shatter.

She liked her whiskey neat and her dinners at the Larkspur. Her cooking
repertoire was a can of beans heated on the office stove, a potato baked in the
coals. She insisted on sharing her supplies with me, her pots of jam and tins
of corned beef. She had several correspondents: Mr. Harold Crump, Esq., in
Denver, Colorado. Her lawyer? And who was Miss Jenny Thomas, c/o Mrs.
Daisy Redmond Thomas, Denver, CO? Was this the niece? I took her letters
to the P.O. and didn't snoop.

What I imagined: her wild adventurous youth.

What I heard: gossip from the bakery, where rumors about my employer rose in the air with the motes of flour, baked into the bread that Dottie Weeks fed the populace of Moonstone. *Trina was jilted, you know, poor thing, left at the altar*, apparently the worst fate that could befall a woman. The half-true and the untrue were repeated, embellished, then hardened to fact. The "fact" that K. T. Redmond hated children. The "fact" that one of her legs was shorter than the other. "She limps," said Bull Baxter in the bakery one day. "She wears a lift in her shoe."

"Not true!" Dottie Weeks confronted him. "It's lumbago, from a girlhood riding accident."

"Riding her broomstick, no doubt," Baxter said, and went outside, laughing. "Redmond the witch. Redwitch."

To me she was kind, though there was a gruffness about her, like a shield of sandpaper. She scoffed at my ignorance and tried to correct it. "Here's instead of a decent salary," she might say, handing over the latest from the Book of the Month Club: *The Pit* by Frank Norris, or *The Last of the Mohicans* by James Fenimore Cooper. "Here's to keep you company on a cold night," said a note on my desk with Helen Keller's *The Story of My Life*. At the rate of a book every few days, I read everything she gave me.

"Go to college, why don't you?" she said, and might as well have suggested the moon. Instead, I studied her. How she scuffed her feet in slippers, gnawing the nail of her thumb, lost in her thoughts. She was a pure American. Her people were from Pennsylvania, and "before that, who knows?" The riddle for me was how to be American like her, but not a knocker, not a snoop, not an Abercrombie, not a *socialiste*, not a Frenchy, not a witch. Not a nincompoop. Not jilted.

One cold morning she came downstairs and dropped a book on the table. "Here's this. A lovely novel about horrors in the Belgian Congo, country of the Padgetts' pet King."

"I don't care for horrors," I told her.

"Read it anyway."

"Yes, boss," I said.

The book was *Heart of Darkness*. Perhaps the author, Joseph Conrad, would offer some clue about Jasper C. Padgett, who had resumed his faraway silence. The absence of a reply from him after I'd accepted his apology and sent him my own confessions was a purgatory. Was he in the grip of dipsomania? The arms of another? If *Heart of Darkness* would provide some insight, I would read it. I got lost in the tale of torrid jungle terrain more hostile than our own icy mountains. But the book was no use in solving the mysteries of the heart. It made me shudder, the story of men enslaved, iron collars around their necks, chained, worked to death, whipped.

"I thought you said King Leopold was in this book," I told K.T. "But he's not."

"Old Leopold himself never went to the Congo," she said. "He merely sent his executioners to the jungle to seize it for his kingdom. To loot and mutilate. Just like the book. Just as today the moneycrats send their flunkies to do their dirty work. These are the inspirations and friends of your sweetheart's family."

"They aren't," I said. "And he's not."

She smiled a knowing smile. "Oh, right, he's not."

My thoughts stammered and balked. Winter stayed. The snow fell. George Lonahan did not arrive with the cavalry. Jasper did not write again. I appeared to be doubly jilted, the worst that could happen. Or so I believed for a few weeks more that winter, until the twelfth of March 1908.

Chapter Twenty

THE SIREN SOUNDED. THE WAIL of it came under the door at the post office, where I waited for the mail sack. Everybody froze, alert as elk at the crack of a stick.

A long blast, then a short, then a long. The call for all hands. The sound sucked the air out of our lungs and filled each of us with a terrible prayer: Please let it not be mine. Not my son. Not my father, husband, sweetheart, brother.

I ran down the icy street to the newspaper office, where K.T. was on the telephone, alarm in her eyes. She hung the earpiece on the hook. "You'll have to go up to the quarry. Find out what the devil is going on." Her expression was grim. "There's been an accident. Nobody will say what happened. Men are hurt. Company's orders are not to talk to me. Go find out."

"The road's not clear."

"You're hardy as a bighorn."

"Don't flatter me," I said. "Cornice on Mill Ridge is set to break. It's a bad risk."

The phone line buzzed. K.T. picked up and listened, wrote on her notepad, and then dropped her pen. Her face drained of color, and she pressed two fingers to her eyes, stroking down the point of her nose. When she put the phone down, she came over to me by the composing table.

"Sylvie." She put her hands on my shoulders, big red hands with freckled knuckles and short bitten nails. Her kind face in front. "I'm afraid . . . your papa."

"No no no," I cried, looked around the room as if something in it could save me.

"There was an explosion. Injuries," she said. "The names—these are the ones the gal thought she heard but she was not sure—Pelletier and Berenotto and Elwars." K.T. offered her flask.

I pushed it away, sprang up as if I could get away from the news, breathing in gulps. I took my rucksack off the hook. "I'm going up."

"Are you sure?" she asked. But she handed me a notebook, a pen. She took cans of potted ham from her private store and put them in my pack. "For your mother."

Dread wound around my neck with the scarf. Outside, the siren wailed. I strapped on *raquettes* and went along in light snow toward the quarry road. By the bridge, a party of men assembled. They carried shovels, long choppers, broad-bladed scoops. Some had webs, strapping them on, and tried to wave me off. "Hey! Hey, girl!"

But I was fast on snowshoes and went right past.

The quarry road was unbroken white. Dread propelled me. Left foot. Right foot. Uphill ten minutes, twenty, poling along, winded. The only sound was my own hard breathing, the thump of webs on snow. The word *explosion* in my thoughts. *Your father.* I blinked against the wind, wiped ice from my eyes. On I went. Forty minutes. Fifty. A mile. A step. Another step. The sky was lowering fast, and a hard snow began, flakes driving sideways. The rescue party was behind me still. Perhaps there was no alarm after all. It was a mistake. The all-clear was sounding now, surely. The wind had drowned it. All clear. We'd laugh about how I rushed off, risking the dangerous path. Walking and praying. My father. *Notre Père qui est au ciel.*

On icy steeps I stepped sideways to leverage along with the pole, handholds of branch, knobs of exposed rock. Move. Step. Again. Climb. Slip. And then: crack.

My heart jackknifed. The sound was not thunder. It was a slide coming fast for me. A whole ridge loosed, but where? The rush built and roared. I braced for it, fifty tons of snow in sixty seconds, wreckage a quarter mile wide. *Imbecile Sylvie.* I would be swept away.

But the noise died, and in the open quiet was only the sound of my breath shaking. *Go back.* I went on. *Mon père.* At Scab Rock, through the white swirling murk, I saw it: the slide across the trail. Trees lying down like slaughtered soldiers, boulders tossed light as hay bales. There was no way forward but over the wreckage. Folly to try. Each footfall triggered a small avalanche, clumps of snow, tumbling over the crag. I did not look except at my feet, the webs placed just so, stepping over a tree trunk, around a boulder. Wind solid as waves pushed against me. I swam in it, made it across the slide path, talking to myself as my father would. *Enwoyé-toi, Oiseau.* Breath froze and clotted the wool across my face, ankle tendons pulled raw by the straps.

Three hours on, I came to the smell of coal fire, the fork of the branch road to Quarrytown. Along the snow-walled lanes, I passed Cabin One. Cabin Two. Cabin Six. *Dear God.* Around the entry to our place, a trampled track led toward the quarry. A mash of too many bootprints by our door. I fell up the step, still strapped in *raquettes*, and banged on the wood. *Maman.* The wind ripped her name out of my throat and flung it away. I called again.

Henry on the other side said, "Leave us alone."

"*C'est moi enfin*," I said. "Your sister."

I fell inside toward a pucker of heat in the center of the room. They did not speak. They did not fall on me with blankets. They were old mummified people, even the baby. When I looked at him, Nipper's gaze was blank. *That's odd*, I thought. *That's bad.*

"*Papa est mort*," Nipper said. "He's dead."

PART FOUR

The Art of
Troublemaking

I began to see that the only friend on earth was money,

and not only a friend, but power.

—Ellen Jack,
The Fate of a Fairy, 1910

Chapter Twenty-One

WHILE WE WAITED TRAPPED IN Quarrytown, the remains of my father lay wrapped in canvas inside the guts of the mountain. The wind's keening matched the sounds we muffled in the dark. For two long days no one came to us. The storm had grown too fierce. We stayed lost in a small room. Maman's face was drained of life, as if she too had died. She lifted her hands, ready for a task, but there was nothing to be done. Henry kicked the floorboards. Punched the doorjamb. Grief had come into the house to suck the sap from us, as little as we had. Nipper did not understand and tried to cheer us with his usual chatter. When we gave him our watery smiles, he grew serious. *Papa est mort*, he said, shaking his curly head.

All we knew: An explosion had killed him. Dan Kerrrigan came at last to tell us. "The compressor was rusty. Jocko refused to start it. But Tarbusch ordered him."

"Why?" Henry cried. "Why'd Dad do it? He could've—"

"No choice," Kerrigan said. "Boss told him, 'You don't start it, you're fired.' Your dad says, 'No. It's rusted.' Boss stands at a sweet safe distance and handed Jocko the match, says, 'Do it, you sonuvabitch. Fire it or you're fired.'" Here Kerrigan faltered. "And so Pelletier just . . . said a wee prayer . . . and—lit the pilot."

Henry sat opening and closing the blade of his pocketknife.

"The compressor blew," Kerrigan said. "Boss didn't want to wait three weeks for a new canister. He's nothing but a bloody savage. Won't say it weren't deliberate. To shut a man up."

When Kerrigan left, Henry threw his knife across the cabin; the blade stuck in the doorframe as if Mr. Tarbusch stood there himself. My mother put her hands over her face and prayed to accept that neither her fear nor prayer itself had saved her husband. Seeing her face covered so long, Nipper climbed on her lap to pry her hands away from her eyes, to see—was she still there? *Maman*, he howled, a shriek that pierced us, but she would not show her face even as we came around her, Henry with his furious eyes leaking and me with them all in my arms, four of us now, not five, the ache in our chests hardening like mortar.

The third day Christe Boleson managed to ski to town for supplies. He returned with a canned ham and condolence messages from the Company (*Your distressing loss. Our valuable employee*). Dottie Weeks sent a funeral cake. K.T. sent a sympathy card, a box of chocolates, and a copy of the newspaper. *Read this when you are ready*, said her note. *It is not for the faint of heart. Or don't read it at all*, she should have said. To this day I wish she'd never sent that paper. What she wrote will haunt me as long as I live.

FATALITY AT THE QUARRY

Mr. Jacques Pelletier, a machine operator employed for nearly three years at the Padgett quarry, was instantly killed there Thursday morning. He was making some repairs to one of the compressor tanks for a channeling machine when the tank blew out. Pelletier was in the path of the explosion and his body was hurled with tremendous force against the quarry wall, with the result that he was literally blown apart. According to witnesses, pieces of his skull, arms, and hands were scattered. Mr. Brian El- wars and Mr. Sal Berenotto were also injured in the blast, by flying metal, but are expected to recover.

Colonel Bowles has promised an inquest. The *Record* hereby advises that the inquiry be con- ducted by an impartial outside party.

Mr. Pelletier, age 39, called "Jocko" by his many friends, was a beloved and skilled worker, a family man. He came to Moonstone in 1905 from Vermont, where he was employed at the Rutland Fine Marble Works. He leaves a wife and three children. (His daughter, Miss Sylvie Pelletier, is a valued employee of this newspaper and is known as a cheerful friend to the village.) Our deepest condolences go out to the family. Funeral arrangements are pending.

I managed to keep this article away from my mother, banished to the bottom of my trunk, where it has remained all these years. But the scene it painted is conjured in my mind whenever I think of my poor lost papa. To this day I am furious about what happened to him. A crime. An outrage.

"An accident," Mr. Tarbusch claimed. When the snow slacked on the fourth day, the timekeeper visited from his cozy lodge "to pay respects." He had a raccoon coat and a scarf over his mouth like the bandit he was. He sat himself at the rickety table across from my mother and took up her hand in his rodent paw. She removed it as if she'd been bitten, and still he went on blaming the dead, unable to look the living in the eye.

"Mr. Pelletier, misfortunately, didn't start the channeling machine prop- erly. A terrible tragedy. 'Course we all know the work is dangerous. Your hus- band knew that, Mrs. Pelletier, when he signed up. Poor old Frenchy did not check the valve."

"My father always checks," Henry said, twitching. "He's a class-one ma- chinist."

"There will be an inquest," I said.

"The Company extends condolences." Tarbusch smiled his undertaker smile.

"Bring him to us, please," said Maman, regal in her steel and dignity.

"Not possible, Mrs. Pelletier." He lied again, about the reason we weren't to see our dead father. I was the only one who knew the truth from the newspaper, the condition of his corpse, that he was blown to smithereens. "We can't get the body up from the accident site," Tarbusch said, and blamed the weather. "The ice is bad. A danger to carry him up. For the safety of the men, we wait."

You did not think of the safety of the men when you told my father to light that match. I feared my violent thoughts, their murderous fury. I would leap at his throat to strangle him. Henry sat in the corner and mashed his fist into his palm as if to pulverize it.

"We would like a priest," said my mother.

Tarbusch patted her arm again and set a paper bag on the table. "The Company would like you and your family to have these."

Six withered apples inside, the last of Quarrytown's rations. When he was gone, Maman swept the bag violently to the floor, where the apples rolled in the grit. "*Cochon salaud,*" she said. Pig.

That was all she revealed of her fury. A single flash.

The good women of Quarrytown picked along the troughs of snow, Mrs. Irina Tchachenko, Frau Anna Bruner, Mrs. Quirk laboring down from the boardinghouse. They brought us what they could not spare, but still they gave it: Potatoes. Lumps of coal in a sack. Dry crackers. Cans of sardines. The women sat, shaking their heads, offering solace and religion.

"He is in a better place."

"Death is not the end. Death does not separate us from our loved ones forever."

It is. It does. I listened as they spouted *conneries,* propaganda, *finesses.* Mrs.

Setkowski sat in her greasy coats and held my mother's hand. In grief Maman forgot her fear of foreigners and prayed with them in their different languages but with the same rhythms and rosaries, eyes raised to the crucifix on the cabin wall.

Three weeks passed. Trapped there. His shoes still by the door. His tobacco. Shaving razor. Fiddle. The bits of leather piled beside the chair where he restrung *raquettes*. Evidence of absence. He would any minute walk in, *Halloo!* hang his hat on a peg. The snow fell. The track remained impassable.

At the boardinghouse, Mrs. Quirk took a message by telephone from K. T. Redmond: *Thinking of you, dear Sylvie, and your family.* Maman prayed with her eyes raised toward the ceiling, where creosote fumes had darkened the wood and the tears of heaven had formed icicles in the rafters. *Je crois en Dieu.* When I prayed, I said, *I believe*, but when my father died, faith was hollowed out of me. In its place was the weight of *tristesse* and this anger, sharpening grief into metal.

After three weeks the Company sent a crew into the quarry, and the men lowered a sling to raise my father out of the white stone cathedral. We brought him down the mountain, wrapped in a canvas shroud. For the last time we followed Jacques Pelletier. His remains went ahead of us on a sled, ushered by Christe Boleson and Henry on skis, holding guy ropes. We followed in our strange funeral procession under a blue Colorado sky. This event was reported in the *Moonstone Booster*. Editor Frank Goodell himself wrote it up as if the rescue of a corpse were a job well done.

A FUNERAL PROCESSION

Last Friday morning, a group of men appeared on the high line above Moonstone, sharply sil-houetted against the snow and moving slowly along the trolley line. Word spread through the town: They are bringing down the body of Jacques Pelletier. The men were from the quarry. They had been shut in there by the storms for weeks with the remains of their companion, a machinist killed in an accident. Provisions were running short, and they knew, too, that it was urgent that their friend should be given a proper funeral. The entire force at Quarrytown went ahead to break trail. It was a sight to be remembered—those men coming single file down the mountain, the body wrapped and lashed to a pair of skis, followed by the family. At the end of the trolley line, the deceased was loaded into a wagon and removed to a manager's empty cottage adjacent to the *Booster* office, where the family was lodged at Company expense. At the request of the widow, a funeral Mass was conducted by the Monsignor DeVivo of St. Mary's Church, who came here over the pass. The widow and children are expected to return to relatives in the East.

This article was the first we heard that we were to return east. It was news to us and a warning. We were no longer useful, thus not welcome.

Chapter Twenty-Two

THEY THREW US OUT THE first week of the thaw, when the April mud was running, birds arrowing through the blue. Three Pinks came to Quarrytown to evict us. These were Company-hired private guards from the Pinkerton Agency, brass stars on their lapels as if they were agents of the actual law, which they were not. In history, Pinks have been the pals of bosses, the coddlers of scabs, bigshot fellas who broke heads, broke strikes, and once hanged a union man off a bridge. It doesn't matter to me that Pink detectives caught Jesse James and the outlaw Butch Cassidy. The list of Pinkerton crimes is long and includes the use of Gatling guns and water cannons to blast picket lines of striking women and workingmen. They were known to spy and double-cross and claim their bloody violence was all for "public safety." That morning the Pinks who came to our door sported double-action revolvers. Agent Harold Smiley had one for each hip.

"Sorry for your grief, ma'am," Smiley said from the steps. He was a swaggering, handsome type, six-two with square shoulders, square jaw, square teeth, and a soul crooked as a dog's hind leg. "Time to pack up. Moving day."

"Move to where?" Maman blocked the door, arms across her chest, facing them brave as a Barbary lion. We had nothing but right on our side. Nowhere to go, no money to travel. Our plan was to stay in Quarrytown. Henry would finish school. I would work at the *Record*, Maman at the boardinghouse laundry.

"We won't leave," I said.

"This is Company property," Smiley said.

"It is our home," my mother told him. Henry and I flanked her. Nipper pushed through our defenses, a thumb plugged in his mouth. "*Bonjour, Monsieur Policier!*"

"Just carrying out orders," he said.

"We've had a death in the family," I said.

"You got a debt in the family too." Smiley rummaged sorrowfully in his vest and handed me—a bill! Itemized charges of $347, for store debts at the Mercantile, back rent on Cabin Six, and $75 outstanding for Jacques Pelletier's original ticket to Moonstone from Rutland three years previous. Also: burial fees.

"The nerve," I said. "To charge us when they killed him."

"With all due respect in your time of sorrow," Smiley said, "it's time to pay up."

"We paid already," Henry said, fierce in the Countess's old fur-collar coat. It flared at the ankle and gave him the air of an outlaw. "We are *owed*. You owe *us*."

"Colonel's orders." Smiley's smile had turned cruel from the poison of his job.

"Our father is due ten weeks of back pay," I said. "Owed." *For his very life*. I'd have us all in debtor's prison before they got one copper penny from us.

"Take it up with the Colonel," Smiley said. "This cabin is reserved for a workingman, so unless sonny boy there is gonna go work in the pit—"

"He is a child," said our mother.

"Not," said Henry, bristling like a man. "I could work, Ma."

"Orders are to load you all into that wagon there." Smiley pointed to Jenkins's team of nags arriving. With a sudden tackle, he picked up our mother like a sack of chicken feathers and threw her over his shoulder while his fellow Pinks snickered and made remarks about her petticoat.

"Put her down!" I cried. Henry roared and my mother flailed, shouting. Nipper hit at Smiley's legs, his fists like gnats. But Maman was carried out and tossed in the wagon, as we were tossed, with our belongings, such scraps as we had, sticks and bits.

"It's the policy, ma'am." Smiley smiled. "Can't be helped."

To this day I hope hell's death traps yawn wide to receive Harold Smiley.

We spent the night on the floor of the train depot without a plan, crackers for our dinner. To cheer the dismal party, I reached in my pocket and surrendered the secret guilty purse of money I'd hoarded for myself.

"Where have you got this?" Maman asked, like a reproach. "*Où là*, so much?"

"*La Comtesse.* She told me to save it for emergency."

"The angel of the camp," Maman said, brightening. "Enough for tickets."

Her plan was for us to return to Rutland. *Ma tante* Thérèse would keep us again. *Le curé* would help our mother find stitching work, find me a husband in the parish. The prospect filled me with dismay, like water in the lungs. But the Devil had plucked twenty-five dollars from the velvet pouch and put it in my pocket, so the money I relinquished was only enough for three tickets, not four. As we waited at the depot with our pile of belongings, I screwed up the courage to tell them: I'd made my own plan.

"You go, Maman. I'll work for the newspaper and send more. As soon as I save enough, I'll follow." But I knew I wouldn't. I'd take my chances in the West.

"Sylvie," she said. "*Ma seule fille.*" Her only daughter.

"I stay for the money," I said, not admitting my other reason: Jace Padgett, some idea that he would return to Moonstone—and then—what? A new wish had taken shape in my mind: to make somebody pay. Jasper. The Company. How I'd extract a tax on them, I had no idea, but the blister of resentment had burst.

———

How cruel was the beauty of the blue sky that April morning, lunatic birds singing in the happy sun as my family prepared to leave. Fresh crews of men were arriving up from Ruby, whistling and ready to work. Women unloaded their foreign bundles, their chickens and kids. *Turn back*, we did not say.

"Only one year ago," Maman said. "A year since we arrive. And now."

Henry loaded boxes into the baggage car. He pushed the flop of hair off his forehead and scuffed his foot in the dirt. "See ya, Syl."

When I put my arms around him, he shrugged away so I would not see his face. I held Nipper and pressed him as he squirmed. "Slivvie come too." He clung to my waist. Henry pried him off me while the boy yelled over the blast of the train whistle.

"*Au revoir, ma fille.*" Maman left me with a fast embrace and dipped her chin to hide her faltering eyes. They climbed up.

"Goodbye." My hand waved high in the air, and when they were gone, it fell down like a bird shot out of the sky.

K.T. helped carry my trunk inside, examining the stickers. "Thessaloniki?"

"We always go to Thessaloniki in the high season," I said bravely.

She laughed but did not razz me as usual, only gave me a lantern for my closet, a blanket for my cot. She fussed about, making tea, with a splash of rum, "to help you sleep." She gave herself two splashes.

When she went upstairs, the first thing I did was betray all her kindness and training by writing a letter to *la Comtesse* Mrs. Jerome Padgett at Belle Glade in Richmond, Virginia, requesting a return to service as her social secretary for the summer months at Elkhorne. My intention was to go back to the castle and get what was owed us. As I sealed my letter, I wished I had photographs to enclose, of my father's grave, my mother's wrecked visage as she boarded the train. I did not write: *Madame, see what they do? Put it in your sociology report.* I'd wave the facts in their faces and insist they make things right, so that my father had not died for nothing.

Two weeks after my plan was stuffed in the mail sack and sent east to Belle Glade, word arrived on a typed page. "Thank you for your inquiry," it said. "Elkhorne Manor has no need of additional staff this summer." Written in neat script below was a note: "Mrs. Padgett has employed me as her social secretary for the coming year and sends best wishes. Sincerely, Hélène DuLac."

Hélène DuLac. I did not yet know she was more than a secretary, but already wished her afflicted with boils and pustules, a slow wasting disease. In the supply closet, I lay in a miserable coil and pictured myself charging into the Company office to make demands. Before I wanted hearts and flowers, but now I wanted a rampage of revenge.

K.T. knocked, pushed in the door to stare at me under the blankets. "Aw, heck. You've had a terrible time, kid. Let me take you to supper."

At the Larkspur Hotel, she ordered us whiskey. "Here's to your pappy." She took a long swallow and I copied her. "You know he stuck his neck out for the boys? Jocko was the one who invited Union George up here to start organizing."

"Union George?" My ears perked.

"Lonahan. Twenty-five years old and already an official in the national headquarters. He could negotiate his way into Buckingham Palace. He knows all the bargaining angles. Jocko brought him in last spring to organize the boys, but the Company kicked him out. But this year? He's back in town. It's going to happen. The men are boiling."

What headquarters, what was boiling? I could hardly pay attention. Barely remembered that letter I'd sent asking George to rescue us. I liked the sound of K.T. talking, but better than that was the medicine taste of the alcohol, the oily swirl in the glass. "Thank you for your kindness, K.T.," I said.

"You might not want to thank me yet. These Padgetts don't like us."

"Comrades. May I join you?"

"Speak of the Devil," said K.T.

"Am I the Devil?" George Lonahan pulled up a chair.

"A charming devil," K.T. said. "You've met the printer's devil?"

"Miss Pelletier!" George looked across the table at me in my cellar of gloom. "I'm here at your request."

"Whose request?" K.T. said. "What're you talking about?"

"Young lady here wrote to me back in the winter. So I grew this disguise"—he pointed to his new mustache—"and resolved to get up here and see what's what. I heard about—" He faltered and cast his kind gaze on me. "I'm sorry about your father. A good man."

My eyes filled. "They claim it was an accident."

"Not an accident!" K.T. cried. "Tell her, George."

Lonahan raked his fingers through his wild crop of hair. He ordered a drink, took a swallow, then explained, "A special commission was convened by the labor department in Denver to investigate. A coroner's inquest."

While he talked, I pressed my fingertips to my eyelids, so dark geometrical shapes swam in patterns.

"The commissioners inspected the compressor. And do you know what they found?" George answered himself: "The metal was *corroded. Rusted.*"

"It was the compressor that blew," said K.T., writing notes. "Right?"

"A hundred PSI of air—forced into rusted metal like that? It's gonna blow. Witnesses say Pelletier told the boss and refused to start the boiler. That bastard foreman Tarbusch threatened him. Made him fire up that machine anyway, and—Boom!" He slapped his hand on the table with a thunderous clap.

I startled as if he'd shot me, hand on my heart.

"Sorry, kid," he said.

K.T.'s pen hovered over her notebook. "So it was purposeful. It was murder."

The word stuck in my throat with a swallow of whiskey. I coughed so violently Lonahan thumped me gently between the shoulder blades. "Easy, now, Sylvie, we shouldn't've troubled you."

"Never mind." I shrugged his hand away. Kindness made it worse, the grief.

My two companions talked over my head, like doctors do to spare patients. Their conversation was about labor troubles: contracts, bargaining chips, demands. Talk went between my ears to swim with the liquor. The waiter brought more whiskey. He brought us chicken dinners, a shellac of gravy over the dumplings, steam coming off. I pushed peas around the plate with that word: *murder.*

"Eat something, Sylvie, dear," K.T. said. She and Lonahan glanced in my direction as if they were sorry to have such a dreary companion.

"Not feeling well." I swayed in my seat.

Lonahan steadied me by the shoulders, the pity in his eyes unbearable. I left the table to wobble outside. George followed. "Steady up, now, kid. There you go, that's right. Left foot, right foot." His voice was calm and safe in the night air as he steered me back to the *Record* and my nook. K.T. brought me tea and made me drink it. She tucked a blanket over me as my mother had done when I was a child. I missed Maman so acutely I turned my face to the wall.

"You'll feel better in the morning."

"How do you know?" I said, drunk. "You don't know."

CORONER'S INQUEST

The County Commissioner has reached a finding of grave negligence in the death of Jacques Pelletier, killed in the quarry. Colonel Bowles, Company President, did not mince words, telling the *Record* just what he thought of the county officials and what he called their sham of an inquiry. In no way intimidated by his bully tactics, the Commissioner fined the Company $200.

It was left to me to roll up that issue of the *Record* for mailing. There, a hundred times, was my father's name, the fine ordered by the court: two hundred dollars for his life. Who got that money? Not us. The inkstains on my hands washed off, but I could not scrub the word *murder* out of my mind.

Chapter Twenty-Three

SPRING CAME TO THE GILDED Mountains. Trills and warbles of birdsong conspired with the frolic of happy woodland creatures to twit me, *Cheerup, cheerup,* while I thought, *Shutup, shutup.* The mountains thawed, and the slopes came alive again with leaves and green unraveling shoots, meadows blooming. The Diamond River spilled melted snow over its banks clear as glass. But it was the mud I noticed. Mourning. Missing my family, *mon père assassiné.* Gripes and grievances that had germinated under the snow all winter sprouted up on the pages of the rivalrous newspapers. Arguments burst forth in rank epithets, fistfights at the mill. Discontent spored in the dank saloon.

Now that the weather was fine, the bosses were determined to get as much stone out of the quarry as possible. Bowles ran twelve-hour shifts around the clock. The men demanded eight hours only and overtime pay. George Lonahan sneaked up to Quarrytown to meet with Dan Kerrigan and left over the back trail before the Pinks could catch him. The *Booster* and the *Record* were dueling over two versions of the argument.

RECORD: Workers at the Padgett Company's
marble operation could vote as early as June on

a proposal to join the United Mine Workers of America.

BOOSTER: Outside agitators! You are not welcome in Moonstone. The men have a right to work as they choose.

RECORD: Our town needs a hospital! Thousands have been taken from the paychecks of our workingmen for such an institution. Where is the money? Where is the hospital?

BOOSTER: Cheer up! Bright Days for Moonstone are ahead. The mill is running at full capacity, and contracts are pouring into the offices from points far and wide. Only the knockers in town are dishing out tommyrot about elections and kicking sand about union demands.

On the delivery route, I left a stack of *Record*s at the saloon, at the laundry, in the lobby of the Larkspur Hotel. The townspeople were friendly to me as they would be to any harmless familiar apparition. *Hello, Sylvie! What's the news? Good morning, dear.* I gave them a brave face but could not escape the pity in their eyes, tongues clucking in my wake, *Poor girl, alone in a mining camp without a mother.* I was the subject of talk and at risk of disgrace.

All over town that spring I looked for my father as if he'd emerge from a blizzard. By the lakeshore where he once skipped stones four-five-six times, ripples circled out like consequences. I saw him among the cattails, a redwinged blackbird perched on a stalk, head tipped, peering at me. "*Allo*, Papa," I said. He puffed his red epaulettes and let out a song, *coke-a-leeee*. A flock rose from the reeds, wheeled like a school of fish, then settled in a tree, the branches alive with birds. My father was nowhere. Gone. I didn't speak of him or of my family far away. I lay lonely in my closet and read a letter from Maman. They'd arrived safely, *grâce à Dieu*. Henry had started school again. Nipper could say his ABCs. "Do you say your prayers?" she wrote, and said nothing about our lost papa. She told her sorrow only to the Holy Father. "Do you ask Him to protect you and forgive your sins?"

I did not. Prayer was useless. "All is well," I wrote, and sent money, half my pay.

In the middle of June, Mr. Koble at the Mercantile refused to take delivery of the *Record*. "Get that bum fodder out of here." He was a Company cog with a stack of *Booster*s out front of the store, with its potshots at Miss Redmond.

BOOSTER:
KNOCKERS BE GONE
The editor at the *Record* news is a Knocker and a Know-nothing. It is hard to believe that the publisher of our printed competition is a female, and openly boasts that her skirts have saved her many a licking. Why any citizen who cares about his future would read that "birdcage liner" defies common sense.

Miss Redmond printed her rejoinders based not on slander but on facts:

RECORD:
SPIES & OUR PUBLIC WELFARE
The local Bell telephone line is under constant surveillance of Company spies who eavesdrop on town talk and spy on our citizens. The switch-board inside the mill plays a part in their secret work. If Ma Bell is to serve the public as guard-edly as Uncle Sam is charged to protect com-munication through the U.S. mail, it will allow a service cut off from the Company.

As for citizens: Where men are subject to un-lawful spying and over-government, the inevi-table tendency is resistance—such resistance as marked by the Boston Tea Party in 1776—such

> resistance as heads of corporations wrongly call "anarchy"—should be made.
>
> UNION VOTE: A vote to join the United Mine Workers is urged for the men as soon as July Fourth. Wouldn't that be cause for patriotic celebration?

Outside the mill gates, I thrust this risky issue of the paper at the workers as they came out of the sheds. The headline blared UNION VOTE. The word *spies* jumped off the page, along with its friend *anarchy*. A few of the fellows waved me off. But others gave me a nickel and took the paper with a thumbs-up and a wink. One fellow said, "Now we're talking."

That made me proud, as if I were doing my part for a cause.

Then, from behind my back, a claw clamped around the paper in my hand. "I'll take that, little lady." It was Smiley, that Pinkerton lackey who'd carried my mother out of our house. "You'll take your leave."

I'll take your mustache out by the roots, I didn't say.

"You can't spread that manure here on Company property."

"Where isn't Company property?" I said. "I'll go stand there."

"You'll be standing on the top of Dogtooth Mountain," he said. "'Cause this town belongs to Padgett Fuel and Stone."

But now it seemed that Moonstone belonged to handsome Harold Smiley. He strutted his pair of six-shooters through the streets. He set up target demonstrations, showing off. He could fire both guns simultaneously and hit two cans off a fence rail. He shot a blue jay through the eyeball. Everybody knew the rumor: that he'd shot a Japanese railroad man from the back of a moving train, as if picking off a crow in a cornfield. "Nobody'll miss a coolie," Smiley was supposed to have said. Instead of filing murder charges, the Moonstone Citizens' Alliance appointed him Sheriff and awarded him a bigger badge made of solid silver. In the pages of the *Record*, Susie Society reported that Smiley was seen at the soda shop with Millie Havilland, the supervisor's daughter, hobnobbing with Bowles and friends, all those Citizens' Alliance types.

Dismaying letters began to arrive at our print shop, one or two per day.

To the Record: Please cancel my subscription.

To the Editor: I no longer wish to read your so-called newspaper. It has anarchist intentions.

To the Record: We now subscribe to the Booster. Two newspapers are too many and so it is with regret I cancel my subscription.

"Cowards!" K.T. cried. "Why won't they stand up? The whole town's afraid of the Padgett Company. These people are sheep in thrall to the false gods of profit."

I was too sunk in the damp root cellar of myself to suggest their fear was well founded. Their thrall. I knew it myself. Hadn't we lost our father to their false gods? And in my thrall, had I not kissed the Prince as well as the hem of the Countess? Not one letter of condolence from a single Padgett. From a particular Padgett. Nothing since his torrid communiqué last winter. I was a stunned grieving girl, and Moonstone was a town afraid. No wonder. Smiley and the Pinkerton Agency had set up an office by the railroad depot where security men watched arrivals to make sure no "agitators" showed up. Members of the Citizens' Alliance, men like Phelps and Baxter, the banker and minister, the managers and architects and local merchants all wore white lapel buttons that proclaimed: *Moonstone Proud.*

No worker sported such a pin. The town was organized same as a system of serfs on the steppes of wherever it was serfs toiled, the underlings and human mules, the middle managers and functionaries of Moonstone falling in line.

I stayed quiet and watched myself move toward summer as if my eyes were outside my head. I cleaned ink off the platens, set type and ran pages, taking in advertisements. I dragged the delivery wagon around Moonstone town in growing alarm. The gossip was troubling.

Bulldagger was the word I heard from an injured man at Doc Butler's clinic. Buck Farrell was there in a truss, one leg suspended from a ceiling pulley, his face cut up. I approached gingerly to introduce myself. "I write 'Infirmary Notes' for the *Record.*"

"That bulldagger who runs it," Farrell said, "orghta run her outta town."

"Our readers would be interested to know, how did you come to be injured?"

"Curl up here with me, petunia, and I'll tell ya." He reached lewd beneath his coverlet and produced a liquor flask.

"Don't speak that way to a lady, please."

"Lady bulldagger." He doffed his flask and drained it. "Us in the Agency gonna run you off like our man Smiley says, 'less you can prove yourself otherwise valuable. C'mon over here, sweetheart."

So he'd revealed himself to be a Pinkerton, not just a lout. Whether his particular slander was true or false I didn't care, except it unsettled me, how we were tarred by it, K.T. and me both. Such rumors were spread about suffragettes and lady gunslingers and women who wore trousers. I'd worn them myself, and why shouldn't we? I shuddered away from Pinkerton Farrell and pictured how the contraption that suspended his leg would hoist him to the ceiling, dangled and gutted like a bull elk killed in the hunt. I wrote nothing about the compound fracture of his leg or how he'd been injured falling off the Quarrytown trolley in a drunken stupor.

A shame he wasn't crushed by the wheels, I did not type.

K.T. agreed I would not have to write any more about accidents. What had happened to my father played too much in my head. I couldn't stop seeing it. A lurid imagination troubled me increasingly.

In the first week of June, on the way to the post, I was thrown into a worse condition by the sight of a *loup-garou*, the flying wolf demon, peering in the window of Moonstone Fine Jewelry.

J. C. Padgett. Jasper. Jace.

On his arm was a stylish young lady, her spring coat a pale lemon color, her hat tied under her chin with a length of yellow gauze.

I turned and fled into the Mercantile. Through the window glass, I saw: Jasper and his elegant friend. Who was she? They laughed. She leaned against him, pointed at an item there in the jeweler's window. They tacked away on the other side of the street, elbows linked. The sight of him with this Lemon Drop flooded me with jealousy, a wish to strangle the stalks of their necks. When they were gone, I retreated to my closet, where grief came in gusts. I stoppered it down, hands pressed to my eyes. Jace Padgett had returned, as I willed him to with my stupid incantations. I should've gone back east to a nunnery. I'd suffer now for my delusions, forced to see him and that Lemon Drop everywhere in town, in my sleep.

"Did you see young Padgett with the Countess's new secretary?" Dottie Weeks was chattering in the bakery with Florrie Phelps. And thus I learned that the Lemon Drop was Hélène DuLac, who had written to say I was replaced. Rejection curdled with the outrage of my father's murder and nurtured my vengeful impulse to prove I was not some scrap shoveled over the hillside in a pile of scree. I feared, however, that's precisely what I was.

The next afternoon, as I turned a corner by the bank, there Jace was again, alone in a summer suit, checking a pocket watch. He looked up, startled. "Sylvie Pelletier! As I live and breathe."

I could do neither. *Run him through the throat with a fountain pen.*

"I thought you had left town," he lied out of his lying mouth. "I didn't know where to find you." He swayed, as if stirred by the breeze. "Didn't you get my letters?"

"One letter arrived in February," I said, wintry, "that you wrote before Christmas. You claimed you sent others, but—"

"You didn't get . . . ?" He scrambled. "The mail here is lousy. I plan to fix that. And *you* never wrote back, you marble-hearted jezebel." His eyes were unfocused, squinting without glasses. He was plainly drunk at noon. "And here I thought you were a well-mannered girl. Turns out you were bent to break a man's heart."

He did not appear heartbroken. I examined him in the hard sunlight, his hair slicked down from a new center part. He was paler, thinner than before, his eyes hollow.

"You said were banished," I said.

He made an actor's face of exaggerated shock. "Did I say that?"

Scourge of a hot poker in your throat.

"And I did write back. I sent a letter to your college—"

"Aha. That's the reason. A change of address. Apologies for any misunderstanding," he said. "I finished my degree in January and went back to Belle Glade. I was ill. But I've now been—rehabilitated. Reinstated. My father has offered a chance at redemption."

"Redemption commonly costs a penance," I said.

"Penance, yep. I'm sentenced to run the Company, under the tutelage of Colonel Bowles. But the exciting part is that my father is allowing me to have free rein."

"So they crowned you," I said. "Free reign for King Jasper."

"Ha-ha, Sylvie the wit. How'd ya make out this winter? Snowy, I betcha."

Bloody, I betcha. Brains on the walls. My lip trembled.

"What is it?" he said, concern on his face. "Sylvie?"

Damn his damn kindness and his familiar touch on my arm.

"My father was killed in the quarry," I said, watery.

"Your father? Frenchy?" The smile died off his face.

"It was in the papers."

He looked away, stammering as the news settled on him. "It's— What a terrible . . . I'm so very sorry. I didn't know. I heard about—a fatality, but had I known . . . I had no idea who . . . I only arrived in town yesterday—" He swayed again, his sincere hand resting on my arm. His sympathy was like food for a starving person, only rotten. "I know how much you loved your father."

A curdled noise escaped me.

"Oh, dear, Sylvie, I— Oh." He massaged the crown of his head, reached in his pocket to remove a silver flask, offering it. "Here's a tonic."

"I don't want your tonic."

"What can I— What do you want?"

To bash your face in. For you to rest me on your shoulders hide me under your lapels feed me a walnut fight me in the river.

I said, "I want you to do one—just one—right thing."

"One right thing?" He sipped his flask, looking utterly accused. "What . . . do you mean, one right thing?"

I let him ponder without answering while he twisted in discomfort.

"When do you go up to Elkhorne this summer?" he asked.

"There's no position for me there."

Jace turned red, seeming to remember the Lemon Drop. "I'll talk to the Colonel," he said. "I'm in charge now. I've got the authority. Leave it to Jace." We walked down the lane uneasy. Twice he seemed about to utter some anguished word. Once it seemed he'd turn on his heel and run to escape my suffocating silence. We arrived at the mill.

"I'm meeting the Colonel now," he said. "I'll find you a position."

I did not want a *position.*

In the loading yard across the way, a white stone block dangled in midair. In my mind's eye, the chain snapped and the load fell to crush the men below.

"You ought to come to Elkhorne," Jace said. "Say goodbye to our friend Inge."

"Goodbye?"

"She's going to Newport for the rest of the summer, then Europe. I don't know why or when. You'll have to ask her yourself. I don't pretend to understand women."

"What do you pretend, then?"

"Tssch. Sylveeee . . ."

My name in his mouth was a reproach, as if he had never murmured it at my neck or confessed his desires in writing, those acts of carnal abandon in his bourbon-soaked letter. "Inge would like to see you." He touched my arm again, with his *coupable* lopsided face of sympathy, and fled inside the offices.

I would roast him in a stone pit and turn the spit myself. Mine were the thoughts of a jealous woman, and I do believe now that jealousy was responsible for the ill-advised decisions I was about to make, along with lust and avarice. All those. And love. Even now I cling to the idea that *amour fou*, curdled as it was, still had me in its grip. I want to believe this. If you do not act out of some form of love, then who are you in the world?

Chapter Twenty-Four

TWO DAYS LATER, SPURRED BY vague and reckless intention, I went up the drive and between the stone pillars guarding Elkhorne Manor. I roared at the lions as I passed them frozen in their stony snarls. I had an idea to present my father's case, to argue for compensation. I wished all Padgetts to grovel in apology but would settle for payment. How to effect satisfactory resolution, I didn't know. Jace had invited me to say goodbye to Inge when what I wanted to say to all of them was *Go to hell*.

Mixed up with my wounded pride was a contradictory idea that I'd somehow reinstate myself in the castle. In the affections of the Prince. Exile from the fantastical *pays de Cockaigne* with its sugar swans was unbearable. Unfair. I was a friend! The favorite of the summer. What had I done to deserve indifference? Perhaps I would at least get some orange juice.

At the kitchen door, Easter answered without her former cheer, a grayness to her skin. Her hair had gone silver and she was too thin, a hollow below her cheekbones.

"Easter? I didn't expect you would be here. I thought—"

"Well, these folks just can't seem to live without me."

"Jasper said you were in Weld County—"

251

"Don't listen to whatever a Padgett say, it's what they do." She went back to the stove. "Me and Grady went out there to Dearfield, sure, and J.C. said he was going to send a supply wagon, and did it arrive? No, it did not. What arrived was snow like the Devil sent it." She held up her left hand to show two fingers missing their tips to the first knuckle. "Frostbit."

"Oh, no, Easter," I said. "How terrible. Let me help you."

She pointed me to a boiling pot full of eggs. "Peel these, please."

"Yes, ma'am." I lifted the scalding pot to the sink.

"How you people live up here in this unnatural cold, I don't know," Easter said, and described how she was caught in a blizzard on the road from Fort Morgan to Dearfield. "This country here is mean as Lucifer's dog."

I drained the pot in a blast of steam and started in cracking and peeling, fifty eggs at least and more boiling on the stove.

"That'll keep you busy till Mrs. Nugent gets back."

"I've come to see Mrs. Padgett," I said, because it wouldn't do to say I had come to smash the statuary.

"Good luck with that." Easter laughed. "Remind me your name again? Gets so you all's alike, all you summer girls. Can't remember one year to the next year."

By *summer girls* she meant *white*, and I saw I was just one in an indistinguishable parade through her kitchen, not special to her, as she'd been to me, teaching me sauces and history. What had I taught her? Nothing.

"Sylvie! Right?" She smiled. "I remember now. From Louisiana with the French name—whatchamacallit? But I do recollect you was a good hand in the kitchen, shucking eggs like that." With a small knife, she cored the stem off a strawberry. "Colorado winter just about shucked all the skin off me here, and I'm still not white enough to vote."

"Women do have the vote since 1893, well, at least in Colorado—my boss at the paper says we will soon get it in all the states, and—"

She rewarded my optimistic know-it-all-ism with one of her stares.

"Anyway, I thought you'd gone home to Richmond?"

"Richmond." She exploded the word. "Nossir. I'm only back in this house because Jasper wrote my son Caleb, begged us here to cook. Promised me good money, now his daddy put him in the boss seat. One more summer, okay? Marcus stays in Dearfield with my husband, building the lunchroom. I call it the Sunshine Café, 'cause we need as much sunshine as we can get." She laughed. "And Caleb's gonna start a college. Yessir. So me and Cal is here now for the money."

"Me too," I said, and didn't mention my other notions, of triumph and revenge. "Jasper is not here?" I asked casually.

"Still asleep. At this hour? I worry about that boy. You tell me how he's gonna be boss when he don't even—you know how he is. I saw you was sweet on him last year. But what can anybody do? He's grown. What I'm saying is, Jasper's good to Easter. I raised him. He got a heart where it should be. But his head is . . . hmmp. Trouble every second day, drinking liquor with Miss Helene."

The Lemon Drop. I rolled an egg along, myself cracked same as the shell.

"He supposed to be running the business," Easter said. "Not running around with such women. Like father, like son." She took the bowl of peeled eggs. "I have to mash these yolks. A hundred devil eggs for one hundred devils."

"What devils?" Her frank talk struck me as new, as if she were somehow unchecked.

"I should bite my tongue," Easter said. "But I won't. It's the Company picnic. Monument Dealers of America or some such. All hundred of 'em up this morning on the railroad. Bunch of grave sellers. These folks care more about the dead than they do about the living, ain't that right?"

"Don't much care about the dead either," I said, bitter. Easter noticed. We had a moment there when she saw me and likewise I saw her, the cracks of red in her eyes. "My father was killed in the quarry," I told her, chin wobbling.

She put down her paring knife and touched my hand with a brush of her blunted fingers. "That is a hard sorrow," she said. "You can't let it eat you, because it will, and don't I know." Her sympathy undid me, and I nearly fell against her, to put my head on her shoulder and weep. "I'm sorry, Easter," I said, "that you know hard sorrow like that."

Just then Mrs. Nugent swung through the door, followed by a rabbity-looking pair of girls in new uniforms. She halted at the sight of me. "Why on earth are you here? We don't need anyone else this summer."

"I came to see Mrs. Padgett," I said. "Only to say hello."

"You're just in time to say goodbye," said Nugent.

I went along the back passages and heard Inge's voice before I got to the Greenery. Outside the door I stopped, queasy at the sight of a butter-haired woman in my chair with a notebook, listening to Inge's lilting French. This would be Hélène. The Lemon Drop. I pictured taking the bottle of ink that sat on the desk—my desk—and pouring it over her head.

"Madame," I said, scarlet with nerves.

"Sylvie! *C'est toi!*" Inge jumped up. She kissed my cheeks, left, right, left, and introduced me to her companion. "Hélène DuLac? *Voilà*, I present you Mademoiselle Sylvie Pelletier. Hélène is my dear *copine* from Brussels."

Hélène looked me over, her eyes the summer blue of lupines. "Lovely to meet you," she said. "*Enchantée.*"

I would enchant her if I could, into a hop toad. Warts on her chin.

Hélène excused herself, tootling her fingers in a wave identical to Inge's.

"Sit, please, Sylvie, *chouchou*, tell me." Inge patted the chaise. "Tell everything. The winter? *La famille?* Your lovers?" She watched me swallow and halt. "Sylvie?"

"My father," I said, and told her.

"Ah, *non*." She covered her mouth in shock. "Oh, poor child." She wrapped me in her lilac arms, murmuring sympathy, so now I did wilt, against her bony shoulder, and forgot to say *Murder, justice, apology*. A strange peace descended between us because of her kindness, and some new sadness clinging to her, not only to me. We sat together, listening to a fly buzz angrily against the windowpane.

"I understand, Sylvie. You see. Bisou also, has died. I cry for him every day." The little dog was crushed by a taxicab on the streets of New York. "How

I wish I could help you. But you can't imagine how terrible it's been for us. The finance collapse. The banks." She waved at the air to fan herself. "My husband, he—maybe *on va divorcer*."

"Madame?"

"I am a scandal. I know you heard it. Everybody hears."

"*Non*, Madame. I came to see about work." It was not what I'd intended to say, but I enjoyed the squirm of discomfort on Inge's face.

"Ah, such a pity, Sylvie. *C'est impossible*. I leave soon for Europe. It's finished. All of it. The King—our friend Leopold—does not put his money down. He does not invest. *Enfin*, the stone company is over for *mon mari*. No more rocks. Duke has only the coal business now. Twenty coal camps to run from New Mexico to Montana."

"But the quarry? The mill?"

"*Pfft*. Marble stone is not for the profit. Only for beauty. It's a toy for the son to play with. His father gives Jasper the operations here, a half share with the Colonel. He wants to make a go of it. The supervisors will show him the cords."

"The ropes."

"Cords, ropes." She shrugged. "The same."

Other restraints still held me back, of law and propriety. I did not rampage through the house or steal valuables as payback. Instead, I listened as Inge tried to guide me along the paths of forgiveness.

"The stone is a hard business," she said. "So we wish good luck to Monsieur Jace. This winter he has become my friend. We passed some months in Virginia while he recovered from his illness—you knew it?"

She saw I did not. Perhaps it was true that he hadn't received my letter at college, because he had left. "He recovers at Belle Glade. *Enfin*, I'm the one who suggests him to own the company. *Jace et moi*—we have the same philosophy. He likes my sociological design ever since—well, let's say that Jasper is more happy now, better, since Hélène—" She saw my face. "Oh, *merde*. I forget how you have the *amour fou* for that boy."

"No," I said, "I never—"

"*Écoutes-moi*: Forget him. That is what I do. I forget, I move along. There are ten million men. I find another. And so will you. This one is *neurotique*. Very angry to himself. To his father. He is extreme in politics. Bizarre. Extreme in the temperament."

"What was wrong with him? What sickness?"

"He loves too much—the whiskey. He drinks, you know. He had the blackouts of memory. Also he is *obsessif*. Too much in his books."

A thread off my sleeve dangled. I pulled it, unraveling.

"Ah, *petite*, don't worry about Hélène. She only plays with him. I warned him, she has other fishes to catch. For her, he's the summer adventure. She never will stay to this town. In August she joins me in Newport. *Bruxelles* for winter. She rests a few weeks here to help settle *mes affaires*. Hélène *et moi*, we are sisters, from the years at *château* Laeken. You see?"

What I saw was the mosaic pattern of the marble floor, the sugar-lump tiles, how the sun fell through the glass, lit up the motes of the air. The blood of severed fingers, exploded men, was nowhere. It was just a fancy floor. I started toward the exits.

"Sylvie. Wait," Inge said. "Another advice for you. Because lately I read your newspaper. And I wish for—to warn you. It's a danger. Do you know?"

"What danger?"

"They do not like that woman. Miss Redwitch."

"Redmond."

"They have a meeting to stop her. Colonel Bowles and my husband. They order Jace to kick her off the town."

"They can't. How would they?"

"I tell him not to do it. But—" She shrugged. "Bowles, he does what he wants. Please, you will be careful."

"Thank you," I said, "for your kindness."

"*C'est tout pour le mieux*," she called after me. "All for the best, you will see."

It was the last time I saw her. During the war, in 1914, I heard she'd gone to the front at Ypres to feed starving Belgian children, the angel of the

camps, and that she was killed in a Flanders field hospital bombed by a battalion of Huns.

"The Company wants you out of town," I told K.T. "Mrs. Padgett said they
had a meeting to discuss it."

"What else is new?" She shrugged.

"Word is the Duke and the Countess are divorcing."

"Really?" She was thirsty for the scandal.

"For all I care, the whole pile of Padgetts can jump in the lake," I said.

"Well, that's a change of tune."

My new tune, of spite and indifference, drowned out the truth: that I'd
mistaken the burn of jealousy for love. The heart wants what it is most denied,
a hard lesson. I could not seem to drop my torch for Jace, wishing half the time
to scorch him with it, but still hoping the Lemon Drop would jilt him, as Inge
said she would. I twisted that old handkerchief with the initials *JCP*, as if those
letters did not spell *l'amour perdu*. Lost love is still love, isn't it.

Within days, K.T. announced her findings: "Our Lady Bountiful is said to
have had an affair with a riding instructor."

I pictured him, Cedric, in his comical jodhpur trousers. "Impossible," I said.

"Or maybe with an English diplomat, or with a stockbroker in New York,
or all three. The Duke has washed his hands of her."

SUSIE SOCIETY REPORTS:
Mrs. Ingeborg LaFollette de-
Chassy Padgett, known locally
as "Lady Bountiful," will not
spend this summer at Elkhorne
Manor. She is reportedly traveling in Europe, but without the
companionship of her husband
or her little poodle dog, whose
antics so delighted townsfolk
last summer as she carried him
on her Samaritan errands. Poor
Bisou has reportedly gone to
pooch heaven. Susie extends
heartfelt condolences on the
loss of a faithful friend.

"You're malicious," I said. "She loved that dog. I'm sorry for her."

"Sorry?" she said. "I worry about you, Pelletier. That you of all people could have sympathy for anybody in that crowd. Think of what I could've written. The bankruptcy rumors. The divorce. The black blood of the son. The financial skulduggery. This column is the picture of restraint. She should thank me."

"Black blood?" I said. "What are you talking about? Also, it wasn't a poodle. It was a schipperke."

"Ohhh." My employer smacked her forehead in mock apology. "A *schipper*-kee. Thanks. I'll run the correction. And you know, that Negro fella—that cook on the *Sunrise*—is his son."

Chapter Twenty-Five

"WHOSE SON?" IT WAS GEORGE Lonahan interrupting. He was holding the office door open for a bird-eyed granny dressed in black, a white lace fichu at her neck. He ushered her in like she was Mrs. Astor. "Ladies, here's somebody I'd like you to meet."

You could put her in a teacup, the woman was that small. A gust would take her, sail her up into the cumulus. Her hair was a white fluff of milkweed silk. You wanted to let it out of its pins, slip it soft in your fingers.

"Here's Mrs. Jones," Lonahan introduced us.

She peered about through little round eyeglasses and inhaled. "I love the smell of ink!" she said, Irish in her voice. "Do you know I once printed a paper? I printed the *Appeal to Reason*, and I've been appealing to it ever since. Do you ladies print the truth? George says you do. Hats off to you. Because it's a hard thing to tell the truth. Nobody wants it. It's a hard thing to wake people up. There is a stupidity about them. We have to get at the papers."

"You got at this one already," said K.T. "Thanks for coming all this way."

"I was already in Colorado, in Trinidad visiting my boys in Mr. Rockefeller's coal mines, so why not?"

"It's a delight to meet you."

"I'd be delighted to rest these feet by your stove a minute. You know I'm eighty-two years old? I've come a thousand miles and had only a crust of bread since Tuesday, but I don't need much. Please don't trouble yourself."

"We have a hot meal for you, Mother," said George.

This ancient was Lonahan's mother? I looked for the resemblance in the rivulets of her face, the merriment in her eyes.

"And there's a bed upstairs for you," he told her, a good son, carrying her bag.

"A bed is luxury, George, love. I've slept on rocks and on the stone floor of prisons, and I'll do so again before I go to my grave. It's worth it for the lads."

"Mother, you are a saint."

"Tell that to the President. He calls me a terror."

K.T. took Mrs. Jones upstairs. George lit a cigarette and perched on a corner of the composing table while I sorted type, glad to see him. "How nice to be traveling with your mother," I said.

"Ha! She's not my mother. That's the great Mother Mary Harris Jones."

"But where's her habit?" I said, confused by the absence of wimple.

"Oh, that is rich. Where's her habit?" Lonahan roared laughing. "She's not a nun. Mrs. Jones's order is the Saints of Toil. Long ago, she lost four children to the Tennessee yellow fever, but now she's called Mother by the laboring classes. The Lioness Mother of a million whelps. She's got 'em wrapped around her pinky and could pluck a mountain out by the roots and set it down somewhere in the tropics, she's that powerful."

She appeared as powerful as a dried-apple doll dressed in corn shucks.

"It's thanks to you she's here," George said. "I showed her your letter and asked her to help rally the men. You're just the one to take her to Quarrytown tomorrow."

"Why'd she want to go up there?"

"A meeting," he said. "We'd be obliged if you'd pass out handbills for us. Redmond said you'd print 'em up and get 'em out." Lonahan took my pen and a scrap of paper, wrote in block letters:

ORGANIZE!
MEETING AT QUARRYTOWN STABLES.
July 14, 1908, 7 p.m.
FEATURING:
MOTHER JONES & THE UNITED MINE WORKERS

Organize. There it was again. My mother's fear. My father's wish. Too late for him. But maybe a union would happen now, with a powerful granny here to wrap everyone around her finger, and George agitating with a cigarette ember smoldering in his grinning mouth. He perched on the table and watched me pick out type from the sorting box. "Your text is backward," he pointed out.

"Ya don't say." I smacked my forehead with the heel of my hand.

"Ha. Just testing you."

I ran the handbills off the press while he fiddled with type at the composing table, whistling. It was comfortable to work alongside him.

"When you're done with those notices," he said, "I've a project of my own for you to print." He showed me his proud row of type. "You're not going to print it?"

Sweet Sylvie lets go next door for ice cream.

"I can read backward." His invitation made me happy.

"Well, then, I'll be forward. How 'bout it? Vanilla or strawberry?"

There was no one to forbid me. At the ice cream parlor, George paid for two cones. We took them strolling and smiling at each other down Marble Street in the dust of the afternoon. I hoped Jasper Padgett would see us and be convulsed with jealousy. I leaned briefly against George in a way that might seem accidental but was not. He was not wrong to think I liked him.

"Tomorrow," George said, "you'll go up to Quarrytown with Mrs. Jones and pass the notices out at the boardinghouse. Put it under the doors of the cabins. Rally the women, like a good comrade."

"I'm a comrade?" I liked the sound of it.

"You're a comrade if you want to be, sweetheart." It was plain that I liked the sound of *sweetheart* too.

"Why wouldn't you join the scurvy likes of myself and the good people of the union camp? Your papa was a fellow traveler." He sang a snatch of a tune under his breath. "'Oh, I had a girl and she was good, one of her legs was made of wood . . .'"

"My father sang that one," I said, stricken to hear it again.

"Who'd you think I learned it from?"

A smile leaked over my face.

"Atta girl!" George said. "Nice to see you brighten up a little. Gives you a certain, je ne say qwa . . . how'd ya like my French, huh? Pretty *bon*, right?"

"*Terrible*," I pronounced in French.

"Terrible! See? I comprennay-voo, exactly! Your father gave me lessons. I can say: *connard*! I can say *sacré cochon*!"

George loped along the street, long-legged in his rumpled coat and sporting his mustache disguise. I had lately turned dour and earnest, but he made me laugh with his attempts at French. "Bon-jurr!" He smiled at Mrs. Phelps. He greeted an old man outside the barbershop, saying, "Miss-shur!" for *Monsieur*, acting as if he'd lived in Moonstone all his life. At the Mercantile, he bought tobacco and saluted Mr. Koble. "Good afternoon, sir!" Under his breath he said, "Bootlicker."

I laughed. "Company cog."

We strolled through town, laughing about toadies and stooges, "the prices in that scalp-me store," and stopped to watch two puppies wrestling in the dust. George caught one and put it in my arms. It squirmed and licked my face and the ice cream off my fingers. You could not help laughing at that creature, and we could not help our eyes meeting, so I saw the mirth and kindness in his, and he saw me, my crush on him. There we were down in the dust, cooing and smitten in love with a puppy, trying out sentiments like code: "He certainly likes you," said George.

"Oh, I love him!" I said, and forgot to be miserable, forgot about JCP.

"We'll keep him for a pet," George said, as if it were a future we'd decided. That dog followed us back to the *Record*, its hopeful tail still going like a metronome.

Before sunrise the next day, I was glad to see George waiting in front of the news office beside Jenkins's wagon. Mrs. Jones came downstairs ready in her hat. "Best get started before the Pinks get wind that the Terror's here," George said. We loaded the packet of handbills and copies of the newspaper.

"I'm off to meet with the mill boys," George said. "I'll come along later."

"Bring that woman reporter," said Mrs. Jones.

"You're riding with her now." He smiled at me, theatrically doffing his hat.

"Take notes!" K. T. Redmond waved us off and went back to bed.

Our lanterns lit long shadows up the mountain. Mrs. Jones patted my arm and made conversation. "George tells me you lost your father in an explosion."

"Yes."

"I tell you, there's more injury and death in the mines and quarries of Colorado than anywhere else in the world. They killed your father, and then they turned you out at the point of a bayonet, no better than a dog. How's your poor brave mother?"

"She took my brothers back east," I said, and missed them sharply.

Mrs. Jones clucked her tongue and pried the talk out of me, good as a crowbar: *How much schooling did you have? What's your ambition? Where are you from?* She was pleased to tell me she'd emigrated from Ireland to Canada. "My people were poor and miserable as yours. Worse! Couldn't read or write." We rode along with the sun rising holy over the Gilded Range, and she put a comforting hand on my arm, in the company of her own grief. "I lost my family in Tennessee. We know the same anguish."

"Oh, Mrs. Jones," I said, "I am sorry."

"Can't stay sorry for long," she said. "We pray for the dead but fight like hell for the living. We're bringing the trumpets up this mountain today, to give the boys a fighting chance."

"Wouldn't count on it," Jenkins said.

"If you stand up to these fat cats and their bloodhounds," she told him, "if you stand together with your brothers and sisters, you'll prevail."

We wound our way up the steep. Birds flitted in the scrub, white-winged plumers and wee gray stumplebekes, such names as I could invent for them. Pleaders and warblers like the rest of us. The sunrise glittered off bits of jewelry in the rocks. Mrs. Jones drew great lungfuls of air and looked around her. We glimpsed the rooftops of Elkhorne below us, and the sight provoked me again with bitterness.

"Did you know?" Mrs. Jones pointed. "That palace of your local czar, Padgett? Two million dollars to build. A fortune in mahogany and gold paint, plus the lives of three men whose names are long forgotten, while the name Padgett is emblazoned on the halls of academe. He calls that philanthropy."

"The house is very elegant," I said, still wide-eyed over it. "I've worked there."

"Does it tempt you, sweetheart, the luxury?" She patted my knee. "It tempts us all. Luxury makes slaves. Never forget it. The paradise of the rich is built from the hell of the poor. I prefer the down road, a comrade's greeting, and the breath of freedom. If I yielded to luxury, I might lose myself."

Had I lost myself? If offered actual luxury, I'd no doubt yield.

"Padgett and his fellow pirates, Rockefeller and Gould—each one has more money in the bank than half the U.S. Treasury! Yet will you look at that?" She pointed at the side of the trail, where a sprouting of white tents had cropped up like snowdrops. "These are the flimsy excuses for a dwelling the Padgett Company calls free lodging. These are the fine conditions of quarry-men and railroad workers. Exposed to the elements and without a soft place to lay their heads at night. They'll be forced to camp here all winter. Stop the wagon a minute."

Mrs. Jones hopped down. The men working on the track took off their conical straw hats as she approached. "Come out for me tomorrow night," she told them. "All you boys. Out of the tents and up to the battle." She took copies of the handbill and distributed them. One fellow translated it in a language exceedingly strange to my ears. The workmen broke into smiles, with foreign bows, bobbing and bending. Jenkins stared at them and I stared. Wasn't it a marvelous thing that one could meet the peoples of the wide world at one's own doorstep? Perhaps one day I'd circle the globe like Nellie Bly, writing famous adventures for a newspaper.

"Come to the rally!" Mrs. Jones called as we left the rail crew behind.

"Nah, Mother, ya donwanna alottachink anafurrner," Jenkins said.

"Pardon?" Mrs. Jones stared at him.

I did not translate his string of slurs, as she needed no interpreter.

"First of all, those folks are not Chinese, they are Japanese. Your grievances are the same." She scolded him like the teacher she once was, offering lessons not taught in school. "So line 'em up for the union. Why should you be afraid of them organizing? If you were real Americans, you'd tell Padgett the nation demands to protect all workers against the exploiters of labor."

"Whoawhoawhoa Nelly, ma'am." Jenkins held his hand up flat to stop her rush of words. "No needa get ugly about it."

"Those boys are not your enemy, son," she said. "You know who is."

I did not know Jenkins's enemies, but I had my own on a list: Juno Tarbusch. Harold Smiley. Colonel Bowles was on it, and Duke Padgett. The Lemon Drop was on it. Was Jace? For the moment, kind George Lonahan had distracted me with quips and ice cream, but I was still mired in rainbow notions about JCP—he was not my foe, but neither was he a friend.

At his Quarrytown barn, Jenkins unhitched the horses. Mrs. Jones stood in the wagon bed and tossed bundles of newspapers to me. She threw down a forty-pound box of potatoes, sacks of cornmeal, provisions for the boardinghouse.

"Missus," said Jenkins, "take it easy. Rest."

"I don't rest," she scoffed. "If these society butterflies would do some lifting, we wouldn't have so many rich doctors." She pulled back a tarpaulin to reveal a long crate, straw spilling from the slats. She poked at it with her small black-booted foot.

"Leave that," Jenkins said sharply.

"If those be rifles," Mrs. Jones said, "I'd advise you to bury them."

"Somebody ordered 'em brought uptown here," he told her. "Won't say who."

"You tell whoever it is: We're for ballots, not bullets. If they find those rifles, they'll put you in a stockade and keep you there all winter without a coat. Then who will give a sugar lump to Sweetiepie and Baby, eh?" She fondled the horses and fed them something from her pocket. "Better bury them shooters, son, or stow them where they won't be used."

"Yes'm," he said, chastened. "I'll tell the customer to take care of it."

She had us eating out of her hand same as the animals. "Sylvie, take me to the women."

I hoisted the sack full of newspapers and handbills, words good as guns. *Organize.* We walked in the cool morning to the boardinghouse, where we found Mrs. Quirk outside, scrubbing over a washtub.

"Sylvie!" She went to embrace me, but a fit of coughing wracked her.

"Madame," said Mrs. Jones, introducing herself. "You need to rest before you sacrifice your very life to the almighty profiteers. Those corporate bandits would take the breath from your lungs."

Mrs. Quirk said, "What kinda talk is that?"

"Let us help you." Mrs. Jones rolled up her sleeves, exposing her speckled arms. From the pile of grim laundry, she plucked a yellowing sheet and plunged it into the suds.

"Thank you," Mrs. Quirk said amid violent coughing. "But there's no need—"

I took up a pair of dungarees and scrubbed them.

"We're only lending a hand," Mrs. Jones said. "These scoundrels have you washing out here in all weather. They've gone and taken our girl Sylvie's house—her father's very life. Will they have your health too?"

"Sylvie, now, who is this?" Mrs. Quirk asked. "Why is she here?"

"She's Mrs. Jones." I presented one of the handbills.

"I'm here to tell the boys how to get justice," said Mrs. Jones.

"The only justice is in heaven," said Mrs. Quirk, wheezing.

"Jesus himself fought for justice here on earth," Mrs. Jones told her. "He took twelve men from among the laborers and with them founded the organization that revolutionized a society. Just so, in our day, the union will hold the Company to rights."

"Don't you let Mr. Tarbusch hear that talk, or the Company will hold you and your union by the ankle and dangle the lot over that cliff." Mrs. Quirk pointed.

"Not if we all march together. Get your mop and your broom. Bang your pots."

"Suicide," Mrs. Quirk told her. "You don't know."

"But I do know, madam. At Paint Creek I faced down the rifles of the Pinkertons, and saw the mothers and children rise up to shut down a coal mine and demand these cannibals offer a living wage for their men. They got it too. It would be a great help, Mrs. Quirk, if you'd rally the women. If the women are strong, the men are strong too."

"Hmmp. Not even five whole women up here in Quarrytown," Mrs. Quirk said. "We don't need any of that ruckus."

Mrs. Jones applied herself at the washboard, scrubbing. Beside us, Mrs. Quirk sank her cracked red knuckles into the suds but had such a fit of coughing that blood came forth onto her hand. "Consumption is well known to be the disease of poverty," said Mrs. Jones. "Profiteers like your own royal Padgett are turning American homes into incubators to hatch out germs among the poor."

"We'd not have jobs at all, without Padgett hires us," Mrs. Quirk said.

"While you build his castles and slave for pennies, he feasts on your blood."

"This is a fine boardinghouse," Mrs. Quirk said. "The men have no complaints."

"They ought to! They are whipped curs too beat for complaint."

"Complaint is the seed of misery," I said softly. "My mother believes."

"Your mother has it backward," said Mrs. Jones. "Misery is the seed, grows complaint, and that brings justice if you'll only speak up."

In this way she tutored us in the Art of Troublemaking and proceeded to charm herself indoors for tea. We sat over steaming mugs. "Rest is as much your entitlement, Mrs. Quirk, as it is Mrs. Astor's," said the old woman, and passed a plate of crackers, "Madame, voulay-voo?" mimicking a society dame, finger crooked, nose in the air. "Some of these butterflies wake up with five dollars' worth of paint on their cheeks. Why, Mrs. Padgett has a toothbrush for her dogs! And yet you hear them say, 'Oh, them dirty miners.' 'Oh, that Mother Jones, that horrible old woman.' Well, I am horrible! I admit. But I must be, to these bloodsucking pirates."

Mrs. Quirk looked over her shoulder for spies. I stayed quiet, thrilled to hear Mrs. Jones bashing royalty. K.T. must've told her about the schipperke's toothbrush.

"Buckle on your armor," Mother Jones said. "A day of reckoning's upon us."

"They will throw us off the mountain," warned Mrs. Quirk.

"And for what would you stay?" cried Mrs. Jones. "It's time for a great uprising."

I left them to their tea and proceeded down the Quarrytown lane, putting the words *RALLY* and *UNION* under cabin doors where the wind had blown frigid drifts all winter. This new notice blew another kind of wind under the door. I hoped for it: *a great uprising*. Among the cabins, the ghost of my father was hanging off a laundry line in the shape of a pair of overalls, a pair of boots on a doorstep. He was dead five months, but if I closed my eyes, I could see him plain, heaving a shovel of snow over his shoulder, heading down this very road, whistling.

I had a girl and she was good . . .

Cabin Six stood weathered, no sign that Pelletiers ever lived there. A stranger came outside, a kerchief around her head. Sockless toes protruded from her shoe.

"Hello. Here's this for you." I handed her a notice.

"Sorry, sorry, no English."

Eva Setkowski emerged from just behind her. "Syl-veee!" She launched herself at me, throwing her arms around my waist. "You're back?"

"Can you read this notice for the lady?"

"She is my auntie. She lives in your house now."

"Read it to her, please."

"You read it," Eva said. "I'll say the Polish."

I read aloud. *Union. Meeting. Tonight.* When Eva translated, the woman spoke in Polish, then went back inside our house, shut the door.

"She says she'll tell my uncle," Eva said. "And I'll tell my brother. Oskar says you gonna marry him."

Her words followed me like a threat. Eva followed too, skipping along while I delivered the notice. "A meeting!" Eva cried. "Come to a meeting!" She was a natural-born carnival barker, luring the women outside. They exclaimed over me like a long-lost relative.

"Seven o'clock!" Eva held up seven fingers. "Tonight! Seven!"

"*Musika?*" Mrs. Tchachenko played accordion keys in the air. "To bring?"

"Yes!" Eva said. "And tell Mr. Bruner: Bring the trumpet."

"It's not a party," I said.

"So what?" Eva shrugged and twirled. "Music is for any reason."

Chapter Twenty-Six

LATE IN THE AFTERNOON I found Mrs. Jones at Jenkins's stables with George Lonahan. They sat out on the back of a wagon, drinking coffee. "Sylvie!" she said, raising her tiny fist. "Are you ready to raise some hell?"

"I'll take notes," I said. "We'll write it for the paper, if that helps?"

"It does!" Lonahan said. "But beware. Mother Jones has caused folks to faint with the force of her talk. She's a fierce terrier at the trouser seat of the oligarchs."

Mrs. Jones looked pleased at the description and more pleased to see I was already writing in my notebook. *Terrier. Oligarch.* It was plain that her words would raise extra hell if the *Record* printed them. I hoped so. What would she say? She adjusted the black ribbon at her neck, tapping her impatient foot. The shift whistle blew.

"Here we go," said Mother.

The sky streaked magenta and tangerine, the mountains black against the garish sunset. I attempted to draw a fierce terrier nipping the trouser seat of a top-hatted man. George angled next to me and looked over my shoulder and laughed at my efforts, so it seemed true that we were *comrades*. I felt an importance, sitting with them, as if I were indeed an inside agitator. Hawky Jenkins lit torches so the air smudged with black smoke.

Nobody showed.

"Spies must've got to them," George said. "Tarbusch."

Then, in the dusk, Dan Kerrigan came from the boardinghouse. Another man approached from the track. Christe Boleson. Two more skirted the shadows along the lane. The Mercanditti brothers. Quarrymen finishing the shift came toward the stables, watching wary as dogs approaching a nest of snakes. Oskar Setkowski came along with Eva. "Hiya, Sylvie!" Her brother gave me his slanting smile. More men arrived, smoking and skeptical.

Mrs. Jones climbed onto the bed of the wagon. "Come nearer, comrades. Don't be afraid, boys, I don't bite."

Now most of the population of Quarrytown herded into the stable yard. Off to the side, Juno Tarbusch parked on a boulder, legs drawn up, necktie dangling. It would serve as a noose to strangle him. Whether he was criminally negligent or had ordered the Snail fired up deliberately to kill my father, no one would ever know, but I needed to blame an enemy, and he was mine.

"That's the quarry boss," I warned Mrs. Jones. She gave him a jaunty salute.

George Lonahan stepped up onto the wagon bed, dashing in his tall boots, his hair too long, thumbs hooked in his braces. "Gentlemen!" he cried. The crowd settled. "Some of you know me. You've heard me talk about the great work of the United Mine Workers, and I'm here again to tell you what a union will do for you. In Cripple Creek, the unions won the men three dollars for an eight-hour shift." (Applause.) "Plus overtime!" (Applause.) "Together we'll do the same here." Lonahan had their attention: Three dollars a day was downright lordly.

"With us," George cried, "you'll have your rights. The bosses can't delay the payroll. Can't starve and freeze you all winter. We're here to sign you for the union."

Lonahan went on, listing the advantages of joining up, and I wrote them down. As he spoke, he held his hands forth, offering us the whole sky. He opened his arms as if he might gather all of us listeners into his embrace for safekeeping. His voice was young and full of hope and possibility and some magnetism of belief that drew me like a spell. The way he raked his hair and paced the platform made me forget for a moment to write down his words. He clapped his hands once sharply, to make a point, and the sound echoed against the mountain like a shot. I jumped.

"No more dead work," he cried. "An eight-hour day. Money in your pocket."

He joked and rallied the men till at last he came to a fiery point, like a ringmaster: "Now!" he cried. "I present! Mother Mary Harris Jones!"

Applause.

Mrs. Jones stepped forward on the wagon bed and began. "Has anyone ever told you, my children, about the lives you are living, so that you may understand how it is you pass your days on earth? Might you imagine a brighter day and bring it to pass? I will do it for you now. I want you to see yourselves as you are. I am one of you. I know what it is to suffer from the schemes of a soulless enterprise."

I copied her words as she said them, her voice ringing out over the rocks.

"You pity yourselves," she said. "But you don't pity your brothers, or you would stand together to help one another. You hard-rock miners have stood for abuse like mules. So have your brothers in Padgett's coal veins, and in the copper mines of Wyoming, and in Rockefeller's oil fields. You have starved your children. Starved yourselves. You have lived in chicken coops and dog kennels. They wouldn't build one for their beagles as bad as yours here. You have permitted the businessmen to rob you, of safety, of the comforts of home. You have given up your leisure. You pay the Padgett Company more than it pays you. You shop in their pluck-me stores and you pay them in blood scrip."

The men prospected the dirt with their boots. Sheepishness grew in the air.

"You are to blame and no one else," Mrs. Jones cried. "You have stood for it. You're afraid! You say you can't join the union because you'd lose your job. Poor wretch! You never owned a job. Those fellas who own the machinery own the job. You have to get their permission to earn your bread and butter. You're laboring under a delusion: that you have no power. But if you were organized, you wouldn't have these conditions."

"She's right," somebody called out. Kerrigan.

"They make you shovel track in the dead of winter for nothing. They call it dead work, and do you know why? Because it's killing you. Men have died here. Of a negligence same as murder. Your friend Jack Pelletier."

My skin went cold.

"The gruesome death of a good man," she said. "A beloved man. You knew him, and know his good hardworking wife and children, thrown to the jackals. The Company replaced him cheaper than a mule. One of you moved right into his house, and the rest of you watched. You watch, yes, while the Pinkerton goons throw wee babies and friendless widows out of their homes as if they were garbage. What's to stop the bosses from throwing you out too? You're next"—she pointed—"or you."

"Organize us, Mother," Kerrigan called out, waving his hat.

Mrs. Jones pointed to Tarbusch on his rock. "See the boss over there? I'm not afraid of a boss. He's just a man like you. And he can act like a man instead of a lapdog. He has a beating heart in his chest. His mother raised him to do right. Didn't she?"

Her daring! It thrilled me. The men vibrated with attention. Tarbusch sat on his rock in a smirk. He had a pocket notebook out, writing in it, same as I was writing.

"Sylvie, lass, come here and stand beside me," Mrs. Jones said. I startled. "You men all know Sylvie Pelletier. Jack's daughter." She beckoned. Lonahan gave me a little push, "Go on, sweetheart," and handed me up next to Mrs. Jones. I stood like a wooden doll, cheeks scarlet.

"Our young lady's father was killed by these criminals," Mrs. Jones cried, her hand around my waist, possessing me. "Killed same as those boys in Ruby roasted alive in Padgett's coal mine. Let's call it what it is. Murder. A human being is killed, and they haul his body up in the cage, and the men go back to work. That man Pelletier was good as slain. And his replacements—maybe your own selves—will die too, if you boys don't stand with the union."

"Will you stand up, men?" Lonahan called out. "Will we take the vote today?"

Something shifted then, a wind blowing through. The smell of kerosene filled the stable yard, as combustible as the men seething in the crowd. They began to cheer.

"Sylvie, lass!" Mrs. Jones called. "You tell them."

Tell them what? My throat filled with liquid fear.

"Speak from the heart, honey," George Lonahan said. The men waited in the fragile quiet. Words were piled on a cornice of my thoughts, and now they would spill to bury me. Who was I to speak?

"Remember your papa," said George. "What would he say right now?"

"Go on, love," Mrs. Jones whispered.

These two agitators pulled words out of my mouth like stitches unraveled, undoing all I knew about silence. That it was golden. *Sink or swim*, I thought, and swam.

"You knew my father," I heard myself say. "His fiddle. His songs."

"Frenchy!" Kerrigan shouted. "Speak louder, sweetheart!"

I fumbled on, my voice growing stronger. "The Company claims the payroll's on the way, but it never comes. They swear the hospital will get built—and then take a dollar off your wage for it. But we don't see a hospital, do we? The only payout is credit at the Company store, nothing to get ahead." Words piled on words, among them Easter Grady's. I blurted them: "Don't trust what a Padgett says. It's what they do."

My voice cracked and shook. "They won't do anything for us. My father, he was for us to help ourselves. He was for the union. He talked about it and sang the songs. He wanted all of you to join. I'm here to ask you to do it. Vote for the union."

Mr. Tarbusch stood up. He stared at me and wrote something in his book.

Murderer. The thought spiked my blood. If I'd had a flaming arrow, I'd've shot it through his glaring eyeball. I gathered myself out of the red poison of the sun sinking behind the dark peaks. "You knew my father," I cried. "You heard him ask for wages when we froze ourselves to shovel the track. You heard the Colonel refuse to pay. They claimed they owed nothing. You were with my father that day he was killed. You know what happened. The inquest said it was no accident."

"Because it wasn't." Dan Kerrigan again.

"Every week the newspaper prints reports of men hurt, crushed under stones, fallen off ladders. Fingers sliced off. Legs amputated. They die frozen in slides. My father can't ask you," I said, "so I will. Sign up for the union. That's all."

I turned away from them with a burning face.

The men began to clap. The applause was not for me, I thought, but for pity. For Papa in his grave, the respect they had for him. I stood blotched and confused about how much I liked it, their approval like medicine. The hand of God would come out of the sky and pluck out my liver as punishment.

Instead, George Lonahan took my hand and held it high. "Hip-hip!"

"Hooray," the crowd answered.

Mrs. Jones took my other hand in her bony fingers. "If the men don't fight, the women will!" she cried. "Your mountain women are fighters! And you men are fighters, are you not? Say you are, boys."

Was I a fighter? I wanted to be, but stepped behind the wagon and was sick in a pile of stone. After that, it was as if shame—for our poverty, for the blasphemy of having spoken out—began to leach from my system. I took up my notebook again and wrote it all down. That habit, to take notes, the impulse to tell what happened, is with me to this day. Writing is a step removed from danger, but speechifying puts a woman right in the middle of it. Even now I have a well-founded fear of speaking in public.

Mother Jones had no such fear and started to wind up the crowd again. "March over here, men! A union will make things right. I'll organize you this very night!"

Tarbusch shouted, "You can't organize them, madam. They have to pay fifteen dollars for a charter."

"Lonahan here from headquarters will give them the cost of the charter," she said. "Raise your hands, all of you, and I will swear you the obligation."

"Union! Union!" the men chanted, fists in the air, and Tarbusch slunk away. To use the pump-house telephone, no doubt, to call out the Company beef.

Mrs. Jones rallied on. "These parasites couldn't live on this earth without us to do the work. Forty-five years ago, slavery was outlawed in this land, and yet most of you have hardly touched a paycheck since last summer. Are you slaves? They give you living quarters same as on the old southern plantations. It's only a few degrees of difference here. Your corporate masters wish they did not have to pay you at all."

Her words settled on me like drops of water and soaked in as if I'd been a wilted stalk of celery but now was crisp and stringy with new leaves. Never had I heard such talk, never heard us held up as miserable and living like animals, or seen the truth about why. And neither had I ever opened my mouth to find out what was in it. The men had clapped for me, and I was altered, charged with a new recklessness, to say what I thought, record what I witnessed.

The pen shook in my hand. I wrote everything. The men swarming to greet Mrs. Jones. George Lonahan taking down names. Lev Tchachenko began to play the accordion. Gustav Bruner joined in on trumpet. It was a party now. Oskar Setkowski made wolf eyes at me and raised his flask in a toast. I inched closer to George Lonahan, hoping Oskar would give up. George was politicking but sent encouraging glances in my direction, the air quickening between us. Was it? Mrs. Quirk watched from a corner of the yard, thumping the flat of her chest, coughing, to get air in her tubercular lungs.

Stars pricked the sky, each one a wish. That I'd stay brave enough to tell some truth, fierce as Mrs. Jones. The air smelled of tobacco and horses. Men conspired outside Jenkins's barn, drinking. Lonahan smiled at me. The terrible musicians fumbled along playing "Stick to the Union, Jack" and "Hold the Fort." Without Papa, the band had no fiddle. Nobody played spoons without

Henry. Somebody ran to the boardinghouse for a guitar, and Kerrigan produced a tin whistle. Eva Setkowski jigged and twirled.

In the horse barn, I sat at the feet of Mrs. Jones, who rested on a throne of hay. She and Lonahan talked with Dan Kerrigan, now named head of the new local union shop. They toasted, drinking. Lonahan offered me the bottle and I took a long drink. Mrs. Jones in turn raised it in my direction.

"Your father would be proud."

"I hope so." I drank more and sang along in the barn. "'Would you have mansions of gold in the sky and sleep in a shack in the back.'" Intoxicating words. Warm looks from George. Mrs. Jones laughing like a girl. In their ragtag company, I was not lonely, not strange or apart, but at home, one of them. A comrade.

At last the men drifted away to the night shift or their bunks in the boardinghouse. Oskar Setkowski eyed me and scooped up his little sister, asleep in his arms. A tenderness he showed toward Eva made me like him, *though not to marry, thank you.* After they left, the stable yard was quiet, the bottle dry. I yawned. It was two o'clock in the morning. "We're offered cots at Mrs. Quirk's tonight," I said, and rose to leave.

"I'm happy here in the hayloft," said Mrs. Jones. "George will escort you down the lane. And warn me if you see those hired gangsters coming with their Gatlings."

George Lonahan steered me toward the boardinghouse. The chips of marble under our feet glowed opalescent, as if many old moons had shattered and fallen there.

"Here we go, step lightly," he said. "Don't let the Pinkertons hear us."

"That speaking," I said. "It was frightening, it was—"

"You did good," George said. "Just like I said: right from the heart."

"They'll call me a *socialist* and a Red and agitator," I said, testing the words. "They'll call me a knocker."

"That's high praise," he said. "I'd call you brave." He put his arm around me like a conspirator, and we marched along in matched steps as if we were in league. *Comrades*. Were we? I wished it, but my legs were weak, my blood thin, and I trembled. Was it the effects of the whiskey or the fault of my escort, holding on.

"Mr. Lonahan—"

"George," he said. He stopped with his hands on my shoulders, inspecting me in the bright moonlight. "Are you all right now?"

"A little bit upside down," I said. "Also backward."

"Are you right side wrong, then, too, Sylvie Pelletier?" He pushed loose strands of hair off my face with the tips of his fingers, so I shivered. "How shall we put you right?" I feared he might kiss me, then feared he would not. He whispered again the word *comrade*, along with my name, murmured so as to steal himself through the cracks in the rackety cabin of my heart. He had me by my hands and I did not pull away. His eyes were kind, searching my face. And then.

Something startled us. A faint singing of metal, the low hum of the electric tram wires vibrating at an hour when no trolley should be running. We froze in our skins.

"Shhh." Lonahan pulled me in, as if to protect me, and I was enveloped in heat and the smell of his tobacco.

We heard a clacking now. Below the ridge, a light moved winking through the trees, and when the tram came to the clearing, we saw the cargo: two dozen men.

"Goddamn Pinkertons," Lonahan said. "Ruin the moonlight itself."

I did not think he meant the moonlight that was ruined. Whatever romance was in the moment got lost in the tumult of events. George turned and pulled me rapidly back to the stables. In alarm, he rousted Jenkins out of the hay. "Mrs. Jones must not get caught. They'll take her to jail. Go fast, Sylvie, and warn her." He sent me to the back room, where Jenkins had given her a bed. She snored away, still in her boots.

"Mother!" I shook her shoulders. "Wake up. Pinkerton agents."

She sat up fast and put on her hat. "Those mongrels. Disturbing the peace."

"Sylvie, take Mrs. Jones to Kerrigan's place and wait there," George said.

"You can't get rid of me yet," she told him. "I want another talk with the men."

"The Pinks will arrest you."

"Let them. Get away to file that charter." She strode down the hill.

"Stick with her, Sylvie, can you?" Lonahan said. He started off, then turned with a look of regret. "I'll have to make myself scarce for a while." He gave me a wistful kiss on the cheek. Our hands caught, fingers lacing then unlacing, reluctant. He disappeared in the darkness.

I wonder still, had he not gone away then, how things would've been different.

Mrs. Jones picked along the branch road to Cabin One. "Here's Kerrigan's," I said, but she shushed me and kept on toward trouble, to the loading yard, where Pinkerton agents were swarming in a mess of torches, hands on their shooters. The quarrymen came pouring down from the boardinghouse, brandishing picks and shovels. The night was split with shouts and whistles, but not shots, not yet.

"This way." I tried to pull Mrs. Jones in a safe direction, but she linked my arm and towed me in a terrifying route through the crowd in the narrow yard. Spills of lamplight cast their shadows against the rock wall in distorted shapes. The Pinks formed a barrier across the tracks. Mother went boldly up to them, smiling in their stony faces.

"Hello, boys," she said.

"Halt." Sheriff Smiley had his pistol out, pointing. "Halt or get shot."

"We're only an old woman and a young girl, son. Why are you afraid of us?" She disarmed them with our supposed weaknesses, age and girlhood, like secret weapons.

"I got a warrant," Smiley said, "to arrest Mary Jones and George Lonahan of the UMW."

"Oh, goodness me!" she said, sweet as syrup. "For what reason?"

"Trespassing. On Company property. We'll put you in jail."

"You do that." Mrs. Jones smiled. "If you're a lapdog for a mine owner, you can be one for me. Get on the telephone and tell Padgett I am going to rouse all his slaves. I've already woken up these ones here. Just look!"

Fifty men had come out in the middle of the night. And all the women. Mrs. Tchachenko had a child on her hip. Eva had her Polish auntie by the hand, both of them brandishing broomsticks. Mrs. Quirk was there, banging a pot with her soup ladle.

Then Mr. Tarbusch pushed through the crowd. "Mrs. Jones! You're nothing but an outside agitator."

"The Pinkertons are the outsiders," I said, as if speaking up were contagious. "We were only peaceful and talking. That's our right."

"Listen up, boys!" Mrs. Jones cried. "Your boss brought these Pinkertons to slam you down. They're not the law of the state. Just the private army of the overlord."

"We'll have you shot," Tarbusch said.

"Will the owner shoot me, or will he meet me? Is he scared of an old woman? Let Mr. Padgett meet me face-to-face. I'm not afraid. Not of him or Mr. Rockefeller or the Governor. Least of all you hired flunkies. If the time comes when a mine owner will intimidate me, I want to die in that hour. Shoot me and be damned."

The men clapped, cheering and raucous.

"We have a warrant." Smiley brandished his paper.

"Keep it in your pill bag," she said. "Goodbye, boys, I'm under arrest. I'll see you as soon as the union pays my bail. If the richtocrats won't give you the eight-hour day, then strike! And when you strike, pay no attention to trained monkeys like these fellas with their tin badges. The judge in Gunnison is a scab. While you work, he serves injunctions for the money class. While you starve, he plays golf."

"Get along, now." Smiley came at Mrs. Jones with a hand on his pistol. She offered him her arm, smiling as if he'd asked for a dance.

Two Pinkertons hustled us toward the pump house, where we were locked under guard. The men skirmished outside. Somebody shot off a gun. Mrs. Jones could feel me jump and tremble beside her.

"We're all right now, Sylvie. They won't shoot the women."

"No," my captor said, laughing, "we'll hang you from that tree."

"I'd like to pull the rope," said his snickering friend. I saw with a start that this was Carlton Pfister, the boy who'd tortured an old mule and scratched my arm bloody. He'd grown into a pimpled variety of rodent, eyes dull and furtive.

"What gives you the right, Carlie Pfister, to keep us here?" I said.

"What give you the right to talk?" he said. "I'm the head night watchman at the pump house. What are you? A loudmouth girl. Oughta learn to shut your trap."

Oh, I hated him. Hated. There's no redeeming a lout like him.

Tarbusch blew his whistle. The shouts faded. When a weak gray light finally sighed under the door of our holding pen, Mrs. Jones and I were brought out to the flatcar and seated behind a load of stone.

"Get that woman outta here," Tarbusch cried.

Behind us in the yard, Oskar Setkowski and Dan Kerrigan lurked, smoking by the derricks. "Stand your ground, lads!" called Mrs. Jones. Her words evaporated in the wind as the tram picked up speed down the swoop. "Whoo-ee." She held on to her hat. "I like the excitement."

"Me too." In the rush, my hair streamed loose like some kind of flag, and as the moon sank over the mountains, my courage rose, tender and pink as the dawn sky.

Chapter Twenty-Seven

AT 5:45 IN THE A.M. the agents prodded us off the trolley into the mill yard. "You have twenty-four hours, Mrs. Jones, to leave town," said Sheriff Smiley. "If you don't go, you'll be held in the jail, then removed to Gunnison."

"Is there a bed in your prison?" said Mrs. Jones. "It'll save me hotel fees."

"Take your young friend with you, that's a warning."

"Oh, Sylvie's been warned," said Mrs. Jones. "She's been warned all her life."

We headed toward town. "Mrs. Jones," I said on impulse, "you mentioned you'd like to meet with the Company President."

"The monkey suits will never talk to the likes of me."

"I am acquainted with J. C. Padgett. He might listen. I'd ask him."

"Would you now?" She beamed. "Show me where to find him."

We marched toward the Company offices, me without a plan, only a strange determination, to appeal to Jace. I'd test his character, show him— what? The mud on my dress, the bits of hay. He would see he couldn't hurt me now. I was a comrade. A columnist. I would bring him Mother Jones.

She barreled along, humming "Turkey in the Straw." I brought her up the steps into the offices, pulled by invisible strings of new recklessness, to run toward trouble.

The front desks were empty. Jace Padgett would hardly be awake at this hour. But then I noticed a man studying some drawings tacked to the far wall. The ducktail at the back of his head was too familiar. At the sight of it, I was afraid again, of the hold he had on me and what I might do now.

"Jace," I said.

He turned around, startled. "Sylvie! What a surprise! Good morning! Who's this charming lady with you?"

"Mrs. Mary Jones," I said. "Mother Mary Harris Jones."

"You?" He stared at her in her widow's weeds. "The dangerous radical?"

"I am indeed. The wicked old woman. In truth, I am harmless as a kitten."

"I'd be well advised to show you out," said Jasper. "But I'll make an allowance since you're here with my friend Sylvie—she's as good a reference as can be."

That's what I was to him, a reference. Oh, he made me so mad, that Jace.

"Young sir," said Mrs. Jones, "I have a particular request."

"I'm all ears, madam." He spoke with the benevolence of a man in charge.

"You say you know Miss Pelletier," Mrs. Jones said. "So you know the tragedy of her father's death."

"I do." He did not meet my eye. "I feel terrible about the accident."

"It was no accident," I said. "The inquest spelled it out. My father died of deliberate malice—because he was organizing a union."

"It will happen again, to another man, and then another," Mrs. Jones said.

"And what will you do about it?" said.

He looked away from my question, sorry as a child scolded. "I—have apologized—" Jace was red, stammering. "On behalf of—"

Mrs. Jones stepped toward him with maternal calm. "Son, I'm here to offer you a surefire salve to your conscience. An appeal to your goodwill. May we sit?"

He ushered us into his private sanctum, his name on the door in gilt. Jasper C. Padgett, President. Within minutes Mother Jones began to work her elfin spells.

"Mr. Padgett," she said, twinkling, "you're an educated man, are you not?"

"Well, yes, I've just graduated Harvard University."

"Then you've read the Stoics and are at least acquainted with the work of the great Victor Hugo or Upton Sinclair's novels of the working class."

"I'm currently enthralled by the work of Dr. W.E.B. Du Bois—"

"Aha!" she said, delighted. "Du Bois is the voice of his people. So I wager you're a man of conscience, not only inheritance. I'm told your moral compass steers you in the direction of justice."

"I hope so, Mrs. Jones."

"The men in your labor camps have just hours ago voted to bring the union in, to join together in the great human struggle for health and well-being. They are worn to the bone. They have been shorted pay all winter."

"We will get the payroll out this week," Jasper said. "I absolutely intend to."

"You must know they can't get ahead without organizing."

"And why shouldn't they organize? I don't have a problem with it."

"I think you do," said Mrs. Jones. "Why else would you hire Pinkerton thugs to stop the quarry miners from the exact thing we're discussing?"

Jace looked baffled.

"Last night they ambushed the workers at Quarrytown," I said. "With guns."

"Ladies, I must correct you," he said. "Colonel Bowles sent a security detail to raid an illegal still of bootleggers—and apparently, a brawling of drunks got out of hand."

"It was not a brawling of drunks," I said. "It was a peaceful meeting."

"To organize the union," Mrs. Jones told him. "If you do not trust my reporting, ask this young lady here. She is a journalist."

In that moment I was not so much *journalist* as jealous jilted jezebel, but I stored up this *journalist* along with *comrade*. Such words had begun to shape me now that *butterfly* was out of the question. If you are called a thing, sometimes you become that thing, for better or worse.

"Sylvie?" Jace said. "You all right? You don't look well, Sylvester."

The soft Virginia vowels of his concern. The trace of sweet talk in it, the odd fond nickname, weakened me a moment, until I remembered myself, pulled the bones of my spine straight.

"It's just as she says," I told him. "The men only wanted a union. But the Pinkertons arrested the organizer and Mrs. Jones. And me. They locked us in the pump house."

My erstwhile beloved swallowed this news with disbelief. "You were *arrested*?"

"For no reason." I found myself proud of it, the arrest like a badge of honor.

Mrs. Jones leaned toward him. "What I plead for is a renewal of the bond of brotherhood between the classes. A reign of justice on earth that shall obliterate the cruel hate that now divides us."

"I plead for that too," cried Jasper. "But—I must ask: Aren't you a Bolshevik?"

"Some people call us Bolsheviks," she said. "Some call us Reds. What of it? If we're Red, then Thomas Jefferson was Red, and a whole lot of those people who turned the world upside down were Red. What is socialism? What is Bolshevism? Who were the rebels of the American Revolution? What, then, is a union? I'll tell you: It is the soul of unrest that is behind all these movements."

"I've been warned," Jace said, "that unrest is antithetical to profits."

"A union is made to quell the need for revolution. I am not with the Wobblies. I am for the workers."

"I see that, madam," Jace said, "and since my father has charged me with running this operation in my own way—"

"Your way might lie along the side of justice," Mrs. Jones suggested.

"My own father," I said quietly, "whom you claimed to admire—"

"I did," Jace said. "Everybody liked Jack Pelletier."

"He fought for the union," I said, fighting to appeal to whatever fondness he'd ever had for me, whatever kindness or honor he might possess.

The look on Jasper Padgett's face migrated from guilt to sorrow, and then it appeared as if an idea had dawned on him, as if it were his own thought, not placed there by us, an old lady and a girl. He raised a philosophical finger. "I'm certainly all for justice," he said. "And I have the authority to begin negotiations with a workers' union. So I'm damned if I won't do it."

At these words Mrs. Jones was all aflower with compliments. "You certainly are a fine young man. The future of our country lies with leaders like you. A model American. Lonahan of the United Mine Workers will be in touch directly, along with Dan Kerrigan, who is president of the local chapter. And then, my new friend," she told him, firm as a schoolteacher, "you'll negotiate in good faith."

"You have my word."

"Speaking is the start of doing," I said, quoting George Lonahan.

"Correct," said Jasper. "I intend to act."

"I'm not here to bust you up in business," Mrs. Jones said. "On the contrary, we hope and pray for your success. Sure, there's enough of it to go around." She headed to the door with me alongside.

"Sylvie?" Jasper said. "Might you spare a minute?"

"Stay," Mrs. Jones said, like an order. "I'll run along before the Pinkertons come to throw me in the clinker."

I was on my own now.

"I'm dying to show you something," Jace said. With great excitement, he led me to the far wall. Blueprint renderings were tacked alongside sketches and diagrams. He pointed to a drawing of a soldier standing on a tall column. "Remember the Daughters of the Confederacy? You recall we won a big contract for this monument to the so-called faithful slave? You must remember."

I remembered.

"Faithful!" He spat the word, pointing to the sketch where *LOYALTY* appeared on the monument's pedestal. This was a frieze of carved human figures: an enslaved woman with a white baby strapped on her hip, a muscular barechested man working a plow. On their backs they held the Confederate soldier aloft, up there with eagles and that traitorous cross-barred flag. "I tried to cancel the order for this—travesty," Jace said. "Too late. The stone was already shipped. But see, Sylvie, here's an antidote—"

He showed me another drawing, of a large formal temple. *A GRATEFUL NATION* was etched on the lintel above a grand entrance. Fountains and a maze of gardens bloomed on a long approach. I peered closer to see what it might be, some mythical place of buttered larks and justice, a design of repair and harmony.

"I should be going," I said, to slight him.

Jace did not notice, only talked fast, eager to explain. "It's an idea direct from Caleb Grady. Inspired by the professor—Dr. Du Bois. This here is the Temple of Gratitude, and I aim for it to be made of our marble and placed on the National Mall to honor generations who built this country without a penny of reward."

"Huh." The flatness of my affect did not dampen his enthusiastic blather. He was thrilled and proud, as if he had cured an infectious disease. He went on about the colonnades and frescoes while I stayed stony, so that I would not be swept again in his dreams or carried away by his charm, his owlish eye on me, smiling, so eager to tell me. Why carry on this way about a statue? Then I remembered—as if connecting two running streams—the unfinished conversation of the previous day.

That Negro fella is his son, K.T. had said. *Whose son, which fella?* It was only gossip. But maybe not.

"My father has given me a real opportunity to run this company," Jace said. "I don't intend to waste it. Because what use is philosophy? Philanthropy? If they're just ideas? Deeds, not words, right?"

"Well," I said. "Words too." *Sweetheart. Angel. Darlin'.* I tried to fend off memory, confused by how I was drawn, still, to JCP. He stood next to me expounding ideals, while I was embarrassed by the dirt under my fingernails. It takes enormous effort to strive against a lifetime of lessons in shame. "Words are deeds," I said. "Tell the Pinkertons to let Mrs. Jones go. Let the workers organize. Don't just throw up your hands and sit there like a poached egg on a wet plate, because you could—"

"Sylvie," he stopped me. "You don't have to be so *angry*."

"No? What else should I be? I should be going." I turned for the door but missed my chance. Duke Padgett came through, blocking the exit.

"Ah, the typist! Good morning!" he said. "Glad you've taken that racket to an office where it belongs."

Next Colonel Bowles bounded inside. "Young lady! You've come to your senses, I see. So J.C.'s hired you for the new typist?"

"She is quite a whiz at it, as I recall," said the Duke.

Do you also recall that my father was exploded in your stone pit? I didn't say.

"Sylvie?" Jace said. "I meant to ask if you'd—"

"Good for you, Sylvie," said Bowles. "Welcome to the right side of things."

But I was on the wrong side, trapped behind a row of desks, the men blocking my escape. Jasper confronted them.

"Father," he said, "I've decided to bring the union reps in for negotiations."

"What the devil—" Colonel Bowles reared back.

"That's a mistake." The Duke pointed a finger at Jasper's chest.

"You gave your word," said his son. "The decisions are mine. I've decided to negotiate. The men have voted to organize."

Jace had listened—*to me.* He showed some spine, that anger I liked in him.

"We've just run those anarchists out of town," said the Colonel. "They're outside agitators. That woman is."

"Mrs. Jones is charming," said Jasper. "I met her and agreed to talks."

"Oh, for crying out loud," said his father.

"Mother Jones is pure trouble!" Bowles exploded. "She spreads lies to suckers and hysterical women like that shrew Redmond, who prints bullshit like it's gospel." He gave me a pointed look. "Excuse my French."

That is not French. I gave him my false appeasing smile.

Duke Padgett trembled with indignation. "You've made a fatal error! You will have nothing more to do with these union people. They'll destroy this operation—"

"I aim to make this operation better than ever." Jace held his father's gaze.

I was enjoying the argument, happy to think I might've caused it.

"Son, you have no idea," said the Duke. "The first time I came to these mountains, there wasn't a damn thing here. Not a human soul."

Except for the Ute people, I did not say, or mention Chief Colorow's curse, but in that moment I wished it on the Duke and the Colonel. Flames. Ruin.

"The point is, I started with *nothing*."

"Respectfully, sir," Jasper said, "did you not have an inheritance?"

"Rot," said his father. "Yankees took it all. Destroyed everything my father built."

His slaves built. With that thought, I understood that whatever philosophy Jace claimed for himself, to support the union or build some Temple of Gratitude, was due to this clash with his father. It was about the Gradys, yes, and rectifying some sordid past, but also about Jasper's wish to declare himself. Perhaps we were, in that way, kindred spirits. We hated the same thing— unfairness—for our different reasons.

His father was purple with righteousness. "I worked from age fifteen! To build up! Not tear down, like these anarchists. They aim to take for free what we have built."

"There'd be nothing for these workers without the Company," said Bowles.

"But Colonel, sir," I said quietly, "there'd be nothing here for anyone without the workers, the men like my father—"

"She's right," Jace said.

A little notch in my heart, of victory.

The Duke looked fiercely at us and shifted his jaw left and right, as if he might bite. "Listen," he said. "Marble is beauty. Beauty is not free. It exacts a price. You don't know the risks. The effort."

"The good honest hard work!" said the jovial Colonel.

"Hell!" the Duke said. "People no longer know what honest work means. Look what we've done for these men. Built 'em gotdam houses. Schools. An entire town."

"And yet you have the very foundations of order gnawed by anarchist rats," said Bowles. "These people carry on like ingrates, who are paid better than workers anywhere on earth."

I cleared my throat, but *You paid them scraps* did not emerge.

"Father," Jasper said, "you gave your word. I only said I would negotiate—"

"Don't you dare—" said Mr. Padgett, his finger under Jasper's nose.

At that moment, two young fellows in neckties came up the steps, draftsmen reporting for work, blocked at the doorway by the bosses in a standoff.

I seized my chance and dodged outside, where a Pinkerton guard scratched himself, yawning as if the day itself were a boredom, when to me it was glaring and new. I looked at my hands as if they weren't my own, and hardly knew myself, who had opened her mouth on top of a mountain and fraternized with the great Mother Jones. Then there was George, who'd nearly kissed me in the moonlight (*had he?*) and called me brave, and Jace with his stunned expression, at my *anger*—but defending me. I fled him and his strange family, breathing the soft air, as if there were such a thing as escape.

PART FIVE

Birds of the Devil

*I asked a man in prison once how he happened to be there and he said he
had stolen a pair of shoes. I told him if he had stolen a railroad he would
be a United States Senator.*

—Mary Harris "Mother" Jones

Chapter Twenty-Eight

THE THREAT OF A STRIKE was equivalent to the threat of dynamite on the mill ridge, one that might trigger an avalanche of ruin. But at the *Record*, K.T. was thrilled by the union news from Quarrytown and Jasper's promise to pay the men. So it was a surprise when she instructed me not to print the speech of Mother Jones or write up the Pinkertons' ambush and our unlawful arrest.

"Printing it will only provoke more trouble. It won't help the men or the union."

I was relieved to agree, which was a mistake. Because of fear, we censored ourselves, so there's no published record of the great Mother Jones's visit to Moonstone, her speech that roused the marble workers.

Instead, K.T.'s idea was "to bury the hatchet with Padgett." She requested an interview with the new young Company President. To her shock, Jasper invited her in for a friendly chat and a tour of the mill operation.

"I'm off to meet the Princeling," she said. "Care to join me?"

I pleaded nosebleed and hangnail and told myself again I was done with the whole pack of Padgetts.

K.T. returned from her interview with Jasper abuzz with changed opinions. She typed while humming. "It's a new era. Padgett Junior has begun negotiations with the union. He is committed to send the payroll out. That young man is a thinker. He reads. And he is more than a little bit odd."

He drinks, I did not mention.

"I was wrong about him." K.T. sighed. "He has a good heart."

I remembered that heart, how it beat wildly in the bony cage of his ribs. The Lemon Drop had stolen it.

"He's in over his head, I'm afraid. A softie never lasts," K.T. predicted. "Bowles will chew him up and spit him out."

She placed a book on my desk. It was *The Souls of Black Folk*.

"Young Padgett gave me a copy of this provocation," she said. "He's inspired by the writer—Dr. Du Bois—lecturing me about some project of his. A monument to honor the black race. Admirable! But improbable. If it ever gets built—not likely—your friend Jace has committed to providing the marble for free."

"He's not my friend," I said.

She smirked. The book of *Souls* sat on the composing table. I buried it under a pile of newsprint, where it smoldered.

About a week after Mrs. Jones had departed Moonstone, I was happy to receive a postcard from George. On the front was a picture of a circus, a lady trick rider decked out in feathers. On the back was one sentence, in a lunatic pen scratch, backward.

SYLVIE I OwE YOu ANOTHEr ICE CrEAM CONE bEFOrE THE SuMMEr's OVEr, FrOM YOUr FELLOW TrOUBLEMAkEr, G.

"Lonahan's sweet on you," said K.T.

"Snoop! You read it."

She saw I was smiling. Since the night of my speech and our lingering in the moonlight, I'd pondered George Lonahan. *Fellow troublemaker*, he wrote now. Was I his comrade? He seemed to think so. He was sweet on me. K.T. had confirmed it.

"Tòo bad he had to hightail it out of here," she said, fishing. "You must be sorry."

It *was* too bad, but I did not take the bait. "Where did he hightail it to?"

"Likely he's with Mother Jones in the southern coalfields" was her theory. "Down in Trinidad, they've been out six weeks on strike."

Strike. The word sounded of sudden sharp danger, random as lightning. It hung over that summer like a dark scribble, despite the dribs and drabs of paycheck that the Company doled out to the workers. Every day was beauty for free, but the glorious landscape fed the persistent ache in my chest. I did my work and brooded about money, demands and concessions, closed shop, open shop, yellow-dog contracts and square deals. Why couldn't things be fair? I was afraid of what violence might happen, tired of the swaggering men. I wished for summer nights by the river and my initials carved in a tree trunk with another's, but whose? It is a tedious chronic condition of youth, the pre-occupations and pursuit of romance.

The newspapers carried on sparring.

> *RECORD*: Negotiations stalled over pennies. Union demands 8-hour day. Walkout set for August first.
>
> *BOOSTER*: The only way Moonstone can fail to enjoy a healthy growth will be for the anarchists to take the country, overthrow the seat of government and cause men to want marble about as much as a starved dog wants bricks.

On fine days that July, Jace Padgett and the Lemon Drop went riding down Prosperity Street and into the mountains, serene Hélène on a gray mottled something, Jasper on a chestnut something. A steed. I did not know the names of horse varieties, only that the Lemon Drop had special riding fashions: jodhpur pantaloons and a squat bowler hat attached to her yellow head. How did it stay on? Perhaps with roofing nails. I pictured hammering it down, the spikes in her skull. One afternoon I watched them from behind the window of the *Record* while they tied up their horses at Mrs. Weeks's bakery next door. Jasper helped the lady dismount, caught her in his arms. The Lemon Drop looked directly into his eyes, the saucepot. Of course he would like her.

"Get away from spying now," K.T. said. She stopped work and confronted me by the glass. "You'll waste a lot of time on that one."

I tried to swallow, but she saw I could not.

"Sylvie Pelletier," she said, "I don't have a daughter, but if I did."

That she didn't, and was alone, was perhaps the reason she'd taken me under her wing. I myself was tired of loneliness, afraid to end up *solitaire*, as she appeared to be.

Outside, the equestrian lovebirds rode away to the hills. Mademoiselle Hélène sat on her horse with an elegant straight back. But Jasper parked in the saddle with his elbows out like turkey wings. He was not a natural outdoorsman or ruggedly strong like the western men who strutted hard-boiled and handsome through the town. Which was a reason he was fascinating to me, exotic as some tropical bird.

"The sooner you seize yourself by the scruff of the neck and leave that dead-end trail, the better it'll be for you," K.T. said. "If somebody'd told me that once upon a time, I'd've thanked 'em."

"Thank you, then." I would've seized my scruff, as she counseled, but it was apparently still in the grip of jealousy. "What was your dead-end trail?"

"It's dead-ended, so never you mind."

"You're allowed to snoop, but I'm not?"

"Precisely."

"You said to ask questions."

"Forget that man, he's a gilded pinhead," she said.

"You said he was a thinker. You said he had a good heart."

"We'll see, won't we? Regardless, he's not worthy of you."

———

Her advice was the same as Inge's, and while I tried to heed it, Jasper Padgett passed me in the town and strung me along with an odd wink in his eye. As if we shared some joke. Maybe I was the joke.

"Hiya, Sylvie. Don't you look lovely this morning?"

Stab me with an ice pick. I could not lance the boil of him no matter how I tried to steer my thoughts toward the agitator Lonahan and his ricochet laugh, his postcards from afar. I exhumed the book about *Souls*, on the chance it might provide a look inside the soul of oddball Jace P. and his preoccupations.

Du Bois had a French name, but his book explained the problems of American colored people, to whom I'd given hardly a thought until my encounters with Easter Grady. *Her sister sold away*. The book was full of sentences that made me itch with discomfort. I wrestled around the chapters, reading about the color line and the sons of slave masters. These essays unsettled me and educated me to truths I was reluctant to know. One story particularly distressed me, of a black woman violated by a white man. Reading it, I remembered that photograph of Easter's sons, so different from each other in appearance, whispers from the summer provoking frost heaves of suspicion.

Because Caleb is— Jace stammering drunk by the river. *Everybody says so*.

The horror of how it could be . . . was unfathomable. I could not stop pondering the puzzle of Padgetts and Gradys, the rumors and the truth. If the rumors were true, who could blame Easter for putting her revenge in the Duke's breakfast? We use what defenses we have, but in the end, hers had not been enough. Now, for money, she was coerced back to toil in the house of her tormentor. I prayed for the Gradys' success in their brave new venture, but knew the odds were stacked against them.

In the middle of August, the strike deadline came and went without a walkout—but without a resolution either. In other news, Susie Society reported:

> Miss Hélène DuLac, visiting Elkhorne Manor
> from her native Belgium as social secretary for

> Mrs. Padgett, has now tied up the work of the
> Company's Sociology Department and departed
> for points east. Miss DuLac told Susie she had a
> delightful stay in our fair town and hopes to re-
> turn someday.

"Saw her get on the downbound train this morning," K.T. said, as if turning over valuable information.

"So?" I said too casually.

That afternoon, there Jace was, walking in the street, not in a straight line. When he saw me, he covered his face as if to hide. "Shylvie, sweet." He held out his hand.

"You're drunk?" I shrank away. "At this hour?"

"Yessh," he said. "Walk it off with me because I. Because you." He turned around toward the lake, pulling air over his shoulder like a swimmer, for me to follow.

Stupid Sylvie do not follow.

I failed to listen to the angels of my better judgment and followed the devil of a weaving Padgett, imagining—what? That he would, *presto*, change into a charming upright suitor and see the error of his ways. I still wanted that. If I had some mea culpa, then I could decide what to do with it. Jilt him back or jump into his arms.

At the edge of the lake, the mountains reflected themselves upside down, so I thought of Lonahan and his postcard. But it was not George who had me wrong side up.

Jace held his arms wide, inhaling the scenery. "Marvelish Lake," he said, struggling to pretend he was sober. "Marvel-lish—*liss*."

"Don't shout," I said. "You'll scare the fish."

"Sorry, Sylvie-ster. I scare myself." He put a finger to his lips. "Shhushh."

We sat on a boulder and watched the red-wings wheeling. The water was dark silk shirred by the breeze. I drew spirals on the rock with a stick.

Jasper took several starting breaths and lifted his professorial finger: "My reason. To explain. My reason. Okay?"

"Reason?" I said, still cold to him. "For what?"

"My behavior," he said. "I've been operating under the impression you did not, you do not, care for me."

"Because you prefer someone else."

"Because I did not hear from you because you did not hear from me and then because your letter was misdirected and did not find me convalescing in Richmond where my stepmother encouraged me to entertain Miss DuLac, in hopes it would improve my spirits and please my father, but—"

I covered my ears. "I don't want to hear about it."

"Also, in truth, I have . . . an affliction. A gloom." He flung a stone side-armed into the water. "See? One stone sinks, and then. What ripples out. I believe you'd know about that, sweet Sylvie. Of all people. Wouldn't you."

"You don't make sense, Jasper. You're drunk."

"Not drunk *enough*. If only you had a bottle up your sleeve. Do you?" He took my arm by the sleeve and lifted the cuff to his eye to peer inside it, clowning.

"Stop." I pulled away sharply.

His gaze was cockeyed. "I am inebriated."

"As always is the case when you speak to me. Or write letters."

"Oh, God, I know." He groaned. "What did I write? I know it was shameful. At that time—I had episodes. Can't remember entire evenings. I apologize to the lady."

The stick I had for tracing broke to a stub. It was not enough, the apology. Some other atonement was due.

"You, Sylvie, are the picture of innocence," Jace said.

"Not so innocent as you think," I said.

"What I mean. Is. I've tried to protect you from . . . myself, haven't I? You don't deserve the torment of my fickling . . ." He grinned. "My ficklement."

"Your ficklery," I said. We burst out laughing at the invented words. "A fickelry would be a place you go to change your mind."

"A ficklement is the predicament of a mind that refuses to change," he said. "Would you change yours, ever? Am I a lost cause?"

"Hmmpf."

"I don't deserve your sympathetic ear." He reached and touched my earlobe.

A violent shiver shook me. "Stay over there," I said. Wished he wouldn't.

"Yes, ma'am. Sorry. I'm desolate. I entangled myself with a she-wolf, and now she has left me here to howl."

"Now you know how it feels. I'm glad you're suffering. I hope your heart cracks open like a walnut."

"Cruel, aren't you?"

"Not more than you."

"True. I'm a dog, not worth a bone."

"My father was killed—but you never asked me one question about it. So I'll tell you: They threw my mother out. Your people did. They charged us for my father's funeral. Billed us for train tickets, back rent, stuck us up at gunpoint—" The words kept coming like punches.

He fended them off with weakling sputters. "I didn't know. I can make it right. I—"

"Your company was fined two hundred dollars for my father's life and paid it to the Labor Department. Not a penny to us, and my mother with holes in her shoes." I didn't care anymore if he knew about the holes in our shoes or the hole in my head where the rest of my timidity had leaked out. What did it matter if he knew we Pelletiers were mountain people with cardboard over broken windows?

"They carried her and the baby out of our house into the mud," I said. "We lost everything. I did. They were sent back east."

"Oh, Jesus. It's unbearable." He grappled with his hair. "I don't know how to stop them. I told Bowles to settle with the men. To release the payroll. But he says leave it to him, and he— I don't know how to run the Company. I'm called a pushover. Truth is, I don't give a damn about profits or rocks."

"I too hate rocks," I said.

"We hate the same things," Jasper said, wistful.

This reminder of our shared loathings softened me further.

"My father gave me his word," said Jace. "But *Bowles* is the boss."

"But you of all people," I said, "you have the means to do whatever you like. Go anywhere you want—"

Jace whipped his head to look at me. "I'd like to get out of here."

"Me too."

"You? You'd leave—? Where'd you go?"

"Away."

He sighed heavily. "I *wanted* to make it right. For everyone here. I tried! Like you said, *one right thing*. A reign of jushtish. On earth. *Justice*."

The red-wings reeled and roosted in the trees. Jasper stayed drunk, lacing and unlacing his fingers. Above us, something fluttered through the early dusk. Darting.

"I'd like to fly away," Jace said, pointing. "Wouldn't you? We could be birds."

"Those are bats," I told him. "The bird of the Devil."

"Of course. Bats." He rolled a pebble between his palms. "I'm not cut out for business. I don't have the heart for it."

"It's news to hear you have one at all. We'll report about it in the *Record*."

"Stab me again," he said.

"Trouble is a pebble."

"Somebody told me that once."

"That was me."

"Oh. Right." He winged the stone into the water, rings spreading out in ripples. His smile was bleary and askew. "If I asked you for help, would you help me?"

"Depends what you asked."

"If I asked you to rob a bank? Or kill somebody? Maybe me. You could put me out of my misery. As a favor."

"Don't be ridiculous." I rolled my eyes. "You're too sorry for yourself."

"Sorry for—everything," he said. "I'm sorry the men are gonna strike and I can't stop it—and I'm sorry that I—that your father was killed. While my father lives another day to break his promises."

"You wouldn't wish him dead, believe me."

Jasper knocked the heel of his hand against his head, as if he could force demons out of his ears. What I did not know was that this day marked a watershed for the son of Duke Padgett. He had failed to convince the Colonel to settle the labor dispute. He had failed to win the heart of a flibbertigibbet. Failed to fit himself to the suit his father had bespoke for him, and now he had to make himself a new suit.

My own failure: misunderstanding how he would stitch me to the linings, design me as part of his plans. I was still afflicted by the common lovesickness of intoxicated young girls kissed in moonlight, so his confusion seemed like something I might use for myself. He might say again, *I'm lost without you,* and we would go forward together hating the same things, fixing broken bones and broken promises. Making things right.

"What do you want then, Sylvie?" he asked. That question.

What I wanted was: *All. Everything.* The flames of sun in a scarlet streak over the mountains. The heat off Jace. His eyes on me were blinking, drowsy. What I wanted was not fancy, only impossible.

"For things to be fair," I said.

"You're a revolutionist, Sylvie Pelletier. I admire it. You'll teach me."

"We're not brave enough to be revolutionists," I said, laughing.

"You made a speech!" he said. "You were arrested! Just you wait. I'll show you."

"If you were serious about revolution, or whatever you call it, you'd do something. You would act—"

"I will, I promise." He smiled at me. "We'll be comrades in anarchy."

He was the second man to propose me as *comrade.* Hardly sweet talk, but as he said it, holding my gaze as he used to, the word had the ring of *darling* or *beloved.* I wished he had said these, but I feared his fickling ficklery and whatever he meant by *anarchy.* That he might do something rash.

"Easter Grady said to pay no attention to what a Padgett says, only what they do."

"I know what to do," he said, and leaned against me.

I pulled away. Lemon Drop not twelve hours gone and here he was, leaning. "We should go. It's almost dark."

"Dark." He sighed. "Shall I escort you home?" The peaches and bourbon in his voice. He rose to his feet, swaying in the windless dusk. He offered a hand to pull me upright, then turned me toward him, too close, his breath at my neck, his mouth. "I remember you," he said. "I remember, you know."

Whatever he remembered, it was bloodshot and untrustworthy, dredged from the bottom of a bottle. I backed away and swatted mosquitoes. A bufflehead skidded to a landing on the water. A fish mouthed the surface. Bats fluttered above our heads. Jasper sighed, "Oh, Sylvie." We headed toward town. "'Lost and gone forever,'" he sang, a fragment of that tune from last summer. I steered him onto the path, home to Elkhorne, where he belonged and I did not.

"Goodbye," I told him.

But he was not done with me, nor I with him.

Chapter Twenty-Nine

Two days later, the union went on strike. August 25, 1908. A hundred cutters from the mill and the hundred-man crew at the quarry put down their tools and walked out into the unhoused world. I stood with the women at the entrance to the sheds. The men filed out, defiant, grinning like boys playing hooky, till they got outside the gate. Then they milled around, angry as sparks in dry grass, cursing. The women beat pots, rattled tin cans full of stones, babies on their backs, children underfoot. Dan Kerrigan started to sing, the picket line joining in like a chorus of alley cats. The tune was "My Country 'Tis of Thee."

"Colorado 'tis of thee, dark land of tyranny, of thee I sing."

Strikes are all the same. Same songs. Same reasons. Same hope and rage. In those years it was struggle and strife all over the mountains, in the cities and on the plains of the country, wherever there was industry or toil.

Our own Moonstone strike of 1908 is long forgotten, as lost to history as a bullet dropped in snow. That first morning at the head of the picket line, Dan Kerrigan carried a United Mine Workers poster asking the question: *Is Colorado in America?* Sheriff Smiley knocked him down, stamped on his hand, and broke the bones. Tony Mercanditti picked up the sign and carried

307

it instead. Kerrigan got to his feet and marched with his men, jeering the Pinks:

"Ya squealers, ya magoofs, ya choirboys. Lousy Company beef."

Smiley barred the gates to the mill. His battalion of goons with badges went house to house, pounding doors, going down a list of strikers' names.

"This house is Company property," the Pinks said, and evicted families from their cabins, threw out furniture, pots and pans, clothes and pictures, toys, icons of Jesus, beds and blankets. All tossed. Mrs. Santorini picked vegetables from her garden and placed a putrid white object on the steps to her former home on Padgett Street. A rotten egg. "This, I leave for the *criminali*," she said, and walked away with her onions and carrots tied in a bedsheet, trailing children with their small bundles.

I wrote what I saw. Quarrymen in an exodus filing down the road, the trolley piled with women and kids. Whole families streamed through town, heading for the union camp on Dogtooth Flats. They hauled handcarts, chickens in crates, goats on leashes. Jenkins's wagon made runs up to the camp, a nickel per trip if he could get it.

A pity we were out of film for the camera. What I wanted was to photograph the women; the claw marks of worry on their faces, the children strapped among the flotsam of belongings, small Clara Bruner clutching her dolly. That would show Jace Padgett. *See what they do?* And where was he? No sign of him, only the Pinks on patrol and Colonel Bowles in his burping motorcar, summoning the Citizens' Alliance to a meeting.

At the *Record*, we worked all night. By morning, the word STRIKE spat out of the press, my foot aching on the treadle. I went to the train depot, where families waited to catch the downbound train, leaving the men behind. There was Mrs. Santorini with her children. When the train arrived, she handed each one up the steps, then gazed to the hillside, where a man waved his hat. "*Addio*, Papa!" the kids cried.

A watching Pinkerton spat on the ground. "Bolshy animals," he said, and worse.

If Jace knew, if he saw, I thought. Some revolutionist. He was not in charge. Bowles was.

"Your friend J. C. Padgett's gone up to the family lodge for a hunt with that fellow—the chef on the Padgetts' train car," K.T. reported. She meant Caleb Grady. Hal Brinckerhoff at the Larkspur had seen "Junior Padgett and a Negro" riding out with a packhorse. "So much for the great negotiator. Halibut says the boy will stay away till he bags a few trophy heads for his wall. Maybe he had a sudden craving for elk-heart stew."

Or anarchy. What was he up to? He could raise wages a dollar a day just by forfeiting the yearly budget for strawberries at Elkhorne Manor. If he was such a revolutionist, why didn't he do that? The more he confounded me, the more I wanted—if not his heart, then his money. Give it all to the people in the strike camp. *Cash, not caramels.* Hadn't he proposed it himself? What I couldn't imagine was that he was plotting his own revenge, his own escape, considering me for the role of accomplice.

A bloom of white tents appeared on the treeless shelf below Dogtooth Peak, pitched on the only patch of local land not owned by the Company. It belonged to a prospector who'd abandoned his claim there after a failed quest for silver. You could still see the orifice of his old mine, one of many dogholes that pocked the Gilded Mountains and Nameless Ranges of the Rockies.

I climbed the trail to see how the strikers would live for the duration. The union had provided them a shipment of tents and stoves, coal and rations. All of it was hauled by jacktrain over the backside of Dogtooth Ridge, where a sharp incisor of rock gave the place its name. The union's supplies started the men off in a festive mood. Strike pay was three dollars a week, plus a dollar for a wife, fifty cents a child. They were hoping the walkout would win them a paycheck of three dollars a day. Cripple Creek miners had gotten it, why shouldn't they?

The strikers dug latrines and ran a sluice to carry water from Dogtooth Creek. While they worked, they sang "We're coming, Colorado, fighting for our rights," to the tune of "The Battle Cry of Freedom." They put up a mess tent, a supply tent, and one for Union headquarters. The American flag flew overhead, and a sign outside read: *UMW of America, One & Indissoluble,* a handshake above the phrase *Eight Hours.*

That's all they wanted: fair pay and a workday of eight hours. "Not too much to ask," Kerrigan said. "A little rest. Overtime." He came into the *Record* sporting a new UMW pin on his lapel. "Talks going good. No more dead work. Pay in real money, not scrip. We're gonna settle soon."

"They won't settle," K.T. said. "Bowles? Never. He's a yellow-dog man."

"We'll be out six weeks, tops," Kerrigan said.

"Should've struck back in April," she told him. "Idiots, to wait till the end of summer. Bowles will hold out till you cave in the cold. Can't survive winter in a tent."

"Bet you a dime we're done before the snow flies."

"I hope you win that bet," K.T. said.

"We'll see who's the idiot, eh, Redmond? We've got 'em dead to rights."

Kerrigan was cocksure, and K.T. kept the walkout on the front page. In the first week of September, my bright idea was to print a famous union poster: the American flag with fighting words on the stripes. *Free Speech Denied in Colorado. Corporations Corrupt. Union Men Exiled in Colorado.* I'd seen it in a union pamphlet.

"Let's put it on the front page."

"It's dangerous," K.T. said, smiling.

MARTIAL LAW DECLARED IN COLORADO!
HABEAS CORPUS SUSPENDED IN COLORADO!
FREE PRESS THROTTLED IN COLORADO!
BULL-PENS FOR UNION MEN IN COLORADO!
FREE SPEECH DENIED IN COLORADO!
SOLDIERS DEFY THE COURTS IN COLORADO!
WHOLESALE ARRESTS WITHOUT WARRANT IN COLORADO!
UNION MEN EXILED FROM HOMES AND FAMILIES IN COLORADO!
CONSTITUTIONAL RIGHT TO BEAR ARMS QUESTIONED IN COLORADO!
CORPORATIONS CORRUPT AND CONTROL ADMINISTRATION IN COLORADO!
RIGHT OF FAIR, IMPARTIAL AND SPEEDY TRIAL ABOLISHED IN COLORADO!
CITIZENS' ALLIANCE RESORTS TO MOB LAW AND VIOLENCE IN COLORADO!
MILITIA HIRED TO CORPORATIONS TO BREAK THE STRIKE IN COLORADO!

"It's art." I smiled back.

"It's truth," K.T. said. "Free speech."

But the moneycrats called it un-American. A defilement of the flag.

This poster had caused a violent furor in Telluride during the 1903 gold mine strike. For publishing it, the local paper was ransacked by the Citizens' Alliance of business owners, the editor run out of town. Now in Moonstone, the image was one more stick of dynamite on the pile of explosives we were building under ourselves.

The day after it was printed in the *Record*, Colonel Bowles came into the bakery, where I sat nursing my coffee and reading the Du Bois book about *Souls*. Instinctively, I hid it. The ideas in its pages were threatening to men like the Colonel. He gave me a smile full of pickle juice and slapped our offending newspaper onto the counter.

Dottie jumped at the sound. She fluttered about, filling the Colonel's cup with coffee and flattery. "What an honor to serve the Mayor! I tell everybody back east our town beats anywhere on God's earth for its beauty."

"Precisely the spirit I like to hear," Bowles said. "Why not apply it to your customer policy? First, you should refuse to serve that anarchist." He jabbed a finger at the *Record* with its striped flag of trouble. "She's responsible for this desecration."

"You mean Trina Redmond?" Mrs. Weeks said, all innocence.

"You serve anyone you like, but when you feed a tapeworm, what happens?"

"It . . . eats you from the inside?" Dottie giggled, nervous.

"Exactly." The Colonel dabbed his mustache. "This town is your home. Your livelihood. How much will your shop be worth if her machinations should be successful? Redmond and her young friend here hurt your interests." He jerked his thumb at me.

That morning I wished to flatten the Colonel like a sheet of paper to write on. *Someday I might.* "I am only the delivery girl, sir," I said, mild as milk— because when you make a man think you're a nincompoop, he'll dismiss you as harmless, less likely to stomp on you.

"Well, young lady, I hate to tell you"—Bowles smiled like a sweet old grandpa—"your employer is un-American."

"I don't take her paper," Dottie Weeks lied. "And I do love reading the *Booster.*"

"Thatta girl," said Bowles with a wink.

We were too innocent, ignorant of the threat in his jocular words, their sugarcoated venom. The Colonel paid for his bread with real nickels clinking on the counter, and leaned over me, placing his finger on the image of the adulterated flag. He whispered, "Socialism in a woman is worse than rabies in a dog."

The next day his company newspaper had a short announcement:

THE BOOSTERS IN MOONSTONE TOWN
ARE THE VAST MAJORITY.
MORE POWER TO THEM! KNOCKERS BE GONE!

Such threats scared half the local subscribers off our list. It was not just Koble at the Company Mercantile who refused to take the *Moonstone City Record.* Hal Brinckerhoff told K.T. that Colonel Bowles had advised him to drop his friendship with her. Instead, ol' Halibut dropped by the office to smoke by the stove. He and Dottie Weeks were loyal friends. Dottie set aside stale bread for me to deliver to the strikers at Dogtooth Camp with the newspaper. Hal threw in a bottle of whiskey for Kerrigan. "Spirits to keep his spirits up."

When I climbed up to the flats, the children of the camp rushed at me and clamped my legs. "Sylvie!" they cried. "*Dolci, dolci!* Sweets!" I could not resist a purchase of strawberry licorice drops and molasses candies, and doled them out while children climbed on me like wild kittens. I told them stories and sang them Nipper's favorite song, "Hallelujah, I'm a Bum," and missed my family. I enjoyed this charity work with a taint of missionary righteousness, like Inge's, that I could do one right thing. I handed little Clara licorice and gave her mother stale old bread and the *Record*.

Frau Bruner was overjoyed at the bread but had no use for the newspaper. For her the news was that her husband, Gustav, had trapped ten grouse. She sat by a fire where several small charred creatures roasted on a spit. "Last year your papa show Gustav how to make the neck trap." She held a bird by its limp neck, plucked the feathers, and put them in a sack, to make a coverlet for the baby. It was only the first week of September, but already the nights left frost on the grass, snow on the shoulders of Mount Sopris.

"Poor dears," said Dottie, offering more bread the following week. "It'll soon be dead cold in those tents. How will they ever last the winter?"

But there were signs that the strikers would not have to last, that their walkout would be a bust, because the quarry and the mill were operating without them. You could hear the clank and hum from the sheds, see the stone carted down on the tram.

In the *Record* we reported the Company's strategy to stay open:

THE SCAB HATCHERY

A scab hatchery has opened in the nearby town of Ruby. The hatchlings consist of forgers, shift bosses, hyenas, chronic toadies, pimples, magoofers, trained beagles, knobsticks, peddlers, foremen, and blackleg herders. It's only a matter of time before these undesirables come up the rail line and into Moonstone. The Labor Commission reports steady complaints that the Company lures these dupes with promises of $2 a day, yet offers them only a dollar when they arrive. The new workers know little of hard-rock mining or stone finishing, and the Company now ships an inferior

quality of marble. Never forget: "Today's scab
is tomorrow's striker."

Scab. The word was dry blood over a wound, and my own wounds refused
to heal. Jace Padgett appeared to have given up on a promise to me. On fairness itself. Giving up was certainly a temptation. I would retreat to a nunnery,
I thought, if there were one without nuns. Someplace where I could avoid
ruminations on romance, get away from these Pinks and scabs.

So-called replacement crews began arriving in the third week of the strike,
imported by train in the darkness. Dan Kerrigan came into the *Record* to report the invasion. "A buncha foreigners shipped from Cincinnati and a few
colored boys brung in from Texas. Sheriff has a whole pen of scabs stockaded."

"Bowles will be training them," K.T. said. "Shadowing the holdouts."

"Ain't no holdouts here," Kerrigan said, threat in his voice. "Not a man
of us would cross that picket line." The whites of his eyes were shot with red.

"This is where things get ugly," K.T. said. "Down in Victor, the Pinkertons smashed the presses. In Cripple Creek, they threw the editor in jail."

"They wouldn't bother us if we wouldn't print—" I started.

"We print." K.T. wheeled on me. "Understood?"

Her scolding stung. I turned away to my sorting trays and missed the fear
in her eyes. After a while, she came and put a hand on my shoulder.

"Last spring I didn't run the story about Mother Jones," she said. "I
thought there might be room for harmony with the new boss Padgett. But I
was wrong, and now the world needs to know what's going on here. The paper
is called the *Record* because that's what it is. I'll pay your ticket home any time."

"Thank you, K.T., I'll stay."

Home, she said. And where was that? Maman's letters from Rutland were about
weather, the price of yarn. Henry had summer work in a lumberyard. She
could not keep Nipper in shoes. *We pray for you,* she wrote. *Le Curé asks if you
might soon take vows at the convent in Montpelier.*

I would rather die, I did not write. *The Devil has me by the throat.* My mother would think so if she saw what I wrote, *finks and magoofers*, printed in the paper. By now I knew that K.T. was not the Devil's envoy. Her defiance no longer shocked me. Instead, what appalled me was the Colonel's refusal to bargain, to raise wages or shorten the workday. What shocked me were the Pinkertons' violent tactics and how we—a little two-sheet newspaper—were the only ones to tell about the outrages in the storybook town of Moonstone.

I think that's why I stayed. To tell about it.

Every evening, we hauled the composing table in front of the door, to bar it "in case those thugs come for us," K.T. said. Most nights, awake in my closet, I heard her pacing above me, talking to Bilious the cat. In the dark, I hummed a tune to drown her out, stifle thoughts of Pinkerton threats and pangs of worry about the freezing children in the camp. Worst was the conundrum of two men: Jace Padgett who stood at the lakeside and said, *I remember you*, then disappeared into the hills to kill an elk, eat its heart. And the other, George Lonahan, who sent cornball postcards written backward.

Stuck in the valley till October. Will have to treat you to hot buttered rum instead of a cold cone. Yours truly, George

The scene on that card was of Colorado's Purgatoire Valley, the name like a message. George in purgatory, Jace in the wilderness, and the rest of us in a standoff.

The strike went on, September nearly gone. The union camp was a bustling town of canvas. The women served soup, knitted socks, hung out the wash. They'd organized a Bible class and English lessons. The children hauled wood and water. The men built barricades and hiked to town for shifts on the picket line, singing their union songs. They dodged the roving Pinks, to avoid arrest on charges of "trespass" or "loitering." They held meetings by firelight. When the wind was right, you could hear their accordions and tambu-ricas coming through the darkness. I fell asleep with their tunes playing in my dreams, "Singing the battle cry of the yooooooo-nyun."

Just before dawn one morning, I was awakened by shouts outside the *Record* office. Somebody yelling for help. I spied from behind the dark window. Pinkertons dragged two men by the arms, jabbing them with billy clubs. "Get off me!" the prisoners snarled and cursed, one of them in a voice I knew. "Get off me!"

It was Oskar Setkowski. "Help, wake up!" he bellowed. "*Syl-weea!*" A melee out front of the *Record* and Oskar calling me. "Sylvie!"

Carlton Pfister and another Pink pinned the two men in the dirt, wres-tling with the twisting fish of Setkowski. He spat and scratched and cursed. Silently, I cheered Oskar. *Beat them. Batter them.*

He broke free and streaked off into the dark. One of the Pinks gave chase while Pfister wrestled the other fellow, wild on the street.

"Ya Bohunk mutt. Shuddup." Carlton whacked the man's head and got a gag over his mouth, then dragged him down the street.

I was furious, sitting in the dark, when there was a tapping on the door. "Let me in, please, Sylweea." Oskar outside, whispering.

When I opened up, he fell inside, panting, his face bloody. "Thank you. They chase me. I don't have—where to hide."

With the lights off, I helped him clean his face and gave him a bandage.

"I'm running faster than those Pinks bastard. You see me?"

"It's terrible what they did," I said. His face was bruised, his mouth bleed-ing. "Sorry, Oskar, but you better keep running. They'll find you here. Go out the back, don't go to the depot. Take the east trail to camp before the sun's up." I gave him an old hat for a disguise and hustled him out the back door.

"You love me, yes?" he said, winking. "You save me."

"Goodbye, Oskar," I said. "Don't go near the depot."

But the depot was exactly where I went. I got dressed and followed Pfister and his Pinkerton friends. Nobody would notice me in the dark. *Just a girl.* Even before I got to the train platform, I could hear the commotion: the Pinks hustling men onto the train. I stood in the shadows and watched.

"Get off me!"

That voice. The hat. They'd caught Oskar again. He twisted and jerked like a trout, cursing. The guards shoved the men into the baggage car. The train began to move, carrying Oskar Setkowski and five other strikers down the mountain. The Pinks dusted their hands. Sheriff Smiley emerged from the ticket office and lit a cigarette.

I approached him. "Excuse me. What was the reason you arrested that man?"

"Having a mouth." Smiley blew smoke. "Also trespassing."

"Trespassing how?"

"Company orders. All shirkers out. Railroad takes them away for free."

"Those men are employed at the quarry."

"Not now they ain't."

"Oskar lives here."

"When the judge in Gunnison is done with him, he can buy himself a ticket back."

"Eighteen dollars?" I said. "How can he pay it? I know him—"

"I bet you do," Smiley leered. "And would you like to know me too?"

I'd like to know how you live with your worm-eaten soul. I backed away, imagining how it would be to poke his eyes out with a pencil, the whites popping like grapes full of blood.

Trina Redmond waited for me by the door in her nightdress, hands on hips. "What was all that about? Where've you been so early?"

"They deported six strikers on the morning train. I couldn't stop them—"

"What were you going to do, Pelletier? Ask them nicely? Write it up."

"I didn't take notes—"

"So what? You saw it, you write it," she said. "Unless you're afraid."

I was. And she was too. "It's reckless—" I said.

"It was reckless to rush out in the dark after those criminals. Did you think of that? Also, it was brave. Type it up."

"Are you sure, K.T.?" I said. "Because if we say what happened—"

"That's what we do," she said. She kept her eye on me while I stabbed at the keys.

I put it all down. I crossed out sentences. Removed Oskar's name so he wouldn't be in worse trouble. But however the words were arranged, the story was the same, and frightening to write, as if the crime—the "trespass"—were to put down in public the truth of what I'd witnessed.

VAGRANCY CHARGES

The Moonstone Marble Company has issued a warning: any "unauthorized" person caught "trespassing" or "loitering" on Company property will be arrested. Already six members of the striking miners' union have been sent over the pass, simply for walking lawfully in town. Pinkerton guards beat and gagged the men and put them on the train. Most of them cannot afford return fare. Unless they hike the twenty-mile distance over rough terrain, they are unlikely to return. Which appears to be the precise intention of the Company.

K.T. read the copy. "There's ink in your veins after all, Pelletier."

I liked to hear it. Praise from K.T. was water on the wilted plant of my spirits. I began to believe I could make myself a real newswoman. K.T. seemed to think so too. She showed me Ida Tarbell's dispatches about Standard Oil scams in *McClure's*, and stories about politics in the *New York Herald* by Cora Rigby, examples to encourage me.

But her headline, ILLEGAL DEPORTATIONS, shrank me again. I'd rather somebody else point a finger. To say *j'accuse* was dangerous. "Don't put my name on it."

"For cryin' out loud," K.T. said. "You saw what you saw and heard what you heard. To write it—to witness!—is the job of the Fourth Estate. If you can't do it, then—"

Then you'll never be a newswriter, she didn't say. "Okay. Print it," I said.

But that night, K.T. paced the floor above my head, and in the morning, she said, "You're right. Let's not print this week. Maybe they'll settle."

"We should publish!" After my chickenhearted reluctance, I was now the one pressing her to run the story. But K.T. had other worries on her mind.

"I've had a telegram from my sister," she said. "Her husband is ill and won't last long. I'll have to head to Denver. I don't want you to put out the paper when you're alone here. Just feed the cat and hold the fort." She put on her hat and flung a pile of mail at me. "And sort that, if you don't mind." She went off to the afternoon train.

Hold the fort. Would there be a siege? Alone with Bill the cat, I worried and found I missed K.T. The typewriter was silent. The doorbell did not jangle. Of late, nobody in town would be seen patronizing a so-called Red anarchist witch bulldagger or her mule of a delivery girl. I sorted the mail, so distracted I nearly missed it: a letter addressed to me, the crest of Elkhorne embossed on the flap, the handwriting familiar.

Mr. J. C. Padgett
Requests the honor of your
presence for dinner at Elkhorne
7 p.m. October 1, 1908

I just about fell over. For what reason would Jace Padgett invite me, the jilted *secretaire*? Perhaps the Company thought I could be bribed to the *Booster* side, seduced by luxury and fancy foods. *Does it tempt you, sweetheart?* Mother Jones had asked. Already I pictured the menu, the array of fruits, the pâté and roast beef. *Luxury makes slaves.* I was trapped in an argument between Caution and the Demon whispering on my shoulder.

Caution: Don't go. Save your pride.

Demon: What's the harm? Think of the crescent rolls with butter. Sparkling wine.

Caution: Do not associate with robber barons. They evicted your family.

Demon: Maraschino. Veuve Clicquot. Kissing.

Oh, kissing. I still thought about it. Beatrice Fairfax's advice column had lately warned about "animal magnetism." It was often mistaken for love.

Stay away, Caution said.

But I stopped listening. I'd go to dinner. If nothing else, I'd write a report for the *Record* about the lovely social evening at Elkhorne: The vast drawing room was lit by fireflies. The guests dined on nectar and sugarplums despite their host owing thousands of doubloons to their haggard workers. Afterward, the glittering assembly was treated to the music of the planets, each invitee anointed by the blood of murdered mineworkers, fanned by servants in turbans.

How could I decline? Not for a moment did I imagine the cream-colored card stock in my hand was an invitation from a madman—was he?—to partner in crime.

"Miss Sylvie Marie Thérèse Pelletier accepts with pleasure your kind invitation . . ." In the formal style, I wrote my reply and mailed it. That week, instead of fretting over the hungry families cold in the strike camp, I occupied myself with the wasting female question: what to wear. The choice was sackcloth or calico. Adele's old navy blue or the too-formal silk of Inge's cast-off green gown. In that last week of September, I could've built a chicken coop or written a book with the hours I spent over dilemmas of fashion. To wear the wrong thing, the Countess taught me, was to reveal your status in a ranking of humans that royals invented to maintain themselves supreme.

In the end, I scraped my pockets. At the Company Mercantile, Mr. Koble followed me around as if I might filch something. At his rack of ladies' fashions, I found a cobalt-blue tea gown. It didn't seem practical, but the buttons in front were shortly to prove useful for stowing what I'd later steal, though not from Koble. With no time to wait for a dressmaker, I paid sixteen dollars cash. When I counted out this fortune into his palm, Mr. Koble's smile was greased with smugness.

"Lovely gown," he said. "Never knew anarchists dressed for tea."

I pictured how it would be to place two of my pennies on his cold dead eyes.

"Easter?" I said, walking past the depot with my parcel. She waited there alone and out of uniform, dressed in a skirt of dark burgundy velvet and matching jacket. Her hat with a feather. A suitcase. "You're traveling?"

"I'm done with the lot of them," she said, not smiling.

"Oh, Easter. I'm sorry. Where you headed?"

"Dearfield. Can't be as cold in Weld County as it is here with these cold people." Her face was twitching, eyes raw.

"You all right? What happened?"

"I told Duke Padgett: Go to hell," she said. "Right to his face. I hope the Devil gets him."

Well, good for her.

Easter hoisted herself to the baggage car and spread her scarf on a crate for a seat, though the passenger car was half empty. And in dawning dismay, I understood she was forbidden by law to sit in it.

What had snapped her? And would I ever have the nerve to tell a Padgett to go to hell? Invited, as I was, to dinner at their castle.

On the evening of October first, I pinned up my hair and clipped on the green glass earbobs. Somebody would say I'd stolen them. But I hadn't stolen anything, not yet. And there in the mottled mirror was the other Sylvie, clean and powdered. *Allez-y*, I said to her. *Seize the opportunities.* Instead, I seized trouble. Not a pebble. A boulder.

Chapter Thirty

A FORCE LIKE GRAVITY PULLED me along the road to Elkhorne, same as a trolley that had lost its brakes. I was fueled by a wish for triumph or revenge. This time I would show these Padgetts . . . what? That I was someone. That I was owed. I went knowing full well that when the brakes on a tram car fail, you'd better jump off and hope you don't die, or hang on and pray the whole enterprise coasts to safety.

That night, at Elkhorne, I could have jumped.

The road to the manor was a long mile to walk in flimsy shoes, so I carried mine, boots laced up under my dress like a mountain woman. I stowed the boots in a milkweed patch and walked the drive in my delicate slippers. A pretend princess. *Good evening, Mr. Nugent. Bonsoir, mesdames, messieurs,* I practiced, and rang the front bell.

But it was not Nugent who flung open the door.

"Sylvie!" Jace took my hand and went to kiss my cheek but hit my lips with a whiff of gin. "*Excusez,*" he said, in a festive condition, going on about the weather, *lovely evening, so glad to see you*. I followed him under the chandeliers, ready for the murmur of conversation, the clutch of guests dazzling on the sofas.

Nobody was there. The fire was not lit. The lamps were dark.

"Am I early?" I said. "Did I mistake?"

"No, no, no, right this way." Jace led me to the kitchen. Nobody there either. "We're skipping the formalities."

Alarms fired my nerves. Who else was in the house? Was the evening to be unchaperoned? People talked. Word would get out that I was a loose woman or worse. What was Jace up to? *If I asked for your help.* He poured wine and set two goblets on the table. A pot perked on the stove, the smell of gravy and unease in the room.

"Jasper . . . you cooked?"

"Elk-heart stew. Cal's famous. You met Caleb last summer, of course."

"Cal's here?"

"We just returned from hunting up at Prettyman's Ridge. Now he's on some errand with my father. Took the *Sunrise* downhill. The old man's heading back east. Hope you don't mind me inviting you under the circumstances. But now, regard." He lifted the pot lid and inhaled. "Two hearts in it. I shot one of the elks. Cal got the other."

My heart was in its own stew. I drank half the glass of wine, to steady my nerves, and stood in a lump while Jace dashed around, rattling a spoon, cutting a loaf of bread. "I didn't know you could cook."

"Campfire cooking, my only skill. Anyway, Easter's gone back to Weld County, gone for good this time, she said, and happy to go, from the look of her. Determined. Our own dear Easter. Not coming back," he said. "This summer, I had to lure her to return with excesses of money. Had to bribe Cal to come too. Marcus and John Grady were not tempted. Sadly, they've convinced Easter to go back with them once and for all."

Easter made the choice herself, I didn't say. *She told your father to go to hell.*

"And now she's gone, and Inge is gone. Nugents are gone. The old man is gone. Caleb will be next to desert me. He's got plans to start a college!"

"A college?"

"Gonna call it Du Bois University. But he needs cash, so maybe he'll stick around. Dad keeps him on his old job on the *Sunrise* train."

Working my old job, I got up warily to set the table. Fork, spoon, knife. *A weapon if I needed one.* Jace did not stop me. "Mamzelle," he said, and held a chair for me. He served the plates with a white cloth over his arm, mimicking Mr. Nugent. "Pour vous," he said in his comical French. Perhaps I would enjoy myself despite the strange circumstances. The elk hearts steamed up from a rich brown sauce, little white onions floating like bouys.

"Jace?" I said. "What is going on?"

"Wait! Candles!" He went cheerfully through the swing door and returned with silver candlesticks. "Promise not to swallow these flames. As I recall, you have an appetite for fire."

Did I? Unable to swallow anything, I sat on guard.

Jace raised his glass. "A toast to Sylvie Fire-eater Pelletier, for inspiring me to be a revolutionist."

"I inspired you?"

"You did." He set his glass down. "You said watch what we do, not what we say. You said: Do something." Candlelight gleamed off his glasses. "So. To begin with the headline. Why I invited you."

"You want me to write a story for the paper?"

"Not this story. No. The news is, I'm fired."

"But you're in charge. How . . . ? Did you fire yourself?"

"I quit on principle," he said. "I sold all my shares to Colonel Bowles."

"What principle?" I cried. "What about the strike? The men walked out weeks ago. They're in trouble—"

"Bowles would only offer a yellow-dog contract. The boys won't sign it. I'm forbidden to concede a nickel or a half hour. I tried. I failed. I quit."

"Jace. What about your project? All your plans? Your promise?"

"My *promise* is the problem. When I said that I'd allow the union in? Disaster. The old man says my entire project is a betrayal of my ancestors." Jasper seethed, mired in a tar pit with his father and the past.

"But you were the boss! You could just—go ahead anyway!"

Jasper had pledged to make it right, for the workers, for the lost life of Jacques Pelletier, but now Jace himself appeared lost, on the heap of Lost

Causes. I sat twisting my fingers in a weave of frustrations, drinking to numb myself against disappointment. Where was the string quartet? The pats of butter shaped like roses? The strike was stalemated after all. Dogtooth Camp could not endure the winter.

"You promised," I said, tipsy.

"I'll make it up to you, so you won't be angry at me ever again—about anything. About your father. Sylvie, I am sorry about him, he was a good man."

We sat in the kitchen of Elkhorne Manor and pondered our different fathers. The wine and the candlelight softened the brittle air. Some current passed in the quiet, from Jace to me, in the migrations of expression on our faces, glances across the table like sips to test the temperature, heating again between us. Flashes of last summer by the river scorched my insides. He smiled as if asking me for something. Forgiveness.

"What my old man won't understand," Jace said, "see, my monument is—not some propaganda lie about *loyalty*—but a tribute to honor the sacrifice and bravery—of the *slaves*." He dropped the word on the table, where it sat heavily.

"That was all a long time ago," I said, distracted by present injustices.

"In living memory!" he said in a flash of anger. "Of millions. Easter. My father. He was born owning people. Even as an *infant,* he owned a human being. And my mother died, you see, and Easter was—my very life is owed to her. Even though my father— " Jasper looked away. The air was contorted by sentences he did not finish.

In horrible fascination, I watched him stammer, grappling with his father's crime. *Unspeakable* was the word employed to bury the appalling truth. The elk hearts sat hardly touched, steam rising like dismay. Jace stabbed his fork at a pearl onion.

"And," he said, "that man won't spare them a lousy block of honorary marble."

"It's the past," I said gently.

"They're the ones who won't leave it there!" he cried. "My father won't. Twenty contracts we have now, for Confederate-soldier monuments in ten states. Tons of marble. Worth millions. His lady friends from the country club are waving the flags of the fallen, waving their dollar bills. All my father cares about is the money."

"My father cared about money too," I said, to stab him with guilt. "The men are counting on you. You gave your word—"

"Sylvie—I tried. Honest. Bowles won't part with a red penny."

Jace impaled an onion on the tine of his fork like the head of his enemy and waved it angrily in the air as he carried on. "Last week Easter asked my father for help, to start Cal's university—and you know what the old man said? He said he'd done enough. Enough for Caleb. That's why she stormed out of here."

"Then do something yourself," I said. "Help Caleb yourself!"

"I tried. My father would not even discuss it, or my plan," Jace said bitterly. "All that marble will be wasted on monuments to traitor Johnny Reb."

"Well, what about the strike?" I pressed him, but Jace had stone on his mind.

"Dr. Du Bois's committee could not secure a spot on Monument Avenue in Richmond, let alone the National Mall. He's lucky the White League didn't lynch him for the suggestion."

"Du Bois?" I said. "I read his book."

"You did?" Jasper's eyes lit, and he leaned across the table. "Whattya know? Kindred spirits. You really read it?"

"Miss Redmond gave me her copy."

"Miss Redmond is a Bolshevik, apparently," he said. "And Professor Du Bois is a menace. My father calls him uppity—refuses to read that book. He says I'm unwell and under the influence of anarchists. He no longer recognizes me as his son." He drank more, muttering, "I'm not the only son he doesn't recognize." He shot a look across the table, to see if he'd shocked me. He had not.

"Why don't you send the stone to the Gradys, then?" I said, exasperated. "Give it to that town or something." It was this suggestion, he later claimed, that set him off, but that night he dismissed the idea.

"Hauling tons of marble all the way to Weld County? Impossible." He poured.

"That's enough wine, Jace. Don't you think?"

"I don't think! I act!" He stood up. "You say act? We must act! Come with me."

He would jump me or murder me or show me the corpse of his dead father. Yet I went, pulled down the staircase by fascination and the hand of Jace Padgett. "C'mon, c'mon." Humming along like a mad river, he swept me into his father's offices.

"Jasper," I said, "I don't belong here."

"I invited you, so you do." He turned to that vault in the corner with its steel door, the gilded crest. He handed me a scrap of paper from his pocket, a tune on his breath. "Read those numbers out to me now."

"Jace, this isn't right."

He would open it. I sorely wanted him to. I read the combination aloud. Jace twirled the tumblers. He had to try three times, while I read the numbers again, heart hammering. It felt wrong, thrilling.

"Don't worry," Jace said. "It's only money. Have no fear. There's plenty."

"Plenty? The Company is in bankruptcy! The payroll—" I stammered through a dry throat. "The Company was wiped out in the panic. Lost everything—"

Jace stopped spinning the tumblers. "The Company is not the family. This here is only the local piggy bank. The big piles are in New York. Hundreds of thousands in the vaults of the Morgan Guaranty."

He got the door open and pulled a cord so a light came on inside.

The sight was enraging. Shelves inside stacked with piles of cash: bills in bundles, coins rolled in paper, felt bags tied with silk drawstrings. I gasped. "Why are you showing me this?"

"Because we're comrades," he said, then blurted, "and it could be yours, Sylvie."

"What are you talking about?"

He steadied himself against the doorframe and sized me up with a conflicted intensity. "It could be yours. Ours. If you do not hate me."

"I'm not a thief," I said, backing out. "I ought to go home now."

"Please don't leave," said Jace. "It's not what you think, sweetheart."

"What *do* I think?" I said. "You tell me."

"You think I have nefarioush, nefarious, intentions."

"I do, yes." And hoped those intentions were to give me some of that cash.

"Wait." He closed his eyes as if doing so allowed him to breathe. "Forgive me, please. This is not going as I planned. It's out of order."

"What was planned?"

"To tell you. The idea. The question—I didn't mean to do this now. In this way or in this—vault. Ask you—" He swallowed, staring with some odd pleading in his eyes.

"Are you all right, Jasper?"

We stood by the open door of the safe. Jasper removed his glasses, his throat working as if he would confess some awful deed.

Then, with a massive exhale of whiskey, Jace Padgett said, "The question is, will you marry me?"

"Ha!" I laughed loudly. Clapped my hand over my mouth. "Ha-ha-ha."

"Why would you laugh?" He sagged inside his jacket.

"Why would you say it?" The absurdity, the strange hurt. "Unless it's a joke? To make fun of me."

"No," he said. "Never. Never, Sylvie."

"You can't mean it."

"Why not?" he said. "Stop laughing. I'm deadly serious. Sincere."

"Why, then?" I laughed and could hardly stop. "Marriage? Why?"

"Why?" Jace pressed the heels of his hands to his eye sockets and sighed as if I ought to know his reasons. "Why? To do one thing right. Like you said. To be a revolutionist. So, *yes*, I do mean it. Because. I care for you. Sylvie, love. Sorry for everything. We are kindred spirits, don't you see? I would give you all this."

"I'm not your charity case."

"No. You're—Sylvie." He struggled. "You are entirely yourself. Whereas, who I am . . . who knows? My father doesn't. Maybe only you do. You listen. I believe you've always understood me."

He had declared me to be entirely myself. What did he mean by that? Why this outlandish proposal? I stared at him in disbelief.

"Sylvie, if you'll only. Look—" Jace pulled me inside the vault. In a great rush, he began to grab bundles of money off the shelves, cramming bills in the pockets of his jacket, his trousers. He took a brick of cash and thrust it at me. "For you, Sylvie." Taking more for himself too.

"I don't want this," I said. But I did. *Seigneur, pardonnez-moi*, I wanted it.

"Take it, take it, take it."

The command inflamed me. I took that money. It began to heat in my hand like an ember of hell. Jace looked at me with the happy glint of conspiracy in his eyes. "Take it, sweetheart. They'll never know. Never miss this little amount—"

"Little? It's a fortune—"

"A rounding error for the Duke."

"It's wrong," I said, smiling and giddy.

"It's right! You deserve it. You are owed. It's mine to give. It's *ours*. You'll see. I have plans to act, to do the righteous thing, like you said."

My seducer plied me with outlaw words and money, laughing now. He clamped his arms around me with stacks of cash pressed hard between us, his shirt pockets stuffed. We stood in the quiet safe, bound together in a strange romance of banditry, our hearts beating madly with the thrill of it.

"I am sorry, Sylvie," he whispered. "Forgive me. Don't hate me."

My hatred was weak in that minute, as I was distracted by the brick of banded bills in my hand. *It could be yours. If you do not hate me.* And had he said it, *Marry me*?

"I don't hate you," I said. "Let's leave, please. Let's go."

He kissed me, tasting of liquor, and I was carried away as before, by the river, kissing in the safe, my breath stolen, knees buckling.

"Will you?" he said. "You didn't answer. Say you will."

He did not say *love*. Was it insanity or alcohol that made him propose marriage? Did he ask out of pity for a Quarrytown *Cendrillon*? Some notion of himself as a savior? To this day I don't know my own reasons. Was it his lips or his pleading need that swept me? Was it the money? Payback for the murderous sins of the Padgetts? Perhaps it was all these. Perhaps I'd learned last summer's lesson after all: to seize the opportunities. Or maybe it was love. I'd wished for it so long, it could be true.

"All right, yes." I was dizzy to hear myself say it. "I will."

A light of disbelief came over Jasper's face. He smiled as if he'd braced for *no* but got *yes* instead. "Really? You would?"

"I would. Will."

"For real?" He held me at arm's length and beamed his contagious happiness at me. "Honest and true?"

"Yes, yes, of course, yes."

Just like that, I dug myself deeper into the quarry of fate, both of us grinning at each other, such green young fools. And even as I kissed him, obstacles and questions crowded my thoughts like sheep blocking the train tracks, bleating for attention. He was drunk. He was not serious. He was flawed. He was not a Catholic, he was an Abercrombie. A prince. Possibly a thief. Possibly mad. He lived in a castle and I lived in a closet.

"You remember? By the lake?" he asked, his lips by my ear. "You remember how I asked if you would help me?"

"I remember you said we could fly." I stayed wary in the warm crook of his arms. The house held a bad silence of secrets and wrongs.

"We can fly this minute. Leave. We'll hire a ride to Ruby, then—"

"What are you talking about? Ruby?" I said. "Tonight? Are you crazy?"

"Don't you call me crazy! Father said I was. Last spring in Richmond, they would've locked me away—they—Bowles said— Never mind. It's my money rightfully. Yours. Don't think it isn't. We'll get the dawn train out. We'll go to the courthouse in Ruby and find the judge and get the license. I already asked how to do it."

"Do what?"

"Get married," he said.

At that minute came a sudden crash. The shatter of glass breaking. Heavy boots above us. Someone cried out, calling, "Jace!"

He froze, then pulled me out of the vault and closed the door.

"Jace!" A man's voice from upstairs.

"C'mon." Jace grabbed my hand.

"Put this back!" I brandished the money. It was hundreds of dollars.

"Keep it. It's yours." He ran up the stairs ahead of me. Sick with panic, I stuffed wads of money inside the bosom of my dress and ran after Jace.

In the drawing room was a man covered in blood. Caleb Grady. He held one arm at a distorted angle, like a broken-winged bird. His eye was dripping red, swollen shut.

"Cal!" Jace cried. "What happened? You were gonna stay in Carbondale. I told you be careful! My father—"

"We got turned around. They blocked the track."

"Jesus, Cal, you're bleeding. Your eye—" Jace helped Cal to the sofa. He pressed a satin pillow to Cal's face to stanch the blood. "Jesus. Cal."

"I'll get something," I said. "Bandages. I'll get a doctor—"

"Use the telephone," Jasper said.

I went to the foyer and dialed. The switchboard girl answered. "I'm calling from Elkhorne Manor," I told her. "Mr. Padgett is asking the doctor to come right away. Connect me to the clinic."

"But Mr. Padgett is right here in the office," the girl said.

"No, it's his *son*, Jace, who's asking. A man here is hurt. Please send the doctor quick. To Elkhorne."

From the kitchen, I brought a basin of water and towels. Blood dripped from Cal's eye. It splashed in dark blooms on the velvet couch. I wrung the cloth and went to clean his face. Cal brushed me away, scrubbing at the stains with his good hand. "Ruined this pillow, now," he said. His shirt was splashed with crimson.

"Shhh. Cal, don't mind about that," Jace said. Fresh springs of blood dripped from Caleb's eye. Jasper took the cloth and held it to the bloody socket.

"What happened?" I said. "How—"

"He says your union dogs beat the daylights out of him," Jace said. "Thought he was a scab. Mistook him for one of the replacement workers, a whole lot of colored men over there in that stockade by the mill."

"Not my union dogs," I said. *And they are not dogs.*

"Four, five boys come along, claim I'm a blackleg scab," Caleb said. "I told them, 'Nossir, I'm a traveling chef for Mr. Padgett.'"

"The name Padgett only made 'em kick you harder," said Jace.

"Anyway, I did a pretty good number on one of 'em." Caleb managed half a smile.

"I bet you did, Cal," Jace said. "They didn't know what they were getting into when they tangled with you, huh?"

Watching them, I checked for signs of brotherhood and saw the tenderness Jace showed, how gentle he was with Cal.

"Where's that goddamn doctor?" Jace said. "His elbow's dislocated."

"My eye," Caleb said. "Can't see."

"It's just swollen, Cal. We'll fix it up. Who did this? Give me a name."

"Some 'skowski or Houlihan," said Cal. "I couldn't hear it—"

"Bastards!" Jace said. "I'll break their necks."

"Nah, not a chance," Cal said, as if he found the idea funny, wincing. "Young lady, you know this man Jasper won't be breaking any necks. He won't land a punch, even to save his own neck. Too softhearted."

"Shh. Don't go saying that to her, now, Cal, she's my girl. Get him a glass of whiskey, Sylvie, please, would you?"

I was his girl. Was I? His kitchen girl. I went through the swinging door and considered the back exit. I could leave, get my coat, get out with the money. I breathed against the hard lumps of cash stowed beside my ribs and poured the whiskey. I drank a glass for myself, straight down, so the liquor ran with the Devil's influence along all the channels in my head.

There was more shouting. "Jasper!"

That voice froze me. The Duke himself had arrived. The thickness of bills burned in my guilty bosom. It was wrong to keep it, wrong all around. *Dump the money in a drawer*, was my thought. Hide it under the sink. Why didn't I? Because: *You are owed*, said the Devil or the truth talking. Blood money. Jasper himself said Padgetts owed us Pelletiers, and who didn't they owe? Caleb was bleeding. In a split minute I decided. With the cash still stowed in my bodice and the whiskey bottle on a tray, I went back out to the scene on the couch, where Cal sat with the bloody towel pressed to his eye.

Duke Padgett stood over him, shouting, "What the hell! Get up, Caleb! What are you doing there, boy? Get up!"

Cal stood. "Hello, sir."

"Let him rest. He's hurt." Jace stepped in front of his father.

The three men in a row like that. A frieze. *Padgett & Sons.*

"Take Caleb in the back," said the Duke. "Look at this mess."

Duke was looking at the blood on the carpet. Jace was looking at Cal, who stood stoic, his one good eye on the middle distance, some future far away from these people. I was looking for signs and found them. Unmistakable. The ear. Cal had it, the protuberant Padgett ear, same as the grandfather, Brigadier General Padgett of the library portrait. The ear of the Duke himself. Three generations of cup-handle ears.

Cal's breathing was strained, and Jace put a hand out to steady him.

"Take him out of here," the Duke said.

"He's injured, Dad," Jace said. "Leave him alone." The liquor had burned through him and colored his flaming cheeks. "I'll take care of him."

"He doesn't belong here," Duke said.

"Then I don't belong here either."

Duke Padgett stared at his son. "You're sick, Jace. You're not right in the head. Remember what the doctor said? Not to get excited. Over this—nonsense."

"It's not nonsense. It's truth."

"Please," Duke faltered. "Son. You had me out of my wits. Those anarchists blocked the track. We had to turn around. When that girl called—I feared that you were killed. She said"—he pointed at me without looking and misquoted my telephone call—"that my son was badly hurt."

His son. Caleb Grady smiled, bits of grit in his expression. He glanced at me as if he knew that I knew, that I had seen him denied.

Duke was still looking at Jace as if accusing him—of what? I did not want to play a part in this drama, yet I had—had I?—just consented to marry—to join the family. Caleb Grady would be my brother-in-law, outlawed.

"I'll just be leaving now, Mr. Padgett," I said.

"You'll stay," said Jasper. "Sylvie, stay, please."

"My son's had too much liquor," said the Duke, apologetic. "He's not well."

"It's Caleb! Cal who's not well!" Jace roared. "Christ! Look at him, Dad. They tried to kill him. They left him for dead."

"He's not dead, though, is he?" the Duke shouted. "Didn't I tell you not to let that union in? Thugs. I told you! But you don't listen, and this is the result!"

"I told Bowles not to bring those scabs up here—"

"Don't you lecture me," the Duke said. "You made a hash of it, and you wanted out. So you're out. You quit."

"Come with me, Cal," Jasper said. "We'll fix you up."

"Cal's fine," said Duke. "Aren't you, boy? You're fine."

Cal grimaced to show he was fine, just dandy, when obviously, he was gravely hurt. Caleb Grady was a master of a defense tactic that I recognized: silence as shield. "Yessir," he said. If you looked, you could see the cold superiority in his coiled smile.

"Attaboy," said Duke Padgett. "Get on over to your place now, Caleb."

"I'll take him upstairs," Jasper said. "He'll sleep in my room."

"Damned if he will," said Duke. "This is my house. I won't have that boy bleeding in every damn room. Look at the mess he's made already."

"The mess *he's* made?" Jasper cried. They stood bristling at each other.

"Jace," Caleb said sharply. He started toward the kitchen door, the distorted elbow propped in his hand, bones at sickening angles. "Let me get out of here."

The Duke watched the two of them with narrowed eyes.

"All right, Cal, good man," Jace said. "You'll be okay. Doc's on the way." His voice was full of worry, his hand gentle on Caleb's shoulder.

I liked him so much in that moment.

Duke went to the sideboard to pour whiskey, the bottle shaking. Did he tremble in remorse? Or in fear—that he might be exposed, condemned to hell

for what he'd done to Easter? He blamed Jace, or Caleb Grady, *union scum.*
Anyone but himself.

"The audacity," Duke said. "To bring that boy in here." He drained the
glass. The bell rang in front. "Get that, will you?"

Go to hell, I did not say, lacking Easter's nerve.

Doc Butler was at the door with his black bag. "Ah. The young lady of
'Infirmary Notes.' Where's the patient?"

In the kitchen, Caleb Grady rested his distorted arm on the table. I cleared the
plates in a rush, an apron over my dress, watching from the sink as the doctor
examined him. Cal breathed in a stutter of pain and drank down a second glass
of whiskey. The doctor cut the bloody shirt, peeling it off. Cal's bare ribs were
purpled with bruises and bleeding cuts. Butler pressed his fingers along the
wounds. He tipped Cal's head to the light and parted the lids of the swollen
eye. Cal inhaled sharply.

"A bad business here," the doc said.

"What about the elbow?" Jace asked. "That's his pitching arm. Nobody
gets a hit off Cal Grady."

"Well, I'll reset it," the doctor said. "And he's gonna yell. After that he'll
wear a sling. And rest these ribs. You cracked a few."

"*He* didn't crack them," Jasper said. "Goddamn lynch mob did. Lucky
those boys didn't hang him."

"Two of 'em went for a rope, but I outran 'em," Cal said. "Done with
running."

The doc rolled up his sleeves. "Gonna yank it good now. You brace him,
Jasper."

"Give him a shot of morphine," Jace said. "For Chrissake."

"He had plenty of that whiskey," said Butler. "They don't feel pain like
we do."

"Like hell." Jace was livid. "You go on and give him a goddamn shot."

"Doc, please," I said. "Give him something."

The doctor went to his bag and removed a vial and syringe, muttering, "Waste of a dose, but all right."

"That'll dull the pain, Cal," Jasper said. "You won't feel it."

"Hell, it's you who won't feel it." Caleb laughed with some ironic bitterness.

"I should be out of the way now," I said. "I ought to go—"

Jace did not stop me. He stood with his hand on his brother's shoulder. I knew it for sure then. Anyone could see it if they looked. He blew me a distracted kiss off his fingertips. "I'll come for you tomorrow," he said. "I'll come for you."

Would he? I went out the back door with my doubts, my spinning head, and two hundred dollars stuffed behind the buttons of my dress.

Chapter Thirty-One

SAFE IN THE RETREAT OF my closet, the smell of paper and ink like home, I sorted the cataclysms of the evening and wrangled the Devil over the soul of Sylvie Pelletier. The warm lumps of money had left red dents on my skin. I broke the paper strip around the stack and thumbed the bills in a fan, relishing the crisp of new greenbacks. Each twenty was an Aladdin carpet to fly me away—with Jace Padgett? Or not. I could take it and flee alone. My thoughts were a welter in the aftermath of the blood, the whiskey, the wild untethered offer.

If you do not hate me.

A low standard for matrimony, wasn't it? The absence of hate. And a bribe. *This could be yours.* He would offer me marriage as payoff, as if he would save me. Was I some penance he must pay? Not a word of love. Perhaps his people did not say it. Or know what it was.

In the tossing darkness, I pondered the Padgetts. The monstrous equation that made Caleb Grady one of them—yet not. I did the math of it, subtracted ages and decades and tracked events backward to when it happened. The year 1883. Easter was a young woman then, the Duke older, neither of them married. After Caleb was born, Duke married Opal and Easter married

John Grady, who raised Cal as his own. Marcus Grady was born. Then Jace months later. When Opal died, Easter nursed both those babies, her son and a dead white woman's child.

Everyone knows, Jace said. Except Jace had not known.

How the mind, my mind, stammered and balked, pondering the shock of it . . . the secret shames of Padgett history. That the rumors . . . that the talk . . . that his father . . . that Easter. And now she had quit at last. Told him to go to hell.

Duke's crime was the root of Jasper's anguish. The father's sin arising from the original sin, as Dr. Du Bois called it, of slavery. Up until that time, the Confederacy of the South for me was a dusty lesson of boring battles, a sweating swamp of snakes and sausage curls, as exotic as a foreign country. But Jasper had invited me to live in it with him, alongside his monumental obsessions. He was called delusional, as if to care about his brother and the Gradys were a sign of insanity instead of what it was. Just love.

How drawn I was to Jasper's torment; how romantic it seemed that I alone understood him. And to confess: I was also drawn to those piles of greenbacks.

Oh, money. Two hundred dollars. A pittance to Jasper, with a vault of dragon loot, but a fortune to me, under the mattress. That night I lay awake on it as if it were a dried pea and I were a false princess, tossing in a nightmare of gore and money, Cal's bloody eye. Alcohol kisses. That question.

I had answered yes but might still say no.

At dawn, before I could be accused of stealing it, I sent a hundred dollars, five twenties, in a letter to my mother. "I was able to secure extra work at the manor," I wrote, with other fibs of news: "The union will soon resolve the strike. Miss Redmond sends best wishes. The autumn leaves are *magnifiques*." Another hundred dollars stayed in my bodice, scratchy and damp. I might need it.

All morning I was agitated, waiting. Before I lost my nerve, I wanted Jasper to hurry and fetch me, as he'd said he would, to stand in the courthouse and get married. It seemed more likely that the Sheriff would take me to jail, accused as a safecracker. I wished Jace would come before I changed my mind. Before he changed his. We'd run away eloping, and then together we'd give thousands to the families on Dogtooth Flats, as fair compensation, to pay what they were owed, to make things right.

All good judgment was lost in the undertow of events, wishful thinking, and a fatal resolve to prove my worth to this Prince. Did I love J. C. Padgett? His oddness and drinking and erratic affections were marks against him. His jokes and talk about books, his anger and idealism, were marks in his favor. His kindness. Kissing. Also the money. *Does it tempt you, sweetheart?* What love I felt for him was all tied up with money. I wished he would hurry.

For distraction, I tidied the piles of newsprint, cleaned the press platens, emptied the ash barrel, and struggled to ignore the roar of silence from Elkhorne Manor. Perhaps the Duke had killed his own son (which one?) in a furious fit. Or the sons had killed him, striking the Duke over the head with a piece of statuary, pushing him down the stairs. More likely, Jace had gone off without me, the cash in his pockets. That odd proposal of marriage was only liquor talking, the words of a delusional.

Just after the noon whistle, I was in a state at the press, printing a notice for the UMW, when Jace burst in, looking frantic as a bird does, flying indoors by mistake. "Sylvie!"

My foot stopped on the treadle.

"Is anyone else here?" he said, agitated.

"Miss Redmond's gone till tomorrow."

"I'm taking Cal," he said in a rush of words. "To see a doctor in Ruby. Not sure his eye can be saved. The socket is fractured. Maybe the retina's detached. Butler here at the clinic—he's . . . not hopeful."

"I'll find out who did it," I said. "I'll ask Kerrigan."

"Come with us. Caleb's at the depot already. I don't want to leave him alone for long. Get your things, will you? Hurry."

"What things?"

"Whatever you need for—" Jasper turned a shade of red. "We can buy new things, whatever you want, Sylvie, we can—"

"Jasper—"

"Pack up, if you're coming," he said. "Train's in thirty minutes." His eyes were wild and bloodshot, his hair disheveled. He had not made another mention of marriage. He'd said *doctor*. He checked his watch. "Sylvie. Let's elope right out of this. You said you would— " He smiled boyishly. "You said."

And I *had* said. It was what I wanted, or so I thought: Ease and elegance. Sink or swim. Flee or fly. "All right," I said. "Five minutes."

"Angel!" A smile broke across his nervous face. "We'll find a judge this very day. Meet me at the depot quick as you can." He went out in a mad rush. Was somebody after him? His father? I packed too fast. New blue dress stuffed down in a valise with all my misgivings. I wrote a dissembling note to Miss Redmond: "Headed to Ruby to investigate the scab hatchery." I deceived her as easily as I now deceived myself. That Jace and Sylvie would elope in a pure romance.

If you repeat wishes enough, sometimes you can force them to come true.

At the depot, I looked around for Jace. In my agitation, I paid no attention to the train's cargo: a block of marble the size of a whale, chained to the flatbed car and hooked behind the locomotive. There was no reason to question it—not then. Such blocks were ferried out every week on this route. Heavier matters weighed on me. Here was Jace with Caleb Grady.

Cal's head was wrapped in a fresh white bandage, one eye patched, that elbow in a sling, his hard bright smile like armor. "Congratulations, Miss Sylvie," he said. "I heard the good news."

"Let's hurry." Jace looked over his shoulder and took my arm to help me up to the passenger car. Cal came next and then Jace after. We found seats near the door, Cal in the last seat with Jace beside him. I sat across the aisle with my bag.

A couple came to find seats, and Jace pulled the brim of his hat to shade his face, as if he did not wish to be recognized. The man appeared to be one of the prosperous potato farmers from the valley. His wife was the color and shape of a sack of McClures freshly dug, her mouth pinched into a scowl. Looking at Caleb, she blanched in terror. "Oh, Lord Jesus."

The farmer moved his arm around her protectively. They continued down the aisle, whispering. The woman sat as far away from us as possible, looking in our direction with nervous outrage. Was she praying? Her eyes were closed. She moved her lips with her hands folded in a theatrical display.

The man walked back to confront us, pointing at Cal. "He cannot ride in this car. Take him around to the baggage car."

"Sir, I'm traveling with this man," Caleb said, in his hard cordial voice.

The farmer ignored him and spoke to Jace. "I know my rights. Take him off, I demand it in Jesus's name."

I wanted to ask: *Was it Jesus who said, "What shall it profit a man if he shall gain the whole train car but lose his own soul?"*

"My friend will sit here," Jace said through his teeth. "He's injured. I'm taking him for medical attention."

"For the safety of my wife, and for the protection of this young innocent girl"—he looked at me with righteousness in his small potato eyes—"he belongs in the baggage car."

"Mr. Grady is sitting with us," I said. "There is plenty of room."

"Not for him." The farmer moved his hand to his hip, and we saw the gun.

Jace stood up, fist clenched. He would be a savior, but it was folly to confront a man with a pistol.

"J.C.," Caleb said in a low warning voice. "Not now." He rose from his seat and went along the aisle of the car. When he passed the farmer, his demeanor changed, and he offered the fellow a smile wide enough to contain forgiveness, or pity, or venom. "May the Lord be with you, sir," Cal said. "I will hold you in my prayers."

The man's hand on his gun again. "I'm gonna teach you a lesson."

It was Caleb who offered the lesson that day, from the moral high ground. He left the car, and Jace followed him, angry. After a minute he returned and flung himself into the seat beside me. The potato couple sent superior smiles in our direction.

"I should've fought him," Jace said, fuming. "If you weren't here, Sylvie, if it were a different circumstance, I'd have done it. Please don't think less of me—"

"Certainly not. Those are horrible people."

"I didn't want to raise a scene. You don't know what they'll do."

"There was a court case, right? Isn't it the rule to have separate cars?"

"Not God's rule," said Jace. "Or mine. If it were a different circumstance, Sylvie, I would put that fellow in his place. I sure would."

The train started down the steep, propelled by the tonnage of stone behind us, brakes screeching on steel. We hurtled past ravines marked by small crosses nailed out of sticks so that I prayed not to run off the tracks. *Turn back.* Was I really doing this? Tension stretched between us like a membrane or a net.

"You're pale," Jasper said, and offered me sips from a flask. The alcohol dissolved the knots in my chest, and Moonstone receded behind the swerving train. The farmer and his wife had fallen asleep, heads lolling back, mouths snoring wide.

"Look." I pointed. "We could drop feathers in."

"Oh, you are a wicked girl," said Jace.

"Or bumblebees," I said.

"Worms," Jace said. "Your demented imagination."

"Same as yours."

We were cheerful now, cackling, imagining the righteous couple coughing and gagging on a list of things we could drop down their throats. Fire ants. Minnows.

Then Jace turned abruptly serious. "You should know something before we—in case you change your mind."

"Are we outlaws?"

"No!" He laughed, bitter. "I didn't steal that money, if that's what you think. It's a lawful inheritance. I am talking about Caleb. Do you mind about him?"

"No." Except that I did. Not in the sense Jasper meant, that they were brothers. What I cared about was that our elopement, our romance—such as it was—was tangled up not just with stolen cash but with such sordid family secrets. Was I snared in the swamp with them now? I was. "I don't mind."

"Everybody else does. At the club, they mind terribly, as if half of 'em don't have colored servants related by blood. I never knew till . . . they never talked about it."

And he still hadn't said it aloud. *Caleb's my brother.* He only skirted and stammered and insinuated.

"You're the only one." He took my hand and examined it.

"Ink stains." I pulled away, embarrassed.

"Ink will wash off with soap," he said. "Unlike the sins of the father. These are a lady's hands now. You won't have to work ever again."

"What would I do all day?"

"Read novels. Whatever you want."

"I thought to be a newswriter." It sounded good, said out loud.

"I'll buy you a paper," he said. "I'll buy you two. Whatever you desire. If only you'll be sure of me before we see the judge. Think about it."

How could a person think, propelled as I was by the weight of my own wish—to seize the opportunities. *Does it tempt you?* Mrs. Jones preferred the breath of freedom. But freedom appeared to be a choice between a supply closet or—this volatile Jasper, who was strange and angry, as I was strange and angry. Evicted from his home, as I was evicted. The train hurtled in a lurching racket. Jasper turned the screw top on his flask and worked to empty it.

"Is this . . . eloping?" I said at last.

"Yes!" He grinned. "Next summer, we'll have a proper big party."

I said, "Who would we invite?" to tease him.

"Inge, for a start. She's always one for the lavish event. And she said I'd be crazy not to go after you while I had a chance. To win you."

"To win me? Inge said that?"

"She likes you very much. So it's all right, then? You're truly sure?"

"Sure," I said, full of doubt.

The train slowed, then strangely stopped altogether in the middle of an empty valley. The engineer came through the car to say the crew had to clear debris off the track, "left by infernal unionists deliberately to slow us."

"Deliberately," I told Jace. "To make a point. To get what they're owed."

"Don't remind me," he said. "Same reason my father had to turn around last night, and Caleb got attacked."

While we waited, Jace laid out instructions, what we'd do when we arrived at Ruby. Arrangements for Caleb at the clinic. The courthouse procedures. But he said nothing about *afterward*—the deranged journey he had in mind.

At Ruby, I waited on a bench while Jace spoke to some teamsters on the freight car. He pointed at the stone. "Take it as far as Greeley. I'll pick up there." He again tilted his hat over his face, signing papers and looking over his shoulder.

Cal got down from the baggage car, wincing.

"Cal, over here!" I waved and he came toward me, walking stiffly. "Won't you sit down? You're injured—"

"No, thank you, ma'am."

Too late, I saw it was a mistake to make room for him on the bench, as I had. People on the platform stared. The potato couple stood with two white ladies and talked behind their hands. More white men came to join the little mob, arms crossed over their chests, watching us. One of them, a large florid cowboy, worked tobacco in his jaw with deliberate menace. Jace was still directing the teamsters. The man spat yellow juice and planted his boots in front of Cal. "Leave this young lady alone," he said. "Hear?"

Cal inhaled, as if fuel were required to maintain his composure, and stepped back.

"He wasn't bothering me," I said. "I know him."

The cowboy narrowed his eyes, hand on his holster, and I felt a mere moment of the menace Caleb had faced his whole life; the threats from farmers, cowboys, country clubbers. Union men. I did not want to think it.

It was a relief when Jace came to join us. The cowboy retreated with a sneer.

"Sylvie," Jace said, "I'll see you at five o'clock sharp. And . . . darling? You can still . . . change your mind."

"I won't." Couldn't now, even if I wanted to. Which I didn't. It was true that Jace had failed certain tests, but he'd passed others, standing up to his father and the farmer on the train. To me, the way he cared for Caleb was evidence of his essential kindness, his good character.

Jace and Cal set off for a doctor's office in a hired wagon. Jace would secure a bed for Caleb, and I'd go to the Ruby Arms Hotel to reserve a room under my own name, as Jace had instructed.

I walked through the village, past charming cottages with gingerbread trim, picket-fence yards. On the main street was the Ruby Social Club, a library, a hospital. These were the good works of the Padgett Company Sociology Department, Inge's pet theories and experiments made real. Not one saloon. Down a side lane was the boardinghouse where we Pelletiers had stayed once in another life. In my mind's eye, they appeared so clearly, my mother and my brothers, and I missed them. There were more than mountains between us now.

At the Ruby Arms, I signed the register, "S. Pelletier." Up the carpeted stairs, I opened the door to all the luxury I'd ever want. It would've suited me to live out my days in that room. By one window, a writing desk, letter paper and pens provided. By the other, a vanity table arranged with perfumes and powder puffs, a vase of carnations. The bed had four posters; the mattress was a cloud on springs. I fell back on the pillows, braced for whatever was next. What I'd gotten myself into.

In the vast porcelain tub, hot water ran straight from a spout and soaked everything off me: Quarrytown and Mrs. Jones. Papa's murder. K. T. Redmond and the union strike. George Lonahan and his postcards. The brawling kiss of Setkowski. The bloody scene last night. Caleb's poor blinded eye. All of it washed down the drain with the ink stains and marble dust, or so it seemed then. I was clean now, and dried off with a white towel, spritzed my throat from a bottle labeled *attar of roses*. At the mirror, I pinned my hair and fastened on the sparkling earbobs. There in her new blue dress, for the last time, was Sylvie Pelletier. Who was she, anyway, who would leap from the lip of a crag? Who thought she could fly. A bat. A bird. A trick rider on a trick horse. It was my strange wedding day, October 2, 1908.

Chapter Thirty-Two

I WALKED ALONE TO THE courthouse, a gray-painted shack. Jasper waited for me on the steps, drumming his fingers on his silver pocket flask, which was again full, like the miraculous pitcher of Greek myth, never empty. "A sip for courage," he insisted, as if we faced a firing squad and not a wedding ceremony. "Ready? Steady, go." But he was not entirely steady as we walked inside, stumbling over the threshold.

The justice of the peace was an ancient man whose hand shook with palsy as he extended us a piece of paper to sign. *MARRIAGE LICENSE*, it said. My own hands shook as I read the words. Age, it asked for. "Eighteen," I wrote. Color, it wanted, a separate line for that.

"Color?" I hesitated, with the odd thought: *Blue*.

"You ain't a Negro," the old justice said, cackling. "If one of you was"—he pointed at us—"then it'd be a crime to license you."

My thoughts snared on the word *crime* (what was illegal?); and then I wondered, why was Jasper acting so oddly? As if he were hunted. Haunted. *Wedding jitters*, I told myself, and smiled at *jitters*, a *pluralia tantum*. I must tell that one to George Lonahan, I thought, but then with a stab realized I would not see George again.

Jasper wrote his age as twenty-one, his birth date as March 13, 1887. Till that moment I hadn't even known his birthday. I was marrying a stranger.

"Jace?" Perhaps he'd hear the hitch in my voice, notice my shaky handwriting. But he was occupied by paying the marriage fee. We signed.

"Winnie!" the justice called. "Come witness!"

A bright-eyed wren of a woman came in, untying her apron strings. "Felicitations to the lovebirds! A momentous occasion." She peered at the paperwork and peered at Jasper. "Padgett? Of Padgett Company?"

"No relation." Jasper shot me a warning look. "A common enough name."

Doubt pooled in my throat. Why did he lie?

"Join your hands," the justice ordered.

"Are you all right, Sylvie?" Jasper whispered.

The justice tapped his fingers. "Ain't you ready? I don't have all night."

"Patience, now, Dad," said Winnie fondly.

I thought of my own father, dead and cold, my faraway mother and brothers. What was I doing? Where were my people? After all our grief and trouble because of the Padgetts and their Company, here I was at the courthouse, willing myself along, to become one of them. Hitched.

"Join your hands." Winnie smiled. "Don't be shy."

Do you take this man? The justice asked questions, extracted promises. To love honor and cherish, for him. Love honor and obey, for me. *I do*, we said. *I will.* Jasper removed a small box from his pocket, a ring inside, flashing a diamond grain of ice set in claws. He attempted to slip it on the proper digit, but it would not fit my sturdy peasant finger. *Sorry.* Both of us in an awkward cringe.

"Here, now." The cheerful Winnie fit the band on the left pinky instead. *So long as you both shall live.*

The justice pronounced us married. "You may kiss the bride."

Jasper gave me a peck on the lips, whiskey in it.

"Look at you two, blushing!" Winnie presented me a posy of goldenrod and Queen Anne's lace. "Here you go now, sweetheart. A bride should have flowers."

"She will. Roses every day." Jace was beaming. He took the marriage license and stowed it in his vest pocket, whispering, "Just you wait, my love. Flowers and finery and whatever festoons you like, Mrs. Padgett."

"Oh." I clapped my hand over my mouth.

"What?"

"Mrs. Padgett. How strange."

Jasper took my arm. In a light rain, we walked out married. He helped me over a puddle as if I had no ability to leap it myself. Perhaps I'd leapt enough for one day. Trills of happiness burst out of me, laughter and disbelief, as my husband kissed me out in public, our hands entwined, grinning madly at our own audacity. We'd eloped. Now what?

In the dining room of the Ruby Arms, at a table set with white linen, my new gentleman husband held a chair for me. The waiter brought champagne. Jasper raised his fizzing glass. "To my bride."

"To the groom."

We toasted shyly with strange new words for ourselves, smiling. And then not smiling. As air leaks from a balloon, we grew silent in the enormity of what we'd done.

"I'm sorry it was so . . . complicated," Jace said. "I meant to court you properly. When I asked you to dinner last night, I planned—I had no idea how . . . bad things would be with Caleb. My father. I wanted to get you out before all hell breaks loose."

"What hell?" Spikes of alarm in my blood.

"Sooner or later—sooner, I think—Bowles will break the strike."

"Strikebreaking is illegal."

"Shhh. Let's not talk of it tonight, sweetheart." He reached across the table and put a finger over my lips to shush me. And I was shushed, as ever. What had I done? We were not comrades. We were married.

He took up my hand and fiddled with the wedding band on the wrong finger. "It was my mother's. Left for me, for my wife to have. I took it from the safe last night."

"That's not all we—you—took," I said.

"The law won't be chasing us. Don't worry. Duke knows it's a rightful inheritance. What he won't know is that we've eloped. I won't tell him."

Another pulse of alarm rippled along my scalp. "Why not?"

"Let's not spoil this day. Our wedding day," Jace said. "Please don't worry. We can go where we like."

"We," I said carefully. "Us. How strange to think it. So sudden."

"We'll get that ring resized for you. I know a jeweler in Denver who can fit it perfectly." He smiled behind his glasses and drank more.

Why did he know a jeweler? *Hélène the Lemon Drop.* Why would he not tell his father? Mistrust and confusion filled my glass along with the champagne. I studied the menu and looked around the room, inhaling the smell of pine fire and attar of roses. *Calmes-toi,* I told myself. *This is your wedding supper.* I determined to enjoy it. Jace ordered us roast beef *aux champignons. Champ-pig-nons,* he pronounced it.

"*Non non non,*" I teased him. "Pronounced *sham-peen-nyon.*"

"Oh, *zoot,* I'm bad at *français,*" he said in his accent. "But *je t'aime,* Sylvester." *I love you,* like a joke.

"Do you?"

"*Mais oui.* You swallow fire."

I did like his sweet talk, whipsawed. Could this be love? It was surely there in his warm glances, his happiness. All the rest of it—the union mess, Cal, the money—was apart now, strangely outside the circle of candlelight around us. The reflections in the window glass, of Jasper's watery shape and mine, watched us from outside like phantoms of our former selves. I pulled my veil of a smile over uneasy questions and listened, practicing the ordained devotion of a wife.

"I have big ideas, Sylvester! You have made me a *revolutioniste.*"

"Ha-ha. Not likely."

"But it's true. I have a plan. It's quite radical," he said. "After we go to Dearfield, we'll travel. First to Italy—there are some expert carvers I want to meet, and—"

"Wait. We go to Dearfield?"

Jace checked himself. "We're going to bring that stone out there. You and me. Okay? It'll be a grand honeymoon adventure. A tale out of *Robin Hood*."

"To Weld County? That quarry block this morning? It must weigh thirty tons. A hundred miles, at least! The train only goes to Greeley—" Was he entirely sane?

"It was your idea!" He winked and carried on with his travelogue. "After Italy we'll go to Morocco and Madrid and Istanbul. Where else?"

"Paris?" *When the slaves of the caves are free*, I thought. But they weren't, and was there something I could do about it, now that I was Mrs. Padgett?

"Of course, Paree," he said. "Also Vermont! To see your family. We must make them comfortable. We'll send funds."

"Jace, thank you." It was touching that he'd thought of them. My brother needed schoolbooks. My mother needed a surgery. Jasper's offer had saved me from pleading on their behalf and opened a door to another question. "I have something to ask of you."

He reached to hold my hand across the table. "I'd do anything for you, angel."

"What you said about the union," I started. "That the Company will break the strike. What about the families? What will happen?"

"I don't know. We can hope—"

"Not hope. I want to help the people in the strike camp. Pay them."

"Of course. It's only right. I promise."

"They'll need thousands of dollars. Enough to let them get ahead."

"We'll figure it out," he said, sincere as a priest. "As soon as we've delivered the stone to Dearfield."

I beamed, thrilled, so distracted by the idea that he could snap his fingers and money would shower onto the strikers in the camp, that I did not stop to question: *If he's banished, where does the money come from?* I forgot to focus on his wild plan to deliver tons of marble across the mountains. Instead, I heard what I wanted to hear, that we would *figure it out*, as he said, *ensemble*, like partners. "You mean it?"

"Really," he said. "It's why I love you. You stand on principle. You even read Du Bois!" He ordered wine and smiled across the table, discoursing about Dr. Du Bois while we ate our filet mignon. Slurred with drink, he quoted the book from memory. "'Only by a union of intelligence and sympathy across the color-line in this critical period of the Republic shall justice and right triumph.'"

It was intoxicating to listen to talk about *justice* from a man who had the money to affect it, and now, it seemed, so did I. He promised thousands. He had said love. It was this above all that I wanted, thought I'd found. He would be a "revolutionist" yet. I would make him one. It seemed the future would offer a grand adventure—plus luxury.

We strolled out to the porch of the Ruby Arms. The rain had stopped, and the new October stars were strewn across the darkness in a salting of silver, the air washed and clean. The vast spaces between the cold sparks made me shiver. Jasper embraced me, his smile crooked with romantic intention. The blood and liquor in our veins roiled me with desire like an ache.

"Come on now, sweet Sylvie Padgett." He pulled me indoors and upstairs, where the vast bed awaited. Wordless in the dark, I covered myself under the sheets, grateful that they hid us, our own strange bodies and souls exposed.

"It's all right," Jasper said.

And it was. Animal magnetism fierce and transporting. He kissed me and murmured pretty things, *adore* and *heart. I cannot live without you.* I wept soundless tears that he brushed away in the dark.

"No, oh no." He kissed my forehead, my hair. "It's all right, sweetheart. Shh. I'll never hurt you. We're married, so."

So. I went on into that new territory, where we whispered and grappled in the awkward wanton darkness. Laughing and happy. It would be a fine romance after all. Yes.

Chapter Thirty-Three

IN THE BRIGHT MORNING, A rustle of paper woke me. Jasper at the desk, folding a letter into an envelope. Seeing me stir, he came to sit on the side of the bed. He took my hand and kissed me. I smiled, half in a dream, till I saw his eyes were tender with something like dread.

"Listen, angel," he said, "I have to go."

"Go?" I was drowsy, in a raw newlywed state.

"Shh. Don't worry. Go back to sleep. Rest, my love."

He seemed close to tears and looked away with my hand in his own, twirling the band on the small wrong finger. "Let me take this for adjustment," he said. "To get it fitted exactly for my Sylvie." He slipped it off.

I sat up with alarm, as if he'd robbed me. "Jace?"

He was dressed but uncombed, a dust of golden whiskers on his face. "It's Caleb," he said. "I'm sorry to— I know you'll understand, won't you?" He managed to flash a wide grin, a wink. "Send to the kitchen for breakfast in bed! Lounge in the palm court! Wait for me, sweetheart. I'll be back very soon. Don't worry."

"But where are you going?"

"Caleb has to get to Denver immediately. It's all explained," he said, and kissed me again, the kiss of a soldier off to war and not to breakfast. "*Au revoir.*" The door latch clicked and he was gone. To this day I regret that in the dreamlike confusion of the moment, I did not fling myself to stop him, or beg him to stay, or hurry to go with him.

On the desk was the envelope, my name on it. When I broke the seal, more cash fell fluttering to the floor. Padgett confetti. And a letter.

Dearest Sylvie,

This morning I've had an urgent message from Cal's doctor at the clinic. His injuries are grave, and Cal is in considerable pain. I am compelled to get him to a surgeon in Denver with all deliberate haste. For this reason I've made the difficult—but chivalrous, I hope—decision to leave with him this morning.

Too late I've realized that it would not be safe for you to travel in his company. Perhaps you did not notice the stares of those men yesterday while you conversed with him, but I was much alarmed. Such men will lynch a Negro on any excuse.

And, as I did not have a chance to fully explain last evening, my "big idea" is this: to bequeath the stone that was intended for the Temple of Gratitude to the people of Dearfield. Yesterday I had it routed to Greeley at the end of the line. When Caleb is healed, he and I will bring it on the last leg by teamster wagon. Then I'll return to you.

Please forgive me. I intended for you to be by my side on this journey. But violent types are everywhere these days, and travel to Weld County will take us over treacherous roads. It would not be fair to subject you to such a punishing trip. For this reason I believe it's best for you to stay here at the hotel until I send for you. I trust you will understand, and promise to make it up to you in several weeks. We'll be together before you know it, sweetheart. I enclose funds to tide you over. You will lack for nothing.

Your loving Jace

There were three green bills. Each featured the portrait of a balding man in wire glasses. John Jay Knox, Jr., was his name. Three Knoxes, each worth a hundred dollars.

The nerve of him. To pay me off—to leave! He'd taken that ring back, and why? Because I'd let him. I sat piercing myself with thorns of regret, disgusted by my own impulsive *yes*. It was not love, it was the Devil who snared me, and now I was punished. In the dark of our wedding night, Jace had seen his mistake. I was too tall, my fingers too thick, my French the wrong French. He took the ring to annul what it stood for, and paid off his guilty conscience. Three hundred dollars. Was it meant to be consolation for the absence of one Padgett? The death of one Pelletier? It was not even a fraction of the thousands he'd promised for the strike camp.

I sat in my chemise and looked at the trio of bills lined up on the desk like a hand of cards. I would buy a ticket to Paris. *When the slaves of the caves are free*, Lonahan had said. *Do not think of Lonahan*. Seize the opportunity. Hanging over my thoughts was the marble block Jace had commandeered and the rest of the money taken from the safe. Probably I was a criminal suspect, and was full of suspicion myself. What was he up to?

I held my head under an icy faucet till it cleared, and looked in the mirror with cold eyes. *Hello, Mrs. Padgett*. Was I? Who knew it? Apart from Caleb Grady, only the decrepit justice and his daughter Winnie. No relation, they thought. *I haven't told my father*, Jasper said. Caleb would not tell anyone, as he was off with his half brother, Jace, on a strange mad mission to Weld County.

All hell's about to break loose.

Of the risks, the worst was to wait here at the Ruby Arms, squandering the Knoxes at fifteen dollars a night just to sleep in a feather bed. It was money better saved in case J. C. Padgett never flashed his baleful crooked grin at me again.

But what if he returned in two weeks, as promised?

The least bad plan was to go back to Moonstone. Keep the money for emergency escape, if it came to that. I dressed and descended to the lobby, where I asked the clerk a favor: "If a letter or telegram arrives here for me, for Mrs. Padgett, kindly forward it to the Moonstone P.O., care of Sylvie Pelletier." I gave him five dollars for incentive and another five "for a freshly addressed envelope and new stamps." I did not want the name of Mrs. Padgett on the mail, to cause questions I couldn't answer.

At the Ruby depot, the uphill train pulled in, hissing and smoking and packed with men, brass stars on their lapels, guns on their hips. Pinkerton agents, bound for Moonstone. I boarded the car and counted nineteen Pinks among the ranchers and farmers coming to sell apples and potatoes. Also on the train: seven hungry-eyed men in thin coats. Scabs from the scab hatchery.

"Make way for the lady," one fella said. All along the lurching aisle, men sized me up, till I found a safe seat next to a jolly woman and her darling puppy, named Chowder. He settled on my lap, happy to be scratched behind the ears.

"He sure do love you," said my companion.

"If only all love were simple as a dog's." I sighed.

"Chowder is a rat terrier," she told me. "He can catch any small pest."

"What can he do about a Pinkerton infestation?" I whispered.

She harrumphed. "Ha. Some of these boys is in love with their guns, is all."

They were boys, half of them still without whiskers, emboldened by their uniforms. The train wound up the mountain while they swaggered along the rows of seats. One of the youngest—with the slack-mouthed appearance of a halfwit—loudly bragged, "My uncle Harry, ya know, Harold Smiley, he's the sheriff there now. Yessir. He's a famous sharpshooter, and he's gonna shoot every damn shirker on sight. We got sights on that agitator, the ringleader, Houlihan."

Lonahan?

"Uncle Harry don't stand for trouble. Just rounds 'em up, ships 'em out."

I heard the word *strikebreak*. I heard the name *Colonel Bowles*. Somebody said, *Torch the place.* All hell about to break loose.

"Where the dickens have you been, miss?" K.T. asked when I came in the door.

"Ruby," I said, breathless, and told her how many Pinkerton agents I'd counted, what they'd said they'd do. I never did tell her, or anyone, the true reason I'd been to Ruby, about my change of title. Missus now, not miss. "They're going to break the strike," I said. "It's a raid on. Scabs—"

"Cripes! Thought you'd bring back a story, not the dogs of hell. Go tell Lonahan."

"George is here?" The way I jumped in my skin told me something I was reluctant to know.

"Since last night. Looked for you this morning. You better get up to the camp quick and warn him."

I didn't want to go to Dogtooth Flats, was afraid to see George. More afraid of his sharp eye than of the message I had for him: *All hell.* In my closet, I hid the three Knoxes in the pages of Conrad and Dickens and Du Bois, then laced my boots and set out at a fast clip. Soon the climb and the altitude forced me to calm down and absorb the beauty of the Gilded Range, in slants of sun. The glowing gold aspens and the slashes of green pine arranged the endless patchwork of a rocky world. The hike detached me from the events of the past two days. They were not real. Not the deranged episode in the vault. Not the wedding posies or the long night or the mad morning letter of Jace. I was a half-day married. Not real.

These tents were real, staked like white moths on the flat ridge. The smell of cook fires was real, the sound of an ax splitting logs. In the dirt lanes, everywhere was noise and activity. Lev Tchachenko scraped hides. His wife beside him gutted a squirrel. A whistling boy cleaned fish. Where was George? *Find Lonahan.* Inside one of the tents, a man shaved over a bowl. Not George. In another, a woman worked a sewing machine: Mrs. Bruner. She called out, "Sylvie!" but I hurried on, looking. When he saw me, George would know by a glance: I was married. *To the overlord,* he'd say, and write me off as a turncoat.

I had made my bed and lain right down in it. *Do not think of beds or lying down.* Inside the big union tent, the light was ghostly through the canvas.

Stacked around the perimeter were boxes of supplies. Canned food. Potato sacks. Coal in a bin. And that long flat crate, straw escaping through the slats. Guns? If so, they were not buried, as Mrs. Jones advised. *We're for ballots, not bullets.* I prayed that philosophy would win the day, but I'd seen the armed Pinkertons on the train, and I was afraid.

Dan Kerrigan sat inside wearing his UMW pin.

"Sylvie!" He broke into a smile. "A sight for sore eyes." Kind Dan Kerrigan, friend of my father. Was he the union man who had beat Caleb bloody? Who went for the rope? "You know, you look just like your papa," he said. "Minus the beard, of course."

Papa's beard. *The nest of a goldfinch.* I swallowed against the sudden water in my eyes. What would my father think of me? Who I'd chosen.

"We could use your dad now, in these wicked days," Kerrigan said, sorrowful.

"I've a message for Mr. Lonahan," I said from a thick throat.

He pointed me toward a corner, where someone lay sacked out on a cot. "Wake up, boss." Kerrigan whistled sharply. "Hey! It's Sylvie here to see you."

George sat up, a dent of sleep printed on his face beside that terrible scar, his hair in a tousle, blinking with a broad smile. "Sylvie Pelletier, darlin'!"

I did not correct him. Said not a word about my new title: Mrs. Padgett. Only told him what I'd seen in Ruby. Pinks. Scabs. Guns. He unfolded his long praying-mantis legs from under the blankets in a hurry.

"At least twenty agents," I reported. "They're after some agitator, Houlihan. Is that you?"

"Sonovabitch." Standing up, he tucked his shirt into his trousers.

"Be careful, George."

He held on to my gaze with his own so I had to look away. "Just my luck," he said, half asleep. "I was intending to wine and dine and serenade you with my fine operatic skills."

"You have operatic skills?" I said with a faltering smile.

"'Sweetly sings the donkey, at the break of day,'" he sang. "'If you do not feed him, he will run away.'" A theatrical hand on his heart. "How sad to run away just as you appear, like a beautiful dream."

"A nightmare, more like," I said. "The Pinkertons are mustering at the depot."

"Aw, hell. I'll go talk to Bowles, see if we can't smooth his hackles."

"Hackles." Our joke. I suppressed a pang. I did still like George Lonahan very much. Too much.

"Hackles!" He slapped his thigh. "You're a stitch, Sylvie Pelletier."

I was a stitch. A dropped stitch, which results in a great unraveling.

George rushed out, shouting. Somebody sounded the alarm, beating a skillet with a clanging spoon. In minutes the whole camp crowded in the big tent. All the strikers, men with stubbled cheeks and drooping mustaches, braid on their odd-brimmed hats. Tchachenkos and Bruners and Mercandittis greeted me like old friends. There was Christe Boleson with his yellow hair, red cheeks. Everybody pressed together, anxious. I stayed in a corner.

Kerrigan stood on a crate to speak to the crowd. "It's a raid coming," he said. "Rumor is, they aim to torch the camp."

"It's not a rumor," I said, too loud. People turned to stare and left me no choice but to go on, voice shaking. "I saw a carload of agents coming up from Ruby, and heard them say they'd burn the tents and run everybody off."

"Listen to her, now," Kerrigan said. "That's our Sylvie Pelletier. Frenchy was her dad. May he rest in peace."

My father was not resting; he was possessing me. His eyes stared out of my sockets at the faces here. Nobody shushed me. "They will break the strike! I worked in the castle here and heard their talk about it. You can be sure the Padgetts have vaults of money in the Morgan Guaranty Trust. You, yourselves, earned it. There's plenty to go around. Don't let them tell you different."

This was not some rallying cry, such as Mrs. Jones delivered, only information, only reporting. Still, the strikers clapped. Nobody knew I was Mrs. Padgett talking, to make herself ill, to dig her own grave. I pushed out of the tent and was sick behind a stack of split wood. I wish I could say it was the last of my fear and cowardice departing, but that would not be the truth.

While George ran to town to head off a raid, the strikers worked fast to build a barricade. They stacked rocks and boxes, flipped a wagon bed on its side, to block the road. They stationed lookouts. The temperature was dropping into the sunset. I was shaky. Hungry.

The smell of Mrs. Bruner's fire led me to her tent. She nursed her infant while stirring a pot on a camp stove, blond braids wound around her head. "*Wilkommen*, Sylvie!" She insisted on giving me tea and a baked potato, too proud to take the dollar I offered for her kindness. I slipped the bill under the jar of goldenrod she'd picked for a centerpiece on her crate for a table, to make the place a home, as Maman would've done.

"Let me take the baby," I said, and rigged a sling for little Albert to hold him on my back. "You rest." She slept while I washed out the baby's grim diaper in a bucket and played with his sister, Clara. We made a crown for her rag doll out of bunchgrass. "What is the dolly's name?"

"Ingeborg Princess," Clara said. She chattered away until she fell asleep in my lap. I did not want to move from under her warm weight and thought of my small faraway Nipper. For him, I was only a story by now. For Maman, I was a prayer and a worry. For Henry, a shrug. I suffered with homesickness, missing a home I didn't have.

It grew late. The wind came up, battering the canvas walls. The night was moonless, too dangerous for me to go back to town. Frau Bruner gave me a blanket. I settled myself on the floor as if I belonged there. The feather mattress of the Ruby Arms and the arms of a husband were remnants of a preposterous fever dream. Somebody started a tune on a harmonica. An accordion joined, and a graveled voice began to sing, "As I walk along the Bois Boolong, with an independent air . . ." The singer was heckled, "Shut up, ya maggot," but he kept on singing, "You can hear the girls declare, there goes a millionaire . . ." The men jeered him, scoffing at the absurdity of millionaires, while scraps of millionaire money festered in the pillow of my rucksack. I fell asleep on it.

Chapter Thirty-Four

LONAHAN'S MISSION TO CALL OFF a raid was successful. The good news traveled through the camp: Negotiations had resumed. I was quick to leave before George returned. The rest of the morning was uneventful, without violence.

But in the ensuing week, as a response to acts of vandalism, "that debris blocking train tracks," the Company increased the ranks of Pinkertons. Swaggering Sheriff Smiley deported two more strikers, but his goons did not attack. Not yet.

"Their intent is to deport them one by one," K.T. said. "And let the camp fold when the snows arrive. Won't say I told ya so."

In the early days of October, my routine resumed as if I'd never married. The fact of the wedding seemed vague as a mountaintop is in fog. The weather grew as cold as my recollection of the courthouse vows, the night in the arms of *mon mari*, the down of clear hair on his wrist, blue veins there carrying his very blood around to his heart, which he said was mine, as mine was his. It was an obsessing mystery, how I could have been his heart when, only weeks before, the Lemon Drop had him riding around bewitched. He'd promised *till death us do part*, but I had no proof, no sign, no photograph. Only this inward shift, as if a magnesium flash had burned through my flesh and left a pulling ache. Dread gathered like the clouds that lowered onto the surface of Marvelous Lake. In the mornings now, the bowl of it held a cold white soup of fog, winter cooking like trouble. No word from Jace. I grew angry at him again, worse than before. I wish now I'd confessed, alerted someone about his mission. I wish I had.

The town was crawling with Pinkerton agents. They bullied around the streets, accosting people on any excuse. They chased and beat a boy for jeering, "Pinks are finks!" waggling his fingers in his ears. The guards' camp was by the river, next to the mill. A hundred scabs were penned there too, in a new stockade nailed up "for protection" against "violent anarchists." Talk of a raid hung in the air, spiked the days with threats. Everybody on edge. The strikers kept to the flats and hauled meager supplies over the difficult trails from Rabbit Town on mules. There was a shortage of blankets. A rationing of coal. I worked and sent my wages to Maman. K. T. Redmond published an editorial demand:

RECALL THE ILLEGAL PRIVATE MILITIA.

The *Booster* responded:

STRIKE HOLDOUTS SAME
AS BLOODSUCKING LEECHES.

Somebody left a scrawled note under our door: "You beter leave this part of the mountins, as you are to free with your mouth."

Mid-October, when I was twelve days a bride, somebody threw a brick through the window of the *Record* in the middle of the night. "Firebombs are next," K.T. said. We nailed boards over the broken pane. The next night, somebody threw a hunk of marble at the front window of the Company offices. It shattered in the shape of a web.

"Serves 'em right, those spiders" was K.T.'s verdict.

"Was it you?"

"We don't throw bricks," she said. "We throw words and reason."

I threw myself into the work of the newspaper in order not to throw myself into the river, holding a handful of reasons, like stones, why Jace would never return. *He is false, a drunk, deranged.* I tried to picture his eyes, lit blue as the center of a flame, with what? Revolution? Alcohol? Delusions?

My own delusions were too painful to examine, so I studied Dr. Du Bois's book of *Souls*, parsing it for insights, trying to understand my husband's mad mission, to be ready when he returned. *If.* What if he didn't? I decided to go to Chicago, where a woman could disappear in a crowd. In K.T.'s unsorted mail, I found two copies of the *Chicago Defender.* To my surprise, it was a newspaper published and written by Negroes. It contained articles about the plague of lynchings, heinous acts in the southern states, written by Mrs. Ida B. Wells-Barnett, fearless in her reporting, sickening to read:

> The lynching mob cuts off ears, toes, and fingers, strips the flesh, and distributes portions of the body as souvenirs among the crowd. If the leaders of the mob are so minded, oil is poured over the body and the victim is roasted to death. This has been done in Texarkana and Paris, Tex., in Bardswell, Ky., and in Newman, Ga. In Paris the officers of the law delivered the prisoner to the mob. The railroads ran excursion trains so that the people might see a human being burned to death.

The *Defender* reports had me again in shock. In his tortured confessions, Jace once told me his father had brought him and the Grady boys to see a man hanged, *as a lesson.* My own lessons continued with the articles in the *Defender*'s pages that called on black people to move west, to migrate for their own safety. I began to further understand the forces at work on the Gradys, what they were escaping. *A town all our own.* Easter had not wanted Jasper to follow, yet he was following, dragging that stone. I couldn't imagine she would be happy to see him or it. A stone inheritance.

———

Two weeks, he'd said. But it was more than two already. I looked at the post office for a letter or a telegram to summon me. Jumped at the ring of the party-line phone, in case Jace might be calling. Listened like a spy for talk of Padgetts and scandal, a robbery of money and diamonds from the vaults at Elkhorne, valuable marble missing. An assault by union thugs of a chef. But nothing was rumored or reported. K.T. would get wind of it, some detail would expose me. As Jasper's accomplice? His wife? A dupe? And then what?

A summons. On the morning of October 16, a Company messenger delivered a note on official letterhead addressed to me. I was to appear at the office for an "interview" the next morning. The request came from the owner and president and mayor, Frederick "Colonel" Bowles.

Here it comes. Was the interview some kind of a trap? I scrambled for reasons to refuse. Something contagious. Smallpox? Measles? But at the same time, I was hoping Bowles had news of Jace, so I went.

The Colonel greeted me, all smiles and welcome. You would never peg him for a snake, this jovial man. "Well, good morning! And how's the anarchy business?"

"I wouldn't know, sir."

He held a chair for me and sat at his desk. "Doc Butler tells me you were working at Elkhorne a few weeks back. The same night some union criminals thrashed a Negro, the Padgetts' cook." Bowles did not say *Negro* but uttered the common epithet. "Doc says he saw you when he went to tend the fellow, about nine o'clock."

I affected the blinking of a slow-witted child. *Silence is a woman's best garment* was advice often handed to me, and I wore it now as a disguise.

"Mrs. Padgett"—he paused and I startled at the name—"suggested you might know the whereabouts of young Jasper. She is worried about him. No one's heard from him since that evening. His father is concerned. Any idea where he might be?"

I shook my head.

"He left with the injured man," the Colonel said. "We searched up at the lodge. We interviewed the train conductors. He was rumored to have gone to Ruby, but there's no word of where he went after that. Miss DuLac has gone abroad, and we thought he might've followed, but he did not. We've contacted his classmates and friends. No luck."

"I wish I could help," I said, glad the Lemon Drop had thrown them off the trail.

Bowles swiveled his chair. "Miss Pelletier," he said, "young Jasper is not— you must realize—he has foolish ideas. He is prone to rash actions. He goes off half-cocked."

"Oh, dear," I said, with big eyes blinking.

"Mrs. Padgett mentioned that you and Jasper are friends. Or more than friends?" His eyebrows lifted with insinuation. "Inge thought perhaps he'd had some little . . . dalliance and might've confided in you?"

I blinked again, like a mooncalf.

Colonel Bowles lit a cigarette and conducted the air with smoke. "Duke Padgett has asked me to find his son. He and Mrs. Padgett are traveling in Europe. The family is no longer connected to the marble operations here, but out of a sense of loyalty and friendship to his father, I'm left to untangle the mess the boy made."

"The mess, sir?"

"The boy made a fatal mistake. He allowed the union in. We've lost time and revenue. Shipments are missing. We've got to get these agitators out of town. Resume normal business. You and that Redmond woman are not helping."

"Sir?"

"Her articles claim our Company is nothing but a stock swindle. Do you know anything about investments? Stocks?"

"Nossir, I don't."

"Darn right you don't. And your lady editor is equally ignorant."

"She studies the markets."

"Phh. In places where we expected investment, that miserable sheet—the so-called *Record*—has been waved in our faces and timidity encountered."

Timidity. I knew it well and clung to it yet, for a strategy.

"Investors will not put their money in." Bowles looked me over. "You always did seem like a nice girl. A good, quiet girl."

"Thank you, sir." My mother would've been proud in that moment at how I bit my lip appeasingly and looked at my shoes.

"You're a friend of the Padgetts, are you not? Mrs. Padgett gave you a great opportunity. Despite the unfortunate accident in the quarry, they've treated you well."

Killing my father. Evicting us. The hackles rose at the back of my neck, and I imagined leaping with wolf fangs at the wattles of his throat. *Le loup-garou.*

"Please understand," he said, "if you were not yourself a friend of the Padgetts, if your editor had been a man, you both would've been ridden out of town a long time ago."

"I am just an office girl."

Perhaps the Colonel heard the gnashing of my teeth, for now he warned: "Do not bite the hand that feeds you. Do us the courtesy of convincing Trina Redmond to cease her attacks. Tell her we mean business. If she doesn't quit, we'll shut her down."

"Like I said, sir, I'm just an office girl." I attempted a little shrug in the style of the Countess. "But I don't expect she'll ever stop printing the paper."

"Shiftless and uneducated workers here are susceptible to her anarchist lies," the Colonel explained.

At the word *shiftless*, I lost my restraint. "Sir," I heard myself say, "the men are worked to the bone. They were forced out on strike because no one had a paycheck since last fall. They only want to go back to work and feed their families. Can the Company not settle and pay back wages—"

"We made our offer!" The Colonel hit the desk. "These boys only listen to outsiders like this fellow Houlihan—"

"Lonahan. He negotiates—"

"Lonahan, Houlihan, hooligan, you know who I mean. You gals will never understand this business. The sheer difficulty and danger. Perilous transportation. The constant snowslides. The fickle investors. We are trying to make a go of it in impossible conditions. Ten thousand feet above sea level. For crying out loud!"

"Trouble is a pebble, sir," I suggested. "My mother always says."

The Colonel snorted. "Trouble is where you're headed if you keep on associating with low types of people. I'd hoped you'd be reasonable. I'd hoped you knew where to find Jasper. His father is distraught. If you hear any word, I'd appreciate your telling me."

Chapter Thirty-Five

No word. The mercury fell. The nights were freezing now, snow in the wind. On several excuses in those darkening weeks of late October, George Lonahan dropped by the *Record* after his attempts to negotiate with management. His habit was to blast through the door, the bell jangling, gusts blowing ice flakes and paper, rattling the nerves and the conscience of this dissembling woman, me, Sylvie P., guarding her secret.

"Halloo, ladies of truth and justice!" George stamped snow off his boots.

"Wipe your feet, savage," K.T. said.

Lonahan scraped each one with exaggerated care and never failed to exclaim over the weather and his enemy, Colonel Bowles, in the same breath.

"Goddamn cold as Bowles's left onion."

"Goddamn cold as Bowles's amphibian heart."

"Goddamn wet out there as the fish-slime soul of Colonel Bowles."

We had the same enemy. I loved how he named Bowles as a *sonuvabitch* and a dog-faced boor, a mealworm, a blue-blooded city boy making bargains in bad faith. "Today Bowles made the union an offer of air and threw in daylight as a bonus."

Between outbursts, he checked to see was I laughing (I was). "You're sweet on Colonel Bowles," he said, to bait me. "You think he's swell."

"No! He's—"

"Bootlicking. Say *bootlicking*. You can manage it. Say *boot . . . lick*."

"You're vulgar."

"You're laughing. Come out with me now, Sylvie, for a ginger beer."

"George, please," I deflected. "I'm trying to get this printed."

"Let me at that type tray. I will spell 'b-e-a-u-t-y.' I'll spell 'What does Sylvie want for Christmas?'"

"Get away, you, Lonahan! I have to set the page." I swatted at him and escaped as a hairball of lies gathered in my throat. The longer my bizarre elopement stayed undisclosed, the more it seemed invented out of fairy books. The longer there was no word from Jasper Padgett, the more I looked forward to George's distractions. My work at the press suffered from mistakes. The air was wiry with tension, leaps of guilt in the blood. I was at all times aware of Lonahan's location in the office. The bell that announced his entry jangled my nerves until he went out again. I followed news of his negotiations, his meetings at Dogtooth Camp. George stayed up there, and the Pinks left him alone for now because he was an official from UMW headquarters.

K.T. the instigator encouraged his visits. Invited him for whiskey, coffee, and cards. It was comfortable, the three of us talking about events both local and global, such that I developed an addiction to the newswires that has lasted all my life. George hung about smoking, drying his wet socks by our stove. One night he borrowed my scissors and cut shapes out of paper, a bird, a daisy, a fish. Another night he fashioned a straggly palm tree out of rolled newsprint and planted it in an empty whiskey bottle. "Now we are in the tropics!" He joked and composed sentences on the jobsticks, messages and doggerel for me to read backward:

Sugar is sweet and so are you.

He persisted in teasing me. I feigned ignorance. A head cold. He hid type so I'd have to hunt for it, finding the S on the windowsill, the G balanced on a tea tin.

"Darn you, George, where's the Q?"

"Just before the R," he said. "After the P."

"Darn you."

He called me "Primrose" or "Rosie" to mock me for my refusal to curse. "Repeat after me: Shitcan the bosses."

"Profanity is just an excuse for a poor vocabulary," I said, then spilled ink and cursed. "Dammit! Look what you made me do."

"Attagirl, Rosie, now you've got the hang of it."

Thus he corrupted me with his jokes and swigs from his flask. "We've got their testicles in a vise!" he announced one day, so I refused to speak to him till he apologized for talking that way to a lady (who was laughing anyway). "Sorry, Primrose. Where's the soap? I'll wash my mouth out."

I missed his distractions when he went with Kerrigan to Denver for a meeting with the Labor Commission. But it was a relief that he wasn't around. I was weak and he was bold. He lingered too close at the printing press, a comradely arm around my shoulder. He was a pirate with the hands of a pianist, long thin fingers, flat blunt fingernails, very clean. The white path of that scar led across the cheek to his mouth.

"How did you get it?" I finally asked him.

"Rescued a kitten from a sawmill," he said, winking. "Or was it the time I fell upon the switchblade of a bandit in the Pine Barrens? Possibly it was that fight with a broken window." Half his stories were true and seventy-five percent of them were not. I could hardly admit to myself how much I liked him. I was married. A married woman. Was I?

The days of October dwindled, and then it was November. Something was terribly wrong. Jace had not written. The mail service was no excuse: I received regular letters from my family. Why had I trusted JCP? Naive idiot Sylvie. Layers of reproach and anger built in me like snow on a scarp. He'd found solace in a bawdy house in a railroad town, or returned to Virginia and the arms of a debutante. Such ficklery had happened before, but I hadn't learned my lesson. My skull was a cauldron of hurt. Jace was free. He could do what he wanted. He was a man. Armed with money. What was my weapon?

Just before Thanksgiving, K. T. Redmond packed her bag and went to Denver again to visit her sister, Daisy, a widow now. "It's a three-week vacation from this cussed burg." She left me in charge of the office, with instructions not to print any news till she returned—only invitations, posters, or handbills. I was to feed Bill the cat and shovel the sidewalk. She left me to celebrate Thanksgiving with Dottie Weeks and her husband, then wallow in self-pity and a copy of *Pride and Prejudice*.

One evening, December already, I lowered the shade and had settled down by the stove when somebody rapped on the door.

"Knock-knock."

"Who is it?"

"Joe King."

"Who?"

"Joking around to get a laugh outta you." It was George Lonahan, whistling out there in the weather. "Unlock the door, Sylvie Pelletier."

"Not funny," I said.

"Then why are you smiling?" He came in with a blast of snow, kissed my cheek, hung up his hat like he was home, and dropped his pack. "It's Dr. Lonahan with a cure for the sours."

"I'm not sour," I said.

"Rumor says you are. I saw Redmond in Denver, and she hinted." He produced a large bottle of whiskey. "Here's medicine."

"George, you'll cause a scandal—"

"The shades are lowered," he said. "The storm is fierce. Are you going to throw me to the wolves? The arctic winds? I am an honorable fellow. Also cold as a frosted frog. And I have good news for you to print, so lemme just thaw here awhile and tell it. Kerrigan's gone to Dogtooth to tell the boys."

I handed him a glass, obviously pleased to see him. Quite pleased with himself, he poured whiskey and toasted. "The Colorado Labor Commission has fined our infernal Company for infractions and breach of promise. Bowles and the bosses have pledged a wage hike and an eight-hour day. I just came from their offices where we made a handshake deal. All that remains is for those rat bastards to add a signature, and we have a contract."

"It's thanks to you," I said.

George flashed a smile of triumph. "Not only! It was your father who started things a year ago. And it's thanks to those brave boys freezing their onions, holding camp up on the flats. But I'll take any thanks. Even only one thank."

"Thank," I said. That joke again, I was not tired of it. We smiled at our own cleverness. By the stove, George turned his hands over to warm them. He threw more coal into the fire pan, and left the doors open to stare into the embers, and sighed. "Soon as these boys sign, sorry to say, Primrose, I'm off again." He watched me to see what I thought of it.

"So soon?" I said. "You just got back here."

"Job's done, pretty much, now we have an agreement."

"Will they really sign, George? I don't trust that Colonel. I'm afraid they'll just pay another measly fine and carry on as usual."

"This time I'm hopeful. Either way, there's nothing left for me to do now. District boss is sending me to the southern mines. There's a coal strike in Trinidad."

"To the Rockefeller camp there? It's dangerous. The Governor sent in troops. They have machine guns."

"They do, the bastards." He cocked his eye at me. "If I were machine-gunned, would you feel a pang?"

"Don't talk like that. They wouldn't shoot you."

"I'm exactly who they'd shoot. And I indulge the idea, not infrequently, that you might shed a tear for me if I died for the cause. That you'd be sad."

"Of course I'd be sad. What are you talking about?" I could not look at him.

"*Je t'aime*," he said.

"Pardon?" I'd misheard him.

"I went to the Denver Library and looked it up in the French department. Learned three things: *J'ai faim. J'ai soif. Je t'aime.*"

In his endearing thick accent, George had said: *I'm hungry. I'm thirsty. I love you.* To deflect him, and to ignore the last bit, I corrected him like a schoolteacher. "*Non*, Georges, you pronounce it *J'ai faim, j'ai soif, je t'aime.*"

"You do?" he crowed, and thumped his chest. "You love me!"

"I didn't say that!" I cried. "No, I said—"

"*J'ai soif,*" he said. "*J'ai faim.*"

He was hungry. He was thirsty. And the third thing. I pretended not to hear it, tried to act as if I did not return the feeling, dug deeper now in trouble. I said nothing in French or English about myself as Mrs. Padgett. I laughed. "If you're hungry, here's a sandwich!" I escaped to the cupboard and buttered bread. He ate it while I helped him to drink the rest of the liquor in his bottle. I should've confessed then. But the heart wants. I was in the grip of loneliness. *Je t'aime*, he'd said, and I was hungry myself, for such words in any language. I should've sent him on his way. Instead, I plied him with questions about the union, the Wobblies, his hobo life on the road, stumping for the UMW. While he talked, I pretended not to see the burn of his eye, the smiles in my direction, how he plucked his long fingers at the crease in his trousers, raked his dark head of hair, parted like crow's wings. He tucked it behind his ears and caught me noticing. "I do need a haircut," he said.

"Your *hairs* cut," I said, tipsy. "Like my mother would say. She used to cut my father's hair."

"There's an idea! Fetch the scissors!"

"Scissors!" I said.

"Shears!" He plucked them off the desk and we laughed ourselves stupid, the *pluralia tantum* like a code for what was singular between us. With George, I did not feel myself to be *less*, not poor or Papist or foreign. We were cut from the same cloth. I took the scissors from the composing table. George took off his tie. I put an apron around his neck and snipped the air behind him with theatrical menace.

"Yikes," he said. "I'm having qualms. A qualm."

"One yike or two?" Roaring again, both of us cracking up.

"Stop," he said. "Do you have a mirror?"

"You won't want to look after I'm done with you. Hold still."

I worked around his head with a comb, leaving tracks in the dark hair. Now we did not talk. George closed his eyes, so I was free to study the arch of his eyebrows, that scar tracking across the blue shadow of whiskers. The noise of scissors cut the quiet. Snips of hair fell to the floor. I folded down the cartilage of his ear, trimmed around the crest of it, above the frayed collar, along the back of the neck. His eyes stayed shut. Some concentration of feeling came over his face, his breathing. The air thickened and turned strange. I grew afraid, not of the scissors working close to the arteries of his neck, but of the heat off his scalp, the whiskey in us, the rise and fall of his chest. I leaned over the long bones of his legs to trim the wings of his curls, my knees brushing his knees. My fingers forked along the scalp, lifted a lock of hair. George opened his eyes and saw the workings of my throat. I nearly fainted at the plain raw intention on his face.

"Sylvie," he said, a husk in his voice.

I was weak beside him, the scissors dropped. He pulled me to his lap and kissed me, and I kissed him, abandoned in adulterous betrayal, wondering was it only kissing that I liked so desperately, or was it George himself or both at once? Was the window shade open? Could the whole town see? Did my lawful wedded husband, Jace, know somehow and would he smell infidelity on me and would the world and God now know me for a traitor to my sacred word? George was not the Devil, I was. I kissed him till I sprang up for breath, wiping at my bruised mouth with a sleeve.

"You'll be lopsided if I don't finish," I said, drunk on kissing.

"Lopsided is a new fashion," he said, pulling me back, his hands along my rib cage, down my one leg and up the other. I did not stop him, only craved to fall away to the floor. I confess it, now that it does not matter. How the chair tipped and lurched. My clothes in a dishevelment. He moved my hands where he wanted them, his own at my buttons.

"Stop," I said. "Stop."

"I'm sorry," he said. We were shaking, both of us rattled. "Forgive me, Sylvie. For a long time I thought of—kissing you. And did you ever think— ?"

"Yes." It was the truth. "George," I said, verging on tears. "George, please, I have to confess that I am—I must tell you—"

He grew cold, watching me stammer, as if a door had been left open in January. Gusts of winter blew in. Gales.

"I'm sorry, I—" A sob escaped me. "I have to tell you."

"There's someone else," he said, hard as a hammer.

I nodded.

He stood up from the chair, his hair half cut. "You're a bad person." He looked stricken then sad then angry. He put his coat on fast and made for the door.

"Your hair—"

"Delilah," he said, and was gone.

George did not return. Jace did not write. The strike did not settle. As I'd feared, the sanction and fine had done nothing to convince the bastards of management to sign the contract. A decoy agreement was drawn up by Bowles only to stall and frustrate. His handshake was as worthless as his word. The women in the camp boiled soup bones to feed their children, and the Pinks were itching—had been for six weeks—to raid the ragged camp, only thirty stalwarts left there. The scabs scabbed in the mill. George was gone, so there was no union rep to hold management feet to the fire or put their testicles in a vise. I blamed myself for driving him away. It was almost Christmas, the season of giving. As penance, I spent forty of Jace's dollars on cornmeal to donate to the freezing strikers, and hauled supplies to the camp in the snow. I visited a little girl quarantined with measles and brought her a box of crayons. At the schoolhouse, I tutored a Slovakian boy who spoke no English. I helped Dottie Weeks to paint the walls of the bakery and got spills of her sunny yellow paint on my father's old overalls, "like the blood of daffodils," I told her.

"Aren't you very strange," she said. "Daffodils do not bleed."

I sent Maman one of my three Knoxes for Christmas. "I've saved my salary, and send it to you. *Joyeux Noël, Ta fille, Sylvie.*"

"*Grâce à Dieu*," she wrote back. "A hundred dollars! Your brothers have new boots and coats for the winter. I have tithed to the church. We pray for you to be home soon." Home was nowhere but my closet. I longed for my family. But when I thought about Rutland, Vermont, the very name of the town matched my despair, land of ruts, not roots. I mailed Maman copies of the *Record* so that she would know the state of things, as K.T. wrote them upon her return from Denver.

STRIKE STILL ON

> An eastern stockholder, on a visit to Moon-
> stone, would think it false if he were told the
> marble workers' strike continues. Company
> managers assure stockholders—poor victims—
> that the strike did not amount to a row of pins
> because the owner and the visible employees
> scoff at the truth: The strike is ongoing. They
> claim the union is finished. But meander over a
> ridge of Dogtooth Mountain and there you will
> find a tent colony inhabited by a stalwart group
> of walker-outers. These are the true employees,
> none of whom will budge until Kunnel Bowles
> signs a fair deal. Meanwhile, an inferior quality
> of marble is shipped, as the replacement crews
> would not know a fine picarillo chisel from a
> sledgehammer.

December hurtled onward. The wind raved in the creaking pines and sent branches crashing down, narrowly missing the heads of sledding children. Gale forces ate shingles off rooftops, and snow fell to muffle the creatures digging under it, human and animal. The board shacks crusted over; the tents up on Dogtooth Flats sagged in depressions of snow.

It was two months since my elopement. Nothing but silence from Jace Padgett. *Pas un mot* from George Lonahan. He had left the day after his lop-sided haircut, "for urgent business with Mrs. Jones," K.T. said. "Or perhaps he was disappointed?"

"I wouldn't know."

"You would," she said, "if your big fat head were screwed on straight."

I took my ears in my hands and straightened the head on my neck. "There."

"Devil," she said. "Take the paper up to the camp. Dottie has bread for you to bring. And blankets." She handed me an old coat of hers. "Somebody'll want it."

"Load me up, sure. I'm the underdonkey."

"We're all underdonkeys now. I'll hire you out to that old mule skinner Jenkins if you don't bring me back a story."

"It's the same story up there," I said. "Nothing new. They still expect a settlement. Same as last week. And the week before."

"Eventually, something's gotta give," she said. "Don't miss it."

Dottie and I loaded the sled. Newspapers. Potatoes, blankets, three cast-off coats, bread. I strapped on webs, strapped my skis to the top of the load. The temperature was twenty-nine degrees, the sky blue, snow glittering in all its hostile glory. The cold braced me for the climb, hauling that sled up the track, an underdonkey in snowshoes. With every step, my ankle ligaments burned like the punishment I deserved. *Les chevilles enflent.*

Threads of smoke rose from the camp. Somebody there was singing. "Hello ma baby, hello ma honey, hello ma ragtime girl." That was Dan Kerrigan. "Hello, Sylvie Pelletier!" he said when he saw me. "Did you bring us bread and roses?"

"Bread," I said. "Slightly stale."

"Roses in your cheeks," he said. "Take the bread to Bruner's. The baby is sick."

In their tent, I found Frau Bruner ragged with worry. The shivering children were piled under blankets. The little year-old boy, Albert, had a barking cough and red chapped cheeks. His arms and legs startled up with each bark, his eyes wide with the effort of gasping. "Oh, Sylvie, thanks God." Frau Bruner took the bread and I took the baby. The poor child coughed, exhausted, on my shoulder. I sang to him softly, "Hallelujah, I'm a Bum." His mother put a pot on the stove and boiled snow. When it was steaming, we held him over it to breathe the mist and loosen his chest. All day we took turns, walking him, trying to get him to eat a little. But he refused the spoon pried between his new teeth. Toward afternoon, he finally slept.

"I'll stay the night," I told his mother. "I can ski him to the clinic in the morning."

"Please Gott," she said.

I bedded down by the stove and fell asleep to the sound of Gustav Bruner snoring, the fitful wheeze of Albert in his mother's arms. And that's how it was that I came to be in the camp at dawn that violent day, December 14, 1908.

We woke to the clang of a spoon on a skillet. Shouts. A dog barking.

"Alarm!" Herr Bruner pulled on his boots and ran out of the tent. Frantic, Mrs. Bruner lifted a section of flooring. Underneath was a cellar. A rocky hole like a grave.

"Fast, fast." She began to throw bedding down, cans and clothes, and descended the ladder, holding her arms out for little Clara and the coughing baby. I handed them down. "*Komm*, Sylvie." Her white face looked up at me from the pit like a swimmer's underwater. "Please hide!" she cried. "Der shooting."

I threw her boots in the hole and ran out.

All hell. Shouts and Pinkerton curses. "Out! Go! Get out!" Up the slope in surprise attack, a pack of thirty agents came raiding over the mountain, two of them sliding on toboggans like demon schoolboys. War whoops echoed off the rocks. Strikers ran out of the tents, yanking up their pants. Children panicking. *Mama, Papa.* Somebody shot off a gun. One of the tents was burning.

Fire! The people woke and scattered and fled. *Get out!* Everything wild. A Pinkerton agent had a broom in his hand and held it to the flaming tent. The broomstraw caught fire as another bandit took up a tin of kerosene and poured it. His friend lit the fuel with his torch of a broom. Something exploded. A camp stove or a charge of dynamite. Debris scattered down, metal bits, bedding, and a shoe. Pops, shots. Bullets. Impossible to tell who was shooting, where. I ran, dodging like a rabbit.

"Get the hell outta here! All of you!" the Pinks hollered, and brandished their shooters. "Time's up! Strike's over!" The cowards toppled tent poles. Canvas crumpled to the snow, mounded over women and their scraps. The Bruners' tent was collapsed but not yet burning. Beside their wilted heap, I found Clara, crying, her dolly buried in the cellar with baby Albert and her hysterical mother. I crawled under, pushing at canvas. "Frau Bruner!" She was down in the hole, struggling to climb the ladder with Albert in one arm. I gripped him by the scruff. We fought our way under fallen canvas into the snow, where Clara was wild for her lost dolly. "*Meine* Inge."

The raid at the flats was over in a snap. Like a pack of jackals, the hired marauders left behind a wreckage of tents and people, bleeding and stunned. Tony Mercanditti had a bullet in his shoulder. Mrs. Tchachenko walked the ruins with her hand over her mouth. Some other men were rope-tied in a line, Gustav Bruner and Dan Kerrigan among them, prodded down the trail by Pinks.

The strike was broken. And then everything was.

Chapter Thirty-Six

THE *RECORD* PUBLISHED EVERY SCRAP of news about the raid, the fire, the breaking of the strike. I delivered that copy to the seventy-one subscribers left in town, rolled and mailed it out to the list of faraway readers.

If you only read the *Booster*, you'd never know it happened. That paper would have you think you lived on the Big Rock Candy Mountain, with its lemonade springs, bluebirds of happiness, a place where raids and fires, strikes and unfairness, were merely inventions of malicious lying traitors to the Company. *Booster* Editor Goodell reported only that the Christmas pageant at the Moonstone schoolhouse would feature a manger with two live sheep. Caroling would take place in the square on Christmas Eve. Their headline story was about a prizefight coming up on December 26, Boxing Day, when black boxer Jack Johnson would be pitted against the white Canadian Tommy Burns in the first-ever heavyweight championship fight featuring a Negro.

The *Booster* wrote:

> It is expected there will be lynchings if the Negro wins.

I stood reading in the cold outside the bakery, hoping the Gradys had escaped that threat for good. *Jace would have a lot to say about it*, I thought, and a picture of his earnest face appeared in my mind like an apparition.

And there, heart-stopping at the bottom of the page, was his name.

JASPER C. PADGETT
1886–1908

> The *Booster* has the sad duty to report that Mr. Jasper Cleland Padgett has died at the family home in Richmond, Virginia, of influenza.

I read it again and then again. The paper trembled in my hands. Strangled sounds came from me and flew up like birds into the pines, scattering sharp dead needles.

> Mr. Padgett was 22 years old, a graduate of Harvard College and Phillips Academy in Andover, Massachusetts. He ably served his father's company, working here in the stone mill, the marble quarry, and in the business office.
>
> His grandfather Brigadier General Sterling Padgett (1833–1891) fought for the Confederacy and was decorated for the wounds he suffered at Manassas. Mr. Padgett is survived by his father, Jerome "Duke" Padgett, founder of the Padgett Fuel & Stone Company and of the town of Moonstone. Also surviving him is his stepmother, Mrs. Ingeborg LaFollette deChassy Padgett, of the Belgian royal court.
>
> Funeral services were held in Richmond, attended by a large crowd of two hundred mourners.
>
> The citizens of Moonstone extend our profound condolences to the family. To honor his son, Mr. Padgett requests donations be sent to the Arlington Confederate Memorial Fund, c/o Mrs. Randolph Sherry, 42 General Robert E. Lee Circle, Richmond, Virginia.

The wind tore the newspaper out of my hand and down the street, then lofted it into the bare winter branches. Jace was dead. No. It seemed impossible. He had died.

In Richmond of the flu.

"You've seen the news." K.T. read it on my face.

I held myself against the doorframe. She gathered the shards of me in her arms, and I crumpled, shuddering and heaving.

"He was the one?" she said softly. "I thought so."

I mashed a fist to my teeth.

"Ah, it's too much, too much," she said. "Poor girl." She pulled the shade down and turned the sign in the window to *Closed*. She sat with me by the stove and did not speak of God's Will or the Eternal Peace of Heaven or say Time Heals All Wounds. She did not say *I told you so*, or try to peel the skin off me with questions, but brought her chair around next to mine and pulled my head to her shoulder. She fed me tea and whiskey. "The best medicine for grief."

She welcomed me into her sisterhood of the brokenhearted, and still I did not tell her the precise nature of the break. The compound of the fracture. Neither the heat of the tea nor the burn of the whiskey nor the warmth of her kindness fixed the facts: I was a widow after sixty-two days of marriage.

I could not confess. Who would believe it? That we had ever married seemed untrue, even to me. *If I could go to Ruby and get a copy of the license—* what then? Would I claim title as the Widow Padgett and present myself to the Duke? He would call me a gold digger, accuse me of stealing from the Elkhorne safe, ask me to get him coffee. Worse—the hard pain of it—Jace had gone to Richmond! And had not told me. He did not write, not a letter or a call. That family. They had bad blood or bad luck or both. I had two hundred dollars.

I could leave. *We could be birds.*

But I didn't leave. Sorrow and regret froze me like the winter. I stayed in Moonstone, a secret widow, waiting as if spring would reveal a plan. It would sprout up, I hoped, a green shoot from the gray and rocky scree.

Snow covered the sad ruins of the camp at Dogtooth Flats. Blizzards closed the trolley track to Quarrytown for the season and blocked the train from Ruby. Moonstone was cut off from the outside world. And all the while, scabs in the mill hammered and sawed what stone they had stored. They were not scabs now but transformed into the new employees of the newly named and reincorporated Moonstone Marble Company, Colonel Bowles, President and Owner. The name was new, the owner was, but everything else about the Company was unchanged.

Orville Prem fell off a mill hoist and broke six ribs, both clavicles, and his jaw. Fourteen-year-old Tip Bascomb crashed on the bobsled course and stayed in a coma for a week. Robert Drain shot Tinker Dillishaw in a brawl. Molly Andropol, age six, was found half frozen on the quarry road. She'd tried to hike to school from Quarrytown in bad boots and would lose three toes.

Death and blood in the mountains, fever and flu, broken trees and fractured bones, all of it common as the moonrise. *Lord deliver me from evil and lead me not.* All my prayers were unfinished. I could not muster the will for religion, only for sleep and tea spiked with whiskey, medicine shared by my kind employer. Jace stayed dead and George stayed gone and I drank liquor now with K. T. Redmond, reading the telegraph wires for news, as if I might learn there had been some mistake.

The day after Boxing Day, December 27, headlines announced that the fighter Jack Johnson had become the first black heavyweight champion of the world.

On New Year's Eve, a glittering electric ball dropped from a tower in New York City's Times Square, heralding the start of 1909.

In January, the U.S. demanded an end to atrocious acts in the Belgian Congo.

In February, on what would have been Abraham Lincoln's hundredth birthday, Dr. W.E.B. Du Bois and journalist Ida B. Wells-Barnett founded the National Association for the Advancement of Colored People, to defend against the rise of atrocities against Negroes, the lynchings and massacres from Tulsa to Memphis.

I read about these events but remained preoccupied by my own predicaments, grief, betrayals, the hole in the leaking sole of my left boot, the raw chap of my skin, the snow coming under the door. I shoveled the sidewalk and delivered the paper to our dwindling list of subscribers. I typed in the cold wearing gloves with the tips cut off the fingers, and wrote letters to Maman.

Tout va bien. All is well.

Some lies we tell to make them true, like wishes. *All is well.* Then there are the lies laid carefully on top of lies, sediment hardening to stone, covering shame and secrets. It was one of these lies—another of Duke Padgett's *finesses*—that was blasted free as if by dynamite, on a day late in February 1909, ten weeks after Jace died "of influenza."

A package arrived, addressed to me.

Chapter Thirty-Seven

THE PARCEL WAS FORWARDED BY the faithful clerk at the Ruby Arms Hotel. Inside was a wristwatch, a penknife, a small notebook, and an envelope: "Please read at once." The letter inside was written in a familiar beautiful penmanship, from Mr. Marcus Grady.

> Dear Madam,
>
> Perhaps you already received the tragic news, but I am at pains to deliver it with these enclosed items. Our friend Mr. Jasper Padgett has gone to God. It happened the 3rd of December, a grievous accident. My mother suggested I write you, to explain.
>
> Jace arrived here some days after Thanksgiving with my brother, Caleb, and a crew of men. J.C. was in a weakened condition after the trip from Greeley. They hauled a load of marble here with a notion to erect a statue. While some of our homesteaders thought it a peculiar idea, Mayor Toussaint agreed to take the stone.
>
> On that morning, the team drove it out to the arranged place and put up a lifting jack, tall as a three-story house. It was a beautiful day, not too cold. Most all the town came out to hear

the speech. My mother kept everybody supplied with hot cider. Mr. Jace poured out rounds of whiskey. We did warn him, Take it easy, but he was feeling celebratory. He had talked of his plan to meet you by Christmas, and was happy about it. When everything was set, he stood on top of the stone to make remarks. The marble was a gift from a grateful nation, he said, and other noble sentiments.

He gave the signal and the horses turned the winch. My mother cautioned Jace to climb down. But he said, Nossir! I will ride the white swan! He looked as proud and happy in that moment as we ever had seen him.

The stone raised up off the wagon. Jace stood on top of it and had a hold of the lifting chain. Then, I hate to tell you, when the rock was up high, the whole load tipped so Mr. Padgett was thrown off just as the chain snapped and the stone came loose altogether. He was caught underneath when it fell. His legs were pinned in as terrible a scene as I have witnessed.

We worked fast as we could to pry that rock off him, but it was near impossible. My mother prayed and held on to his hand and he told her he did not feel any pain. He said, Tell Sylvie I'm sorry. He asked her to send all his things to you and no one else.

One of our citizens ran to fetch Dr. Ames, but by the time he arrived, J.C. was gone. The men worked into the night to get him free. We took him back and laid him out at the house. My father made the box for him and the Reverend came to pray with us.

Caleb notified the family by telegraph. Mr. Padgett wired to ask my brother and me to bring Jasper home to Belle Glade, but I regret to say it was not opportune for us to risk a trip to Virginia, the situation being what it is. Greeley Funeral Service made arrangements, and Mr. Jace was sent on to his rest. The Grady family offers our prayers to you in these days of sorrow.

Sincerely,

Marcus Grady, Dearfield, Colorado

I sat with that letter a long time, leaning against the wall of my closet. Jace Padgett was not dead of influenza in Richmond. He was killed in an accident. Dead in a utopian town. Drunk when he died. I pressed my eyes to shut out the scene. But the accident, the snapped chain, the fall and crush, played in my head like a gruesome film.

The parcel also contained a small pocket ledger, the word *Finances* embossed on the cover. After a while I opened it, expecting only numbers. The pages were lined in a grid, figures entered in columns, charges for hotels and meals, the purchase of equipment. Wages were recorded for men I didn't know. Slips of paper fell out: ticket stubs from various railroads, receipts for the purchase of tools and tents, wire rope and sacks of feed, a camp stove and kerosene. I flipped the pages but did not find it: the marriage license. But at the back of the book was a scrawl of tormented writing in Jasper's hand. Words crossed out, paper torn from the binding and tucked inside: a half-written letter.

Dear Sylvie, my heart,

When I left you in Ruby, I expected a speedy trip, but much to my dismay, Cal was refused treatment at the doors of Denver's hospital. At last we found Dr. Williemae Parker, a Negro surgeon (a woman!) who operated on Cal's eye. She is not hopeful of a good outcome and insisted the patient rest blindfolded in a dark room. We'll know results when the bandages are off, in about ten days.

I've rented rooms and stayed to help him. We are located above a saloon, in a poor quarter. For obvious reasons I think it best for you to remain comfortable in Ruby until Cal is recovered and we have delivered the stone. Despite his condition he puts on a brave face and can find his way blind around a stove, like a magician. He has taught me to cook a passable roast. At his request I read aloud to him and find he likes to argue the philosophies of Du Bois versus Washington as much as he likes to cook.

~~I'm plagued by the fear that Father will try to contact you~~
~~to discover my whereabouts. I hope for your trust, dear Sylvie,~~

~~and ask you to remain silent on thxxx unless your —xxxx We~~
~~will be~~

His words were crosshatched. The letter never sent. I paged through the ledger looking for clues and comfort, my own name anywhere, the words *wedding* or *wife* like proof, and found neither. The book appeared to have served as a diary, and I conversed with it as if it were Jace himself, alive. The entries followed his journey from the moment I last saw him at the Ruby Arms, twelve hours married.

October 3. Train from Ruby to Denver. Left my darling
asleep in her dreams.

Your darling? Is this how you treat a darling? In hurt and sorrow, I read on as Jace recorded the trip in harrowing detail. *In a devil of a blizzard,* they had gone through Gimlet Gorge, the railroad clinging to the sheer rock wall, a long drop on the other side. Crosses marked where men had died. Jace wrote:

Oct. 20. I fear the weight of the cargo will flip the train over
the side to smash in the gorge below. Out the window is the
blinding whiteness of the storm, the glass frosted in beautiful
lace patterns. I distract myself with thoughts of showing such
lovely things to S.

So he was thinking of me—unless there was another S. Sally? Sukie? *Salope?* Perhaps he did love me. I still prefer to believe so.

Their trip to Denver was a parade of delay and catastrophe. A slide blocked the track. A rescue team came by snowshoe to take some—the white women and children—off on sleds. Jace and Cal were stuck for days, drinking up the supply of liquor on the stranded train, and distracted themselves by singing hymns with a Negro preacher and his daughter. When the brothers reached Denver, Jace sent not a single word to me. Did the city not have a telegraph line? A post office? Or was my *husband* too drunk to buy a stamp or too cowardly to write me the truth: he was a thief. Was he? Meanwhile, Cal's arm healed. His eye did not. For consolation, young Caleb Grady courted the girl he met on the train.

> She sings like a nightingale and has convinced Cal to put down the bottle. He's not inclined now to go with me to Dearfield.

Next came a scrawled entry with crosshatched X's like secrets badly disguised.

> I'll start for Greeley with or without Cal. We argue a good deal. He says my plan is folly. I say it's a tale out of Robin Hood! Sylvie gave me the notion to do it. ~~XX~~ She must wonder ~~XXXXX~~ Think what Father will do when he finds I've chosen the maid, as he calls her. Like father, like son, I could say. The apple doesn't fall, etc. He'll never fathom my feelings about her. How my angel listens so quietly, so calm. She is most tolerant of me, and stands on principle. Do "one right thing," she said. It's because she inspired me to give the stone to the Gradys that I have taken the challenge.

The maid.
I was not calm.

> This monument enterprise has begun to appear, even to myself, like madness. Father insists I'm suffering a "mental delusion," my project born of some unhealthy fixation on the past. Is it? Why do I give a goddamn? Why me and not all the other Dixie boys with secrets in the woodpile? All of them related by blood to the servants back through the ages. Father won't speak of Caleb. Will not acknowledge. So I ask myself, why am I here offering . . . what? Stone. Marble.

Jace Padgett feared himself to be deranged, but it seemed to me it was the Duke and the other "Dixie boys" who were crazed. I read on, intent on finding evidence of my marriage, and turned the page to another half-written unsent letter.

Greeley, Colorado, November 2.

Dear Sylvie,

A thousand apologies for my delayed correspondence. We got to Greeley yesterday and will soon set out on the last leg to Dearfield. Cal is not keen on the mission, but he'll come round. He is going to marry! He met Ellen Graham on our trip through the mountain passes, and the wedding will be in the spring. He is quite in love as I am! I long to see you. Soon, my darling.

In my plans, I'd imagined you'd travel by my side, keep me on the straight road. Caleb tries, but we invariably end up in the saloon, arguing and fired mad about the state of things. As it is now, all over the South gangs are out killing Negroes for sport. You've surely read about them, the hoods over their faces, etc. These same people are building monuments to the Lost Cause. Cal and I are fairly sure Duke's friends from the country club are part of this crew. Is my father? The question torments me. Years ago, after Booker Washington dined with Roosevelt at the White House, my dad told me that a thousand Negroes would have to be strung up to learn their place again. I like to think of Duke's shocked face when he finds out about my plan to honor the colored people who built this nation, who toiled with no earthly reward.

Sylvie, you have every reason to be angry at my failure to get these letters to you. Perhaps reading this, you can forgive your Jace. I've taken a pledge and am changed to a better man by the hardship of this task I set for myself.

Tucked behind this page was a certificate printed on heavy stock.

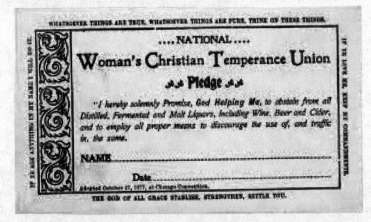

I, J. C. Padgett, have taken the Abstinence Pledge this 11th day of October, 1908.

The scroll around the border read: "Whatsoever Things Are True, Whatsoever Things Are Pure, Think on These Things." I did not know what was true or pure, or how to think about these words from the pen of a dead man who died drunk despite his pledge of abstinence.

It was alcohol that killed Jace, and his own folly.

He did not write any more in the diary about me, or to me, but did exhaust several pages reporting his disagreements with Caleb over the different philosophies of Booker T. Washington and W.E.B. Du Bois. Their other arguments were about the trip. Cal begged Jace to call it off, warning about blizzards and bad roads. But muleheaded Jace went ahead and hired three teamsters:

> All these men are eager converts to the idea of Dearfield and plan
> to buy land there. I promised to make their down payment if we
> arrive with the stone and ourselves in one piece.

On November 13, Jasper and his party set out in two wagons, one for the stone, one for supplies. After that, his entries were sparse, the ink runny, the pages buckled. They'd left too late, and winter hit hard. The men camped under the wagons, tarpaulins down the sides.

> Snow like death falling. Cold to the bone. The ice in the wind
> makes our faces bleed. The breath freezes in the horses' nostrils.
> Cal cursed me and my mission in most foul terms. I told him,
> I am doing this for you. But he said, No, it's for yourself. His
> accusation cuts me. We've fetched up tonight near Hardin with
> a farmer. His advice is, Turn around.

It was "slow progress." Conditions were "hideous." The stone held them back. The hired men voted to abandon the load. Jace argued. For two days, they rested in a deserted sod house on the bank of the South Platte River. And then Jace got sick. He took whiskey for his medicine, which—I surmise now—must've led to the breaking of his short-lived pledge to abstain.

> High fever. Chills. Cal gave me tea made from roots. Tastes like
> poison but it gave me strength. He said I would poison myself
> if I keep on like I do with my friend whiskey but it's all that
> warms me enough to write this down. That and thoughts of S.
> Returning to her.

It was a comfort to know that he intended to return, that our long, silent honeymoon was not abandonment—it was due only to his ill-advised mission, and drinking. In undated entries, he gave all credit to Caleb for saving his life, describing how his brother carried him over rough drifts, doctored him with teas and medicines.

On November 30, the frostbitten party arrived at Dearfield in bad condition, Jace still feverish. They pulled up in front of Easter's pride, the Sunshine Café.

> Easter was in a shock to see us, hysterical at the sight of the
> stone lorry. Is it Cal? She thought by the shape of the cargo
> that it was his coffin. When she saw her son drive up in the
> second wagon she fell to her knees. Marcus and John Grady
> came outside and embraced Cal like he was returned from the

dead. She thawed us by the stove. I insisted they come outside for the unveiling. When I pulled back the tarpaulin I expected joy on their faces, applause at the gift of valuable marble. But Easter didn't say a word. What you brought that for? she asked. You dragged that all this way? Are you crazy? What in God's eternal name were you thinking? Etc.

We went through hell to bring it, I told them. But John Grady only scratched his head. Yessir, you certainly did. Easter was more interested in showing us her luncheonette, pleased to hear my compliments about the peach cobbler and the impressive progress in the town.

The Gradys gave him a tour of Dearfield, where the settlers had built a clinic, a church, and a general store. The schoolhouse—Marcus Grady, schoolmaster—was finished, unlike the one at Moonstone. The hired teamsters picked out plots of land for themselves and planned to settle at Dearfield to raise families. The population stood at 356 already, refugees from violence in Virginia, Georgia, Alabama, Tennessee.

Ten pages in the journal were devoted to Jace's discussions with Mayor Toussaint Jackson, who expected the Fort Morgan–Cheyenne railroad to route through Dearfield soon. The settlers would have a good market for crops of sugar beets, melons, and so on. The Mayor asked Jace for investment: equipment and supplies, irrigation from the river. Jace explained that the donated stone was worth thousands of dollars, a draw for tourists on the new rail line. He proposed to put the monument right in the town center.

It was Easter who rejected that plan, Jace wrote, his last entry in the diary.

Dec. 2: It's just going to remind me, Easter said. And that was the worst of it. How I'd failed to think—what it would remind her of. It's decided instead to place the marble on a rise looking over the river, far from the town center. Worst despair yet. What was I thinking? Dearfield is bustling; folks greet me pleasantly, but with a wariness like I'm a ghost or a threat. Perhaps eventually they'll see the vision. Either that or the stone will be hollowed out for a horse trough. Tomorrow I'll be shed of it forever and go back the way I came. Should reach Denver in good time, to pick up the ring and meet S. before Christmas. I'll send that letter finally. The guilt weighs on me but ~~If only~~ Telegram better. I'll make it up to her. She must think me a first-class heel. She must

The writing stopped here. Jace was dead the next day.

A widow cries. A brokenhearted woman weeps and wails. I didn't. I sat alone in a closet. A packet of paper was what I had left of Jace. In the dim silence, I considered what I knew about him, laid bits of information out like an alphabet of type to sort. They would not form sentences of any coherence. Some grief is too deep, my mother said. Was mine buried too far down in the bones for tears? Gravel in the veins, eyes parched. Thinking of Jace's life expired on the prairie, the motherless boy he was, carrying the sins of the father, I could not cry. He tried to do *one right thing*, some act of charity that he alone had decided was right, and for what? For whom? For himself, to make himself right in his own eyes.

Think what Father will do when he finds I've chosen the maid. The phrase rankled. He'd married me to spite his father. And spite was half his motive too, for taking that stone, carting it across the plains.

I knew Spite. It was one reason I'd broken my own promise, betrayed vows, kissed George Lonahan. *Do not think of George.* By my own lights, I did not deserve sympathy. In the days that followed, a sad relief came over me that Jace was gone. Relief not to be plucking petals from the daisy of *He loves me, he loves me not.* A fraction of my solitary mourning was lightness, like a flake of snow blown upward in a tendril of air, freed from the falling blizzard. I had loved Jace. He had died. He would not get to live more life; I would not have him in mine, for better or worse, in sickness or health or this drowning disbelief. I was numbed and tender with sadness and memory.

And yet. There was business unfinished.

Chapter Thirty-Eight

JASPER'S DEATH AND HIS DRUNKEN confessions haunted me. Was I responsible in some way for his ill-advised mission? *Why don't you give it to Dearfield?* I'd said, never thinking that he might try it, hauling stone across the plains. A tale out of *Robin Hood*, he'd called it. After a few days, seeking distraction, I took *Le Prince des Voleurs* from my shelf, thinking of *mon père*, who'd read the story of Robin Hood to us on winter nights. Turning its pages again, I was struck by the words of the Prince of Thieves.

I am what men call a robber, a thief so be it! But I extort money from the rich, and take naught from the poor. I detest violence, and I shed no blood; I love my country.

Was this how Jace thought of what he'd done? And was it wrong?

I formed a vague idea to go to Elkhorne. I could not admit to myself what I was after.

That Sunday, it was snowing hard. I strapped on *raquettes* and set out from town. I did not go up the drive but risked the high trail, then trekked down the slope of Rosy Dawn Mountain, through the trees behind the manor. The big house was shuttered, empty for the winter.

Kate Manning

The wind was fierce, driving walls of white. I left tracks, but they filled quickly, erased. The snow was piled so high by the back of the house that I was able to swing one leg over the top of the wall and jump down inside the laundry yard. The drying lines were at the level of my knees because of the deep snow. The door was blocked by drifts. Only the summer staff used this entrance. I tried the handle and found it open. Just more Padgett carelessness, leaving it unlocked. Or perhaps someone was here? Duke alone and mad with grief, repenting in some room upstairs. Not likely. He'd fled across the sea, where he could shed his past, though not the rot in his soul.

Inside, the house was cold. I leaned my webs against the wall. I opened a cupboard and saw evidence of mice. On the table was the sugar bowl. I dumped the pure white cubes into my pocket and put one in my mouth, thinking of Easter. There was her apron. Her rolling pin. I went in my coat and mittens, nervous breath frosting along the back passage and down the stairs, past the dark billiard room, the wine cellar. I could've helped myself to a bottle of French champagne, but I was after something else.

The office was musty. The desks tidy. In the Duke's inner sanctum, a dim snowy light came through the window, everything outside obscured by the blizzard. My breath hung in the cold air. The crest of two lions still fought on the steel vault door. The clang of the tumblers was too loud.

Two turns to the right. Twice to the left. Right to land on open sesame.

Who would suspect that I had the combination tattooed in memory? *Eighteen-twenty-ten.* The tumblers clicked on the second try. A sucking sound of wind when I pulled the door open, heart hammering. Even in the dimness, the prize was plain. Fat bundles of money on the shelves.

I took ten of them. Like the woodcutter Ali Baba in the cave of thieves, I would help myself. My pockets were empty, and I filled them.

Most of it I left behind. *He doesn't even count it,* Jace said. *This is only the little piggy bank. They won't notice.*

I closed the safe behind me and twirled the tumblers locked. Upstairs, I went out the back way and strapped on my webs, walked in the snow to the

Moonstone City Record. For the rest of that Sunday afternoon, I feigned a fever, sleeping. When K.T. had gone to bed, I put on a lamp and counted money.

It was not a few lumps of coal. Not two silver forks. It was five thousand dollars.

It's not a crime. It's a right. My father's words were mine now.

I had believed that, married to Jace, I could be a kind of princess, and now I was. Of thieves. *La Princesse des Voleurs.* A story out of Robin Hood, for real. What I stole was not for me. Not for spending on trinkets. It was for recompense and revenge. I hid it behind a board in the supply closet at the *Record.* For myself, I kept only what was left of the three Knoxes Jace gave me at the Ruby Arms, and what remained of the money he thrust at me that night in the vault. My personal nest egg totaled $307, given to me or earned at my job. Not stolen. I was alone now, in charge of myself.

A week later, early March, the train track opened as far as Glenwood. I seized the opportunity and bought a round-trip ticket. At Glenwood Savings Bank, I deposited the stolen dollars in an account under the name of Angela Sylvestri. (*Angel. Sylvester.* His names for me.) Seeing the bundles of money produced from my rucksack, the bank officer raised his eyebrows.

"It's an inheritance," I said, eyes welling. "My husband died." The sadness was not an act. This was the only time in my life that anyone ever heard me say those words, *my husband died,* about Jace.

The banker had just one question: "Angela Sylvestri. What kinda name is that? You Italian?"

"Yes," I said.

I had a cashier's check made out for one thousand dollars, to the Ladies' Auxiliary Strike Fund of the UMW. I sent it to the union hall in Denver: "Please use this as strike pay to any striking miners in the district of Colorado. Signed, A friend." No return address.

This check was the first of the "taxes," as I thought of them, exacting the ones Padgett did not pay for the common good. My plan was to dole the money out, wherever someone needed it, a one-woman Sociology Department. *Sylvestering*, I named it. Mailing that check made me giddy.

To have made people happy is a day well spent, said Robin Hood. *'Tis only just!*

I rode the train back to Moonstone with that brand of justice and my secret new identity: Angela Silvestri, Princess of Thieves.

But happiness is short-lived for a thief as it is for a grief-stricken girl. I tried to be stoic, forced smiles so as not to seed misery with complaint, yet remained preoccupied by the fear I would be caught. Still, I couldn't bring myself to run, to leave K.T. and the *Record*, our familiar routines. I blamed myself for my troubles. It did not occur to me to connect them to an ancient omen, to consider that the curse of the banished Ute tribes had fallen on the town of Moonstone. Chief Colorow's prophecy: that whatever white people did in the Gilded Mountains would bring them failure and death. That curse was only a folk legend spread by children like Eva Setkowski, I'd thought, and had forgotten it.

So, despite old-timers' warnings and stories of slides past, I did not worry too much about avalanche season. There was no reason now for me to go up to the quarry or hike to Dogtooth camp. No cause to risk the train ride through Gimlet Gorge. I would stay in the flats of town till spring, then pack up and go somewhere else. Away. San Francisco or Chicago. Anywhere but a Rutland convent. I brooded, marking time till the track was safe and the train would carry me down the slope. Waving *adieu. À jamais.*

On the morning of March 13, I was outside the *Record* office, shoveling a foot of new snow off the sidewalk boards. Dottie Weeks, digging herself out, waved to me. The day was brilliant, fifty degrees of sun melting piles off the roof, icicles dripping daggers. The snow was as heavy and wet as my leaden bad mood.

I flung snow on top of drifts taller than my head. An icicle fell off the gutter with a crystalline shatter, like a sign from God.

"Feels like spring!" Dottie called. "Beautiful!"

"Ha! Spring!" I said. "Is that thunder?"

We stopped shoveling at the sound of doom out of the blue sky.

A roaring. We turned and looked up to see the side of Millhouse Mountain collapse, a wave cascading, exploding white into the blue sky, trees broken, boulders big as houses bouncing like baseballs. *Slide*, we said in the same breath.

The roar of it rolled over the town, thundering. Then stopped. A siren started, fast-long-fast-fast, a code that spiked the blood. Everybody—the whole town—rushed out, some half dressed, half asleep, everybody in a panic, me, Dottie, K.T. We ran with spades and shovels toward the mill.

It was gone. Crushed. Where the sheds had been, a cloud of snow rose up like smoke over the ruins, small rainbows in it, rising in the sun, sparkling ice drops toward the blue. We stood with our mouths open.

"Well," K.T. said, stunned, "destiny has kept her appointment."

"Not very nice of you," I said.

"Niceness is not one of the virtues," she said. "Kindness is."

"What's the difference?" Dottie asked, in tears.

"Niceness is easy," K.T. said. "It's a smile and a hello. Kindness, now, that takes work." She turned away from the wreckage, sadness on her face. "What a tragedy. I can't bear to look. Write it up, Pelletier."

"Me?"

"You. The big story: the Avalanche of '09."

"But I'm not—"

"I've got a fever," she said with a harsh cough. "Have the copy ready by five o'clock. And no niceness, hear?" She waved me toward the wreckage and went back to bed. Dottie followed. She promised to come back with hot tea for the rescue parties. The women left me there with my notebook.

Men scrambled over the ruins of the two flattened mill sheds. They dug, frantic, and called out, "Halloo! Anybody?" Silence. They peered under fallen timbers and roofing but did not hear a cry or see a sign of anyone trapped.

Not an arm or a leg. It was pure luck that the morning shift had not started yet. The night watchman had left. Mabel Roper had been on switchboard duty in the telephone shed on top of the millworks. The force of the slide knocked her clear through the door onto the roof, tore the clothes off her back. The townspeople watched as she was carried to the clinic, unconscious, wrapped in a blanket. Word went around. *She'll be all right. A miracle nobody else was hurt. Thank the Lord.*

I toured the wreckage, climbing in snow over broken beams, buckled tin, a shattered marble cherub. The slab saws were buried, the machinery hopeless. At the cabins on Padgett Street, I talked to a woman digging out her parlor. Another woman showed me her bed frame, bent in half under wreckage. "Lucky we weren't in it," she said. In the clinic, I visited Mabel, the injured girl. She could not stop shaking. Bruises covered her face; her arms were purpled and scratched.

All afternoon I wrote the story of the avalanche, a winter's worth of grief and vengeance turned into a slide of news.

"Well, Pelletier speaks!" K.T. said, reading it. "I especially love this line about Destiny."

"Because it's yours," I said.

"Pretty good, if I do say so. Your 'Crash of Doom' is also excellent."

"Thank you."

"If I were you, I'd add more information for Company investors about how this disaster affects the marble business."

Ever her eager student, I wrote the lines that sealed our fate, dangerous words about financial loss. I set the type in a banner across the top of the page, loaded the press. If writing itself is silent, a mouse scratch in the walls, printing is loud as trumpets. Brass hard words rolled off the plate, my foot on the treadle. I could see the sound of it: my voice cranked out now in bold type, not upside down or backward but right side up and published. To print the words would cause me a kind of public nakedness, tear the clothes off my back. But for the record—and in the *Record*—I did not care.

DESTINY KEPT HER APPOINTMENT

MILL CRUSHED LIKE AN EGGSHELL BY AVALANCHE

With the awful noise peculiar to such destruction, like the crash of doom came a snowslide that wrecked the company stone mill Wednesday morning.

Warnings Unheeded

For days snow has built and hung threateningly over the mill on a cornice to the south. Old-timers warned and shook their heads over what they were certain was as inevitable as taxes. When the whistles of distress from the siren pierced the air, there was no questioning from these experts: The long expected had happened.

The slide crossed the river, just as previous slides have done in the same place. It swept away the machine shop, the electrical storehouse, and shop number one.

That there was no loss of life was because of "supernatural design," some said. "Pure luck" that the night workmen had left the shop but a short time previous. Miss Roper, the night telephone girl, was blown out upon the main roof without fatal injury. She was unconscious when rescued and suffered many cuts and bruises. She is recovering at the clinic, grateful to be spared.

The Company will no doubt report the disaster as "causing but little damage." But to one viewing the scene, the wreck is complete. Misjudgment, ruin, desolation speak in heaps of twisted timbers and misshapen machinery, shattered statuary in the monument shop and the wrecked office building, one end of which was torn away entirely.

STOCK SELLING

Company Organized by Strenuous Promoters
Its Investment Scheme
Only Worthless Paper Given
For Ruined Human Lives

Never Will Pay Dividends

Stock selling, which has been a great source of revenue to this gigantic swindle, has not recently gone as well as Kunnel Bowles had hoped, and so the Company cannot yet state what will be done about rebuilding the destroyed mill.

It was these last paragraphs that later caused the trouble, just a fraction of what I had to say about Desolation and Human Life in the Gilded Range.

All night I printed and addressed the copies for mailing. The others I hauled on my sled through the stunned village. I tossed papers on porches and tucked them in milk boxes, coal bins, behind storm doors. We beat the *Booster* to the story by twelve hours.

The next day Tommy Phelps, *Booster* delivery boy, went skiing past me, his own sled piled high with rival papers. He stuck out his tongue. "Your paper is—" He leaned over to perform a fake theatrical vomit.

"Poor Tommy," I said. "Delivering lies has made you sick."

True to its name, the *Booster* reported the disaster through boost-colored glasses.

THE MOONSTONE BOOSTER *EXTRA*

It takes more than a snowslide to put the Company marble operation out of business or even to give our boys a serious setback. What yesterday morning appeared to be a complete disaster is today a temporary inconvenience. Indomitable spirit and loyalty have brought quick results, and the damage proved not nearly so great as was first supposed. Work has resumed in all departments. The outlook is very cheerful. The townspeople and employees have rallied to the Company's support in splendid fashion.

Only one thing occurred to mar the general cheerfulness, and that was the appearance of a so-called newspaper on our streets, containing an article which in every line expressed satisfaction that the disaster had occurred. This pseudo-newspaper has upon many occasions attacked the Company, but it was thought that the present situation would call for a square deal from even the bitterest enemy. To print a spiteful article when misfortune comes is just about the last straw. The *Booster* would not be surprised to hear of a summary action being taken against that publication, such is the general feeling of indignation.

"Summary action!" K.T. cried. "If they come at us—" But she stopped with a strange look of panic and did not finish her sentence.

We locked the doors now, even in daylight. On Friday, two days after the slide, a handbill appeared, plastered to the window of the Mercantile. Others like it were tacked up all over town.

MARCH 15

TONIGHT 8 O'CLOCK.

MEETING AT MASONIC HALL.

EVERY MAN & WOMAN IN MOONSTONE

STRONGLY URGED TO BE PRESENT

"Beware the Ides of March" was all K.T. would say about it when I told her.

About seven-thirty that evening, Dottie Weeks burst into the *Record* with great excitement. "Let's go. We want to get a seat."

"Not me," K.T. said, coughing. "Not with that flock of muttons. You two go ahead." She shut the door behind us but opened it again to call: "Pelletier! Take notes."

All along Marble Street, citizens of Moonstone hurried toward the hall. Moonlight smudged the clouds scudding along the ridge, mottled like sour milk. We arrived at the same time as Mr. and Mrs. Phelps, rude parents of rude Tommy the paperboy. Florrie Phelps cut in front of us. Mr. Phelps held the door for his wife, then went through, leaving it to slam in Dottie's face.

"The nerve," Dottie said.

"Muttons," I whispered, and made sheep noises, bleating.

Dottie laughed and clapped her hand over her mouth with scandalized eyes. "Shh, Sylvie." We laughed again, not yet afraid.

Hal Brinckerhoff came to sit with us in the back. The place was packed, more than a hundred people inside, many standing. The room smelled of damp wool and camphor and something foul. Vengeance.

At the front was Colonel Bowles. When the room was quiet, he began.

"I wish first to impress upon you that my position is simply that of an individual. I'm not representing the Company, but merely myself. I have only the interest that every person here should have: that of men and women whose bread and butter rely upon town industries, barber or baker or banker. Your livelihood depends on Moonstone Marble. Let's start by saying this is not a Company meeting."

"Ha!" Dottie Weeks elbowed my ribs.

Next to speak was Bull Baxter, the Colonel's new assistant. "We have met to discuss a common enemy," he said. "A certain newspaper. Nothing has hurt the town so much as these reports from the so-called *Record* that our Company is a stock-selling swindle. A preposterous claim."

The crowd sent glances down the rows as if passing a church collection, gathering nods of approval. Baxter continued.

"The *Record*'s disgraceful article yesterday suggested that Destiny—a divine and deserved retribution—had visited tragedy upon our little town. That's the last straw."

I copied the speeches, dread constricting my chest. In the front row, Frank Goodell, editor of the *Booster*, was writing too.

"Unforgivable!" Baxter cried, his cowlick trembling. "That the paper openly exulted in the disaster! Reading it, one can only assume the editor is sorry no one was killed!"

"Miss Redmond never said that!" I blurted quite loudly. "She is not glad."

Florrie Phelps turned to stare. Tarbusch whispered to Bowles, eyes boring my skull. Surely, I'd be revealed as the writer of the fateful news report. Someone would point the finger and expose me.

"The time has come when the town must be rid of this frightful editress." Mr. Koble held up a piece of paper. "The orders here say that Miss Katrina T. Redmond must get out of town."

The crowd erupted in applause, raucous cheers.

"The floor is open for debate," Koble said. "Then we vote."

Hal Brinckerhoff crossed his arms over his chest. Carlton Pfister glowered at me, his new Pinkerton badge glinting off his coat. I took notes with a shaking hand.

The banker rose to his feet. "Every man here tonight hates to tackle this problem because the editor is a woman!"

"When a woman takes a man's place," somebody shouted, "she must expect to receive what justice a man would receive!"

The crowd was foaming now. They would hang us from a gallows.

Reverend Winthorp: "The Lord instructs us to protect the weaker sex. But—"

Mr. Koble: "In regard to that heinous article, there's no disagreement. This City Hatchet is chopping the blood out of our town."

It was blood they wanted. You could feel the heat of anger rising in the room, winter frustrations pent up and boiling.

Little Mrs. Overby was lifted upon a chair to speak: "Too many people read her articles and do not take pains to find out whether they are true."

Dottie elbowed me to my feet. "Say something."

"The newspaper simply reports the facts," I said with a burning face.

"Miss Pelletier," said the Colonel, twitching, "it's common knowledge that you've been wrongly influenced by outside agitators. For your own health, it would be best for you to stand down." Dottie pulled me, shaking, to my seat.

Mr. Mill Manager Phelps: "The editor is the paid agent of those who try for their own gain to hurt the Company. I'm too much of a gentleman to say what I think of her."

With a smile, as if administering cakes to the poor, Florrie Phelps passed around copies of the resolutions while Bull Baxter read them aloud:

> WHEREAS, the editor of the *Record* newspaper, Miss K. T. Redmond, has endeavored to injure the chief industry of the town by publishing scurrilous and untruthful statements, and
>
> WHEREAS the wrecking of the mill by the recent snowslide was a disaster, and that

the article in the *Record* was untrue, written
with a fiendish satisfaction over the loss to
the Company, and seeming to regret there
was no loss of life, and

WHEREAS such an attitude is in direct
opposition to all community interests, and
the continued publication of this slanderous
sheet a menace to the people as a whole, be it

RESOLVED: That we hereby request
Miss Katrina T. Redmond to take her departure from the town at once, *never to return.*

At those words came a fearsome swell of applause and stomping on floorboards. The windows rattled. The assembly cast cold muttering looks in my
direction.

"Dottie." I nodded for the exits, and we fled.

"Trina!" Dottie burst into the office. "They're going to throw you out of
town."

K.T. sneezed. "They wouldn't dare touch me. I'm contagious. I'll infect
them all with plague." She looked quite pale.

"I tried to speak up," I told K.T. "But they weren't in a mood to listen."

Dottie went home. We pushed the tables against the door and barricaded
ourselves in for the night.

Chapter Thirty-Nine

ABOUT ONE O'CLOCK THE FOLLOWING day, a delegation of Moonstone citizens gathered at Mr. Koble's store across the street. I peered out the window, watching them work up a froth. "Sheep are ruminant mammals," K.T. said. "Look at 'em chewing the same cud they started last night." She went out with her shovel and began to chip ice off the sidewalk in full view of the flock. They crossed the road and stood directly outside the *Record*. Bull Baxter and Carlton Pfister approached manfully.

"Katrina T. Redmond!" said Baxter. "We have a resolution to present you."

"I don't care if you have kittens," K.T. told him. "Stay off my property." She flung a load of snow to the street. Later, at the trial, Pfister would claim she'd threatened him with the shovel.

"Come and hear the verdict, old girl," Baxter said. "You've got to go."

"I've got to go write a headline about your kangaroo court," K.T. told him. "Your sham verdict. It's got no basis in law." She came inside, and we watched the crowd's maneuvers from the window. Hal Brinckerhoff stood at the far edge of the group.

"Brinckerhoff!" Baxter called out. "You're a friend of Trina Redmond's. If you represent her, we'll read the resolutions to you."

"I don't represent her," Hal said. "She's her own agent."

"Then bring her out."

"Bring her out yourself," Hal said. "I don't believe in mob law. We have courts in the land to settle these things now. Not vigilantes."

"Savior Hal," K.T. whispered behind the glass.

"You have a crush on him," I said.

"I might." She smirked. "But we don't kiss and tell around here, do we?"

Baxter came to the window and rapped on the glass. "Katrina Redmond! I know you can hear me. I present you the resolutions." He read them aloud, ending with righteous thunder: *Never to return.* "Come take this paper."

"You can put that where the sun don't shine," K.T. told him.

"We'll drag you out if we have to," Baxter said.

Carlton Pfister pounded the door. "Open in the name of the law."

"You are not the law," K.T. cursed him, but when the lunkhead Pfister threatened to break the glass, she undid the latch.

Carlton barged in, waving his shooter and an official paper. "We have an order here, signed by the Mayor, to take you in custody. You'll come with me."

"To jail?" she said. "That can't be what this says."

"It does. Read it."

"You may not simply take the law into your own hands," K.T. scoffed.

"I'll take you, then," Pfister said. "And your assistant with you."

"Leave her out of it," K.T. said.

"You don't come now, we can't guarantee your safety." He pointed his chin at the window, where the good people of Moonstone pressed their wet noses. They began to chant, "Throw! Her! Out!" Bits of gravel and ice pelted the storefront.

"Get your things, Sylvie," K.T. said, her face pale. She gathered papers frantically. "We'll go to Dottie's."

"Leave everything," Pfister said. "You're only allowed a change of clothes."

When he was distracted, I put my notebook in my skirt pocket. K.T. hurried upstairs. In my closet, I packed some clothes and Jace's *Finances* diary. I took a hundred dollars from the pages of Du Bois's *Souls*. But when I reached for the rest of my nest egg, hidden in Dickens and Conrad, Pfister pulled me roughly by the elbow.

"You're hurting me. Let go!"

"What if I don't?" Carlton smirked and leered.

Mr. Baxter snooped among the papers. K.T. rattled down the stairs with her bag. "The ledger," she said. Just in time, I snatched up the register of subscribers' addresses, all the East Coast financiers she kept informed about stock-selling scams.

"Leave that, now," Baxter said sharply. "It's likely to be evidence against you."

Pfister wrested the ledger from me even as I fought him. When Baxter took charge of it, I saw him smirk, and then understood what the Company wanted above all: to keep the investors from finding out about their business losses and cruel practices. They didn't care a fig for anything but profit. Pfister and Baxter marched us down the street. The good people of Moonstone town stared from their doorways at our sad parade. A mob of dogs and children followed, barking and jeering.

Out by the quarry road, the jail was a small cabin of notched ill-fitting logs, well ventilated through the gaps. One of the two cells was occupied by the bootlegger Mrs. Hurley, serving a six-month sentence for selling hooch in our dry town.

"Hello, Rita," said K.T. "Are the beds comfortable?"

"Unfit for ladies," Mrs. Hurley said from behind the checkerboard of bars.

"Get in there," said Pfister. "Both of you." He shoved us at the empty cell.

"You aren't going to lock us in there!" K.T.'s voice rose in panic.

Pfister puckered his lips at me. "A kiss will buy Frenchy here a mattress."

"How dare you!" K.T. said.

"Like so." He grabbed my face and mashed his lips on my mouth. I tried to bite him, pushed at him, gagging. He shoved us in, shut the door, and locked it. With my sleeve, I wiped off his tobacco slobber. K.T. wheezed for air, coughing. We were caged. Two metal bunks hung chained from the wall. The bedding was a rat's nest of newspaper and rags that stank of urine and grease.

"It's against the law!" I said at the bars.

"I'm the law now." Pfister hooked his thumb under the star on his lapel, smirking.

"I'm sorry, Sylvie." K.T. seemed old suddenly, watery bags like blisters beneath her eyes. Her breath was labored. "I'm so sorry."

"It's my fault. I wrote that story."

"Every word was true. That article was just their excuse. They've wanted me gone for a long time." She sagged on the floor, coughing. Would I lose her too? I feared it. My only friend.

"They will take everything I worked for all my life," she said.

"They won't get it," I said. "It's not legal."

"It's legal if we say it is." Carlton Pfister stretched his legs by the stove and fired a stream of tobacco juice hissing into the fire.

"Go to hell," I said.

"Pretty mouth on you," said the leering goat.

"Bootlickersonuvabitch stooge," I said.

"Attagirl." K.T. laughed. "You tell him."

"*Chien humain,*" I said. "*Maudit putain hosti chrisse de calice tête de marde.*"

My French curses nearly killed K.T. The more I swore, the more she laughed, racked by coughing. "How far we've come, oh, Saint Sylvie of the Mount," she crowed. "Miseducated by circumstance."

"By a wicked employer, you mean. A knocker."

K.T. roared again. "Pelletier, you're a true printer's devil now."

It was high praise from her, fuel to me. Within the hour, we'd cheered ourselves by inventing lines of doggerel for our guard: "There was a young TOADY named Pfister, who made a girl sick when he kissed her . . ." But before we said the next bit, our keeper hurled a can of beans that hit the bars with a clang. Mrs. Hurley shrieked. We retreated to sit on the floor by the back wall. K.T. coughed on my shoulder. Her brow was hot.

"You need a doctor," I said.

"I need a lawyer, is what I need."

"A cup of tea," said Mrs. Hurley next door. "Just wait while I boil it." Through the boards came the sound of a struck match, our neighbor prattling. "They give me a wee camp stove here in my coop, despite I never sold a sip of hooch to nobody! Yet they lock me up and fine me! Three thousand dollars! On no evidence." Our fellow prisoner maneuvered a steaming cup around the bars. K.T. took a sip and spluttered. "Jesus!" The tea was spiked with moonshine.

"Shush, now." Mrs. Hurley passed me my own cup. "Drink your medicine."

Evening fell outside our cage. Guard dog Pfister lit a lamp and took himself off for dinner, leaving us a tray of hard cheese and harder bread. I tried to sleep, but worries kept me awake: What would happen? What about my money? K.T. tossed with fever. In the darkness came a sudden noise like rats scrabbling in the walls. Outside, somebody whispered, "Rita, Rita."

"Joe, darlin'!" Mrs. Hurley said. "Ladies, good news! My own Joe just slipped a bottle to that dunderhead Carlie Pfister. He'll stay away now. And he's brought us a fresh jug. I have my straw, and you'll have yours. Just feel along the south wall."

"Oh, Lord," K.T. said. "A siphon. Genius."

A rubber tube poked through the unchinked logs. K.T. doubled over laughing and had a draft of it. "Tastes like gasoline," she said after swallowing. I myself took more than a swallow. The force of that hooch knocked us out, all three prisoners.

Our guard Pfister was at his own party, a Wrecking Ball. While we slept, he and his Pinkerton friends broke into the *Record* office, smashing and looting. They carted off the printing press to be junked. They seized cases of type and threw them in a box. We learned later from Dottie Weeks how they dumped it all out in a snowbank behind the building. The leads and the slugs, the ornaments and gauge-pin tongues that had composed all the sentences ever printed in the *Moonstone City Record*, sank down buried in white drifts. Perhaps they're still there.

Night in that cell was dark as the inside of a dog. At about four in the morning, we were awakened by spears of lantern light in our eyes. Deputy Pfister had arrived with his fellow partygoers, Sheriff Smiley and Bull Baxter.

"Get up." Pfister unlocked our cage and pulled us out of the squalid bunks.

Mrs. Hurley croaked in hysterics, "Don't take 'em to the gallows! Free the ladies!"

"Oh, they're free," said Baxter. "Free to take the morning train."

We were marched along Marble Road. Beams of lantern light cast our distorted shadows on the snowbanks like phantoms walking alongside.

"Where are you taking us?" K.T. demanded to know. "On what authority? What law did we break? Do you have a warrant? A writ of habeas corpus?"

"You want Latin?" Smiley said. "We'll give you a postmortem."

"You've broken the law, Mr. Smiley," K.T. said.

"Military necessity recognizes no laws," Smiley declared.

Smiley and I each have excuses for our different crimes, I thought, knowing my own Robin Hood motive was superior. What *military necessity* required the jailing of a feverish woman and an office assistant? I was on the side of the underdonkey, whereas Smiley was a bootlicker out for himself.

"Miss Redmond needs a doctor," I said.

"What is this, a gabble of geese?" he said, cupping his ear. "Do you hear honking and squawking, Marshal Pfister?"

"I do, Sheriff," he said. "Like a hen party."

They laughed heartily and pushed us at gunpoint onto the 5:35 a.m. train. "The conductor has orders," Smiley said, "not to let you ladies off till Denver."

"Where we'll meet my lawyer," K.T. told him. "His name is Crump. Do you know he famously has six fingers? The extra one is the long finger of the law. Six-finger Crump will point that one right at you, Mr. Smiley, and the rest of your hired mongrels." With that, we departed the storybook town in the clouds and did not look back.

The train was stuck three days, caught in slides at Grubstake Pass, stopped in the cold. Despite the word *grub*, we had nothing to eat but dry crackers. K.T. slumped with her burning head against me. We slept in our seats.

At Denver, a hackney cab brought us to the home of K.T.'s sister, Daisy Thomas, a motherly widow who put K.T. on the parlor sofa to convalesce. I was given a pallet on the floor of a room with her daughter, Jenny, a freckled girl of ten with sparse eyelashes and rust-colored hair. I climbed under the blankets and did not wake for fourteen hours. When the sun rose, I looked out across Denver city. In the far distance was the sharp ridge of the mountains, where I did not intend ever to return.

PART SIX

The Princess
of Thieves

I shall plunge boldly into Colorado.
Is common humanity lacking in this region of hard greed?
Can it not be bought by dollars here, like every other commodity,
votes included?

—Isabella Bird,
A Lady's Life in the Rocky Mountains, 1873

Chapter Forty

THE SPRING SMELLED OF MELTED snow, green shoots. The birds sang *printemps, prin-temps*. K.T. grew well and downright cheerful, thanks to the doting of her sister and the entertainments of her niece. I washed and cooked and tutored Jenny on her Latin verbs: *Dico, Dicere, Dixi, Dictus*. I wrote a letter to Maman: "The newspaper in Moonstone has closed its doors." I explained nothing, only informed them of my new arrangements: "Miss Redmond's nephew, Robert, is at university, and I've been given his room. In exchange, I tutor the little girl and help as housekeeper." I sent her twenty dollars and tried not to think about the pilfered Padgett money in the bank. It was not mine to spend. In my own pockets, only a hundred dollars was left. Another two hundred was abandoned back in Moonstone, stuck in the pages of novels—or stolen by Pinks.

It was not safe for us to return. K.T.'s possessions and mine could not be retrieved until a judge ruled on her petition to reclaim them. Dottie Weeks wrote to say the *Record* had a padlock on the door. "Your kitty cat Bill came mewing around the bakery," said her letter, "and now catches mice in our kitchen."

"Watch out," K.T. wrote back. "Colonel Bowles will accuse you of harboring a Bolshevik cat."

———

Bolshevism was as far from my mind as Moonstone itself, lost in the clouds as I was in the comfort and carpeting of the Thomas house. I'd planned to be Princess of Thieves, hiding in the forest of anonymity, but spring passed and I took no action; only brooded, reading by the parlor window.

"Why don't you go to college?" K.T. suggested one morning in May. I feared what she really wanted to say was: *Why don't you move out?*

I had never thought of college. College was for men, or women like K.T., who was educated at Oberlin and knew the history of Europe, the periodic table of elements, and Greek philosophy. She had read Spinoza and Descartes. How would a person like me afford the fees? The pilfered money of "Angela Silvestri" was tempting. I supposed I could go to the Padgetts and claim inheritance rights by revealing myself as Mrs. JCP. But there was no proof. Was there? I would check again.

In my small pile of possessions was *Finances*, the ledger of my late husband-for-a-day. I had not read it over since the morning that parcel arrived. The words in it were tentacles that would reach from the pages to sink me down in seas of grief and guilt for what I'd stolen and who I'd married for only a blink of time.

By the window I sat *in the throes*, a miserable singular with the plural construction. *George.* He was a throe if ever there was one. At last I opened the cover of Jasper's diary and ran my fingers over the words. *Dearest Sylvie, my heart.* They traveled up through the skin and bones of my hand and made me watery with sadness. As I turned a page, out fell scraps of paper. Those tickets and receipts, including one I hadn't noticed before, a flimsy folded slip. This was a jeweler's claim check for a "diamond ring, to be resized." The shop was Capital Gems, with an address six stops down the trolley line.

That afternoon I rode the city tram into town, along cobbled rivers of streets, rivulets of people, every contraption of wagon and cart crowding along. Each turn revealed some marvelous new sight: a movie theater, the gates of a brick mansion, a university, a fruit stand of bright lemons. Rocky Mountain Dirigibles advertised balloon rides, and I wished for one, to soar over the fantastical city itself. Every block advertised, *Western boots, Stetson hats! We Buy Gold! Silver! All Precious Stones!* The Diamond Spurs Book Shoppe was the size of a barn. I stared at a meat market where pig heads and whole beef carcasses hung on racks outside. A man in a bloodied apron trundled a wheelbarrow of offal past pedestrians in city fashions. Every corner presented a drama of *tableuax vivants.* My head swiveled, ogling; the city had me enchanted.

I disembarked into a crowd of strangers who surely recognized me as a mountain roughneck. I dodged and squinted at street signs and asked directions till a lady pointed the way to Capital Gems. The window displayed jewels on black velvet, pearls and diamond pendants dangling. On a white mannequin arm, a bracelet of rubies like drops of blood. I stood by the glass and gazed through my own reflection, so the gemstones seemed to float on my transparent face. The proprietor greeted me with a loupe at his eye.

"I'm here to pick up a ring." I fished the receipt from my purse. "My husband left it." It felt false to say *husband*, as if I'd no claim to the word.

He took the paper to a back room and returned with a small flannel pouch, spilling the ring from it onto a tray. "May I?" He took up my left hand and fit it easily on the fourth finger. "Perfect."

"What do I owe you?"

He examined the receipt. "Nothing. It's paid in advance."

"Thank you, sir." In disbelief, I left the shop, then stopped frozen on the sidewalk.

When I was a child, *mon père* taught us geology, that diamonds were made from coal—carbon compressed for eons under heavy rock. My brother and I put lumps of black anthracite beneath the heaviest boulders we could lift, not realizing it would take a million years to become a jewel. We thought we'd return someday to collect brilliants.

What I wanted now was plain, not brilliant. My heart's desire was to possess whatever could not be stolen or killed or buried. If not love, then what?

A way to keep myself. The ring was just a relic, a memento mori. Proof of my marriage. Wearing it made me realize I wanted nothing further to do with the Padgetts, with their power to trap me the same as a tonnage of stone. It would do no good to confront the Duke with this diamond evidence.

"I'm sorry, Jace," I said aloud, and went back inside Capital Gems to ask the proprietor: "If I sold this ring, how much would it be worth?"

He held the band to the light, turned it around under his magnifier. He appraised me anew, and I saw him calculate my reasons: Destitute? Divorced? A thief? "Two hundred dollars," he said. "It's about three carats."

"If it were for sale, would you buy it?"

"I might." He shrugged. "Is it?"

"Three hundred," I said, bold as brass.

He gave me cash, and with it my independence.

Back on the trolley, I got off in front of the Diamond Spurs Book Shoppe. Inside, I inquired about employment. The proprietor was in need of a shopgirl for fifty cents a day. Within the week, I'd moved to a rented room at Mrs. DeRosa's Boardinghouse for Women. Mrs. DeRosa played the piano in the parlor and liked to sing "Greensleeves" in a sorry mew. "Alas, my love." Love, alas, was in thin supply, as oxygen is at high altitude, but I would have to learn to carry on without it, same as my lungs had learned to breathe in the air of the Gilded Range.

K. T. Redmond filed a lawsuit against various parties in Moonstone town for the recovery of her possessions and damages to her livelihood. Four months after our forced eviction, in July 1909, I traveled with her to Gunnison for the trial. The lawyer Crump called for witnesses from the fateful meeting at Moonstone's Masonic Hall. He also wanted to know about our arrest, our jailing and deportation. In addition to K.T.'s testimony, the judge heard from Dottie Weeks and Hal Brinckerhoff. Then I was led to the witness stand and made to swear on a Bible.

Mr. Crump asked me to present my notebook and read from it aloud.

"'Mr. Bowles then said . . . Mr. Baxter said . . .'" It was a long recitation, and as I talked, my palms grew damp, the notebook trembling in my hand. I made the mistake of looking up to see Florrie Phelps at the front of the courtroom, despising me, her mouth pressed to a thin pink worm. I faltered and stopped.

"Go on," said the lawyer.

I was overcome, swallowing. I would be sick.

"Courage, sweetheart," Dottie whispered from the gallery.

The gavel banged, and I found the gumption to resume in a voice that gathered force as I continued recounting the events, naming each one of the townspeople: "'Mr. Baxter presented the resolutions. Mrs. Phelps passed them out. Mr. Pfister took the ledger from me by force. Mr. Smiley took us to the jail.'"

I had to live it all over again till I was told to step down.

"What about what *you wrote*?" hissed Florrie Phelps, livid as I passed her.

Colonel Bowles and others offered an indignant defense, citing the *Record*'s slanderous articles. But the judge refused to show the jury any issue of our paper, not even the articles about the avalanche that wrecked the mill.

"You may not like said articles," the judge said. "You may not like their author or the editor. But these reports are not relevant to the actions under discussion."

The actions under discussion were: our eviction and arrest, the wrecking of the office, the loss of property. The taking of the law into the hands of vigilantes.

After only a day's deliberation, the jury awarded K. T. Redmond a settlement of $10,345 in damages, most to be paid by the Moonstone Marble Company. Seven other defendants—those who'd called for K.T.'s banishment—were also liable, including Colonel Frederick D. Bowles, Mr. Koble of the Mercantile, and Deputy Carlton Pfister. Each was fined and found guilty of malice.

"Malice!" K.T. practically skipped from the courthouse, leading me to a corner tavern to celebrate. "If charges of skulduggery and craven greed were available, that Company of bandits would be guilty of those too."

And murder, I did not say, *by negligence*. My father's ghost smiled at me, winked.

K.T. lifted her fizzing glass: "To Sylvie Pelletier, a printer's devil. And to your article about the Avalanche of Destiny."

"Sorry, I didn't mean to cause trouble—" I said.

"Good Lord, stop apologizing! If the Equitable Surety Company ever collects those payments—which I don't count on—I'll pay your lost wages."

Thus I learned that while silence, perhaps, is golden, speaking up is silver. Sometimes it is even if it gets you thrown in jail. As it turned out, most of the judgment money was never recovered, and I never asked for back pay. K.T. had already given me an education and a calling. Because of her, I tried all my life not to be a nincompoop. To think for myself.

In a private celebration of victory, I sent another "tax payment" from the Silvestri account to the UMW Strike Fund and mailed several hundred dollars to support the striking shirtwaist makers in New York. I went to the Ladies' Auxiliary meetings, and took notes, and saved some of my bookstore wages for college.

Chapter Forty-One

K.T. WAITED TILL SHE THOUGHT Moonstone's anger had cooled with the weather. In September 1909, she wrote to her friend Hal Brinckerhoff to see if it was safe for us to retrieve our things. "Still not advisable," he wrote back. "They'll string you up from a lifting jack." He volunteered to bring our possessions to Denver. K.T. invited me to join them for dinner. How strange it was to see a face from Moonstone in the Thomas parlor, piled as it was with K.T.'s boxes, my Thessaloniki trunk among them.

Hal was eager to show us photographs he'd taken with K.T.'s camera. "I found it in the wreckage," he said. "Sorry to say, Trina, your place is looted." We leaned over Hal's photographs of the *Record* office ransacked, the clock shattered by a bullet, the composing table flipped on its side, papers helter-skelter. "Found a family of squirrels living upstairs when Dottie and I packed your rooms."

"Don't know what I'd've done without you and Dottie." K.T. was giddy to see Hal, grilling him about the gossip.

"You and Sylvie had better not set foot in Moonstone again," he said. "Certain folks are on the hook to pay fines, and they curse you every day. They take it as gospel that they had nothing more to do with driving you out of town than they had to do with driving Adam and Eve out of the Garden of Eden."

"They all signed that petition!" K.T. said.

"What choice did they have?" Hal said. "Bowles's men told everybody, 'If you're a friend of the Company, we want you to sign.'"

"Why are they angry at us?" I asked. "Why not blame the Company? Or Padgett?"

"Duke's done with Moonstone," Hal said. "Hasn't been at the castle for a year."

"Not since his son died." K.T. glanced at me.

I looked away, lost again thinking of Jace, his violent death, the revenge I'd taken. I did not feel guilty, only feared getting caught. Perhaps it was assumed that the money missing from the vault was due to poor accounting. *A rounding error.*

"Bowles promised that the Company would cover all expenses of the settlement," Hal said. "But not one of the liable parties has seen that money."

Money was on my mind as we ate our boiled beef. Was the rest of mine in the trunk? I was impatient to get home and see. At last, after a game of cribbage, K.T. yawned, then Hal.

"G'night, Pelletier," said K.T., and went upstairs to read *Little Women* aloud to niece Jenny. Hal insisted on getting me a cab home. We loaded my trunk in the back.

At Mrs. DeRosa's, when I lifted the lid, the smell of Moonstone wafted up. Inside were old mothbitten woolens, a pair of pretty good Arctics, the Countess's green silk dress, a navy-blue skirt with mud on the hem, all of my notebooks, and, *grâce à Dieu*, *Bleak House* and *Heart of Darkness*. When I flipped the pages, money fell out like plums off a tree. I closed my eyes and wrote a silent letter on the insides of the lids, as if the dead could read. *Thank you, Jace.* Now I would go to college.

I had come to love the money in my pockets, the plumping balance in my personal account, thanks to the sale of a wedding ring and one Knox left from

Jace. Having my own money made it easier for me to be generous with the Robin Hood funds of Angela Sylvestri. I sent two hundred dollars to the striking women of Chicago's Amalgamated Clothing Workers, another hundred for relief to the miners striking Duke Padgett's coal operation in Ruby.

My small acts of charity had me always thinking of Jace, who'd promised to help the families on Dogtooth Flats but had not lived to keep his word. I believed he would approve of me. It was power, to hand that money out, and I relished it, as I relished adding my wages to a nest egg of my own.

At the bookstore six days a week, I made change at the register and impaled the receipts on a spike. I fed Falstaff, the store cat, and answered the telephone: "Diamond Spurs Books! May I help you?" I unpacked boxes and deposited my paychecks. Our best customer was K. T. Redmond, who came in weekly and walked out with armloads of novels for her niece: *The Wizard of Oz, Five Children and It.* She took me to dinner and detailed her various plans: to open a newspaper in Pueblo or Leadville. She speculated aloud, "You could be a columnist."

"I'd like that," I said, picturing the newsroom, the sound of the press clacking.

As the months passed, K.T. did not start a paper. She was growing stout on her sister's cooking, doting upon that niece. *Jenny is smart as a whip. Jenny can recite Shakespeare by heart. Jenny wants to go east for college.*

"And what about you?" K.T. asked me one evening.

Fearing rejection, I didn't tell her that I'd filled out college applications. A weed of ambition bloomed on the scrap heap of me, easily wilted by scorn or the breath of ghosts, the secrets of love and money that still disturbed my sleep. Maybe I would start my own newspaper and hire *her* as columnist, niece Jenny as printer's devil. But first: college. I had enough now to afford it. I waited for the mail and hoped to surprise K.T. with letters of acceptance.

"Lonahan is in Arizona," she said at one of our dinners, and studied my reaction: a small cough. I did not inquire of his health. I did not ask: Was he in danger? Did he have a sweetheart? Had his hair grown back since he'd left half-trimmed, half a year ago?

One afternoon, K.T. came into the shop and threw down a newspaper. The front page featured a photograph of Mother Jones tying the shoelaces of a child on her lap. *New Shoes for the Striking Coal Miner's Children*, said the caption, and I wondered, *Did Angela Silvestri's money buy those shoes?*

"Mrs. Jones is speaking at Union Hall tonight," K.T. announced, and handed me a ticket. "But I'm taking Jenny to the picture show. Go say hello to Mother for me." She purchased *The Scarlet Pimpernel* and left.

That evening I went unsuspecting to the crowded hall. The Princess of Thieves settled her anonymous self in a seat, and Mother Jones came striding across the stage, hat perched like a crow on her head.

"In New York and Philadelphia," she began, "the women gave battle fearlessly. They were clubbed. They were jailed. But they bore it all for a principle. And now the time is here when the woman—the woman!—is going to fight it out to a finish! Write that down, reporters!"

I took it as a challenge. I got pen and paper from my bag and copied her words. I had no assignment, only a note-taking habit and an impulse to spread her ideas like salt on ice, to melt away lies and reveal truth, to say what to *do* about it: *a great uprising.*

"The politicians better go to their mamas and get a nursing bottle!" she said, to great laughter. "They'll do better there than making war on an eighty-three-year-old woman in a state where women vote."

The audience sat spellbound.

"Your Colorado Governor!" she cried. "Is the obedient little boy of the coal companies. He claims I'm dangerous. He says Mother Jones is too radical because she inflames the minds of women! Of workers! He said I'd be arrested if I returned here. To which I say, 'Come and get me!' I'm going down the western slope to see the starving strikers of Rockefeller's Colorado Fuel and Iron and further inflame them."

The lady next to me fanned herself.

"The sewer-rat bosses of the steel companies play golf while your men break rock like prisoners," Mother Jones cried. "Their children have dancing lessons while three hundred thousand strikers' babies eat the bread of bitterness."

"Bread of bitterness," I wrote. "Dancing lessons."

"Women!" she cried. "The destiny of the workingman is in your hands. Go out and picket!"

"We will!" the women cheered and embraced each other with new conviction. The hell-raising spirit was a contagion. I pushed through the throng to find Mrs. Jones. Perhaps I would give her the money remaining in Angela Silvestri's Robin Hood account, new shoes for all the children. Warm coats and hot supper. On the stage, a crowd of supplicants surrounded the tiny bird, Mary Harris Jones. She pressed their hands and looked into their eyes, listening. Sympathy and merriment radiated from her dried-apple face. Great peals of laughter erupted from her bony frame. She spied me on the fringes.

"You!" she cried, and beckoned. Her disciples stared and let me pass. "You're from the top of that mountain! That quarry!"

"Mother, you'll remember Sylvie Pelletier," said a man behind me, stepping forward in a cold draft from the open exit.

This was George appearing, as if dropped from a trapdoor in the ceiling, from the cobweb attic of my secrets. The trap was surely engineered by Trina Redmond, to maneuver me to the meeting where George would be. He had a toothpick in his mouth and a chip on his shoulder. *Delilah*, said his expression, still angry. My face turned scarlet. It was a relief when Mrs. Jones embraced me.

"Young Sylvie of the *Moonstone Record*, is it?" she said. "I want you to tell me all about the great victory in that lawsuit of yours. But I haven't had a drink or a doughnut since breakfast. Let's all go get a jag on." She linked my arm and dragged me to the corner tavern along with a crew of her union boys. George Lonahan strode ahead of us, in conversation with a pair of them. He was frosty. He did not look back.

In the hope of second chances, I joined them, as if running away to join a circus. There was no trick horse, as I had once imagined. No spangles. I went with Mrs. Jones and her crew to drink whiskey. I told her the story of the avalanche, what we wrote, and how we went to jail. I glanced down the length of the table at Lonahan, his face when he laughed, the way he pounded the table and leaned across it and tipped his chair back, scratching his chin. His scarred cheek. The hair too long, past the collar. I would not dare suggest a haircut but hoped he'd watch me, and he did. I talked too loudly, reporting the judge's verdict to Mrs. Jones.

"Ten thousand dollars!" she crowed. "That'll fix 'em." She turned to the men and held court while I suffered, freezing in the glare of George Lonahan.

But then, with the lateness of the hour and the effects of liquor, the chill of his expression appeared to thaw. He came around and drew a chair beside mine to whisper sharp sideways questions, like darts. "So. Are you married?"

"No."

"Engaged?"

"No."

"Why should I believe you?"

"Because you want to?"

The scar side of his face twitched.

"Because I want you to," I said.

"Do you, now?"

"Yes."

"And why would that be?"

"*J'ai soif*," I said, reckless and thirsty and lonely. "*J'ai faim*."

"Is that right? And the other?"

I could not say it. The third thing was so plain on my face, surely he would know. He stared straight ahead, at the shaker of salt, the ash in the ashtray. It was a loud tavern of talkers around us, glassware rattling, a fiddler in the corner, drunkards singing, but the sounds fell away, and the room did. There was his left hand coddling a bottle, the right hand flexing, flat then fisted. There were my own fingers, lacing, unlacing, in front of my mouth. The table was nicked and carved with initials and divots. Underneath it, his leg was a long femur of thigh pressing against mine, withdrawn fast. His boot toe then covered the top of my foot and held it pinned, as if to claim it. Then it was my foot on his, and we traded claims with our feet piling like that under the table, till it made us helpless with laughter. Then not helpless.

———

Six weeks later, I ran off with George Lonahan. I never did go to college, not in any granite building with marble columns. Two letters of acceptance arrived at a Denver postbox sometime after I married George and matriculated at the University of Toil and Strife and went to study along the down road, as Mother Jones called it. We two, Mr. and Mrs. Lonahan, now traveled for the union, sleeping in haylofts and board shacks where miners shared their bread. I did not go to Paris but went instead to jail again.

In 1910, I spent three nights in a Trinidad, Colorado, cell, locked away with coal miners' wives and their babies. George was jailed next door in the men's ward, hundreds of us arrested on charges of incitement to riot, just for marching in the town with our union signs and the Stars and Stripes of America. Arrested for a peaceful march! Can you imagine? In our lockup, we sang rousing choruses and fight songs to wake the Devil. These were days of rage, but we—Mr. and Mrs. Lonahan—were full of another kind of ardor. George called me Primrose, as he used to, for my tendency to blush, but I was not so prim anymore.

In December of that year, we went to New York with Mrs. Jones to rally the striking shirtwaist makers. While she was busy courting the politicians, George and I sneaked off to see the Christmas displays on Fifth Avenue. At Lord & Taylor, snow fell indoors onto a miniature mountain town where mechanical skaters went around a pond and carolers sang in electric moonlight. "Oh, George," I said, "it's so pretty."

"Tinfoil and soap," he said. "A theatrical effect. Give me a real mountain town any day for beauty. New York is all false glitter and grit."

But I wanted it still, some glittering bauble or excitement, and thought about that stolen money dwindling in the bank. It was not mine to spend on trinkets.

"I couldn't never live in this burg," George said.

"Well, where *do* we live?" I asked.

"Our address is like our shoes," he said, borrowing Mother Jones's line. "It travels with us."

Our shoes had us on the road, back to Colorado, to Pueblo and Durango and Trinidad. George organized local chapters of the union and strategized about strikes, arranged for shipments of tents and rations. He went on ahead or followed behind. I took notes and sent dispatches to the *Provoker* and *Appeal to Reason*, whoever would pay me the paltry fees of a scribbler. I wrote what I heard and saw.

In Coeur d'Alene, Idaho, in Cherry, Illinois, in Westmoreland, Pennsylvania, it was the same everywhere, strikes and violence and misery. All this time, without a word to George, I doled out the pilfered Padgett money in the guise of Angela Silvestri. A hundred dollars here, two hundred there, always to strike funds, to feed the families of workers on the picket line.

But as the balance dwindled, I began to see the flaw in Robin Hood's strategy and my own. Charity is a private, whimsical thing, not a system of fairness. It does not last. Once Robin Hood vanished into the forests of Nottingham forever, who would take from the rich and give to the poor? After Angela Sylvestri's account ran dry, the satisfactions of benevolence and revenge would be gone. What then? The amounts I gave away got smaller. Just twenty-five or fifteen dollars, to stretch it out, to gather a little interest. I was scrupulous in accounting. Never spent a dime on myself, not on a pair of shoes or a packet of peppermints, however much I was tempted.

When the balance dropped to $2,526.35, I stopped the distributions. That remaining money gave me a certain secret standing. The notion that I was Someone. If I gave it all away, then—what? How would I move a single rock off the stone pile of troubles rising around us in those years? Struggle, crimes, and wars. Maybe Mr. Rockefeller or J. P. Morgan or the U.S. government had money or means enough to make things right, but I did not. The rest of the Robin Hood money stayed unspent. Because I needed it. Not to buy things— but to *have*. Now I understood something of the miserly covetous instincts of millionaires. I'd grown up with nothing and was afraid to have nothing again.

At the New Year, 1915, we rented rooms in Denver on Quebec Street (which I chose for the name alone) and lived over a cigar store. In that apartment, Jack Lonahan, named for my father, was born in March, his sister Joan barely a year later, their sister Katrina, called "Kitty," after that. What happened to me, once I became a mother, was little of romance, luxury, or adventure. No trick horse, only the trick of stretching pennies, the exhaustion and rewards of toil, raising children, cooking and washing, teaching and minding them, worry over sickness, smiling at all our silliness, singing in the bath. It was the years of picket lines and music on the radio and Saturday-night dancing with George, who turned out to be pretty nimble at the turkey trot and the grizzly bear, the scandalous "animal dances" of our day. He was as good a man as any I've ever known. Which is to say, not perfect. We squabbled over money and ideas in books, petty slights in the kitchen, where he left his dishes, his habit of letting a cigarette burn while he napped, and about my own faults: I was prone to daydreaming, bouts of gloom. I left the window open and let the flies in, or the cold, just for the smell of the pure Colorado air.

But we were happy as it is possible to be, with the porch out front, the lilac bushes. George grew tomatoes and corn in the yard. I stitched curtains and clothes, shoveled snow, raised chickens in a coop for eggs and meat as my mother had done, knitted mittens for the brave soldiers fighting the Huns in Europe, where Inge was reportedly killed. (Was she? If anyone could survive, it would be Inge.) Henry, my daredevil brother, flew over France in 1917 as a dogfighter pilot and shot down four German Fokkers, for which act he won the Distinguished Service Cross. He came home to clear timber for a ski resort he ran in the Green Mountains of Vermont, and named it Miracle Mountain, for the miracle of his survival.

During those years, the 1920s, I did not pen a word of any appeals to reason, or report any firebrand speeches, only wrote family news in letters east, where Maman had married Monsieur Charpentier, a mustachioed widower, in Rutland. Nipper, now Frank, called him Papa. He had no memory of *mon père*.

For fifteen years I did not see my Pelletiers. Then, in the summer of 1923,

George and I bought a Ford roadster and drove the children across the country for a visit. Joanie and Jack showed off their appalling knowledge of French, which consisted of the song "Alouette" and certain phrases: *J'ai faim, j'ai soif, je t'aime.* My girl Kitty, age five at the time, announced that she could say *putain*, "like Mama does," and scalded their ears. Perhaps we should not have named Kitty after K. T. Redmond, my cursing friend who died at age seventy-six in her sleep. In her last years, she was looked after by her own daughter—for Jenny Thomas, the "niece," was in fact K.T.'s child. Daisy Thomas had raised the girl as her own, to save her sister, Trina, from shame. After the funeral, Jenny and I found the truth in a box of old letters. Dickie T. Walker was the scoundrel's name. He'd been an editor at that Denver paper who'd exacted the price a young girl had paid to become a newswriter, a jilting double-crossing two-timing scab of hearts. Secret unto death.

I've kept my own secrets. It never did feel safe to confess a word about Jace Padgett and our elopement all those years ago. To this day, I have not allowed myself to spend the money from the sale of his ring, accruing interest even now in the bank and trust. *For emergencies*, I tell myself. A million times I nearly dipped into it, to pay the electric. To keep the landlord from shutting off the gas. But how would I explain such a windfall to George? He was a dear man, a funny man, though a jealous one too (for a certain reason). He was also a strict accountant and doled out money for housekeeping expenses, putting it in a Mexican pottery jar on the counter. "Here, Mother, for the milkman, and don't be inviting him inside." How would I explain a secret postbox to receive statements from secret bank accounts? If I said anything about Jace to my jealous George, it would hurt him. He preferred to pretend he was my one and only.

When I could, I added to my own separate Pelletier account, dreaming of college for the children or a cottage by a lake. With my small additions, the interest accruing, Jace's several hundred dollars deposited in 1909 grew, by 1930, to over three thousand. (As it turned out, I did have a head for finance.)

The country was in the grip of hard times, the Great Depression. My bank somehow held through it all, and still I did not spend down my secret monies.

And while he did not ask, George knew. He knew something, somehow. "Your mother has sat at the feet of kings," he used to say to the children. "She danced with a duke. She's tasted *foie gras*."

"Tell!" the children always begged.

I only smiled. "Your father is a fantasist."

But George understood, the way husbands understand, what not to ask. We skirted the subject of Padgetts the way the tongue avoids a sore in the mouth, to let such things heal. He had secrets of his own buried. I knew where not to dig. In the early days, he came home a few times with bloody knuckles, a split lip. It was well known that the union men beat scabs without mercy. So there remained a pricking thorn of suspicion because of the name Caleb Grady uttered that night at Elkhorne. Houlihan? I didn't pry. The old scar on his face, George claimed, was from a bar brawl: "Some drunk." After hearing many versions of his tall tales, I surmised that the fight was over a woman. I never asked about his past *amours*. He was kind enough not to ask about mine.

We cannot help how the past is knitted into the calcium of the bones, pressed and hardened as coal is under the great pressure of living, the frenzy and worry. The skin falls and bags around the creaking skeleton, the ache in the spine, the fallen arch, but somewhere in the container of me, Jasper Padgett still resides, his bespectacled face faded to sepia. All this time I've known Jace, if not as a husband, then as a force that formed me in the press of those years in Moonstone, surely as any geological weight forms the good earth we stand on. We wreck ourselves and build ourselves layer by layer, as nature makes marble and diamond, granite and schist, all the beautiful radiant elements of matter and weather.

And now George is gone too, killed in 1932, in Butte, Montana, while picketing the craven owners of a copper mine. The Governor had called in federal troops who fired into a crowd of strikers. One of their bullets hit George in the heart. *I'm exactly who they'd shoot*, he told me once. It was my heart shot along with his. Unbearable to tell. So I won't.

People do not want to hear sad stories. They want cherry pie and bromide. I'll keep my sorrow private, as my mother did. I understand her more as I grow old. Her stoicism and lessons about suffering. Certain *tristesses* are too deep for tears. We move onward, as we must. Bravery is not just for the battlefields of war. Every day, ordinary people climb out of bed and carry on extraordinary, in a fight for their families, carrying sorrow, working for the betterment of us all.

One recent afternoon about six months ago, on a spring day in Denver, 1934, I was on the way to a meeting at the Union Auxiliary, riding the trolley, when I noticed a man climb the steps and pay his fare. It was the dark patch tied over his eye that made me glance twice and recognize him.

"Cal?" I said, "Mr. Caleb Grady?"

He turned, wary, and did not appear to know me. The other passengers stared.

"It's me, Sylvie."

"Why, Miss Sylvie—Mrs. Padg—" he said.

"Mrs. Lonahan. I'm Mrs. Sylvie Lonahan. How are you, Cal?"

"I'm keeping well."

"And your mother?" I asked. "How's your family?"

The trolley started up. Cal shrugged an apology, then went toward a seat at the back. Overcome with questions, I followed. He leapt from his seat. "You don't want to be sitting back here, ma'am," he said with some alarm.

He knew, as I did, that Denver Mayor Stapleton was a member of the Ku Klux Klan. Colorado Governor Morley too, probably, and half the statehouse. They dressed in their ghost hoods and were photographed grinning at the racetrack. They railed against Catholics and Communists and talked against Jews on their campaign stumps. They made sure that black people did not move into the white neighborhoods or swim in the public pools. And those men did worse things we whites didn't hear about, or maybe didn't want to know, because then we would have to act against appalling injustice or change somehow. And if we didn't, weren't we ourselves only one rung up from the white-sheeted goons on Satan's ladder to hell?

Caleb tipped his hat to me and jumped off the trolley as if I were a threat, because I was. But still, I didn't think of that in the moment. I had questions.

"Cal!" I jumped off after him, with my forty-three-year-old legs complaining.

He turned around then, looking—I must say—so startlingly like his half brother, Jace Padgett, that I nearly wept. The round eyeglasses, the skewed necktie, the cup-handle ears. We stood on the corner and traded news. He was a chef at the Albany Hotel, he told me.

"Do you make your famous elk-heart stew?"

"No elks to hunt down here." He laughed. "Unless you mean the Fraternal Order of Elks. We cater their meetings." A fraction of a smile on his face. I returned his smile as if he were a long-lost comrade, though he was not. He made that clear in his reluctance to talk with me.

"Cal," I said, "tell me, how's your family?"

For an answer, he drew two photographs from his wallet, one of his wife, Ellen, "she's a piano teacher and choirmistress at the church." The other picture showed their three daughters in front of a diner: Sunshine Café. "The girls at my mother's place out in Weld County," Cal said. "My dad runs the gasoline station there at Dearfield."

"The town. You really did it," I said, impressed. "You must be happy. And wasn't there a college? Did you start it? Du Bois University, as I recall."

Cal appeared pained by the question. "It's finished in Dearfield. Marcus and his family live here with us." He explained that Dearfield had prospered for a decade on crops of sugar beets and melon. But then, instead of the railroad, it was a drought that came through, all over the Colorado grasslands, same as it came to Texas and Oklahoma and Kansas. The West was a dust bowl of shriveled fields, abandoned homesteads.

"Old people, like my folks, the only ones left there now," Caleb said, something hard in his eyes that stoppered me with sadness.

"I'm sorry to hear it."

"We're starting over here in Denver," he said. "Du Bois College. Thirty-two students already enrolled, night classes."

"That's wonderful news," I said. "Can you tell me, is that—is the stone still there? That Jace took—the marble?"

"It is." His expression told me that the stone remained uncarved, a monument only to folly.

"He believed he was doing right," I said.

"For whom was he doing it?" Caleb asked with his hard smile. "Not for me."

"I never understood—"

"I don't expect you to, Mrs. Lonahan," Caleb said in polite irritation. "J.C. was always talking my ear off about my rightful inheritance. I suspect you know the reason. He said he talked to you about it."

"He did."

"And so, in the end, what was your inheritance?" Cal asked. "What was mine?"

"Did you not receive . . . ?" It was a guilty question, as I already knew the answer.

"Mrs. Lonahan." Caleb straightened his gaze, aimed it at me. "I don't like to speak ill of the dead. And not about J.C. He always talked about the future, how he'd set me up. I believe he meant to do it, but the old man cut him off. Jace was killed. And you can guess the rest."

I guessed, slumped at the thought of it.

"My mother always warned me," he said. "Watch what a Padgett does—not what he says."

"Easter told me that too."

"We Gradys tried to get ourselves away, on our own—and here you are, Mrs. Lonahan, running me down to bring it all back. And so I'm just gonna say it now, what I didn't say that night: Your union boys was the ones that beat the dickens out of me. Cost me my right eye. Them Turks from the marble mill, beating on scabs. I heard that name Monahan or Lonahan. Never did tell it. Would only bring more trouble on myself."

My mouth dropped open. I covered it. Cal kept on. "To this day, the union won't let a colored man in their clubs. I went to get work at the iron-works on Larimer and the hiring hall told me stay away or they'd lose me my other eye."

"Wait—" I was foundering. The pricking thorn was not a suspicion now but a painful truth to pluck from my conscience. "My husband George—he would never—" sputtering, my defenses up so high I did not ask questions but only batted away his words with grievances of my own (as so many of us do, when confronted with painful truth). "I have—my own father was—my husband was killed—"

Caleb Grady looked off toward the spiky mountains in the distance while I flailed in a pond of guilty denial and a realization that the money I stole— reclaimed!—from the Padgetts was dispensed to exact my own brand of justice, for my father and our cause. Had Caleb Grady got that money he would've had his own fight, to make things right for his mother, for the advancement of his own people. It's shame and willful ignorance, such as mine in that moment, which blinds us to unfairness.

Caleb seemed eager to get away from me.

"Cal—Mr. Grady—wait. I apologize if my husband—if he—I didn't know."

"All right," he said. He saw my squirming.

"And I never did thank you," I said. "For what you did for Jace. How you took care of him—when he— he did like his whiskey too much."

"That he did," Cal laughed. "Good to see you again, Miss— Mrs. Lonahan."

With his hands in his pockets, Caleb Grady turned and strode down the street, whistling. You might say it was a carefree tune. But I could swear that what he whistled was "Onward Christian Soldiers." That Temperance anthem. *Marching as to war.* With all the crowns and thorns and the kingdoms falling, as they do, in that hymn.

———

That evening, alone at home on Quebec Street, I climbed the pull-down steps to our attic and found my old trunk. There, under brittle yellow copies of the *Moonstone Booster* and the *Moonstone City Record*, were my notebooks and letters, the ledger of *Finances*, holding secrets. I sat reading under the eaves, awash in nostalgia and tender sentiment for my unknowing girlhood and the first husband I lost. He was only a boy, really.

In a shoebox were years of postcards and letters, mostly from George, writing his travels. I sat remembering the *pluralia* of his affections, his jokes, and how he cared for me. I don't want to believe he'd have hurt Caleb Grady, but that doesn't mean he didn't.

Next morning I went to the bank and emptied out and closed the account of Angela Sylvestri by writing a cashier's check for two thousand dollars. It was enough for a few years' rent. A car. Perhaps a down payment on Du Bois College. A grand sum, to my way of thinking. I sent it to Mr. Caleb Grady, Chef, The Albany Hotel, Denver.

It was the last act of *La Princesse des Voleurs*.

> Dear Mr. Grady,
>
> Please accept this money from the estate of Jasper Padgett, now deceased. He spoke often of you and your rightful inheritance. I know he'd want you and your family to prosper. If he were with us still, he'd have made sure of it. Please send my regards to all the Gradys, and tell Easter that I still cook all her recipes (her chess pie is a favorite), and thank her to this day for her wisdom, and all she taught me, about sauces and pastry and also about history. About right and wrong.
>
> Yours sincerely,
> Mrs. Sylvie P. Lonahan

And I did it why? For Jace? Did I send funds to Caleb to salve my own conscience? To do *one right thing*. Was there a fair price for the lost eye of a man beaten by thugs? A woman violated? These were not equations of equivalents. An eye for an eye. A two-hundred-dollar fine for my father's life exploded by a rusty canister of malice. A summary judgment of $10,500 for a smashed newspaper. Such sums were *rounding errors*. The real money was in the markets, the vault, the three homes big as castles, six cars, servants, a pair of dancing slippers costing the same as a college term, parties that cost more than the yearly salaries of three men.

What I sent Caleb Grady was guilt money. Mailed off as if I could purchase absolution and make myself superior to the Duke or the Colonel. I justified myself, thinking, *Some people would send nothing. Some would offer a block of stone.*

A week later, the check was cashed, Caleb Grady's signature endorsing the back of it, so I knew the money was in his hand. Of course, as the only surviving son of Jerome "Duke" Padgett, Caleb should have inherited a vast fortune, enough to start ten colleges. The amount I sent him was crumbs off a cake, not a fair share of the spoils left behind in the vaults of Elkhorne or gathering interest at Morgan Guaranty Trust.

I am not here to say I am Saint Sylvie. I don't care to be any kind of angel.

The truth is, I kept back five hundred dollars for myself, as payback for the death of Jacques Pelletier. I was now twice a widow and had mounting expenses that a UMW pension could barely cover, a surgery for female trouble, repairs for a leaking roof. Five hundred dollars of stolen spoils still remained in my own nest-egg account to gather up interest. If it were unspent at my death, it would be left to divide among my surprised survivors. A legacy from their Pelletier grandfather's grave. Frenchy, he was called. *Mon père*, who was killed in a marble quarry in Moonstone, Colorado.

These days I find the old fury plaguing me again, violent visions, the urge to strangle. I see the bread lines downtown and read about the suicidal bankers and the caravans of skeleton people crossing the dusty plains wanting only to work, to rest, to eat a square meal, and that impulse to *do something* burns in me still. But what to do? What?

I cannot be a thief. From whom would I steal?

On a train, several months ago, I read my newspaper full of news about the proposed Wagner Act, an attempt by a goodhearted politician to help the struggling classes. The bankers were denouncing it from their marbled offices. Out the window I glimpsed a mule by the side of the tracks, a man lashing the animal with a switch. The sight of him put me in mind of the skinner Jenkins, and that long-ago essay contest. Three paragraphs about abused mules had set my life on its course. In the lurch of the train car, I got out a scrap of paper, and wrote, K.T.'s question in my mind, *Did you know the Liberty Bell is cracked?*

December 1934

A LETTER to MILLIONAIRES

Dear Messieurs Rockefeller, Mellon, Morgan, Dupont, et al,

In your boardrooms, labor people are branded as "violent," "shirkers," "anarchists." We are called Socialists as if it means Satanist, when we only wish for a fair deal. Here in Colorado, the Governor calls in the National Guard if there's even a whiff of protest, doing the bidding of bosses and men of vast fortune, like yourselves.

This year, more than a million US workers have gone on strike: longshoremen, autoworkers and steelworkers fighting for a fair deal. Their protests are peaceful, but the police and private guards respond with bloody violence. In Minneapolis, police shot 67 striking Teamsters, and killed two men, as my own husband was killed alongside strikers in Montana. Like him, these workers were only demanding a living wage, and the right to join a union.

Now in Congress, the proposed Wagner Act will set up a Labor

Board to enforce fairness: it outlaws yellow-dog unions, bully tactics, and requires employers to negotiate in good faith. But the bankers and your money class oppose it; Mr. Mellon at Treasury thinks more charity is a solution. In this long Depression, alms are not the answer.

You gentlemen give away your money to opera houses or college buildings that bear your names, but your charity is a fraction of your vast wealth. Will it solve problems of the unhoused world? It is only for yourselves that you are philanthropists. Why not pay workers what they deserve? Workers do not want charity. Charity is not a system of law. It is not justice that lasts.

The Wagner Act will bring fairness. The Congress must pass this law or face a great uprising. Americans will demand that millionaires be held to rights, and pay a fair wage to the good hardworking people who build our country,

Sincerely,

S. P. Lonahan

Denver

Like throwing a feather dart, I sent that screed to *The Sun* in New York City where the millionaires lived, and asked for a job as a stringer covering labor news in Colorado. To my surprise, the editor sent me a check for five dollars—published the letter, and offered me the job. I got no response from Mr. Rockefeller, et al., but the byline emboldened me to fill these notebooks, pouring out words on troubled pages, trying to make sense of these uncertain days, these perilous times.

"Who is Mother Jones again?" my girl Joanie asked me the day she read that Mary Harris Jones had died, one hundred years old, November 30, 1930. This was when George was still with us. Hearing the sad news, he wept. The newspaper showed her portrait and photographs of her funeral, attended by grateful thousands, her grave at the Union Miners' Cemetery in Mount Olive, Illinois. A granite monument to the great woman stands there today.

"We knew her once upon a time," I said. "Your father and I. And Auntie Trina."

"You *did*? How? When?" Joanie was briefly impressed but lost interest as I began to tell her. "Oh, that tiresome union talk," she said. "All Dad's strike stories are the same, picket this, picket that." She was off to put her hair in rollers, slide silk stockings up over her darling young ankles.

And just in a snap like that, I saw how history is lost. Kept from the children out of exhaustion or our own shame at how the feet suffered in broken boots, leaking in the snow, unbearable to live it over again. *Your grandfather was killed and the Pinks threw your grandmother out onto the gravel and I didn't see my brothers again for fifteen years.* You tell about it, and the children say, *Huh.* They yawn, impatient.

For you, the past is alive in yourself as breath. To them, the young, it's a story, no more real to life than a painting. They're in their own story.

"Hallelujah, I'm a bum," my son, Jackie, sang as a boy, like Nipper did long ago. But our Jack had little idea where the tune came from, what the words were about or how the sunlight cast shadows like bars when Henry rode off through the trees, with our little brother singing on his shoulders, to catch fish in the Diamond River. Jack and his sisters have their own music, new on the radio. They have their own song for the times. "Brother, Can You Spare a Dime?"

What I have are memories, these old newspapers, and—this longing, still, to keep. To *have*—not *things*. Not maraschino cherries or a pearl choker or elephant-hide wallpaper. Just a yearning for something like the snowflake melted in the heat of my hand, my mother's breath. What I want is to save it, a crystal only of beauty, the sharpness of the mountains, that pure cold in the lungs to quicken a body from inside out. Outside in. Here under the attic eaves, that urge grips me, to set it down, the way a painter wants to clutch the sunset, the purpling bruise of light on the underbelly of a cloud. The heart *wants*. To kiss in the moonlight. To hear Jacques Pelletier's fiddle again in the evening, to catch his eyes crinkled above his beard, and taste the *soupe aux pois* my mother stirs, singing so as not to forget, *longtemps que je t'aime, jamais je ne t'oublirai*. To save it preserved, a flowering snowdrop in amber.

Perhaps this wish is the same as one that builds a monument in marble or casts a statue in bronze, carves initials in a rock. But that's not what I'm after. Not the stone glory of important or self-important men. Only to tell how it was: The wind groaned in the eaves. The cold froze the very marrow. The lights of the village winkled in the dark, the towers of Elkhorne spired above the pines. The sound of the rack-rib donkeys split the morning, and woodsmoke filled the wind. Ancient urges stirred the blood by the river, love and fear. A mountain lion snarled. The magpie laughed. Deep in the mountain, a white cave hummed with the sounds of men and machinery, bone crack and groan. Chisel and drill. The glory of the sun stole the breath and released it to the blue sky. The snows gathered on the cornice to thunder down, melted to flood the rivers. The curse of the Ute people lay upon the land, and white drifts built up around the walls of the cabin so that we were in our own little pocket, like animals in a burrow, all together there.

THE END

Author's Note

GILDED MOUNTAIN IS A WORK of fiction, drawn partly from histories of Redstone, Marble, and Dearfield, Colorado, in the years between 1900 and 1915. While real historical figures like Mary Harris "Mother" Jones and King Leopold of Belgium appear in the novel, their scenes are invented, as are the other characters. People whose lives inspired this book include one of my great-grandfathers, J. F. Manning, who served as president and general manager of Colorado Yule Marble during the years that company supplied the stone for the Lincoln Memorial and the Tomb of the Unknown Soldier; Oliver Toussaint Jackson, founder of Dearfield, Colorado; Sylvia Smith, newspaper editor; and John Cleveland Osgood, founder of the Colorado Fuel and Iron Company; and his wife, Alma Regina Shelgrem Osgood. For purposes of this story, I have appropriated some newspaper articles, events, and certain biographical details, but have reconfigured these, and altered dates and circumstances, when it suited the narrative.

Acknowledgments

This novel is indebted to the journalists and historians, photographers and memoirists whose work preserved details of life in the early 1900s, especially the following: *Sylvia Smith: Her Day in Court*, by John F. Bennett, in *The Denver Westerners Monthly Roundup*, July–August 1970 and *Marble: A Town Built on Dreams*, Volumes 1 and 2, by Oscar McCollum, Jr. Special gratitude to photographer Henry Johnson, whose 1910s pictures of Marble, Colorado, inspired and informed this novel.

Other invaluable works include: memoirs of J. F. Manning, 1935; *The Fate of a Fairy*, by Ellen Elliott Jack; *I Await the Devil's Coming*, by Mary MacLane; *The Life of an Ordinary Woman*, by Anne Ellis, *Cripple Creek Days*, by Mabel Barbee Lee; *Tomboy Bride*, by Harriet Fish Backus; *A Lady's Life in the Rocky Mountains*, by Isabella Bird; *From Redstone to Ludlow: John Cleveland Osgood's Struggle Against the United Mine Workers of America*, by F. Darrell Munsell; *Mother Jones: The Most Dangerous Woman in America*, by Elliott J. Gorn; *Mother Jones Speaks*, Philip S. Foner, Editor; *King Leopold's Ghost*, by Adam Hochschild; *Camp & Plant*, the Colorado Fuel & Iron Company magazine; *Marble, Colorado: City of Stone*, Duane Vandenbusche and Rex Myers; and *Dearfield, Colorado*, by Stephen Hill, from Blackpast.org.

Two newspapers were immeasurably helpful: *The Marble Booster*, issues from 1911–1915, and *The Marble City Times*, issues from 1908–1912. No journalist was bylined, but some reports from these papers are copied here or altered to suit the novel. They contain text likely written by Frank Frost, editor of *The Marble Booster*, and by Sylvia T. Smith, editor of *The Marble City Times*, who was evicted from Marble for writing negatively about company matters.

Many people helped my research in Colorado, including the late Sue McEvoy Strong, who gave me a fascinating tour of Redstone Castle and shared her deep knowledge of local history. I'm indebted to Daniele Treves of R.E.D. Graniti for a tour of the astonishing quarry at Marble. At Marble Historical Museum, Alex Menard, Kimberly Perrin, and Lynn Duane Burton were exceedingly helpful. For local knowledge, great thanks to Gary Bascombe; Vince Savage; Patsy Smith, Sam Smith, Glenn Smith, and Tim Hunter of Crystal Jeep Tours. Thanks to Lisa Wagner of Crystal Dreams B&B, for lending me her jacket.

Bouquets of thanks to a crackerjack publishing team. First to a marvelous and wise literary agent, Sarah Burnes, and crew at the Gernert Company; to my wonderful editor, Kara Watson, for bravura work and outdoor editorial meetings in the 2020 pandemic; and to Nan Graham and the team at Scribner, including: Stu Smith, Sabrina Pyun, Jason Chappell, Beth Thomas, Brianna Yamashita, Katie Monaghan, Mia O'Neill, Ashley Gilliam, and Jaya Miceli. Gratitude to Wendy Sheanin at Simon & Schuster; and to Nicole Dewey, Dewey Decimal Media. Thanks to Savannah Frierson of Tessera Editorial for fine-tuning historical details and authenticity.

For ongoing editorial expertise, wisecracks, and wisdom, I owe everything to my dear friends Roberta Baker, Amy Wilentz, and Nick Goldberg. Big thanks to Margo LaPierre for pro help with an early draft and all things Québécois. For encouragement and shop talk, thanks to Diane McWhorter, Christina Baker Kline, Marisa Silver, Erik Larson, Rachel Cline, Helen Benedict, Robin Marantz Henig, Sally Cook, Ann Banks, Laura Popper, Carroll Bogert, Barbara Jones, Ellen McLaughlin, Shira Nayman, Lisa Beyer, Sara Nelson, Ann Marie Cunningham, Lisa & Joel Benenson, Susan Ades Stone, Anne Edelstein, Jeanmarie Fenrich, Alexander Papachristou, and the late Anthony

Acknowledgments

Weller. For community and support, gratitude to Roxana Robinson and the novelists' group Word of Mouth.

For instilling and fostering a sense of the ridiculous and the sublime, I'm indebted to my family, a bulwark against pandemical plagues and giving up, starting with my magical mother and father, my brothers, and in-laws. A kiss to all the nieces and nephews. Deepest gratitude and love to my three children, and to my husband for his jokes, his keen editorial eye, and his ability to leap tall buildings with a single bound.

About the Author

KATE MANNING IS THE AUTHOR of the critically acclaimed novels *My Notorious Life* and *Whitegirl*. A former documentary television producer and winner of two Emmy Awards, she has written for the *New York Times*, the *Washington Post*, the *Los Angeles Times Book Review*, *Time*, *Glamour*, and *The Guardian*, among other publications. She has taught creative writing in the English Department at Bard High School Early College and lives with her family in New York City.

BOOK CLUB FAVORITES
READER'S GUIDE

GILDED MOUNTAIN

Kate Manning

This reading group guide for **Gilded Mountain** includes an introduction, discussion questions, and ideas for enhancing your book club. The suggested questions are intended to help your reading group find new and interesting angles and topics for your discussion. We hope that these ideas will enrich your conversation and increase your enjoyment of the book.

Introduction

HEROINE SYLVIE PELLETIER RECOUNTS HOW she leaves her family's snowbound cabin to work for the Padgetts—owners of the marble-mining company that employs her father. At first, Sylvie is awed by the luxury around her. She's fascinated by her employer (the charming "Countess" Inge) and confused by the erratic affections of Jasper, heir to the family fortune. But Sylvie discovers that the Padgetts' lofty ideals are at odds with the unfair labor practices that enrich them.

Outside the manor walls, the town of Moonstone is roiling with discontent. The editor of the local newspaper is publishing unflattering accounts of the Padgett Company. The Padgetts' servants, the Gradys, are preparing to form a utopian community on the Colorado prairie. And a union organizer, along with labor leader Mary Harris "Mother" Jones, is stirring up the quarry workers. Sylvie must navigate between these vastly different worlds and find her way amid conflicting loyalties.

Topics And Questions For Discussion

1. Sylvie frequently mentions that she feels restrained, tongue-tied, squelched, and silenced, but seldom expresses resentment or anger aloud. What are the causes of her silence? Who else in the book is silent? About what and why? How is silence useful? Destructive? When characters do speak out, what are the repercussions?

2. *Gilded Mountain* might also have been called *The Education of Sylvie Pelletier*. What does Sylvie learn—about herself and about the ways of the world—over the course of the novel? Where does she get her education?

3. Five women act as role models for Sylvie: her mother, Cherie Pelletier; newspaper editor K. T. Redmond; the "Countess" Ingeborg; the chef Easter Grady; and Mary Harris "Mother" Jones. What choices are available to these women at the time in which the novel is set? What lessons does Sylvie take from each of them? How do they ultimately change or shape her?

4. Discuss the many ways in which characters "reinvent" themselves in *Gilded Mountain*. Who succeeds and who fails? In your opinion, what does it mean to reinvent yourself in the context of this story? Does every character in this novel have the power or opportunity to self-invent?

Which characters do, and which characters don't? Is it a privilege or a right?

5. Moonstone is a "company town," while the Grady family aims to create a utopian community for the descendants of enslaved people in Weld County. What are the founders of each place hoping to achieve? How do they aim to control what happens in these places, and why? Quarrytown and a certain neighborhood of Moonstone—given a name that uses a slur for Italian immigrants—are also called "towns," but are they?

6. Trace the effects of great wealth on the lives of the characters. What does Sylvie learn about wealth and charity by the end of the book?

7. Sylvie is a child of Québécois immigrants. On page 20 she asks, "How was anyone to be American?" How do various characters answer the question of what it means to be American? How does Sylvie navigate the tension between her parents' culture and her own? And how does her immigrant perspective inform how she sees herself and others?

8. *Gilded Mountain* predominantly takes place in 1907–08, during a financial panic, an enormous influx of immigrant labor, violence against African Americans, and workers' struggles over fair wages, workplace safety, and the right to unionize. How do these "external" forces and events shape the individual lives of the "ordinary" people in the story?

9. The town of Moonstone has two newspapers, each with a particular editorial point of view. How do their different approaches to news reporting affect what happens in the town?

10. *Gilded Mountain* features a number of sympathetic characters—including some who also perform or are complicit in harmful acts. While reading,

did you find yourself drawn to any one character (besides Sylvie)? Discuss your favorites and how they are portrayed.

11. Early on, Sylvie mentions that marble stone is used for building "statues and bank pillars, monuments. Gravestones" (page 4). What is the role of memory and memorializing in the book? Who and what is honored and why? What do the different characters believe about what is owed to the dead? What purpose do monuments and memorials serve in the story?

Enhance Your Book Club

1. *Gilded Mountain* is a historical novel, and the author blends fictional characters and places with real ones. Research the historical figures, as well as the models for some of the fictional people, places, and events in the book, and discuss them with your book club. Does it surprise you that some characters and events are based in fact? What about locations? (Hint: Try googling Marble, Colorado!)

2. Draw parallels between the events of this novel and events that have occurred in recent history. Discuss these connections with your reading group.

3. Consider an event from the past that has shaped or influenced the course of your life. Try writing about this event the way Sylvie does—narrating from a retrospective point of view. Has your perspective of the event changed with the passage of time? Why or why not?

4. Read Kate Manning's prior novel *My Notorious Life*, about a renowned midwife, and discuss the differences and similarities between the heroines Axie Muldoon and Sylvie Pelletier.

FOR THOSE WHO IMBIBE AND ARE OF AGE,
TRY A *GILDED MOUNTAIN*–THEMED DRINK:

THE FIZZING SWOON

A frontier twist on a Soixante Quinze, or French 75.

Sylvie says of her sip of champagne at the Hunters' Ball, "A swallow went down my throat like a zipper unzipping, the taste of fizz" (page 154). And later that night she has her first kiss on the banks of the Diamond River: "I was ruined now, by pineapple and electricity, champagne in flutes, the drunken swoon by the river" (page 181).

Enjoy this champagne cocktail, but don't let it ruin your reputation!

INGREDIENTS

3 tsp powdered sugar

1 oz freshly squeezed lemon juice

1.5 oz rye whiskey

Ice

2.5 oz champagne (cava or prosecco work too)

Lemon peel, for garnish

DIRECTIONS

Ground powdered sugar with mortar and pestle and squeeze fresh lemon juice. Combine sugar and lemon juice in the base of a cocktail shaker until sugar dissolves. Add whiskey, shake vigorously with ice, then strain into an ice-filled glass. Top with champagne and stir. Garnish with a lemon peel.